# THE CURIOUS CALLING
# OF LEONARD BUSH

# THE CURIOUS CALLING

## —OF—

# LEONARD BUSH

Susan Gregg Gilmore

— BLAIR —

Printed in the United States of America
Cover design by Laura Williams
Interior design by April Leidig

Blair is an imprint of Carolina Wren Press.

The mission of Blair/Carolina Wren Press is to seek out, nurture,
and promote literary work by new and underrepresented writers.

We gratefully acknowledge the ongoing support of general operations by the
Durham Arts Council's United Arts Fund and the North Carolina Arts Council.

This novel is a work of fiction. As in all fiction, the literary perceptions and
insights are based on experience; however, all names, characters, places, and
incidents are either products of the author's imagination or are used fictitiously.
No reference to any real person is intended or should be inferred.

Library of Congress Cataloging-in-Publication Data
Names: Gilmore, Susan Gregg, author
Title: The curious calling of Leonard Bush / by Susan Gregg Gilmore.
Description: Durham : Blair, 2025.
Identifiers: LCCN 2025010260 (print) | LCCN 2025010261 (ebook) |
ISBN 9781958888551 hardcover | ISBN 9781958888582 ebook
Subjects: LCGFT: Bildungsromans | Novels
Classification: LCC PS3607.I4527 C87 2025 (print) |
LCC PS3607.I4527 (ebook) | DDC 813/.6—dc23/eng/20250310
LC record available at https://lccn.loc.gov/2025010260
LC ebook record available at https://lccn.loc.gov/2025010261

*For Dan*

*Just as I am and waiting not*
*To rid my soul of one dark blot*

———

"Just as I Am" by Charlotte Elliot

# — Leonard Bush —

IN THE BEGINNING, Leonard wasn't thinking about God or other high-minded things. Nor was he concerned with talk of sin and salvation or destiny and calling, although those words swirled about him mightily once news of the amputation spread. He paid neighbors' prophecies no mind. He was only twelve years old and not yet ready to consider how loss and contrition might shape his life's journey. For now, Leonard was certain of only one thing—his leg needed a proper goodbye. One that came with a preacher, prayers, and a bit of hymn singing.

From the start, his mother, June, argued that it was too soon for such a public show, that Leonard's skin was pale as milk and his thoughts muddled from the trauma of his recent loss. Abundant evidence, she told him outright, that his judgment was not sound. "Besides, your leg ain't some souvenir for safekeeping," she said. She wiped tears from her eyes, then kissed his forehead and checked the stump for any lingering signs of infection. But Leonard's thinking was straight, and years later, his memory of that day would remain clear.

The sun broke hot on the foothills of East Tennessee the last Saturday in September 1961. A band of clouds was mustering strength to the west, but the TV weatherman reported the rains would hold until evening. Leonard's father, Emmett, a seasoned dairyman who regularly mined the sky for meteorological clues, agreed. At one o'clock in the afternoon, he stepped onto the back stoop, trussed up in the only suit he owned, and gazed up at the sky.

"Time to go," he said.

Leonard waved goodbye to his mama who stayed at the house

to prepare another batch of lemon squares for the wake to follow. Although June had fussed and fought about the leg funeral, once the date and time had been set, she insisted their guests be served a satisfying meal — ham, deviled eggs, yeast rolls, dessert, and a cold drink. She had spent two long days preparing the feast, neatly packed in three Coleman coolers and loaded in the bed of the truck. She followed Emmett into the yard. "No need for Leonard to be out in the heat at this hour. It ain't even been a good three weeks since the operation." She wiped her hands on her best apron, the one trimmed with a ruffle of blue gingham. "Besides, preacher won't be up there for a while yet."

"Don't baby the boy." Emmett tossed Leonard's crutches into the back of the pickup. "A crowd's coming, and we got to ready the cemetery for the service."

June slumped into another blubbering fit.

"Dammit." Emmett's tone turned sharp. "You could water the garden with all the tears you've cried and not reap a thing from it." He laid his suit jacket on the seat and climbed into the truck beside Leonard. "It was his leg or his life." Emmett slammed the truck door. "At least your son's getting on with it." He started up the engine.

Like his daddy, Leonard had grown tired of his mama's sadness, even though he was to blame for most of it. He imagined it would be painful for any mother to see her perfectly normal son suddenly become lopsided. Still, as he studied her standing on the concrete stoop, her body heaving in a pitiful, unrelenting meter, he wondered if his mama missed his leg more than he did. Emmett patted Leonard's shoulder and shifted the engine into gear.

As the pickup lurched forward, Leonard glanced back at the house, suddenly remembering he'd left his baseball cleats, muddy from an afternoon of play, on the stoop right where his mama was standing. The shoes were gone. His mama had probably thrown them out for fear seeing them would be too upsetting for Leonard... or for herself. Maybe it was for the best. He'd never need those shoes again. He tossed his mama a wave and settled against the seat.

The gravel drive wound its way around the milking parlor and feeding barn, and a field stubbled with stalks of fresh-cut corn muted the northern landscape. Doves, nibbling on the remnants, flew away as the truck rattled past. Emmett cocked his finger out the window and pretended to fire. Leonard laughed at his daddy's play, and Emmett shifted into a lower gear. The old truck churned farther up the hillside, squeaking and grumbling as if it were apologizing for the rough ride. None of the discomfort mattered to Leonard. He was happy to be out of the house and free of his mama's care. So while the cicadas' roar climbed and fell, he settled deeper against the seat and closed his eyes. For the first time since the injury, his body drained of worry.

Outside the cemetery gate, Emmett cut the engine. The motor idled a few seconds before sputtering to a stop. He leaned over the wheel and glanced up at the sun. "Don't like to admit it," he said and tugged on his shirt collar, "but your mama might've been right about you staying at the house til closer to time."

"I'll be fine," Leonard said.

Emmett winked at his son. "Okay, let's do it." He pointed to a towering oak, its leaves already hinting at the fiery colors to come. "We'll set up over there, in the shade." Emmett helped Leonard from the truck, then pulled a folding chair from the back and turned toward the oak. Leonard steadied himself on the crutches and followed close behind his daddy, every step slow and careful. When his good leg buckled and the crutch gave way, Emmett froze but did not reach for him. Leonard righted himself, and Emmett smiled. At the oak, he opened the metal chair and dusted it clean with one of June's dish towels. "Sit here," he said.

Leonard yanked the tip of his left crutch from a patch of soft ground and did as he was told, glad for the chance to rest. His stump throbbed, and his stomach ached. But he did not complain, not even when a mass of gnats took frenzied aim at the swollen nub still sutured and bandaged in layers of white gauze. He swatted at the bugs, but they circled back around. After he shooed them away a third time, he gave up and fixed on his daddy, pulling weeds crowding the family's graves.

With each tombstone Emmett touched, Leonard called out the name of his ancestor. He knew them by heart, had seen photographs of them in a scrapbook. Most of the men and women held the same gaunt cheeks and tired eyes Leonard saw in his daddy. Until today, they'd felt more like strangers than kin. Now he was trusting them to care for a piece of himself. His mama always said that the dead keep a close lookout for the living. A shiver whisking down the spine was proof enough that a spirit was near. Leonard had felt no such chill yet and speculated that the loss of a leg might not be enough to garner their attention.

When Emmett finished weeding, he knelt beside one of the smallest headstones, one of a dozen adorned with a little lamb resting on top. *Sarah Elizabeth Bush.* Leonard tossed her name into a building wind, trying to conjure a picture of the girl missing from the scrapbook back home. She came to him fuzzy and faint, the child never mentioned in family stories, Emmett's baby sister who had died of scarlet fever before her fifth birthday. Clutching a bouquet of wild aster, Emmett appeared to be talking to her, maybe even crying. Leonard squinted for a better look. The thought of his strong daddy tearing up made him uneasy. He felt better when Emmett patted the lamb's head, stood, and brushed his pants clean.

Another gust of wind and the sun took cover behind a bank of clouds. Emmett reached for a thermos of water. He held it up. Leonard shook his head. "I'm fine," he hollered back. Emmett carried the thermos to him anyway. "You should drink something," he said. Leonard sipped the cool water while Emmett unloaded the Colemans and folding tables and peppered the lawn with more metal chairs borrowed from the Baptist church. Leonard counted forty chairs, forty-one including his own.

"If that ain't enough," Emmett said as he set the last one in place, "folks'll just have to stand."

"Ain't that many coming. Not for a leg." Leonard took another sip. Faraway thunder rumbled closer.

"I don't know about that," Emmett said. "It ain't so strange to spot a farmer with a missing finger or two." He held up his hand. "Guess I been lucky. But not everybody's seen a boy missing a whole leg. You okay with that? Them coming just to gawk?"

In the sky, a red-tailed hawk spiraled above the oak before settling on its tallest branch. Through the leafy cover, Leonard caught sight of him, preening and fanning his tail. He wondered if the hawk was searching for his next meal or if he'd come to the hilltop to get a first glimpse of the one-legged boy. "Yeah, I'm okay," he said. He set the thermos on the ground.

Emmett rested against the oak, wiping his face with a clean edge of the dish towel. "From up here, the world looks perfect, don't it?"

Leonard surveyed the valley, the hundred acres of dimpled pasture his daddy farmed, a clutch of rooftops and steeples farther to the west, the waters of Big Sugar River winding between them, friends' homes scattered like seed. From the hilltop, Leonard could see everyone and everything he loved. "Yeah, Daddy, it's perfect."

Emmett smiled. "All right. Just one more thing to do." He tossed the cloth under a folding chair and walked back to the truck, his perfectly starched shirt soaked with sweat. At the tailgate, he bowed his head as though offering up a short prayer, but Leonard knew better than that. His daddy was not a church-going man. Emmett bit his lower lip as he hefted a small box onto his shoulder.

Leonard quivered at the sight of the box shaped from scraps of pine. He had come to the hilltop to bury his leg because of a gnawing in his gut, a strong tugging that pulled him to this very spot. He couldn't explain it any better than that. But now every bit of him twitched and squirmed, and he wondered if his leg might be twitching inside that box, too. Suddenly he was nervous about the whole idea of a leg funeral.

Emmett set the casket at the tree's base, nestled between two gnarled roots pushing their way free of the ground. A fresh grave, small like Sarah's, lay empty a few feet away. "I hope this brings you peace," he said to Leonard. He pulled a half-empty pack of Salems from his shirt pocket and slapped the package against the palm of his hand, then yanked a cigarette free with his teeth and lit it. A thick tail of smoke curled up and clouded his eyes. Before the accident, Leonard had never seen his daddy with a cigarette. Emmett took another drag. The stench of burning tobacco, harsh and woolen, drifted underneath the oak.

"Hello to you, Brother Emmett!" Brother Puckett appeared on the far side of the cemetery, carrying a Bible in one hand and waving a white handkerchief in the other like a woman might. His belly jiggled as he walked, and he paused every third or fourth step to press the handkerchief to his balding head. Leonard stifled a laugh. Emmett offered his hand to the preacher.

"Good to see you, Emmett." The preacher tucked the handkerchief in his pants pocket. "Hope you're doing fine," he said and shook Emmett's hand. "Thought I would've seen you in church Sunday." He nodded in Leonard's direction. "Considering."

Henrietta Ooten walked up behind the preacher, toting her Autoharp in its black leather case. Emmett flicked the cigarette to the ground and turned to greet her. Plump with graying hair, the spinster lived on a small tract of neighboring land and wore the same orthopedic shoes whether working in the yard or attending Sunday church. As she waddled across the hilltop, Leonard imagined a mother duck leading her brood to water. She took a seat beside Leonard, nodded hello, and began tuning her instrument.

The notes rang out like a call to supper. Soon, men and women arrived in carloads and on foot, their children filing along behind them. The adults greeted Emmett and Leonard, offering hugs, handshakes, and fresh-baked pies. The men helped Emmett set up the last of the church tables outside the iron gate. The women decorated the tables with checkered cloths, jars filled with Shasta daisies, and their own homemade foods, leaving ample room for June to add her share. When the work was done, the men gathered around Emmett and talked about the heat of the day and the rains sure to come. The women took to the folding chairs, crossed their ankles, and reprimanded their little ones for pointing at Leonard as if he had two heads. Leonard caught the grown-ups staring, too, but he didn't mind their ogling. He guessed he would've done the same. Truth be told, he preferred them staring long and hard rather than catch his mama looking away.

In the distance, Leonard spotted Eddie Burl Ford. The boys had known each other since birth — born on the same day, in the same hospital, their mothers laboring under the same full moon. Leonard had always understood that their friendship was rooted more in a shared history and a mutual love of fishing than a genuine liking of one another. The two had been together on Big Sugar when Leonard cut his foot, and even though a part of him wanted to blame Eddie Burl for his loss, faulting his buddy was not going to change Leonard's circumstance. Eddie Burl looked to his mother. Vivienne Ford nudged him forward, fingering her pearl necklace as they took seats on the back row.

Little Henry Reed, whose mama, Margaret, had died in early July, walked a few paces behind their friend Hoyte Lattimer who'd come to the hospital to visit and thrown up at the foot of Leonard's bed. June had not wanted Hoyte, Little Henry, or Eddie Burl at the service, but Leonard had telephoned each one, even though it was Azalea Parker he most hoped would come. Azalea had been with him, too, when he stepped on that shard of glass on the bank of Big Sugar. She'd tended his cut that day, but Leonard hadn't seen her since the amputation, and he worried that Azalea felt partly to blame for the way things turned out. He sat up straighter and scanned the crowd for her red hair.

Miss Roberts, his sixth-grade teacher, arrived next, smelling of roses and bearing a manilla envelope chock-full of spelling and math assignments. "Thought you might be feeling restless." She waved the envelope in the air. "Maybe now you'll focus on your schoolwork better." Her eyes grew big. Her cheeks colored up a deep shade of pink. "I'm so sorry. I don't know why I said that." She fanned her face with the envelope, and Leonard caught another delicious whiff of her perfume. "I knew I was going to say something foolish. And there I've gone and done it."

"It's okay." Leonard took the papers from her. "I'll be back to normal before long."

Miss Roberts pulled a tissue from her pocketbook and tucked it under her blouse's sleeve. She took a seat behind Leonard just as June walked up to the iron gate. Conversations stopped and a piteous moan rolled across the hilltop. Leonard knew the other mothers must be secretly thanking God that they were not June Bush, that he was not their child, that this tragedy was not theirs to own. Leonard imagined his mama shared that longing, but she hid her truth behind a pair of dark glasses.

A bevy of women gathered around June as she unloaded the trays of lemon squares and deviled eggs she had carried up in her car. June then walked straight to Brother Puckett. Since Leonard's return home from the hospital, she had called on the preacher nearly every day. Almost as regularly, he had come to the house just as lunch was being served, never once refusing a turkey sandwich and a slice of June's pound cake. He'd huddle over Leonard, washing away sin and sickness with a long-winded prayer and a cold bottle of RC Cola. On her knees, June, bound between preacher and son, echoed his plea.

This afternoon, Brother Puckett leaned in close to June and whispered in her ear. She nodded, then took her place beside Leonard. Brother Puckett greeted the guests, raising his Bible toward the heavens. "Dear Father," he shouted, "it's time we turn to You to heal what is left of Your poor, wounded child, Leonard Marlowe Bush." Leonard's friends snickered hearing his middle name, and their parents offered up a collective "*Hush!*" The preacher continued: "We know that without You this boy will never be whole again. Without You, he will never know the true reward of eternal salvation." The preacher placed his hand on Leonard's head, invoking the faithful to tender their own sins and shortcomings.

As the *amens* faded away, the preacher called Leonard to speak. He pulled himself up on his crutches and faced the family and friends gathered on the hilltop. "I ain't thought much about what to say," he started, his eyes fixed on the pine box. "It was just that burying my leg seemed important." He cleared his throat and looked at his daddy. Emmett proffered a reassuring smile.

"I never thought I'd be a boy with only one leg. So far, it ain't been too bad." He loosened his grip on the crutches. "But to be honest, I think I'm going to miss that leg. I learned to walk on it. I learned to catch a fly ball and hit a line drive on it. I caught my first fish on that leg. Remember, Daddy?"

Emmett's smile crumpled. He pulled a handkerchief from his suit pocket and blew his nose.

Leonard's throat tightened. "Yep, it's been a real good leg," he said. "And no disrespect or nothing, Brother Puckett, but I ain't sure God had a hand in this like you say. Just don't seem like the Almighty would will a boy like me any harm." Leonard looked at June. "It was an accident, Mama. That's all it was. Getting infected like it did, well, that might've been my fault for not speaking up about it sooner. But I don't think God or anybody else had anything to do with taking my leg from me."

June pursed her lips and pushed a handkerchief underneath her dark glasses. Emmett dropped his head. The hawk shrieked from the oak. Thunder boomed in the distance. Little Henry gazed up at the darkening clouds.

"Daddy says that a man ain't measured by his size or shape. I think he's right about that. At least I'm hoping so."

Another clap of thunder drummed along the foothills. The hawk lifted from his perch in the oak and flew west over the treetops. "Also hoping God can make something of me ... of what's left of me ... like I am ... one-legged and all."

The hilltop fell silent until a man hollered, "Amen!" Others echoed

his call while Miss Ooten plucked the first notes of "Just As I Am."
Leonard lowered himself onto his seat. Emmett reached across June
and patted him on the shoulder. June pointed at the tip of the bandage now stained yellow. She unfolded her handkerchief and draped
it over the stump.

Brother Puckett leapt to his feet, seemingly eager to seize one
last opportunity to lead his flock to repentance. "All rise," he said.
"Not you," he mouthed at Leonard. He opened his Bible to Psalms.
"He shall not delight in the strength of the horse," he read, his voice
reaching a commanding measure, "nor take pleasure in the legs of a
man."

The Bible verse made no sense to Leonard, but the preacher grew
fierce as he sputtered on about the legs of men and the destiny of God,
beads of spit spraying from his lips. Miss Ooten shifted her rump
on the metal seat, not missing a single chord as she led the crowd
from one hymn into another. "Onward Christian Soldiers," the men
and women sang. Emmett reached for June's hand, but she slapped
it away. The voices swelled, and the preacher called out for one
last hearty *amen*.

The funeral for Leonard's leg was done.

# — June Bush —

 THE MORNING AFTER THE leg funeral, a bird chorus roused June from her sleep. She woke cold, and for a few foggy moments, had no memory of the amputation or yesterday's service. She pulled the sheet to her neck, wishing she had placed a quilt at the foot of the bed last night when the room had been too hot for sleeping, even with both windows open wide. She had worn her thinnest cotton gown and pinned her hair on top of her head. Emmett had set the fan oscillating on high and promised the air would cool soon enough.

"Just lie still," he'd said.

Emmett possessed little patience for complaining of any kind, but it had been too hot and June too agitated to *just* lie still. Pushing back the covers, she'd fussed about the heat and recounted the conversations from earlier in the day. "Leonard will be *fine*," her women friends had promised. "God's watching over him," they said. "He's such a very *special* boy," Vivienne Ford had trilled above the others. "Surely Leonard is meant for something, well, *special*." June scrunched her mouth as she mimicked Vivienne's words. Emmett raised an eyebrow.

"I don't want a *special* boy," June said. "I want a *normal* boy. *My* boy. The way he was when he came into this world. *Perfect. Whole.* A boy who plays baseball and builds forts, who chases after lightning bugs and climbs trees." Emmett had listened for a while, then told her to hush, and rolled onto his side.

Now with sunrise looming, June cast off the chill and woke to the reality of her loss. She gasped as if she were learning of it for the first time, reliving that moment when the surgeon had told her and

Emmett that the infection was spreading fast. He had pulled a pen and notepad from inside his starched white coat and sketched a leg. "The incision will be here," he said, drawing a sharp line where he intended to cut above the knee. "God, not the joint, please not the joint," June begged. But the doctor had ignored her pleas and prattled on about a speedy recovery and the use of prosthetics, only stopping to make the occasional note with his ink pen.

A throaty wail gurgled up inside her, blending with the songs of the wrens migrating to warmer climates. June buried her face in her pillow. Her body heaved. When she was done with her crying, she looked at Emmett sound asleep beside her, his face porcelain-like in the last glow of moonlight. Out in the pasture, the cows, their udders bulging with milk, would be calling for him soon enough if he didn't rouse on his own. That man could sleep through the fiercest thunderstorm, she thought, remembering how he'd balled up in a chair and napped during Leonard's operation. She hated that about Emmett, the way he could carry on with the simple routines of living even on the darkest day.

There was a time early in their marriage when June would have snuggled up close to her husband on a morning like this, pressing her body into his every curve and bend. She'd have confessed her worries in whispered tones and kissed his muscled back. Emmett would have pulled her into his arms, brushed the hair from her eyes, and called her his precious Junebug. He would have been quick to reassure her that everything was fine, that she and Leonard were safe in his care. But after fifteen years as husband and wife — the daily demands of managing a dairy and keeping a home wearing on their patience for one another — Emmett kept to his side of the bed and June to hers.

She dried her eyes and reached for the terry robe tossed over the arm of a nearby rocker, not bothering to cinch it around her waist or feel for the matching slippers on the floor beneath the bed. A week before the amputation, she had hinted for a new robe, one with satin trim and a matching satin collar. A frivolous request from the mother of a one-legged boy, she thought. Tiptoeing to the dresser, she plucked the bobby pins from her hair and held them between her lips while she ran a brush through the brown mane that fell below her shoulders. A black cloth, draped across the oval mirror with the walnut frame, hid her face from view as she reset her hair in a tight bun at the nape of her neck.

Emmett hadn't allowed her to cover the other mirrors in the house. Only this one. "Ain't tolerating another of your silly superstitions. Ain't nobody died here," he'd said. "Besides, you ain't making a lick of sense. First, you want nothing to do with the funeral. Then, you go acting like that leg is a living, breathing thing, deserving of a fancy wake and all this hocus-pocus." He snatched at the cloth, but June snatched it back. Emmett didn't understand. Where June came from in North Carolina, folks shrouded their mirrors when a body died. And that leg was part of their son's body, dead and gone, and she wasn't taking any chances.

When Leonard had first asked for the funeral, she'd fought him on it. That much was true. Then she prayed, down on her knees, and counseled with the preacher, who admitted the service might do Leonard some good. This morning, with the leg safely buried on the hilltop, June was glad they had done it. Everyone said it was a lovely ceremony, a true testament of Leonard's abiding faith. She looked at the mirror, then at Emmett, lingering in a peaceful sleep. Maybe it was time the official mourning came to an end. Although she was scared of what another day might bring, she was growing weary of her grieving. She folded the black cloth into a square and placed it in the bureau's bottom drawer, hoping the ritual would provide some protection going forward.

"Lord Jesus, watch over my boy," she whispered and eased the bedroom door shut behind her. She skimmed down the hall, pausing in front of Leonard's room. A growing child needed at least eight hours of sleep. She'd read that in the *Reader's Digest*. A crippled boy likely needed more.

When she married Emmett, they had imagined a big family,

two or three more kids at least. But that had not been God's plan. Now she felt guilty about wanting more, as if Leonard had not been enough. She leaned against the doorframe and dabbed her eyes with the back of her hand. "Stop it. No more." She patted her chest, a quirk of hers when trying to stave off tears, then pressed her ear to the door. Satisfied Leonard was sleeping, she slipped into the kitchen and flipped on the overhead light. The sudden brightness stung her eyes, and she held her hand to her face for a moment. Once her eyes adjusted, she reached for the percolator, already set with coffee and water, and plugged it into the wall.

She tied her robe closed, then pushed the rubber stopper into the sink drain and cranked the faucet to high. She poured a long splash of Clorox into the water. The dirty dishes from yesterday's wake had been cleaned and put away, and the floor and Formica sparkled from the evening's last scrubbing. But June never began a meal without disinfecting her sink and counters. Emmett said she wasted time repeating the chore. But the kitchen was June's to manage as she pleased, and she cleaned and polished it like a precious jewel. When the sink was full, she dunked a dishcloth into the water, wrung it out, and began wiping down the countertops. She reached behind the faucet and underneath the tin canisters that held flour, sugar, and salt, spots, she figured, other housewives likely ignored.

Growing up the daughter of a poor farmer who reaped more desperation than tobacco, June had never dreamed of living in a house as fine as the one Emmett built her. The Bush family home where Emmett was born and raised a quarter mile down the road had no indoor plumbing and a sagging roof. Nothing that can't be fixed, June had told him when he first brought her to Sweetwater, but Emmett insisted his bride have the very best. Two bedrooms, a bathroom off the hallway, a brightly lit kitchen, a generous-sized room for gathering, and a tiny sewing room at the end of the house tucked between her bedroom and living room where she kept her Singer. As more babies came along, Emmett had promised they would add to it. Snug as it was, June loved her cheery yellow house and the garden of vegetables and herbs out back. But it was her kitchen, with its pale blue counters and blue linoleum floor speckled with gray and white like a beautiful robin's egg, that she cherished most.

Done with her cleaning, she tossed the cloth into the sink and poured herself a first cup of coffee. Outside, the deep black of night was giving way to shades of blue. June walked to the front porch and looked to the East. From this familiar perch, the Smokies that had held her so tightly as a child, sometimes choking the air from her lungs, posed no threat. Those mountains carried the pain of a little girl, but she came to this porch every morning to stare them down, never once flinching. All these years later, she hoped to find the same courage to face her troubles here at home. She took a sip of coffee. The bitter drink warmed her throat.

Emmett would be waking soon, looking to be fed before tending to the dairy. He'd sit at the kitchen table, compare the newspaper's forecast against his own, then gobble down his breakfast of scrambled eggs, sausage gravy, and warm buttered biscuits. *Cows with aching teats got no patience for a man lingering over a cup of coffee,* he'd say. *Well, I got something to say to you, Emmett Bush. I ain't wasting my time on the porch. I'm squaring my day.*

There were two facts of marriage June learned early on. One was that it was easier to argue with Emmett when he wasn't there, and two, that the cows came first on a dairy farm. Lately it seemed Emmett looked for every opportunity to spend time away from the house, either tending to the herd or holed up in the milk room, the small cinder-block space next to the milking parlor where tanks of fresh milk were stored. There he watched his black-and-white TV set and calculated the dairy's losses and profits. He never talked about the amputation. In fact, some days it was as if he hadn't even noticed Leonard was one-legged or that June was left to care for him on her own. She drank the last of her coffee and turned to face the day ahead.

The kitchen was growing warm. June opened the window above the sink a little wider, and the cotton valance she'd made after arriving in Sweetwater fluttered against the morning breeze. A cow lowed in the distance, and a red-eyed vireo jabbered from the pin oak out back. "Hush up. You're going to wake my boy," she said, reaching for the stoneware mixing bowl kept on a high shelf on the opposite wall. June set the bowl on the counter and opened the canister of flour, measuring out two cups, some baking soda, and a pinch of salt. Working a handful of shortening into the mixture, she smoothed out the coarse lumps between her fingers before dialing the oven to high. While the oven ticked as it heated, she added cold buttermilk to the bowl and hurried to shape a soft, moist dough. When she was done, she turned it onto a floured board, rolled it out, and cut it up with an old jelly jar. Pleased with her efforts, June slid the biscuits into the oven and poured herself a second cup of coffee.

Twenty minutes to six, the sun was peeking over the top of the foothills, tossing broad ribbons of pink and orange across a clear sky. No doubt this day, like yesterday, would prove hot. Too hot for late September, in June's opinion. During spells like this, she could almost smell the burley ripening back in North Carolina. Emmett said ain't nobody got a nose that good. *Well, you're wrong about that, too. I know when you been sneaking a drink or a cigarette, and trust me, I know when tobacco is ready for picking.*

Standing in her pretty blue kitchen, June could smell the burley. Her eyes watered just remembering the pungent stink of it. She was barely six years old when her daddy first set her out in the field to work a row of tobacco, squishing hornworms between her fingers and snapping off the low-growing sucker shoots. At the end of the day, her hands, cut and bleeding, were covered in a sticky black gum, her head faint, and her stomach churning. "Baccer sickness ain't going to kill you," her daddy had told her, "and you ain't stepping a foot in that house with them gummy hands neither." He made her wash with his own concoction of lye, hog fat, and water. *Like I said, Emmett Bush, I know when tobacco is ready for picking.*

The electric clock above the sink hummed as the long hand swept from one minute to the next. June peeked at the biscuits. Browning at the edges. Nearly doubled in size. She dialed down the oven temperature a few degrees. Another two minutes more was all they needed. As she reached for a crock of butter on the table, she spied specks of dried dirt scattered across the floor. Leonard and Emmett knew better than to muddy up her kitchen. Shoes and boots were to be left on the rear stoop. That had always been the rule. June instantly regretted her frustration with her son. Leonard wasn't the boy he once was. Since the tragedy, he hadn't picked up a baseball or tromped through the fields, racing after rabbits with his twenty-two. How could June blame him for this mess? It was surely Emmett's doing, and dirt couldn't be ignored. She glanced at the bleach water in the sink, grateful she hadn't drained it, then fished for the cloth and squeezed it almost dry. As she knelt down, a ghost image of Emmett and Leonard appeared, sitting at the kitchen table just as they had the morning when Leonard went fishing at Big Sugar with Eddie Burl.

"I made him a new lure," Emmett had told her then. Now appearing haint-like, he said it again with a proud smile. "Told the boy he could try it out after his chores."

"I told you I don't want him at the river, and you got no right to cross me like that," June snapped back. "I got a feeling, and it's growing stronger by the minute. And you know good and well that a bad crowd of men are always drinking and carousing down there."

"That's further up the river," Emmett said.

"I don't care what you say. Leonard don't need to be hanging out with Eddie Burl for one thing. He ain't a good influence on our boy. Spoiled like his mama. For another, it's filthy at that river what with old man Harlan's cattle using it as a watering hole. Hear me plain and clear, Leonard don't need to be anywhere near Big Sugar till the last of the bad luck passes. It's dangerous," June concluded. "Margaret's death was only the first strike of three. There's more to come."

"Hell, June, milking a cow is dangerous, but I can't live my days in fear, tallying up every cut, bruise, and broken bone," Emmett had said. "Besides, it's been weeks since Margaret Reed's passing. There ain't more bad luck hanging about."

*Leave me be.* June shook her head, rubbed her eyes, and the vision passed. There was no good reliving what was done. She had tried to move forward like the doctor advised. Focus on the time ahead. But every morning she woke moored to the past, desperate to change one second of the day that had led to their tragedy. If only she'd argued harder with Emmett, stood her ground, insisted Leonard stay home. If only Emmett had trusted her worries concerning Little Henry Reed and the bad luck she was certain he carried after his mama's passing. If only she'd gone to the river and checked on Leonard when the chill washed over her, nearly leaving her faint. If only Emmett hadn't made that damn bottle cap lure.

June wiped up the last specks of dirt while the electric clock whirred away, and the red-eyed vireo hollered the same old song. "Told you to hush up once already," she said, but the bird and the clock carried on. June rinsed the dishrag, then scrubbed at the baseboards even though they were clean. But the ghostly images of Emmett and Leonard circled back around. This time, Leonard, hot with fever, begged for his mama's help. June reached for her son, his foot scarlet red and swollen three times its normal size. "I got you, baby," she said. "I got you." His body flopped and jerked on the linoleum floor like a fish yanked from water. Each time she relived the nightmarish memory, June always saw a worse ending play out, one where Leonard never woke, his lips fading to a grayish blue, his body falling cold. Whether it was grief or another omen coloring her imagination, she wasn't sure, but these visions left her skittish, scared more bad luck was drawing near.

*Stop it.* She flung the wet cloth across the room. *Leave me be.* She cast off another cold shiver, fetched the cloth, and dipped it in the bleach water again. The vireo picked up his song while June rested on her knees and began washing her linoleum a second time.

## — Azalea Parker —

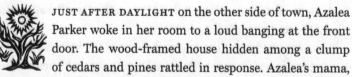 JUST AFTER DAYLIGHT on the other side of town, Azalea Parker woke in her room to a loud banging at the front door. The wood-framed house hidden among a clump of cedars and pines rattled in response. Azalea's mama, Rose, scurried down the hall and greeted the visitor with a sugary hello. "Beginning to think you'd forgotten about me," she said.

A man's voice answered. "Forget you? No way." He mumbled something, and Rose giggled. The front door slammed shut.

Azalea reached for her baby brother, Atlas, who was whining in the rickety crib beside her bed. "Hush," she whispered in his ear, straining to identify the man's voice.

"Sure hope you've been missing me half as much as I've been missing you," Rose said with such exaggerated affection it caused Azalea to shudder. "Give me a minute to doll myself up. You deserve something extra special for coming such a long way for little ol' me."

"Damn straight, I do," the man replied.

"Make yourself comfortable, handsome. You know where I keep the beer."

Although Rose called every man who came to the house *hand-some*, Azalea recognized this voice. Deep, harsh — it belonged to a man seemingly suffering from an incurable case of laryngitis. More specifically, it belonged to Mack, a long-haul trucker who drove tim-ber from Canada to New Mexico. He'd shown up the first time in early May, a few weeks after Atlas was born. He'd been a regular at the Parker's house ever since. Once he'd even stayed the night, sat at the kitchen table and ate a ham and tomato sandwich like Aza-lea imagined a real daddy might. But Mack was nothing like the daddies Azalea had seen on television. And with ham costing fifty-nine cents a pound, Mama only made a sandwich for Mack.

He talked sweet in one sentence, rough in the next, calling Rose beautiful and stroking her hand, then barking at her for sitting too close or not sitting close enough. A picture of a big-bosomed woman clad in a skimpy, two-pieced bathing suit inked his left forearm. A dove with an American flag waving behind it colored the other. His body stank of alcohol and Old Spice. His breath of snuff. Azalea cuddled Atlas and sang a lullaby in his ear.

Across the hallway, Rose knocked about in the bathroom, likely taming her auburn bangs with some Dippity-Do and smearing her cheeks with rouge, her lips with Revlon Red. Azalea thought her mama beautiful without all that color on her face, but the men who came to their house seemed to like it, particularly Mack. He even brought Rose fake eyelashes once. Made her go put them on that very minute.

A moment later, Rose stepped across the hall to Azalea's room. Azalea closed her eyes, feigning a deep sleep. The door creaked open, and she felt her mama's gaze, heard her breathing, smelled her scent of tobacco and lilacs. Rose lingered a moment, then shut the door, and walked into the front room. Azalea wondered if she'd glued on those fancy lashes she kept in an envelope in the medicine cabinet.

"Better, handsome?" Rose asked.

With the door closed, Azalea couldn't follow their conversation, but she heard feet shuffling across the floor and the crisp pop of a can of beer being opened. By her count, nearly three weeks had passed since any good-paying man had come to the house. She thought their home would be a hard address to find with nothing but a giant forsythia marking the dirt path that wound its way to the door. But it seemed half the men in Sweetwater and most of the big-rig truckers traveling north and south on US 11 knew where Rose Parker lived and how she earned her money.

Azalea didn't care for any of the men Rose entertained, but despite his stink, Mack was better than most. He usually brought a bag of groceries — sausage and a dozen eggs, Spam and white bread, milk for Atlas's bottle. Last visit, he'd pressed a shiny quarter into Azalea's palm, said it was hers to spend on candy or ice cream. Time before that, he'd left a yellow hair ribbon on Azalea's dresser for no reason. He said he had a little girl back home that liked those kinds of things. Azalea glanced at her dresser where the yellow ribbon was dangling from a knob.

Odd noises seeped through the walls and under Azalea's bedroom door. She plugged her ears and hummed another lullaby.

Azalea had heard plenty of mean talk about her mama. Kids at school teased her. Grown-ups tossed about words like *tramp* and *slut* whenever she was within earshot. Azalea never debated the truth of it. Still, she cringed every time she heard the hurtful words. When Atlas was a week old, the righteous women from Piney Grove Baptist Church showed up with a basket of diapers, a loaf of banana bread, and a small quilted blanket. Tied to the basket's handle was a card with a picture of Jesus on it and the Ten Commandments numbered in bold block type on the back. The women agreed raising children was exhausting work, whether a father lived in the house or not.

The preacher's wife begged to hold him, pressing Atlas against her ample bosom. She sniffed his neck and kissed his bald head, then professed that babies were God's sweetest gift. Rose thanked them for their kindness, even offered to make a pot of coffee. But when she refused to repent and admit she lived contrary to Scripture, the women gathered up their pocketbooks and Bibles and left in a huff. The preacher's wife handed Atlas back to Rose, kissing his head one more time before following the others to their cars.

Rose had probably broken at least one commandment by birthing a baby out of wedlock, although Azalea wasn't exactly sure which one. But what those church ladies did not know was that Mack, with his wavy brown hair and pale white skin, who'd shown up at the house only a few days before they did, looked the spitting image of Jesus Christ on that Ten Commandments card. Surely that should count for something in terms of her mama's salvation. Azalea wished she could tell those women that, even if it meant sitting through another afternoon of Scripture.

Atlas fussed and kicked at the covers. Outside the window, a lick of orange crowned the treetops. Most mornings, he'd already downed his first bottle by now, and Azalea knew there'd be no explaining to a five-month-old that his breakfast would have to wait until his mama finished her work in the other room. Hoping to distract him, she lifted his undershirt and blew on his belly. Then she kissed his feet and pretended to gobble up his toes, games that usually left him smiling. Instead, his cheeks reddened, his fussing grew louder. "Shh, shh, shh," she purled, pulling off his plastic pants and a soaking wet diaper.

Working fast, she slid a clean diaper under his bottom. Atlas fought against her. Sometimes she felt like she was wrestling a bear cub and wished for a third hand. She placed her fingers between the diaper and his belly like her mama had taught her. "Better to stick yourself than the baby," Rose had explained. Azalea worked the pin through the thick cotton and pulled his plastic pants up around the diaper. "There you go," she said, but still Atlas whined and his belly gurgled. She offered him her pinkie finger to suck, but he shook his head and balled up his fists. Azalea knew better than to leave her room when men were visiting. Rose had drilled that lesson deep. But she'd be pissed if Atlas started caterwauling. Men don't like crying babies, Rose had told her more than once. Azalea wasn't sure what to do. Atlas shook his head harder and straightened his legs, priming for a full-blown tantrum.

"Okay. Okay," she said. Holding him against her chest, she tiptoed into the hall just far enough to see into the living room.

An army blanket, pocked by the jaws of hungry moths, covered the only window, but a splash of morning sun dappled the floor beyond it. The muted television flickered light against the room's bare walls. An ashtray, a school picture of Azalea taken last year, and a pink crystal vase decorated the top of a wobbly table set at the far end of the sofa. Rose had bought the vase years ago just because she thought it was pretty. Azalea always admired it, too, and kept it filled with cedar in the winter and dogwood and mountain laurel in the spring and summer.

A few feet away, Mack sat on the blue sofa. His bare, muscled arms sprawled across the back cushions where bits of white stuffing poked through the cloth. Rose knelt on the floor in front of him, her head, hair teased high on top of it, bouncing up and down.

Azalea felt wrong for watching but couldn't look away. Atlas squirmed in her arms. They were nearly out of milk, and Azalea's own stomach clamored for something more than saltines. Maybe Mack had brought the makings for her mama's macaroni and cheese with hot dog bits baked in it. He'd promised he would next time he came to visit. She licked her lips just thinking of it. This wasn't the first time she'd found herself struggling to square her mama's vocation with her own aching belly.

Atlas stiffened. Azalea jostled him in her arms. When he started to whimper, she tightened her grasp on him and scudded across the back wall before ducking into the kitchen, careful not to make a sound. She poured the last of the milk into a bottle and tickled his lip with its nipple. Atlas cooed and settled into the crook of her arm. Azalea's heart sank. There were no groceries on the counter like last time.

"Look-a-here, woman," Mack growled.

Azalea peeked into the front room. Mack's shoulders tensed whenever Rose touched his privates. "Slow it down."

Rose tried to kiss Mack on his mouth, but he pushed her away. She sat back on her heels and shrugged off the pink satin robe she wore for the men who came to the house, then again dropped her head between his thighs.

Azalea's stomach pitched.

"Yeah, woman," Mack said, his words coughed up between breathy gasps. "That's it. That's the way."

Atlas slurped his milk. His eyes grew heavy.

Mack's grunts turned deep. His head bounced back and forth like a bobber on the end of a fishing line. "Shit," he said, snorting and heaving forward before falling limp against the sofa. Rose dropped onto her bottom.

Disgusted and confused by what she'd seen, Azalea dashed to her bedroom and locked the door. She pulled on some shorts and a collared shirt dirty from days of wear, scuffed on a pair of flip flops inches too long, and wrapped Atlas in the quilted blanket. She froze in the middle of the room, angling her head toward the door. Mack and her mama were quiet for now.

Keeping Atlas close to her body, Azalea slipped through the room's open window, slithering alongside the house like a copperhead searching for summer shade. Holding her breath, she looked back at the front door before darting across the clearing.

A crow cried out from a brush pile and took off for a spindly pine. Azalea yelped and ran faster, skirting past low-growing cedars and swatches of goldenrod that scraped her bare shins. Her side was quick to ache, but she lengthened her stride, kicking up dirt and pine straw with every step.

She caught sight of the forsythia, a grand old bush whose bright yellow blossoms had long since faded. Rose said it had bloomed for the very first time the day Azalea was born. She'd even considered calling her baby girl Forsythia before deciding on Azalea instead. A morning breeze ruffled the shrub's leafy branches, making it look like a squatty, long-haired crone flailing her arms, encouraging Azalea to run harder.

"Four, three, two, one," she counted off her last steps, then crawled underneath the bush where she had culled the lowest branches to better shape a hiding spot. Choking on fear and dust, Azalea rolled onto her side and clung to Atlas, her stomach still knotted from what she'd just seen. Atlas tugged on her nose and grinned.

"Lucky boy," she whispered in Atlas's ear. "You got no idea what's going on in that house."

Atlas squirmed. Azalea pulled him closer. She could see the wheels of Mack's truck parked on the roadside.

Those upstanding Christian women who'd come to the house with their Bibles had promised Scripture and prayer could solve any problem. "Hand your troubles over to the Almighty," they'd said. "Trust the Lord in all things. His love knows no bounds." They had talked big about God and love that day. Apparently Rose Parker and her two ragamuffin children were deserving of both. But at twelve years old, Azalea had already figured out that in Sweetwater, Tennessee, you had to be sick with the cancer or lose a leg like Leonard Bush to get a chicken casserole or homemade pie with no strings attached. Couldn't those women see that a man like Mack just filled in the gaps between an empty belly and a full one?

Azalea gazed through the forsythia's leaves to blue sky. Was God up there, looking down on her? Could He hear Atlas fussing or Mack grunting? Could he see Rose on her knees? Her face flushed hot. For her mama's sake, Azalea hoped God was as forgiving as the church women had promised.

Azalea herself had never prayed on her own. She'd gone to Vacation Bible School one summer and always bowed her head at school when Miss Roberts led the class in a morning devotional. But she had never come up with her own words. Now balled up in her secret burrow, she pressed her palms together and studied a patch of blue sky. Atlas began squealing. Across the road, a bullfrog started croaking and quickly grew more and more insistent. "Shut up," she hissed. "The both of you. I can't think." Again she tried to find the words deserving of God's ear, but Atlas and the bullfrog only cried louder. *Ain't no point*, she thought. God wasn't likely listening anyway. She lay beneath the branches a while longer until she was sure her mama and Mack were done with business. Then she picked up Atlas and scooted out from under the forsythia. A clump of butterfly weed across the yard caught her attention. She plucked some to add to the cedar in her mama's crystal vase. Maybe Mack had left the bag of groceries in his truck.

# — Emmett Bush —

EMMETT TUCKED A gnawed number two pencil behind his ear, then rolled his desk chair closer to the milk room's open door. On days like this when a gentle wind blew from the west just right, he could hear the river's rushing waters nearly a mile away. His heartbeat slowed, and his breathing grew deeper. The river had always held the power to lull Emmett to a gentler place. As a boy, he had fished Big Sugar and bathed in its gentle pools. He had carried his fears and dreams to its banks and trusted the river to keep them secret. As a father, he had cradled his infant son at the river's edge and sprinkled its water on his brow and fingers, eager for his baby to love this place from the start. Now Emmett closed his eyes and listened a while longer. In his mind, he traced the river's circuitous route as it spilled over rocks and fallen trees, winding its way to deeper, broader waters.

"Dammit." He smeared a tear into his cheek. "Enough already." Emmett reached for the pencil and a leather-bound ledger that held the dairy's daily successes and failures. Turning to a fresh page, he noted the date in the upper-right corner, November 9, and the pounds of milk he'd collected this morning, 503. A single tear dripped onto the page.

June blamed him for Leonard's loss. Most days, Emmett blamed himself, too. He was the one who had promised their son he could fish Big Sugar that September afternoon. He'd dangled that home-made lure in front of Leonard, guaranteeing the bass would go for it. June had protested, said the river wasn't safe, although her only reasoning for such a claim was a haunting premonition, a twisted feeling in her gut. More of her silly superstitions, Emmett had told her. June didn't understand the joy that came from casting a line and teasing a fish onto a hook. She didn't understand the magic of the river, wading knee deep into its cold waters and balancing on rocks smoothed with age. If there was a God in heaven, as June insisted, then surely He intended a boy to fish Big Sugar whether he stood on one leg or two.

Emmett tapped the pencil against the ledger's open page, then jotted down numbers in a column and quickly totaled the sum. He scribbled computations on a scrap of paper, ignoring the electric adding machine June had bought him last year. He checked his addition a second time. The cows had milked particularly well this morning, putting out a hundred pounds more than they had any other day this week. Behind him, two stainless steel tanks stored a generous three-days' yield. Any other farmer in these parts would've been pleased. He closed the ledger, pulled two cigarettes from his shirt pocket, and slipped one between his lips and one behind his ear.

The day he married June, Emmett had promised never to smoke again. He was in love then, a deep, gaga kind of love that left him weak-kneed and tongue-tied. Young and impetuous, he would have lassoed the sun and the moon had she asked for them. A thick puff of smoke hovered in the air before thinning and stealing its way out the open window. He'd kept that promise, too, until Leonard's surgeon had offered him a Salem, warning that he'd need to be strong for his family. "Besides, your wife won't mind you smoking these," the surgeon had said. "They're menthol."

The cigarette dangled from Emmett's mouth, and the tissue-thin wrapping paper stuck to his bottom lip. He had tried to be strong from the very moment June had screamed for him from the kitchen door, blubbering something about Leonard and fever. Later, when she fell into his arms, begging him to save their son's leg, Emmett had not cried. When he first caught sight of Leonard's stump, raw and sutured with black thread, he had not gagged. When a nurse handed him the amputated limb packed on ice in a Styrofoam box, he had not flinched. June accused him of being heartless, but she was wrong. Emmett's heart ached, and the pain was never ceasing. In the month and a half since the surgery, his guilt had only festered, burrowing deeper into his heart like a worm finding its way inside an ear of corn. He feared his heart might truly break.

Emmett scanned the room as if he were scouting for enemies lying in wait. He puffed on the cigarette, then reached inside his pants pocket and pulled out a child's ankle boot. The brown leather was polished to a high shine, the lace tied into a neat bow. He placed the shoe in the palm of his hand, then gently closed his fingers around it as if he were cradling a baby bird. He pressed its toe to his lips. This was the only physical memento left of his baby sister's short life on this earth. And he'd always kept it close. Sometimes in the dresser drawer in the bedroom where June set his t-shirts and briefs. But more often, he kept it in his pocket, reaching for a quick touch without even thinking. A silly quirk, he told himself. A long-held secret between him and his baby sister, Sarah. He knew it wasn't normal behavior, but he couldn't stop it either. Since the amputation, his need for the shoe had grown stronger. Emmett relaxed against the chair. He pressed its toe to his lips a second time.

Just outside the milk room, a calf shuffled inside her hutch, padded thick with straw. He rubbed the shoe against his lips, kissed its toe, then slipped it back in his pants pocket before taking a last, long drag on the cigarette. "Bet you're hungry, baby girl," he said and fetched a stainless pail filled full from the herd's last milking. Without spilling a drop, he poured the creamy liquid into a bottle and clamped a rubber nipple to its top, then called to the calf. Sure-footed at two weeks, she bolted from the hutch and lunged for the bottle, her tongue grabbed hold of the nipple, nearly yanking it from his hand. He laughed, and the pink-nosed calf gulped down the milk, cooing dovelike as she suckled.

Before the accident, bottle-feeding calves and scraping the feed barn floor were Leonard's chores. These days, June was against that, too. Although Emmett was in no mood to fight her, he missed the hours at the dairy alone with his son, especially in the late afternoons when he could ask Leonard about his day.

"Good girl," Emmett said, patting the calf's head. She nudged his hand. "Ain't got no more." He pulled the empty bottle from her mouth.

The calf was growing strong. Emmett would add more grain to her diet in the next few days. Before long, he'd turn her out into the field. "Go on," he said, but the calf pressed against the side of the pen and licked his hand. He pulled the cigarette from behind his ear and held it to his nose but didn't strike the match. Instead, he flicked the unlit cigarette into the straw and slid to the ground, cross-legged, his back against the pen. The baby calf nuzzled up behind him. He slipped his hand in his pocket while Big Sugar crooned in the distance.

# — Leonard —

LEONARD LOCKED HIS BEDROOM door, then propped the swollen stump on a bed pillow wrapped in a crisply starched case. He dipped a clean washcloth into a pan of soapy water and dabbed where the skin had rubbed clean away. A blistering pain licked down his left calf although it was no longer there. He gripped his thigh and squeezed, trying to choke the fiery ache.

He had walked on the fake leg too long today, then gone and done something foolish. At recess, Eddie Burl had challenged him to race from one end of the football field to the other. Leonard knew it was wrong to do it, but he'd missed competition of any kind — catching a touchdown pass, holding a runner at third base, sinking a basket from the foul line. Coaches and teachers were as skittish about his well-being as his mama was. But none of them were around when Eddie Burl had dared him, only Azalea and Little Henry cheering him on from the bleachers. In the end, he'd fallen twice and lost by fifty yards.

"I ain't even run my hardest," Eddie Burl had jeered, before challenging Little Henry.

Tonight, Leonard wasn't sure which hurt worse — his leg or his pride. If his mama saw his stump, swollen and oozing, she'd make a fuss, keep vigil by his bed during the night, and call the doctor first thing come morning. She'd claim something new and sinister was brewing, another infection maybe. Or worse. Most likely, she'd chant a prayer while burning sage and cedar, careful to waft the smoke throughout the house. Still anxious, she'd call the preacher and beg him to pray for Leonard by name, come to the house and lay hands on him despite the late hour.

Leonard imagined Emmett rolling his eyes and quickly excusing himself, suggesting he had books to balance, a tractor engine to repair, silage to ready for morning. In response, June would accuse him of not caring, not loving Leonard like she did. Emmett might shake his head, mumble something under his breath, but he'd be certain to slam the door on his way out. The window would rattle. June would throw a hairbrush, book, or metal spoon, whatever was handy. When they argued last, she'd reached for Leonard's baby shoes, bronzed and rock solid, but thought better of it and set them back on the console television. After the fighting was done, the house had fallen quiet, a sickening quiet that left Leonard raw at the edges. He knew this routine too well. His mama and daddy had always fought, usually about him or the dairy. But this felt different.

Gritting his teeth, Leonard swabbed the wound with the damp cloth. This was not the first time the fake leg had rubbed his skin raw. Whenever he wore the prosthetic too long or didn't get the fit tight enough on the stump, he faced this kind of blistering. The doctor had warned this was to be expected from time to time. "Kids handle these little setbacks better than adults," he'd said. Leonard had always been reticent about sharing the full truth with his mama, knowing her tendency to worry and fret. The cut on his left foot he'd suffered at Big Sugar was an unfortunate example of his caution. But since leaving the hospital nearly three months ago, he'd become even more expert at hiding things like this.

He dabbed at the wound some more, then squeezed some ointment onto his finger and smoothed it over the nub, wrinkling his nose at the pain. He covered it with a thin layer of gauze, adding another layer, and another after that, wishing he had a second box of the sterile cotton so he could build a thicker pad. Come morning, his mama would frown if he came to the breakfast table on crutches. June liked things looking tidy and perfect—her kitchen, her garden, her sewing, her family. Leonard taped the bandage in place. In the next room, June's and Emmett's voices scratched at the wall. It was starting up again.

Leonard pawed at the air just below the stump. The pain was bad tonight, but the ache of being duped into thinking his leg was there was far worse. Some nights, lying in bed, he was certain it was. In the dark, he could see every detail of his old leg—the shape of the birthmark on the back of his calf, the once-fine blond hairs growing coarse and thick, the curve of his knee and the scab he usually carried there, the contour of his ankle and how it looked more like his daddy's than his mama's, his second toe that was slightly longer than the first, another trait he took from his daddy. A Bush from head to toe, June would say. Come morning, though, when Leonard drew back the covers, he would be reminded that he was indeed a one-legged boy, one who would never beat Eddie Burl in a race.

He dropped the washcloth into the water and slid the pan under the bed. The pillowcase was stained with a yellow seepage. The surgeon had warned the stump might ooze like this whenever the skin was rubbed raw. "You keep it clean, young man," he'd said, placing his hand on Leonard's shoulder. "You don't want to see me again." Leonard hid the pillowcase under the bed, too. Tomorrow, when June wasn't looking, he'd get rid of both.

Leonard scooted to the dresser on the other side of the room and opened the middle drawer. He pulled out a pair of pajamas and tossed the shirt he was wearing on the floor. Someday, he feared, he'd remember nothing of the boy he had been before he lost his leg, the boy who could beat Eddie Burl at almost anything—running, casting, even adding and subtracting. The day he cut his foot on the shard of brown bottle glass, he was chasing Eddie Burl to Big Sugar to catch the biggest bass. Before leaving the house, June had made him promise not to wade into the water barefooted.

Leonard still got riled remembering how Eddie Burl had smarted off that afternoon. "Ain't no fish in Tennessee that'll bite at that bottle cap, and your daddy's a fool for thinking so," Eddie Burl had said before pitching a rock into Big Sugar. He laughed and called Emmett crazy. Worse than that, he doubted Emmett could catch a bass or any other fish even if it swam right onto his hook. He tossed a second rock farther than the first.

Eddie Burl picked on everybody, and his jabs grew sharper when he needed to feel stronger. Usually Leonard ignored him, but this time he was determined to prove him wrong. Despite his mama's warnings, he kicked off his shoes and waded into the water so he could cast a better line. He snagged a smallmouth right away and held it up for Azalea to admire. She clapped and begged Leonard to catch another.

"What you got on the end of your line, Eddie Burl?" he'd asked with a taunting grin.

"Big deal," Eddie Burl said.

"Yeah, big deal, seeing how I caught it with my daddy's lure, the one you said was no good." Leonard wiggled the hook from the fish's mouth. "You need my daddy to make you one?" he asked, dangling the lure in his hand.

Without warning, Eddie Burl tossed his rod aside and picked up Leonard's shoes. He held them up like he was primed to play keep-away but then flung them into the water. "See if you can catch those with that crazy thing," he said, his smile cutting.

"What the hell, Eddie Burl?"

Eddie Burl cackled and pointed to the shoes floating downstream.

Swiftly casting a line, Leonard caught one and yanked it to shore. Azalea grabbed it from the hook, and Leonard cocked his arm and cast again. But the lure plopped into the water inches short of the target. "Dang it," Leonard said and hurried to reel in the line.

Eddie Burl, doubled over, laughed harder.

"You're a jerk, Eddie Burl," Azalea said.

"Boo hoo," Eddie Burl sassed back.

The other shoe, trapped in churning waters, bobbed up and down. Leonard waded waist deep and cast again. The shoe popped up, a tiny speck of white against metal gray water. Leonard tugged on the line, but the shoe had slipped away. Leonard smacked the water's surface, then spun around, aiming the tip of his rod at Eddie Burl. A broken bottle lay buried just beneath the shore's silky clay. A piece of glass that changed his life.

Now alone in his room, a flash of anger washed over him. At the leg funeral, he'd felt mostly at peace with his loss, promising his mama and everyone there on the hilltop that it was an accident. He'd kept Eddie Burl's behavior a secret, holding no grudge. But maybe his mama was right. Maybe his head had been muddled with fever that day. Tonight, with the stump aching and the missing leg clamoring for attention, Leonard wanted to spill the whole truth, point his finger at Eddie Burl and blame him for his part. But what good would come of it? It wouldn't change a thing. He shook off the memory and slipped on his pajamas, tying the dangling pant leg into a knot while his parents' voices grew louder. He scooted across the floor, gripped the top of the mattress, pushed up on his foot, and hoisted his body onto the bed.

The throbbing in his stump was strong tonight. He lay flat and stared up at the ceiling. He didn't have a good idea of what he looked like anymore, having carefully avoided the plateglass window at the IGA supermarket and the large mirror in the boys' bathroom at school, anywhere he might catch his likeness staring back at him. When his daddy drove him out to the pond in the late afternoons to check on the herd, Leonard refused to walk near the water for fear of seeing his reflection floating on its surface. He knew he was one-legged. He didn't need to see it.

If he had to guess, he figured he looked most like the boy pictured on the tin can at Mitchell's Hardware, the one collecting spare change for the crippled children attending the Easterseals camp in Middle Tennessee. That boy didn't have any legs and only one good arm. Once he and Eddie Burl had poked fun at him, sitting in a wheelchair with an oversized grin spread across his face. "What's he got to smile about?" Eddie Burl had joked, then tipped the can over, robbing it of a nickel for the gumball machine. Thinking back on it, Leonard hated himself for laughing at that boy. Maybe Brother Puckett was right. Maybe the Lord was a vengeful, punishing God. But that didn't make sense. Eddie Burl still had both his legs. Leonard shimmied underneath the covers and turned out the light.

In the next room, June and Emmett's fight strengthened, a wild vine sprouting new growth with every mean word and accusation. It seemed they were dedicated to its nurturing, watering and feeding their anger nearly every night. Leonard feared it would wrap itself around their necks and strangle the breath right out of them.

He shoved his head under the downy pillow.

If there were a greater purpose to come from his loss, a potential salve for his parents' wounds, he wished someone would share it with them. The preacher, their friends and neighbors, even Miss Ooten, had chanted this singular refrain: *God will make His divine purpose known in good time.*

There was biblical proof for their reasoning. Baby Moses had been plucked from the bulrushes of the Nile and handed over to a queen. Joseph had been sold into slavery, his own brothers exchanging his young life for a bag of silver. In the end, great things came to both Moses and Joseph, but Leonard had no dramatic story to tell. He was simply a dairyman's son who'd cut his foot on a piece of glass. The talk that had swirled around the hilltop the day of the leg funeral, talk about him being "special" and "blessed," only caused his stomach to sour. He was *special* all right. But *blessed?*

A one-legged boy never won a footrace or attracted a pretty girl like Azalea Parker. At best, his mama and daddy might send him to the Easterseals camp, and he and that boy in the wheelchair might end up best friends.

Leonard shifted to his side. His mama's words grew sharp. He plugged his fingers in his ears and tried counting sheep. At 2:35, he started counting the heartbeats in his stump instead.

# — June —

 JUNE KNEW BETTER THAN to trust her cake baking to Betty Crocker. At the time, she'd worried she was cheating, not baking from scratch. But there had been canning and laundry and a run to the co-op for another roll of barbed wire Emmett needed before dark. Miss Ooten had reassured her that there was no fault in taking a shortcut on occasion and that adding a heaping cup of love and a dash of vanilla extract to the batter would make it nearly as good as homemade.

"You ain't got to be perfect, June," Miss Ooten had told her. "That's Mrs. Crocker's business."

Yet the one day June used a box mix all hell broke loose. Funny, she thought, she never did get a taste of that yellow cake, having left it to burn up in the oven while she and Emmett raced Leonard to the doctor in town.

When she woke this morning, June thought of baking another cake, from scratch, maybe a pumpkin spice for the Thanksgiving holiday. Emmett was at the dairy. Leonard was watching cartoons in the front room. She had most of the morning to do as she pleased. But the memory of Leonard convulsing on the kitchen floor while that Betty Crocker cooked in the oven had robbed her of the pleasure she'd once found in baking. Instead she set the kitchen radio to her favorite station, then fetched the iron and board from her sewing room. She reached for one of Emmett's work shirts and sprinkled the cotton with starch water while the iron heated up. Patsy Cline crooned about love and heartache and falling to pieces over a man.

June licked her index finger and touched the iron. A slight sizzle. She held the iron firmly against the cotton, just below the collar, then swept it down the front panel in a single stroke. Pleased with her work, she adjusted the shirt on the board, first peeking at the outdoor thermometer tacked to the window's frame. Temperatures were finally turning cold, and a lacy frost had decorated the foothills. Again, she swept the iron across the cotton, spritzing it with more starch whenever a wrinkle proved stubborn. Emmett said there was no need to starch and iron his work shirts. "Them cows don't care how I look."

*Them cows. Them cows.* Sometimes Emmett acted like they were the only women in his life. *My husband ain't going nowhere looking a wrinkled mess.* Finishing the first shirt, June folded it with sharp creases and set it aside. Glancing out the window, something at the far end of the drive caught her eye. She leaned over the ironing board, squinting for a better look. Miss Ooten had called yesterday evening claiming a black bear was poking around her yard. June had not believed her. Miss Ooten was more lonely for company than worried about a bear trespassing on her property. June looked again, though, just to make sure. The wispy figure lingering at the end of the drive was no animal.

It was Little Henry Reed. June knew the boy hated it when people called him *Little*, but he was the same age as Leonard and only two-thirds his size. Not long before her death, his mama, Margaret, had admitted that the men in her family tended to measure abnormally short. Muscled and strong, but short. A distant uncle was a circus worker for Ringling Brothers, and though Margaret seemed proud of that fact, she had also admitted that Little Henry's daddy, Wayne, was rough on the boy for not growing faster. Now in the silver mist of early morning, Little Henry kicked at the Bush's mailbox. "Go home," June whispered. "Please. Go home."

Margaret had been her best friend. Kind and soft-spoken, mother and son were alike in that way. They even shared the same crooked front tooth and sky blue eyes. June smiled, wishing she could tell her friend how the loss of Leonard's leg grieved her. Margaret would understand her pain.

The newspaper had reported Margaret's passing was an accident. Apparently, Wayne blubbered to the sheriff, swore he never saw his wife pinning bedsheets to the line while he sat on the porch, cleaning his shotgun, shooting off the last shell. Sadly, Little Henry had been a witness to it all. And June was convinced that the round of bad luck that took Leonard's leg started the moment Wayne pulled the trigger, immediately tethering itself to Little Henry. Days later, like Typhoid Mary, the boy carried the bad luck right to their own kitchen table. He had shared a meal with them the night before Leonard fell ill.

This isn't to say June didn't hurt for Little Henry. She did. She had been about his age when she lost her own mother, so she knew firsthand how his heart ached. No matter, the boy needed to leave. A final round of bad luck was certainly circling around him like a kettle of vultures. June pressed the iron to the cotton collar of a Sunday shirt, never taking her eye off the boy still kicking at the mailbox post.

Emmett would be furious with her for not inviting Little Henry in for breakfast, but June couldn't worry about that. Emmett had longed for a house full of children as much as she had, and she'd seen him worry over lesser things than a motherless boy. Yet he rarely put words to what pained him. June had hoped fatherhood might change that about him, help him open up about his fears and worries. She sighed and doused the shirt with more starch while Patsy Cline's throaty contralto reminded her how much she missed the way Emmett had loved her in the early years of marriage.

Leonard laughed out loud in the front room. And Little Henry started up the drive.

"Dammit, Little Henry, I can't be your mama." June untied her apron and tossed it on the counter, forgetting the iron weighing heavy against Emmett's shirt. She took off down the drive, running toward the post box. "Go on, Henry," she waved her hands, shooing him like she might a feral cat. "I mean it. Get on home."

Little Henry scrambled backwards and took off running. He

stumbled, pitched forward, caught his balance, then took off again, his arms pumping hard at his sides. June watched the boy until he disappeared behind a thick patch of chokeberry. Satisfied, she hurried back to the house, tucking loose hairs behind her ears. She stepped inside the kitchen to find Emmett with the iron in his hand, the shirt smoking on the board.

"You trying to burn down the house?" he asked.

"No! Of course not." She snatched the iron from Emmett, set it on the board, knotted her apron around her waist, and tossed a dishcloth across one shoulder. "Thought you were at the barn." She glanced out the window, then at Emmett's ruined shirt.

"I was. Thank goodness I came in for something to drink." He pulled a glass from the cupboard.

June shook her head. "Leave me be. I got a lot on my mind."

Emmett opened the refrigerator door and reached for a pitcher of tea. "You get the morning paper while you were out there?"

"Paper wasn't there yet," June said without looking up.

"At this hour?" Emmett glanced out the window.

"I said it wasn't there." June examined the burn mark. There was no saving the shirt. That too was Little Henry's fault. She set the shirt aside, hoping she could stitch some of it into a quilt.

Emmett poured himself a glass of tea and gulped it down in three swigs. Wiping his mouth on his shirtsleeve, he reached into the refrigerator and pulled some meat from the ham June had cooked day before yesterday.

"Get a plate," she said, disgusted when Emmett grazed like one of his cows, filling his mouth full of food and smacking as loud as those four-legged beasts chewing their cud.

"Don't need a plate. Ain't making a sandwich." Emmett stuffed more meat into his mouth.

"Here," she said and handed him a paper napkin, remembering the first time she had laid eyes on Emmett at the Blue Ridge Coffee Shop in Sylva. A few days earlier, she had turned sixteen and was finally working away from her daddy's farm. Emmett said he'd come to North Carolina to look at a bull offered up at a fair price and would only be in town for a day. Maybe two. "That's a shame," she'd told him and brought him a thick slice of freshly made pound cake. She'd felt a prickling in her stomach then, but now her husband's drinking and eating annoyed her, the sound of his chewing enough to make her shudder with disgust.

"Seriously, what were you doing out there?" Emmett wiped his mouth and dropped the napkin on the counter.

"None of your mind."

"Just a simple question, June."

"I ain't got to report to you what I do or where I go."

Emmett refilled his glass. "Ain't everything got to be an argument neither."

June adjusted a shirtsleeve on the board and pressed the iron to it.

"I'm taking Leonard fishing later today." Emmett fingered the rim of the glass. "Think it'll do him some good to get back out there before the weather turns too cold. Don't want him growing afraid of it."

June set down the iron and flicked off the radio. "No, you ain't." She knew her words rang harsh, even she was surprised by the shrillness of her voice. But Emmett had no right to take their son back to Big Sugar without asking first. It was too dangerous. The last of the bad luck, the third event, had not yet struck. Sometimes it was sneaky like that, waiting weeks or months before its final blow. By June's count, Margaret's death was one. Leonard's leg, two. How could Emmett tempt fate knowing more was due? Little Henry's coming around this morning was a surefire sign. *This time, Emmett Bush, you're going to listen.*

Smoothing the front of her apron, she said, "I'd think you'd be more respectful of my wishes, considering all we've been through. You know bad things come screaming out of nowhere. You got to pay attention to the signs, Emmett. They ain't silly superstitions. They're gifts from God."

Emmett banged the glass against the counter. "You think our

son losing his leg was some kind of gift?" He pushed past June and shoved his feet into his boots left by the back door. "It's Saturday, and I'm taking my son fishing. I don't need your permission." The door slammed shut in his wake.

*You're twisting my words, Emmett Bush, and you damn well know it. If nothing else, you'd think losing your own baby sister when you were a boy would leave you more understanding of my fears.* June wanted to run after Emmett, force him to see things her way, but she knew no good would come of it. She also knew her husband was tight with a dollar, snored most of the night, and littered the bare floor with his toenail clippings. But when it came to other things — his fears and hurts — she knew very little about him. He was a secret keeper like Leonard, and she hated that about them both. *Go on, Emmett, run to the barn. Hide like you always do.*

June washed his glass and placed it on the dish drain to dry. Outside the window, a squirrel scurried down the pin oak, a nut clenched between his teeth. Farther up the drive, Emmett tugged on the door to the milk room. June had known so little about men and love when she'd married. Her daddy hadn't taught her much about either. She'd kissed only one other boy before Emmett — Bobby Renfrow, and he'd nearly gagged her with his tongue. The only women to guide her — her mama, Margaret, Miss Ooten — were either dead or had never married.

The smell of scorched cotton hung in the air. First the Betty Crocker cake and now Emmett's shirt. She couldn't do anything right. No doubt, she'd done wrong by Little Henry this morning, too, but nothing Emmett could say would've changed her course. She picked up the iron and ran it down the left sleeve of his second-best shirt. Maybe later, Emmett would come around and sweeten his talk, sneak a kiss on the back of her neck, slip his arms around her waist. At the very least, he'd look fine in his crisply pressed shirt.

# — Leonard —

 IN HIS DREAMS, Leonard took his mama by the hand and led her to Big Sugar, silence hanging between them as they crossed pasture and navigated woods. Outfitted in the same black dress she'd worn to the hilltop service, June stood steadfast on the creek's shore, the cold water lapping at her feet. Her long hair whipped across her face. On the far bank, a heron, balanced on twiggy legs, arced, and leapt for the sky. June waded into deeper water, the hem of her dress floating about her waist.

Standing firm on two feet, Leonard pushed his bare toes into the shore's clay, the river stones slippery underfoot. June dangled the bottle cap lure in front of him. The sun struck its metal, a blazing orb dancing over the water.

"Come back, Mama," he called.

June smiled and waved him forward.

Leonard took a step, but his foot gave way. "The water's too deep."

"The water is fine," she said and slipped beneath its surface.

———

A KNOCK CAME LOUD at Leonard's bedroom door.

"Come on, son," Emmett said. "Your mama's got breakfast on the table, and we got fish to catch." Emmett poked his head into the room. "Might want to wear your leg," he said and nodded toward the kitchen. "She's in a mood."

Leonard rubbed his eyes, the dream still clouding his thoughts. He didn't understand its meaning, or if it even had one. But he'd dreamed it three nights, and it taunted him every time it came around. He always woke from it fearing for his mama, swallowed up in Big Sugar in one long gulp.

"You hear me?" Emmett knocked on the doorframe. "Get a move on."

Leonard tossed back the covers. "Yes, sir."

He rushed to dress, first slipping a heavy sock over the stump, then shoving it into the prosthetic. Through an opening above the knee, Leonard reached for the sock, tugging and tugging until he held the whole of it in his hand, the stump sucked tight inside the wooden leg. The fit was a tad loose, but he had no time to reset it. Emmett was waiting. Leonard yanked on his jeans and hurried down the hall, swinging the fake leg awkwardly with every step.

Already seated at the table, Emmett pushed back a chair with his foot. "You better eat them eggs real quick. There's a bass waiting for me out there." He held up a paper sack. "I got ham sandwiches for later." He leaned close and cupped his hand to his mouth. "Even stole a couple of cookies your mama baked for Sunday church. Don't tell her. She might send the deacons over here to pray for us." He handed Leonard a paper napkin. "Use this," he said, "not your shirt-sleeve," and stood up from the table.

Leonard scarfed down a few bites of egg then pushed the plate aside. "Ain't really hungry," he said and followed his daddy to the truck. He hollered goodbye to his mama, busy pouring birdseed into the feeder hanging from the pin oak's lowest limb. She stared back but didn't speak, reminding Leonard of his dream. He didn't believe in superstitious notions like his mama. But he hadn't been back to Big Sugar since the amputation. He wondered if his dream held a message, one he needed to heed. Leonard glanced back at June, scattering the last of the seed into the yard.

"She'll be fine," Emmett said, starting up the engine.

Leonard didn't believe that to be true. He feared he would always be the source of her worries. But the excitement of fishing with his daddy outweighed any guilt he might have felt in that moment, even if they were driving to the water and not walking as they always had in the past. Part of the day's fun had been crossing the field together, scouting for dove in the fall and turkey in the spring. "Don't worry," Emmett said as he set the poles in the back of the truck. "It won't always be like this. Your mama will come around." Leonard nodded, then pulled himself onto the seat and waved to June. When she went inside without a goodbye, Emmett gripped the wheel, his knuckles coloring up white. Leonard settled against the seat, already thinking about the fish he'd catch.

Leaving the truck on the ridge top, Emmett and Leonard hiked slowly through thick patches of faded reeds and tall grasses. Big Sugar gleamed below them. Oaks, maples, and hickories stood nearly bare in late November while the smell of cedar and pine grew stronger where the land altered its pitch and sloped sharply to the water's edge. On the far side of the river, someone was burning brush, the smoke of it slightly charring the otherwise sweet woodsy air.

Tracking close behind his daddy, Leonard zigzagged around clumps of suckers and mountain laurel. His left hip started to ache. Thinking back on it, he wished he'd taken more time to better secure the prosthetic to the stump. He plodded along, placing most of his weight on his good foot and reaching for stray branches to balance his next steps. Emmett glanced over one shoulder with a concerned look. Leonard shook his head. "I'm good," he said.

Up ahead, the water lapped against the bank. He lengthened his stride, dragging his fake leg behind him, eager to beat his daddy to the first cast. Leonard dropped his tackle box in the grass and plopped down on the ground, his breath puffing up a cloudy white against a dazzling blue sky.

Emmett pointed downriver. "Try over there. Where them logs are jammed up. That's the honey-hole where we'll find us a fish." Emmett threaded his line, his strong hands nimble as he tied a black-dotted jitterbug to the end of the nylon. The reel hummed as the lure sped across the water, dragging the line behind it.

"Nice," Leonard said, his good leg curled up beneath him, his other one sticking out straight. He had not looked inside his tackle box since the day he'd come to the river with Azalea and Eddie Burl. A chill beset him seeing the box just as he had left it, packed with brightly colored lures, a cleaning knife, spools of extra line, a half dozen bobbers, and the bottle cap lure. He'd caught a bass with it just like his daddy had promised, proving Eddie Burl wrong. Leonard traced the cap's circumference with the tip of his finger but picked another one crowned with a wisp of yellow feathers instead.

Emmett tugged on his line. A single maple leaf, tinted deep orange-red, spun and twirled before landing on the water. Every color was brilliant and sharp, leaving the world looking both dreamlike and overly real. Leonard's heart thumped harder, and he'd have sworn his left toes were stretching for the water if he couldn't see for himself it wasn't so.

He rolled onto his knee. Emmett held out his hand and pulled him to his feet.

Big Sugar had always given Leonard a courage he couldn't fully explain. It was a rejuvenating power, Emmett told him once, that sprang from a mere trickle on a wooded mountaintop that grew deeper, wider, and stronger with its descent. Leonard didn't doubt that, but what he knew for certain was that on the river's banks, father and son had once talked about everything. Sports — Leonard's heroes, baseball's Hank Aaron and Willie Mays, football's Jim Taylor and Jim Brown. The farm. Girls. The birds and the bees. Even doubts about heaven and hell. And Big Sugar had washed it all away. Emmett claimed every generation of Bush men had found a similar solace in this water. But the world had shifted since the amputation, and Leonard wondered if either Big Sugar or his daddy could bear the troubles of a one-legged boy. If he did confess them, what could his daddy say to reassure him? And could the river be trusted with his secrets?

At the leg funeral, Eddie Burl had brought presents, Yahtzee and Risk. Sitting-down games his mama Vivienne had called them. Was that all he was good for anymore? Sitting-down games? Leonard carried a burden of worry that grew heavier each day, and he wanted to share the load with his father. But standing beside Emmett, their elbows nearly touching, Leonard feared what his father might think. Would he blame himself for his son's worries? Or might he think Leonard was turning weak, a little less of the boy he had been before the amputation? Leonard shook off the thought and looked to the logs jammed up in the river. He pitched his weight to his right foot, struggling to find a steady balance. He cast his rod forward, without releasing any line, and pretended to reel in his first catch.

"Go on, son. Get your line out there. There's a big one waiting for you."

# — June —

JUNE'S HANDS BURNED from the bleach water in the kitchen sink, but she was too angry to care. The counter didn't need a second scrubbing. She recognized that. But Emmett made her seething mad — dropping a half dozen trout on her clean Formica, telling her to cook them up for supper, then announcing it was time for Leonard to pick up his chores again. "Rake the barn and feed the calves."

June dipped the cloth into the water and wrung it out.

"Any boy who can fish like he did today can work the dairy," Emmett said. "He needs to get back to normal." He sidled up behind her and placed his hand on her waist. "We need to get back to normal, too, Junebug."

*Normal? What was that man thinking? Did he not see Leonard was still one-legged? Nothing about their lives would ever be normal.*

She pulled the drain plug and tossed the cloth on the counter. She had no taste for trout tonight. These would go in the freezer. She was cooking pork chops instead. She'd picked up two pounds at the market along with new Playtex gloves and some Bartlett pears. The pork chops were marinating in the refrigerator, her kitchen gloves hung across the faucet spout, and the pears were ripening on the windowsill above the sink.

"It's too soon for Leonard to be working the dairy," she had told Emmett.

"No, it ain't," was all he said, so matter-of-fact about it.

But Emmett wasn't a mama. He'd never understand her concerns. Nor did he trust her intuition. The other day, after Little Henry had come lurking about, Miss Ooten caught the tip of her finger in a rat trap, snapping the bone clean in two. Adding that incident to Margaret's death and Leonard's amputation, June had counted right. One. Two. Three. She was thankful this cycle of bad luck had passed, but she wasn't ready for Leonard to fish Big Sugar or work the farm. "There ain't no point in tempting fate," she said.

Emmett shook his head and walked out the door. June followed behind him. "I ain't finished talking to you," she hollered. "Come back here."

Emmett spun around. "Why don't you try stepping out of that kitchen once in a while," he said. "You might find there's a real big world out here where danger ain't lurking at every turn." He climbed into the truck, revved up the engine, and sped down the gravel drive, a trail of dust marking his getaway.

June slammed the door shut, rattling the plate glass. "Go on, run away like you always do!" she cried, then for no reason filled the sink full with clean water.

Seething, she pumped lotion onto the palm of her hand. *Damn cows.* She grabbed a pear from the windowsill. *Fine, Emmett, do what you want. You always do. But you ain't putting our only child back to work in that damn barn.* She cut a thick slice of pear and set it on a CorningWare plate. Emmett had bought the dish set from the Sears and Roebuck catalog Christmas a year ago. Pretty blue flowers trimmed the plate's band, a perfect match for her kitchen. She had kissed Emmett on the lips, right in front of Leonard, when she opened the box. So much had changed since then. She bit into another slice of pear, regretting she'd said the word *damn* twice, even if it had been spoken in her thoughts.

Leonard shuffled into the kitchen.

June lit up seeing him. "You shower that river off you?" she asked.

Leonard shoved his hands in his pockets. "I wasn't dirty."

"You smelled like fish when you came home." She hugged his neck and caught the clean scent of Ivory soap. "Keep me company," she said, pushing aside her argument with Emmett. She hurried to cut another pear and added the slices to the plate. "I saw these in the store yesterday."

Leonard sat at the table.

"Mr. Lykins said they came from California." She set the plate in front of Leonard and sat down beside him. "Can you imagine a pear traveling all the way from California?"

Leonard wrinkled his nose. "Got an apple?"

"Good to try something new." June smiled big as if she were encouraging a baby to take a first step. "Go on. Take a bite."

Leonard picked up the pear and held it to his nose.

"Go on."

Leonard nibbled the end of it.

"Take a real bite."

Leonard bit a little more. "Tastes like an apple some, but it don't feel the same in my mouth." He set what was left of it on the plate. "Don't feel right exactly."

"That's because it's a pear. Ain't the same as an apple." June held up a piece and admired it. "I read in the newspaper that Jackie Kennedy served poached pears in the White House. For dessert. Not exactly sure how to poach one, but if it's good enough for the First Lady and the president of the United States of America then it's good enough for Leonard Marlowe Bush of Sweetwater, Tennessee."

"Don't call me that, Mama."

"It's your name. Your God-given name. Marlowe after my mama's people." June popped the piece of fruit in her mouth. "Miss Ooten says I look like Jackie Kennedy." She pushed her hair a little higher and pursed her lips. "What do you think?" She preened like a fashion model in *Look* magazine. "Think your mama looks like the First Lady?"

Leonard shrugged. "You both got brown hair, I guess."

"Is that it?" June stood up and shoved the chair underneath the kitchen table, tired of the men in her life only seeing her as another hired hand. She set the plate in the kitchen sink, not even bothering to wash it. She reached for an apple in the wire basket, rinsed it off, cut a thick slice, and handed it to Leonard. "Your daddy don't like pears neither."

# — Azalea —

 VANITY WAS NOT THE reason for Azalea's early morning primping. The Olan Mills photographer was making his once-a-year visit to school today, and she wanted to look her very best. Not for beauty's sake. For historical accuracy.

In the third grade, Azalea had read an article in *My Weekly Reader* about famous photographers like Dorothea Lange documenting the country's *story*. That was the very word, *story*, and it stuck with Azalea. Ever since, she thought it important to have a photographic record of her own growing-up years. Without it, there could come a time when no one in Monroe County would remember Rose Parker's only girl. They would know nothing of her story.

She adjusted the collar on the cotton shirtwaist with the fake pearl buttons and practiced her smile in the bathroom mirror.

The dress's slightly gathered A-line skirt was a little big on her skinny frame and the hem a little too long, but she felt pretty in it, particularly the way it fluttered against her knees when she walked from one end of the room to the other. She'd snuck the dress out of her mama's closet, washed it, and pressed it with a cool iron. A belt at the waist tightened the fit, maybe even hinted at tiny bosoms up top. And the yellow ribbon Mack had given her tied around her hair proved the perfect finishing touch. Although Rose rarely dressed in more than nightclothes these days, she might snap at Azalea for taking from her closet without asking and worse for spending money on Olan Mills.

When Azalea brought the Olan Mills order slip home weeks ago, Rose had tossed it aside, explaining there was no money for such trifling things. "Sorry, baby, maybe next time," she'd said and fetched a couple of aspirin from the bathroom cabinet. But Azalea had planned for this day for a full year, saved since last December for the fee, stealing pennies and dimes from her mama's purse whenever she wasn't looking. Today, she'd leave the house early and wait for the bus a stop farther down the road just to make sure her mama didn't spot her dressed like she was going to church.

Ten minutes after eight, Miss Roberts tapped the blackboard, drawing everyone's attention to a lengthy list of equations, long division, and three-digit multiplication, printed in bold, neat numerals on the blackboard. Azalea pulled out paper and pencil and began calculating. Eddie Burl leaned over her shoulder. Azalea covered her answers. Working sums and quotients came easy to her, and a few minutes later, Miss Roberts called her to the blackboard. "Solve this one for the class, Azalea," she said, holding out a piece of chalk. "It's triple digit long division—your favorite."

Azalea wove around desks, angling toward the oversized windows that lined the far wall. Dust motes floated about her path, and the sun warmed her face. Around her, soft giggles bubbled up. The snickering grew louder. Eddie Burl reached across his desk and pointed. "*See-more* Parker!" he shouted, and the class fell into riotous laughter.

Azalea quickly fingered the buttons on her dress, checking that it was not gaping open. But when she looked down, she saw what Eddie Burl and the others had seen—the silhouetted shape of her legs, the slight curves of her hips. The cotton was too thin, and without a slip underneath, Azalea had bared her body in front of the sixth-grade class.

Miss Roberts rapped a ruler against her desk. "Get back to work," she said, handing Azalea the sweater draped across her shoulders. "Tie it around your waist," she whispered. Azalea hurried to her desk, her cheeks burning hot, her throat closing up. She scribbled down long stretches of numbers, not bothering to find the answers. Miss Roberts walked up and down each aisle like a sheriff keeping the peace. She touched students on the shoulder and dropped a tissue on Azalea's desk, drifting from her hand like a giant snowflake. Azalea crumpled it up in her fist. When the bell finally rang out and the class lined up outside the gymnasium for their turn with the photographer, Azalea threw the order form in the trash and hid in the girls' bathroom.

At lunch, she sat alone while the other kids clustered around long tables in the cafeteria. Their talk and laughter swirled about her. A few of the boys walked past, calling her *See-more* Parker as if that were her name. She gritted her teeth and pushed aside the carton of milk.

"Can I sit here?" Leonard set a paper sack on the table without waiting for an answer.

Azalea scooted a few inches to the left. She hated everybody at school today, even Leonard Bush. He lifted his fake leg up and over the bench seat and settled down beside her. "You look pretty," he said, flipping the bag upside down. Two sandwiches, two brownies, both wrapped neatly in wax paper, two apples, and one banana spilled onto the table. "Mama worries I'll go hungry before I get home for supper." Leonard laughed. "I think she's hoping that if she feeds me enough I might sprout a new leg." He held out a sandwich. "You want one? Can't eat them both."

Azalea took the sandwich, unwrapped the wax paper, and held the sandwich to her nose like she might a fine perfume. "Roast beef." She hadn't had much appetite for the cafeteria's chicken patty and carrot salad, but the roast beef was tempting.

He handed her a brownie. "You want this, too?"

She nodded and bit into the sandwich first.

Leonard rubbed one of the apples against the front of his shirt. "Never seen you looking so fancy."

"Shut up. I look a fool."

"No, you don't."

"Look again," Azalea said. "Unless that doctor cut out your good sense when he took your leg." Azalea took another bite of the sandwich, savoring the meat smeared with a thin layer of mustard and mayonnaise. She unwrapped the brownie, eager to try that next.

"Your mama make you wear that dress?"

"No," she snapped.

"Mama made me wear the leg." Leonard knocked his fist against the prosthetic. "Told her the picture was from my waist up."

"At least she cares."

Leonard nodded in an exaggerated way. "Oh yeah, she cares."

"How come you don't wear it every day?"

Leonard flicked a crumb across the table. "I don't know. Don't always feel right."

Azalea signaled as if she understood, but she couldn't imagine lugging around a wood leg. In that way, she figured she had it better than Leonard. She slipped the extra apple into her canvas bag for later.

"You been missing a lot of school lately. You been sick or something?" Leonard asked.

"I'm fine."

"Then how come you ain't been at school much? Barely come at all last week."

Azalea felt her face flush hot. "Dang it. You from welfare or something?"

Leonard fiddled with the paper sack, then crumpled it into a ball. He tossed it from one hand to the other, then raised his arm like he might on a pitching mound and pretended to fling it across the room. "Just wondering. No need for us to keep secrets from one another after you nursed my cut foot." He dropped the ball on the table.

"Didn't do you much good."

"You did your best."

Leonard was always nice. She'd never seen his temper flare, except toward Eddie Burl, and she figured that was justified, especially now. Her tone softened. "If you must know, I ain't been to school because my baby brother's been fussy. Teething. And Mama ain't feeling good lately. Says his crying gives her headaches." Azalea slid her hand over the sweater's cuff.

"Is that why you didn't come to my leg funeral? Your baby brother? You could've brought him."

"Lord, Leonard, that was months ago." Azalea wrapped up what was left of the roast beef sandwich and dropped it inside the canvas bag with the apple.

Leonard nodded. "You know it wasn't your fault, right?" Leonard twirled the apple around and took a bite from the other side.

"I know it," Azalea said, although she didn't fully believe she wasn't to blame. At least in part. When Leonard cut his foot and it started spewing blood, she had bandaged it with a dirty rag, one Eddie Burl had tossed her from his fishing box. She had rinsed the cloth in Big Sugar first and warned Leonard to clean the cut good when he got home. "With soap and water," she'd said, "maybe some hydrogen peroxide if you got it."

Later at school, when she saw the streaks of cherry red running up his calf, she regretted not saying something to Miss Roberts or the school nurse, but Leonard had sworn her to secrecy. He said his mama would fuss about it. Looking back on it, maybe some of this was her fault. But she had troubles of her own to worry over. She couldn't be heaping guilt on top of everything else.

"Don't it bother you, Leonard, the way some of them poke fun?" She glanced over her shoulder at the table where Eddie Burl sat with Icky Greer.

Leonard chewed his apple down to the core and dropped what was left of it on Azalea's tray. "Didn't know they did."

"Really?" she asked, her eyes growing big.

"Well, no more than usual." Leonard grinned. "Look, Eddie Burl can be a jerk. Don't pay him any mind."

The entire sixth-grade class seemed to be chattering at high speed except for Billy Myer shooting peas at Little Henry and Emily Watkins whispering secrets in Julia Armstrong's ear. Azalea wondered what best friends like Emily and Julia talked about. She wondered if they were talking about her and her see-through dress or making up stories about her and Leonard being lovebirds. She looked back at Leonard. He didn't seem bothered by any of it. "I think you're too nice, but I guess even Eddie Burl's got enough sense not to poke fun to your face."

Leonard laughed. "I don't know about that."

Azalea picked at a loose thread on the sweater's cuff. "I lay awake some nights thinking of ways to get back at Eddie Burl for every mean thing he's done. Even thought of killing him once." She cut a puckish grin. "But I ain't got a gun. And ain't fond of knives."

Leonard's eyes narrowed.

Azalea fussed with the loose thread some more. "I ain't ever going to do it. Even I know killing's a big-time sin, but there ain't no crime in thinking it."

"Brother Puckett says thinking and doing ain't much different." Leonard leaned in close like a best friend might, his nose nearly touching her ear. "But I don't think that." He lifted his leg over the bench and grabbed the paper sack. "Besides you're too pretty for anybody to ever make fun of you."

Azalea held her hands to her face, her cheeks flushing hot while Leonard walked to the far side of the cafeteria where Eddie Burl sat stuffing his mouth full of carrot salad. Leonard tossed the paper sack in a trash can, swatted the back of Eddie Burl's head with the palm of his hand, then sauntered out of the room, not seeming the least bit concerned that Eddie Burl might retaliate.

Azalea appreciated Leonard taking up for her like that. But if he really knew the truth of it, she appreciated the roast beef sandwich even more. She retied the sweater across her waist and followed Leonard out of the cafeteria.

# — Leonard —

*TAP. TAP. TAP.* Leonard woke startled. *Tap tap tap.* At the other end of the house, June's rambling about in the kitchen and the smell of fresh coffee brewing reassured him that he was in his room at the start of another day. He yanked the covers to his chin, rolled onto his side, and tried to sleep a while longer.

But the tapping started up again — louder, more urgent — like a woodpecker drumming for his mate's attention. Leonard flopped onto his belly and lifted the bedroom curtain. Little Henry Reed stood on the other side of the window, his face smashed up against the glass.

"Dang it," Leonard said. Little Henry bobbed up and down, grinning, motioning for Leonard to join him outside. Leonard opened the window and shivered in the cold air. "What are you doing here?" He scanned the yard. "My mama see you?"

"Not this time," Little Henry said, passing a cardboard box to Leonard. "Don't open that." He grabbed hold of the windowsill but quickly lost his grip and fell backwards into a clump of wax myrtle.

"What'd you mean this time?" Leonard set the box on his bed, then lifted the window a little higher and held out his hand. "Get in here before she does."

The morning was icy cold, and Little Henry wore only jeans and a sweatshirt. He grabbed hold of Leonard's hand and climbed through the open window, knocking against the bedside table and tumbling onto the floor.

"Keep it down," Leonard whispered. "Mama hears everything." Little Henry scrambled to his feet and snatched up the box. "How long you been out there?" Even in the dim morning light, Leonard could see Little Henry was trembling from the cold, his teeth clattering. His lips were colored a pale gray, the hollows beneath his eyes a shade deeper.

"I don't know exactly. An hour? Maybe two," he said, cradling the box the way a mother holds a baby. "Don't matter. I like being outside. My angel mama can see me better that way." He sat on the bed, then perked up straight. "You hear that?" He angled his head closer to the window. "You hear that whippoorwill?"

Leonard laughed. "Whippoorwills ain't out in the morning."

Little Henry shook his head. "This one is. He calls for me morning and night. Don't matter if it's dark or light." He patted his chest. "He's after me."

Leonard stared at his friend. Little Henry hadn't been acting right since his mama died — sleeping in school, drawing pictures of nothing but angels and rainbows, chewing on his lip until it bled, then chewing on it some more. But this morning he seemed rattled to the bone, and his talk sounded crazy. Leonard considered calling for June but immediately thought better of it. "Why you think that?" he asked. "Why you think a whippoorwill is chasing after you?"

"Because of what's in here." Little Henry tucked the box tight against his belly.

Leonard reached for the lamp switch and a bright light washed over the room. He needed to check if Little Henry's eyelids were drooping or his skin was drained of color. Surely he was feverish. That's what June would say if she evaluated his condition. In the lamplight, Little Henry did not look ill. Skittish, maybe. Scared, could be. But not ill.

"I promise you nothing in that box is causing nature to act a fool. If you make a mockingbird mad, it'll chase you down and dive at you like a kamikaze. But whippoorwills? That ain't their way," Leonard said.

Little Henry shook his head. "Ain't so. That whippoorwill's proof, and you got to help me make things right or he'll never leave me be." Little Henry's voice climbed higher, louder.

"Hush up." Again, Leonard pointed toward his bedroom door. "I don't want to be explaining to my mama why you're here at the crack of dawn." He reached for the box, but Little Henry held on to it. "Let me see what's in there."

"Only if you swear you won't tell nobody."

"I swear."

"On a Bible."

"Shit, Little Henry, I ain't looking for a Bible."

Little Henry gulped, then slowly removed the lid. A cardinal lay inside the box, eyes open and claws curled. Next to the cardinal lay a scarlet tanager, then an indigo bunting, and an orange-chested robin, a bluebird, a mourning dove. A whippoorwill was shoved into the mix, each bird lined up square against the next, posed with eyes open and claws curled as if Little Henry had shaped them that way in their passing. Twelve birds in all. Each one beautiful in death. Leonard stroked the robin's wing.

"I found the dove but killed the others," Little Henry blurted. "I did. I'm a murderer." He bit his lower lip, already cracked and dry. "A cold-blooded killer."

Leonard pulled back the drape and looked out the window. Although he knew it was silly to think so, he wondered if Little Henry's angel mama or the angry whippoorwill really might be watching from afar. Feeling certain neither were there, he nudged his friend. "How come you done it then?"

Little Henry stroked the bluebird's feathers. "So I could draw them right. Their coloring. Their feathers. It's all a blur from a distance."

Leonard nodded. "So you killed them to draw them?"

"I told you, I couldn't see them good. I didn't have a choice."

"I ain't judging you." The box shook in Little Henry's trembly hands leaving the birds to look as though they were rousing from sleep. Leonard checked to make certain they weren't.

"Mama read in a magazine once that a man named John J. Audubon stuffed different sorts of birds and animals so he could study them better. I couldn't figure out how to stuff them right. Tried stuffing cotton balls down their throats but that didn't work." Little Henry wiped his drippy nose with the back of his hand. "Heck, all the famous painters use models of some kind, Leonard. Even naked women. Living ones. But naked."

"I said I ain't judging." For a moment, Leonard imagined a woman sitting butt naked on his bed, posing for a picture. A grin swelled across his face.

"Mama loved my drawings," Little Henry said, his voice calmer now. "She thought they might hang in a museum someday. Maybe one in Nashville or even Paris. That's what she said." Little Henry looked out the window as if he were looking for his mama. "I ain't ever been to Nashville or Paris, Tennessee, for that matter. Sure would like to one day." He set the lid back on the box. "But Daddy says a boy shouldn't be coloring pictures. He says there's nothing but trouble to come of it." Little Henry stared at his collection of dead birds. "Daddy says coloring is for sissy boys."

Leonard had seen bruises on Little Henry in the past, and he worried what kind of trouble his daddy meant. "Drawing dead birds might be a little strange for boy or girl, but I don't see nothing wrong about it."

"No, Daddy's right. I've already caused enough trouble. And if I don't make up for it, I'll never see my mama again."

"How you figure that?"

"Murderers don't go to heaven, Leonard, unless you're a soldier or the killing is on a cause of an accident. Daddy says those are the only two times the Ten Commandments don't count." Little Henry shook his head and placed his palm against the lid. "This whippoorwill, she was a mama. Her nest was full of babies. The babies surely died, too." Little Henry faced Leonard. "The daddy whippoorwill's added it up. That's fifteen killings. He knows—that's why he's following me."

Leonard pondered the strange situation, then lifted his gaze to Little Henry. "For one thing, you ain't going to hell for killing a few birds. I've done that with my BB gun more than once. And there ain't no whippoorwill that can add sums." Little Henry had always been small and weakly, but looking at him now, sizing him up, he seemed nothing more than a wisp of who he'd been when his mama was alive. Leonard felt bad for him.

"It ain't the same—you and me," Little Henry said. "Can't rightly explain it, but it ain't. But I got it figured out, and I won't go to hell if you help me set things straight."

Leonard knew there was no fixing the past, no undoing what was done. Otherwise, Little Henry's mama would still be alive, and Leonard would still be standing on two legs. But Little Henry seemed desperate. "When did you kill these birds?"

"Summer."

"How come they ain't rotten?"

"Kept them in the bottom of the deep freeze. Mama dug out a spot for them."

Leonard studied Little Henry, his good foot knocking against the side of the bed. "Okay," he said at last, "we can bury the birds behind the barn after Mama goes to town. She always goes on Saturdays." He nodded toward the barn. "I'll borrow daddy's shovel, but you'll have to do the digging. Ground's going to be hard."

"No," Little Henry said, straightening up, his tone turning rough. "That ain't going to set things straight. I need to bury them proper, like you did your leg. You got to read something from the Bible. Sing a hymn or two. Up there. On the hilltop."

Outside the window, a cloudless sky was shifting from dim to bright. "You want a service on the hilltop and bury those birds in my family's cemetery?" Leonard shook his head. "That cemetery's for *people*, Little Henry."

"Your leg ain't people. And the birds don't have to be right next to anybody."

"My leg came from a person, though. It's part of me, and I'm a Bush."

"But these are whole birds. Twelve of them."

"Just because you got a dozen of something don't make it right." Leonard noticed his own voice climbing louder. He took a deep breath, cracked the knuckles on one hand, and started again. "I just don't understand why you got to bury them up there." Leonard reached for his crutches.

"I need to bury them *up there* just like you did your leg because of what it did for you." Little Henry placed both palms on the lid of the box. "Look, nobody thought you'd be the same after that operation. Daddy said you were done for. Now you walk around like it's no big deal. Daddy says you're a living miracle. He also says your mama's a pain in the ass." Little Henry shook his head. "But I don't think that."

"Well, I ain't a miracle," Leonard snapped. "And your daddy got no right talking bad about my mama."

"The part about your mama's right. But Daddy says you might be *special*. He says he can't even tell you're a cripple no more when you wear your wood leg, especially from a distance." Little Henry's eyes watered up again. "I just want the same thing. I want to move on. Put my murdering past behind me."

Balancing on one crutch, Leonard held up his hand.

Little Henry hushed, and in that moment the robins and mockingbirds hushed as well. But the word *special* carried on like an echo traveling across flat water. Leonard had heard those words too many times in the days and weeks following the amputation. He'd ignored them then. But now they had resurfaced, and he flinched at the sound of them. *Special. Touched.* Neither fit right — like an ill-shaped sweater or a too-tight shoe. Then again, this wood leg didn't always fit right either.

Little Henry clasped his hands together. His thumbnail was nearly chewed to the quick. "Daddy says me and Bobby got to be good if we want to see Mama in heaven someday." He bowed his head. His back heaved. A tear dropped onto the box. "I want that Leonard. I want to see my mama in Heaven, even if I'm an old man when I get there." He handed the birds to Leonard. "Please do this for me."

---

LATER THAT MORNING, while Emmett tended the cows and June went to town, Leonard, Little Henry, and Azalea bundled up against the cold and set off for the hilltop. Leonard had called Azalea and was grateful when she agreed to help. Her mama felt good today, she'd said, and the baby was behaving.

Little Henry insisted a hymn be sung, and he had wanted to ask Miss Ooten to bring her Autoharp. Leonard refused, knowing she'd spread word of it on her telephone's party line. Azalea didn't play the Autoharp, or any instrument for that matter, but she had a pretty singing voice. She told Little Henry that she only knew one hymn from start to finish, "On the Wings of a Snow White Dove."

Little Henry said that wasn't in the church hymnal and didn't count. "It's on the country station," he said.

"It's about a bird."

Little Henry didn't argue after that. He carried the cardboard box, Azalea the shovel, and Leonard a small Bible he'd been given the day he was born, his full name engraved in fancy gold letters in one corner of the front cover. The three walked single file up the hill behind Leonard's home. Below them barns and silos seemed bolted to the land, the watering pond a tarnished nickel left among it all.

"I bet Mama can see me good today." Little Henry stopped halfway to look at the sky. "Ain't a cloud in sight."

Azalea wrapped an arm around his shoulder. "Bet she can."

Leonard worried he was misleading Little Henry into thinking he could soothe his pain, free him of his murdering past, lift the guilt from his shoulders. He wondered if Little Henry's mama could see what they were doing and what she thought of it. Leonard hoped he was doing right but worried that his own mama might find out he was taking Little Henry to the hilltop to bury a box of dead birds.

She wouldn't like it, not one little bit. He walked on, his thinking jumbled and his pace growing slow. Climbing the hill one-legged was proving tough.

They stopped at the cemetery gate. "Over there," Leonard said, leaning against the wrought iron to catch his breath. He pointed with his crutch toward the far corner of the cemetery, and Little Henry ran ahead, the coat Leonard had loaned him nearly hanging to his knees. Leonard and Azalea walked side by side to the piece of ground that in warmer weather would be thick with wild clover and purple-crowned thistle. A nice burying spot for birds, he thought.

Little Henry took the shovel from Azalea and pressed his weight against it, jumping on it, struggling to push the metal tip deeper into the ground. Azalea snatched the shovel back. "I ain't got all day," she said, digging into the hard earth.

"Make it deep," Little Henry said. "Don't want no dogs finding them."

Azalea dug until the hole suited Little Henry, then brushed dirt from the front of her jeans and cleared her throat. She hummed a couple of notes before singing a number one hit of salvation and glory. As she clung to the last word, Leonard reached for the tiny Bible in his rear pocket. He flipped through the tissue-thin pages until he landed on the one hundred and forty-seventh chapter of Psalms. He found the very words Brother Puckett had read the day he'd buried his left leg a few yards from where they stood now. Little Henry had insisted on it.

"He shall not delight in the strength of the horse," Leonard began, "nor take pleasure in the legs of a man." The words made no more sense today than they had when the preacher spoke them, but Little Henry smiled so Leonard continued. When he finished reading, he slipped the Bible back inside his pocket.

"Little Henry, you came here today to bury these birds so you could quit grieving the past. So you could right a wrong. So you could move on from here."

"Move on," Little Henry repeated.

Azalea reached for Little Henry's hand.

"I can't tell you what coming here and burying my leg done for me. Some good's come of it. I think. Just ain't got it all figured out yet." Leonard paused, suddenly wondering if there would ever be any tangible meaning attached to his loss. A wave of grief washed over him. He tapped his chest like he'd seen his mama do to calm herself. "Maybe there's healing here in this dirt. Maybe it's in the Scripture reading or the hymn singing that soothes the heart. I don't know. But I think it done me some good, and I hope it does the same for you."

A sharp gust of wind pushed past, and Little Henry called out for his mama. Leonard took the box from Little Henry and placed it in the ground. Then he scooped up some dirt and sprinkled it on top of the cardboard. Lifting his arms toward the heavens, he shouted, "Amen." Azalea smiled, and Little Henry let out a big sigh.

"I ain't ever been to a funeral, but that sure was a fine service," Azalea said.

Little Henry nodded. "Yes, it was. Real fine. Every bit as good as the one Brother Puckett done for your leg." He turned his gaze to the sky. "Bet Mama thought it was fine, too," he said and wandered away from the gravesite, following a fleecy cloud drifting past.

"I think you done Little Henry some good today," Azalea said, reaching for the mittens inside her coat pocket and slipping them back on.

Leonard shrugged.

"It sure looked like it to me." Azalea stood at the new grave, packing down the earth under the weight of her right foot.

On the far side of the hilltop, Little Henry lay on the cold ground, pointing toward the heavens. Leonard smiled, then reached for the Bible again and pulled a stubby pencil from his front pocket. On the very last page, he marked an X, a simple reminder where Little Henry's fears were laid to rest.

# — Emmett —

TIRED FROM A full day's work, Emmett took up the hoe under the light of a rising February moon. The winter cold left the ground rock hard, and with every strike of the blade, his shoulder muscles screamed out. But June, anxious to ready her garden for spring, was nagging at him again. She wanted to double her garden's size — add extra rows of cucumbers for pickling, some Cherokee Purple and Golden Jubilee tomatoes, another three rows of beets, and her favorite Peaches and Cream corn.

"It don't need to be done tonight," Emmett had said after supper as she stood at the sink washing the last of the evening's dishes. "Planting season is months away yet. Nobody works a crop this time of year."

"My daddy put seeds in the ground in winter."

"That's tobacco, not beets."

"I don't care what you say." She turned her back to Emmett. "I been asking you about it since the first of January." June reached for a plate from the soapy water in one side of the sink and dipped it in fresh water in the other. "I got buckets of coffee grounds and broken eggshells saved that needed to be in the ground three weeks ago." She buffed the plate dry and tossed the cloth over her shoulder. "Seems you got all the time in the world for them cows and fishing and anything else that fancies you. Guess I'm just supposed to feed off the scraps like an old crow."

"*Them cows* keep a roof over your head," Emmett said and stomped outside, cussing under his breath then immediately regretting it. He knew how much pride June took in her garden, especially her beets.

Her methods, she'd say, were the reason for her three consecutive years of blue ribbons. But it seemed to Emmett that nothing he did pleased her anymore. In the nearly six months since the amputation, June had fought him over everything from his poor table manners to his even poorer church attendance. Tonight, he tilled a full two rows before resting the hoe against his thigh. Maybe his garden work would please her. He dug his hand inside his pants pocket for a quick touch of the little shoe he'd kept with him all day. The sky was crystal clear, the kind only a cold night could offer, the moon full and stars glowing bright. Inside the house June glided from one end of the kitchen to the other, every movement graceful as she stored away the dishes and wiped the counter clean. There was nothing prettier to behold, and from the outside looking in, Emmett understood that his life appeared wonderfully normal. He pulled the shoe from his pocket and rubbed its toe against his lips.

June was still a beautiful woman. The fine lines furrowing from her eyes and lips, the occasional white hair, the slightly fuller hips only added to her beauty. And he didn't need a calendar to know it had been too long since they'd made love. She untied her apron and left it folded on the counter. Emmett grew full of longing for her and felt no shame for it either. But he could not share this need with her, fearing she'd push him away. He lifted the hoe over his shoulder and struck the earth. When he looked at the house again, June was gone.

After he was done with the garden and showered clean, he found June in bed, her eyes closed, her arms clutching a pillow. He whispered her name. She didn't answer. He moved to the far side of the bed, dropped the towel from his waist, and slipped between the sheets. For a moment, he lay quiet, hoping she might reach for him. But only his heartbeat and the house creaking and moaning as it settled into the night answered his longing. Emmett placed his hand on June's belly, a layer of thin cotton separating him from her body.

Her eyelids fluttered. Emmett moved his hand toward her breasts. Her breathing quickened. He ran his fingers through her hair, kissed her cheek. Once. Twice. A third time. June didn't flinch or move away, nor did she pull him close.

Emmett eased his body on top of hers and kissed her lips with an open mouth. June kissed him back. When he lifted the hem of her gown above her waist, June spread her legs and let him settle in between them. He moved on top of her slowly, gently, nestling his head against her neck, nearly smothering himself in her scent.

When he was done, he tucked her gown down around her legs and kissed her cheek one last time. June rolled toward him, her eyes still closed.

# — Azalea —

AZALEA FRIED THE last of the bologna in an iron skillet, barely browning the edges of the meat, just the way her mama liked it. When it bubbled up, she pierced it with a fork, then slid it onto a plate and added a couple slices of tomato and a piece of buttered toast. In the past couple of weeks, coaxing her mama to eat had become a daily burden. Rose claimed nothing tasted good. But bologna was her favorite, and Azalea hoped she would eat this breakfast. She dropped the hot skillet in the kitchen sink, listening to the cool water dripping from the faucet sizzle against it.

*On the wings of a snow-white dove He sends His pure sweet love.* The song she'd sung for Little Henry came to mind, but Azalea didn't dare sing out loud, knowing her mama wanted quiet when she took to bed for long stretches. Azalea had grown expert at singing in silence. In her head, the music was beautiful, a guitar's strumming guiding her from one verse to the next. *When troubles surround us, when evils come, the body grows weak, the spirit grows numb.* She carried the plate to her mama, mouthing the words in an exaggerated way as if she were standing in front of a microphone, an audience cheering her on. Atlas crawled down the hallway behind her.

The vinyl shades in Rose's room were pulled shut, sunshine sneaking past their edges gently illuminating the small space. A three-legged stool underneath the window carried the weight of old magazines and last night's meal, a grilled cheese sandwich and glass of milk. Azalea fumed seeing the wasted food. She flipped on the ceiling light.

"Turn that off," Rose growled. Azalea handed her mama the plate, but Rose pushed it aside. "I ain't hungry for that, honey," she said, her voice eased some. "Just bring me some saltine crackers and turn that light off. Turn the damn sun off if you can."

"You ain't put nothing in your mouth but them crackers since Tuesday. That ain't enough to live on." Azalea again pushed the plate toward her mama. Atlas crawled straight to the stool, but Azalea steered him away with her foot.

"I said I ain't hungry." Rose fumbled for a pack of cigarettes and slid one between her lips.

"Dang it, Mama, I missed school again on account of you. The least you can do is eat what I fix you." Azalea set the plate on a bedside table.

"Go on." Rose tore a match free. "Put the baby on the bed here next to me and go on to school. He'll be fine." Atlas grabbed the bed covers and pulled himself up to his feet, wobbling but proud of himself. He grinned at Azalea, then fell to his bottom. Rose lit a fresh cigarette. "I mean it. You go on. Me and Atlas'll be fine."

Azalea lifted Atlas onto her hip. "Too late. Nearly eleven o'clock." Atlas dropped his head against Azalea's chest. "Been five days," she whispered in the baby's ear. "What's one more?"

Rose had taken to bed early last week even though she had yet to show any visible signs of sickness — no fever, rash, swollen throat, or juicy cough. When Azalea had gone to school, she couldn't concentrate on her reading or her numbers for fretting over Atlas, knowing her mama might fall asleep and leave him crying in his crib without a bottle or clean diaper. Last week, Miss Roberts had found her and Little Henry dozing in class, both of them slumped over their desks. She asked if either of them needed to see the nurse. Little Henry jumped at the chance, believing the nurse bore the spitting image of his mama. Azalea had said no. There was nothing the school nurse could do to change her situation. Now, watching her mama suck on the cigarette, her hair wild about her head, Azalea grew angry. She kicked at the mattress, and Rose smacked Azalea's thigh. "Leave me be, girl."

"Fine. But the bologna's here in case you change your mind. Ain't making you nothing else later on. And we ain't got no more saltines." Azalea had saved back a few for Atlas but wasn't about to tell her mama. She reached for a nightgown at the foot of the bed. A smoky haze already clouded the room. She gathered up the other clothes littering the bedroom floor, kicking what she couldn't carry into the hall. She flipped off the light and closed the door, pulling it shut with her toe.

Azalea feared another baby was taking root in Rose's belly. Her mama had grown lazy, quit eating, even thrown up a time or two in the early morning. She was short-tempered most days and ignored Atlas and the house — all convincing signs that she was pregnant again. Sometimes Azalea wondered if her mama knew how babies came to be. When she had mentioned her concern, Rose laughed and assured her there was nothing to worry about. "I got an angry uterus," she'd said. "Babies can't grow there no more."

Azalea didn't understand what her mama meant by an angry uterus. She hadn't bled yet herself, and some of the mechanics of child-making and childbearing were a little vague to her. But when Atlas first took root, Rose had acted much like this. Ornery and lazy. In another month or two, Azalea feared her mama's stomach would be as swollen as a melon.

She set Atlas on the floor and shoved the laundry onto a tall pile on the back stoop. Atlas tottered behind her, pressing his hands and nose against the screen door. "I ain't forgetting you," she said, handing him a saltine cracker. With one eye on Atlas, she dragged a metal tub into the yard and filled it with icy cold water from the garden hose. Then she added some powdered soap and stirred the water with her hand, making billows of suds before running back to the screen door.

"Come here," she said and again settled Atlas on her hip, this time bundling up the baby in a white jacket she had worn as a toddler. He was growing into it, she could see that, but the hood slipped down, covering most of his face. She laughed. "You look like a marshmallow. Pure fluff is what you are." She kissed his chapped, rosy cheeks. They walked into the yard, and Atlas reached for the tub. "No, sir, you ain't getting wet today. Too cold for that." Azalea placed him on the ground and pulled a plastic rattle from her pocket. "Play with this," she said, tucking the toy in his hand. "And don't be going nowhere." Atlas shook the rattle and squealed while Azalea ran back into the house for a bucket filled with soiled diapers. Pinching her nose at the stench of ammonia, she set the bucket in the yard, deciding to tend to the diapers after she'd done the other laundry.

Atlas dropped the rattle beside the tub and crawled toward the corner of the house. A chipmunk darted past. Atlas squealed and crawled after the animal. Azalea shoved the dirty clothes into the soapy water, careful to keep Atlas in view. Babysitting was a tiring effort. He never stopped except to sleep. And she only slept when Atlas did. She picked up her mama's dress, the one she had worn to school when Olan Mills came to take pictures. Eddie Burl had called her *trash* that day, whispered the word in her ear in the cloakroom where the teacher couldn't hear. "Just like your mother," he'd said. But that wasn't so.

Her mama hadn't always been like this, and Azalea had a black-and-white photograph taped to the back of her closet door to prove it. In the picture, Rose wore a pretty dress that buttoned to her neck, her hair set in neat curls, a gardenia blooming just above her ear. A handsome man in a collared shirt sat beside her, his arm draped around her shoulder. Both were smiling, seeming to make goo-goo eyes at one another. "You were just a tiny speck in my belly," Rose had told her once. "Your daddy was coming back to make an honest woman of me. Promised to buy me a gold ring." Sadly, John Jeffries never showed. A logger from the North Carolina Blue Ridge, he was killed felling a tree in Wilkes County less than a month after the photograph had been taken. But this small treasured piece of Azalea's personal story was proof against the mean words she faced most every day.

"No, sir," Azalea hollered and ran after Atlas, who was sucking on a stick like he might a lollipop. When she grabbed it from his hand, he began to cry. "I ain't mad at you." Azalea scooped him up and kissed his hand. "You might hurt yourself." She tossed the stick toward the tree line. Atlas squealed and yanked on her hair.

While the clothes soaked, Azalea carried Atlas into the house and changed his diaper. His bottom was growing red, but she'd used up the last of the Desitin ointment days ago. She scrounged through a dresser drawer for a tub of petroleum jelly and smeared some on his bottom. Atlas fussed when she touched his raw skin. Azalea blew on it, then applied a little more jelly to the red patch that had doubled in size since yesterday. She pinned a clean diaper on him and left him to play in his crib while she washed her hands in the kitchen sink before mashing up half of a banana. If her mama didn't get better soon, Azalea feared the welfare lady really might come looking for her and Atlas both. She'd heard stories of children being carted off to the orphanage in Knoxville, never seeing their true family again. Some days she hated her mama for putting them at risk like that, but she hated the thought of leaving her even more.

The song she'd been singing in her head came back around. *When troubles surround us, when evils come, the body grows weak, the spirit grows numb.* Azalea slipped a spoonful of banana into Atlas's mouth. He held onto the crib with one hand and reached for more banana with the other. "Not so fast," she said. "Swallow what you got in your mouth first."

When she was done feeding Atlas, she wiped his mouth and dabbed a little petroleum jelly on his lips and cheeks, too. "That ought to fix you up," she said, then dressed him in warm clothes. Out in the yard again, Azalea tied one end of a nylon rope to his leg and the other end to hers. "You ain't getting away from me this time," she said and went about pulling wet clothes from the tub and wringing them dry, her hands growing stiff from the cold. She pinned each piece to the cord stretched between an oak and cedar. Atlas pulled up on the tub's edge and splashed in the soapy water. "Dang it, boy, looks like I'm going to need to hang you out to dry before I'm done here," Azalea said as she pinned her mama's slip to the line. Atlas reached for a washcloth soaking in the tub and put it in his mouth.

"That baby's going to fall in that water and drown if you ain't careful." A deep, familiar voice rolled across the yard.

Startled, Azalea jumped back to find Mack standing at the far end of the house, a duffel bag in his hand. She waved, then reached for Atlas, still sucking on the wet rag.

"Thought I heard noise back here," he said.

"Mama's in bed. She ain't feeling good." Atlas shook the rag as if he were waving at Mack.

Mack threw the bag over his shoulder and walked toward them. "That's a shame. I came a long way to see her. Got a few days to kill." He reached in his shirt pocket and pulled out a silver necklace adorned with a heart-shaped charm. "I brought this for you."

Azalea's smile was broad, her gaze fixed on the necklace dangling from Mack's hand. She owned no jewelry other than a plastic ring and bracelet Rose had given her on her birthday last year. She reached for the necklace, but Mack yanked it away.

"Not so fast," he said.

Azalea tilted her head, her expression confused.

Mack dropped his bag to the ground and stepped closer to Azalea. He drew a circle in the air with his finger, indicating she was to turn around. Azalea followed his instructions and lifted her hair off her neck. Mack's breath felt warm on her skin. The strong scent of Old Spice stung her nose. "A pretty necklace for a pretty girl," he said, clasping the chain in place.

Azalea fingered the pendant, pleased with her new treasure. "Thank you," she said.

"You're very welcome." He patted her bottom, his hand lingering there a tad too long.

Azalea wriggled away.

"Come on now," Mack said, grabbing her shoulder and spinning her around. "First time I met Rose she told me she had a little girl."

His eyes traveled the length and breadth of Azalea's body, making her feel squirmy inside. "But you ain't so little."

Azalea stepped backwards, tripping over the bucket of dirty diapers, and Atlas whined again. Mack grabbed Azalea, but she jerked her arm free and leapt onto the stoop, clinging tight to Atlas. Mack moved quickly, pinning her to the screen door. Her heart beat like a hummingbird's. "You better go. Like I said, Mama ain't well."

"Like I said, I come a long way." His thin upper lip curled at one corner. Azalea was certain his stare bore right through her shirt and jeans. She felt bare in front of him just as she had that day at school when the entire class laughed at her for not wearing a slip. Atlas buried his face in the curve of her neck, and she was glad of the shield of his small body. Mack pressed closer, the hairs on his forearm grazing her skin.

"Well, look who's come to see me." Rose stepped into the doorway behind Azalea.

Mack shifted his attention to Rose. "Just saying hello to your girl here." He backed away from Azalea, adjusting his belt.

Rose opened the screen door and yanked Azalea inside. She reached for the pendant resting against Azalea's breastbone, gave it an odd look, and patted Atlas's back. "Hey, handsome, been dreaming about you lately," she said, beckoning Mack closer. "Lo and behold, here you are. In the flesh."

Mack snorted. "Got a few days to kill. Thought I'd crash here."

Rose smiled and opened her pink satin robe some. She pressed her rosy mouth to Azalea's ear. "Get to your room, baby girl," she said, then welcomed Mack inside.

# — June —

JESUS CAME TO June on a Thursday morning. He floated down from heaven on the wave of a bright shining light, landing smack dab in the middle of her sparkling clean kitchen. With his arms outstretched, He called to her, smiled, then vanished as quickly as He had appeared, riding the wave of light straight back to the Promised Land. June took it as a sign that Jesus was calling her to action. What else could it mean?

The minute Leonard boarded the school bus, June buttoned her coat and knotted a blue scarf under her chin. Although the day was gloomy, she searched her purse for her sunglasses. She didn't need them, but the dark lenses gave her a certain confidence. In the nearly five months that had passed since she'd watched Leonard bury his leg, friends and neighbors continued to treat her as if she were a fragile piece of bone china, *ooh*ing and *aah*ing over her, a few still bringing casseroles as if she'd lost a hand and couldn't cook any more. June hated being treated like she was different from the other mothers in Sweetwater. She could cook for her family just fine, thank you very much. She pulled the sunglasses from her purse and stepped out the back door.

June slid into the Impala, shoving her brown leather handbag to the passenger side of the seat. Beside it, she dropped the Bush family Bible that held the record of some of her life — her marriage to Emmett and Leonard's birth. There was no family Bible back in Sylva, and until lately, June had stored this one on a high shelf for safekeeping. When Leonard had asked if she were going to mark the date of the leg funeral in the same frilly handwriting, loopy with curls and soft-sloping letters, she'd barked a quick "No." Then she saw the disappointment in his eyes and had told him, "Maybe."

She slipped the key into the ignition and patted her dress pocket where she had tucked the week's grocery list. A package of hamburger buns, a jar of mustard, three cans of tuna fish, four cans of Spam, and a box of Corn Flakes, maybe two if they were on sale. At breakfast this morning, Emmett had asked for a potato casserole with Corn Flake topping and hamburgers for supper. Hoping to avoid the market, June had suggested grilled cheese sandwiches and tomato soup instead, but Emmett insisted. He had a hankering for burgers, he said. "And nothing goes better with burgers than your potato casserole."

June had not told Emmett of her plans or of the Lord's recent visit. Emmett would have poked fun if he knew she was headed to church to meet with Brother Puckett. Emmett had tired of the preacher soon after the amputation. "What's done is done," he'd said when Brother Puckett had come calling. "Unless you can grow my boy a new leg, I don't see the point in all this praying." Brother Puckett quit coming by the house not long after that, but June depended on the man, despite Emmett dubbing her commitment to the Lord *newfound. Phony.* "You can't call yourself a Christian and at the same time cling to these superstitions. God forbid you kill a ladybug or cut your fingernails on a Sunday or swallow a watermelon seed." Emmett laughed. "You're going to have to pick, June, your faith in Jesus or your faith in this malarkey. One negates the other."

She didn't see it that way. Both were matters of faith. *A black cat, a broken mirror, an owl flying over the house—these were signs from God, divine warnings, Emmett Bush. And you better quit mocking them and pay them some attention.* In Jesus, Christianity put a divine face to the mystery of life and the hereafter, a kind face with twinkly blue eyes offering trust where some might doubt. Emmett was wrong about God and Jesus Christ, about Brother Puckett and the depth of her faith. Her attendance at Sunday service was near perfect, and she had answered the altar call regularly since the accident, even though Miss Ooten had assured her once was plenty.

So yes, June's commitment to the Lord may have blossomed since Leonard's amputation, but it wasn't newfound or phony. Emmett seemed to forget that she had asked him to drive her to Linville, August a year ago, so she could hear the Reverend Billy Graham preach. Of course, Emmett hadn't known that her interest in the good-looking young preacher had not been purely spiritual. She'd seen pictures of him in the newspaper. A handsome man was a handsome man no matter his denomination, but none of that mattered now. She was a changed woman. Brother Puckett said she glowed with the Holy Spirit. Emmett just couldn't see the transformation in her. He didn't look at her close unless the lights were off and he was feeling his way under her gown. June adjusted the rearview mirror, barreled down the drive, and turned left onto the main road. She would tend to her shopping later. The preacher shouldn't be kept waiting.

"Good morning, Brother Puckett. Mrs. Puckett," June said, waving to them both as she stepped out of the car. The preacher stood on the church's front steps, his hands clasped in front of him. His wife, Edna, stood dutifully beside him, her hair styled and sprayed stiff as a starched shirt, her dress snug across her bosoms and hips.

"Good morning to you, Sister June," he said. "And what a glorious morning it is." Edna nodded in agreement.

June searched the sky, two shades darker since she'd left the house. She reached for her purse, Bible, and an umbrella kept under the front seat.

"Edna's here to witness and lend a helping hand. But first, tell me, how's Leonard?" Brother Puckett asked. Edna smiled, her eyebrows arched high as though she were eager to hear June's answer.

"Good, I guess," June said. "He don't talk about, well, much of anything anymore. At least not to me."

"The Lord has given him tremendous strength. Just like his daddy."

June nodded, but a few kind words from Brother Puckett did little to ease her worry. Before the amputation, Leonard often lingered at the supper table while June tidied up. Now he kept behind his bedroom door most evenings and on weekends found excuses to hole up in the barn with Emmett. Leonard had lost a leg, but June was beginning to feel as though she had lost a son.

The preacher and his wife walked into the church side by side. June ran up the steps behind them, removing her scarf and glasses. The building smelled of old wood and hymn books, seasoned with sweat spent from generations of soul saving. Come Sunday, the space would be filled with congregants squeezed into the pews and two rows of folding chairs already set in place across the back to accommodate the latecomers. Miss Ooten would sit at the piano, banging at the keys as she wove the tail of one hymn into the next until the preacher was convinced everyone committing their eternal soul to the Lord had made their way to the altar steps.

Jesus was here. On a Thursday. June felt His presence like a warm shawl draped around her shoulders.

Halfway down the center aisle, the preacher turned to face her. "You've gained in your faith, Sister June. Out of tragedy, you have found God's grace," he said. "I only wish you'd wanted your church family here to witness your confession of faith." He tendered a sharp *tsk tsk*. "One's commitment can be such an encouragement to another."

June fidgeted with the clasp on her purse. "I'm guess I'm just a little tired of the attention lately, what with Leonard's amputation and leg funeral." June opened her purse and tucked the scarf and glasses inside it. "The good Lord knows my heart, and like you said, Edna's here as a witness."

The preacher nodded. "I'll meet you at the water." He disappeared behind the altar.

Edna tapped June on the arm. "This way," she said, directing June to follow her to a door to the right of the pulpit. "I left a baptismal robe hanging on a hook. Change into that. I'll be waiting for you right here." Edna pointed to the floor. "Then we'll walk to the baptistry together." Again, she pointed for emphasis, this time toward the back of the church.

*I know my way around, Edna*, June thought to herself. *I ain't some simpleminded fool.*

Edna held the door open, smiling warmly. "You know if the preacher and I had ever been blessed with a child, I'd love him one-legged or two."

June's cheeks flushed with heat. She stepped into the changing room and shut the door behind her. *What'd you mean by that, Edna Puckett? That I ain't a good mother? What would you know about mothering anyway?* June tapped hard at her chest, determined to defeat another round of tears bubbling up to the surface. Edna didn't understand that June being here on a Thursday, rededicating herself to the Lord, was because she loved Leonard? Maybe if Edna had a child of her own, she'd understand that.

June unbuttoned her dress and eased it off her shoulders, suddenly feeling bashful even though she was alone. She hurried into the robe and left her dress hanging on the hook, glancing at herself in the full-length mirror before slicking her long hair behind her ears.

She held no clear memory of being baptized as a child, and if she had been, there was no surviving record of it. When she first met Brother Puckett, he'd asked her point-blank when she'd officially accepted God as her personal Lord and Savior. Young and foolish, she'd worried he might not marry her and Emmett if she answered that she had not. So she held up her right hand and affirmed she was a bona fide Christian, baptized at the age of nine in Scott Creek by an itinerant pastor. Any official certificate of proof or a family Bible with mention of it, she said, had been left behind in Sylva.

Lately, she worried that her deception might have been another reason for Leonard's misfortune. There had to be justification for her boy's pain and suffering, right? God wouldn't cause this kind of loss without a reason, and for her family's sake, she needed to make everything right with the Lord. If a Thursday morning baptism was the key to fixing the Bush family, then so be it. Emmett might scoff at this kind of thinking, but June would take no chances. She kicked off her shoes and left them by the mirror, then greeted Edna waiting outside the door.

With God and Edna as her only witnesses, June reached for the preacher's hand and waded into the heated pool of salvation. The water pressed against her body. The robe grew heavy. Her heartbeats slowed. The preacher guided her forward. Chest-deep in the water, she drifted back to her growing-up years on her daddy's farm.

The air was hot and strong with the smell of ripening burley, her fingers raw from a day of picking, her shoulders blistered red. She slid, bare bodied, into the metal tub set in the yard, its water warmed by the length of the day's sun.

Her daddy, his face shadowed by the brim of his cap, tossed a bar of soap into the water and told her to scrub herself clean. Standing behind her, he took a pair of scissors to her hair and cut it short. "You ain't ever going to get a brush through that tangled mess and beggar's-lice," he said, pushing her head forward, the scissor's blades cold against her neck. "Quit that crying," he'd hollered. "It'll grow back soon enough."

All these years later, a similar sorrow washed over June as Brother Puckett held his hand firmly against her back and lowered her under the water.

# — Emmett —

IRENE, MOLLY, LULU, FRAN — Emmett named his cows, always had. He knew each one's temperament — which ones were the first to the milking parlor, which preferred lolling about in the feeding barn, which loved to have their rumps scratched. He paid close attention to them all, especially the heifers calving for the first time. He had checked on two this morning, both already springing up, their udders swollen and full. He'd bring them in from the pasture in another day or two and bed them down with straw.

But that chore would have to wait. A broken fence post along the property's northern boundary demanded his attention. No need to be chasing down a cow in the dead of night, especially an expectant one. He would have mended the fence yesterday, but the tractor engine needed repairing and the milk tanks washed, and he still had acres to plow before the next corn seeding. *Farmer's Almanac* was predicting an early spring, and he wanted to get a head start on the field work. In that way, he was a little like June.

Mountainous clouds edged in gray hinted at afternoon rains. Emmett hurried to strap a new post and some barbed wire to the tractor's fender before hitching the post-hole digger to the tractor's back end. He cranked up the engine. It faltered and fell cold. "Come on, girl," he said, patting the tractor's metal hood. He turned the key again, adjusting the choke. The engine caught. He pushed his foot against the clutch and shifted the engine into gear, steering the tractor up the dirt path, skirting between barn and pasture. Half a dozen cows grazing in the pink light of afternoon stared as he drove past. Emmett reached for a cigarette and slipped it between his lips, then patted his thigh, needing the lumpy proof that his sister's shoe was there.

At the northern edge of the property, he reversed the tractor up to the fence, positioning the auger where the new post needed to be dug. With the brake in place and the engine idling, he reached for a match in his shirt pocket and jumped to the ground. The sun was dropping fast, the days too short for Emmett's tastes, and June would grow testy if he wasn't home by the time she put supper on the table. He hurried to guide the auger a few inches to the right before lowering its bit to the dirt. Keeping one eye on the spiral blade, he stepped back to the tractor and engaged the power. The auger quickly caught hold, clawing its way deeper and deeper, spitting out earth as it bore its way down.

Emmett watched from a distance while he smoked the cigarette. After a stretch, the auger moaned and slowed its pace, sped up for a moment, then slowed again, fighting against hidden rock. *Dammit*. He tossed the cigarette to the ground. At this hour, he was in no mood to deal with a cranky piece of machinery. He revved up the power, and the auger drilled deeper before slowing again, this time nearly to a stop. *Piece of shit*. Emmett stepped on the blade and pushed against it. The auger didn't budge. He stepped on it again, harder, bearing his full weight down on the blade. A groan, a twitch in the blade, and suddenly the auger spun up, catching hold of Emmett's boot lace. The coil yanked him to the ground. It twisted his ankle and tore his boot clean away, chomping it up and spitting the leather out in pieces.

Emmett scrambled backwards as if he were running from a hungry bear. He closed his eyes, afraid to look at his foot. His head grew light and his stomach sick while a few feet away the auger continued digging deeper into the earth. He rolled onto his back and stared up at the sky, waiting for the pain to come. The auger could have severed his foot, maybe eaten up his entire leg. He might die from blood loss before anyone found him. Farming was dangerous business. He was always telling June that for good reason. Tales of farmers losing fingers and toes, arms and legs — even their lives — were not uncommon. Last year, he'd heard of a man in Madisonville whose shirtsleeve caught in an auger and swallowed his arm, stopping just short of his shoulder.

Taking a deep breath, Emmett propped himself on his elbows and saw that he was whole. He wiggled his toes inside the heavy wool sock, then rotated his ankle. Pain shot up his leg. He examined the bone. Nothing was broken. Just a bad sprain.

"Thank you, Lord. Good God Almighty, thank you." He hollered his praises to the heavens as he replayed the moment his bootlace first threaded around the auger, watching every single frame of it in his head. An odd mix of fear, anger, and relief took hold of him and left him gasping for a good breath. Shaking, he pulled himself up on his knees. *Oh God. Sweet Jesus.* He inhaled and exhaled this mantra in steady beats, desperate to calm his racing heart. Emmett had no memory of the last time he'd prayed in earnest, only at the evening meal, and that was always at June's insistence. But out in the pasture alone, he bowed his head and clasped his hands together.

He wondered if he had yelled out for God when the auger grabbed hold of his boot. He had no memory of that either. Nor of a bright light or a voice calling to him from the great beyond as old timers claimed would happen when death finally came calling. Had God shown up in the nick of time and fed the boot to the auger instead of Emmett's foot? Or was it just dumb luck? Surely God didn't pick some to save and others to sacrifice. Why would the Almighty take Leonard's leg but spare Emmett his foot? Why would He perform a miracle for a dairy farmer who never bothered going to church but neglect to save a boy's whole leg or breathe life into an innocent little girl growing cold in her mama's arms? Thirty years after Sarah's passing, Emmett had no good answer for that. Staring up at the heavens, he couldn't make sense of any of it. And he couldn't catch his breath.

He grabbed for Sarah's shoe in his pocket and squeezed it tight. When that wasn't enough, he rubbed its toe against his lips. He kissed the leather. He lay still, the tall grasses tickling his neck, the shoe pressed to his cheek. His heartbeat slowed. Clouds lazed past. A cow mooed in the distance. Another answered back. Emmett lay there a moment longer, then struggled to his feet, his first steps wobbly, his ankle tender. He longed for the rest of that cigarette he'd thrown away, even if it only afforded him a drag or two. He kissed the little shoe, slipped it back into his pocket for safekeeping, and disengaged the auger. Maybe it had been his baby sister looking out for him, yanking his foot out of that boot at just the right moment, not God. He uttered a short prayer to both and climbed back onto the tractor. A sharp pain pierced his right ankle and darted up his calf. He drove forward, hunched over the wheel, the auger left behind him partly buried in the ground.

Every time Emmett pressed the accelerator, he stifled a groan. Across the clearing, he could see the house lit up. June was likely in the kitchen, finishing supper, checking the clock, worrying. Not ready to face her yet, he parked the tractor at the dairy and limped inside the milking room, remembering some Wild Turkey he'd hidden there. Another one-legged Bush was too much for him to consider, and he intended to keep the day's accident a secret from June and Leonard both. He needed to find a pair of worn-out work boots he thought he'd stashed in the metal cabinet, but he had to stop shaking first.

Emmett dropped to his knees in front of his daddy's army footlocker shoved into the far corner of the milking room. His hand trembled as he spun the dial on the combination lock. Then he flung open the lid and dug past reams of tax filings and receipts. He gripped the neck of the whiskey bottle and felt instantly calmer. He unscrewed the cap from the pint bottle and took a long swig. The golden liquid burned his throat, and he was glad of it. He took another swallow, then reached for a fresh pack of Salems at the back of his desk drawer and felt again for the little shoe in his pocket. He needed all three balms this evening to calm his nerves. If he'd bled to death, he imagined June would have cursed him more than she would have grieved him. He couldn't blame her. He tucked a fresh cigarette in his shirt pocket, checked for Sarah's shoe one more time, then took another sip of whiskey before sealing it up and walking into the house, the bottle also tucked inside his overalls.

---

SHOWERED AND DRESSED for supper, Emmett still trembled thinking of his misstep. Standing at the dresser, he opened the bottle he had sneaked into the bedroom. June didn't like alcohol in the house any more than she did cigarettes and would surely smell it on his breath. But Emmett would face that argument later.

Looking in the mirror, he saw the scared boy he'd once been, huddled at his mama's feet when her daughter lay dying in her arms. Sarah had suffered at the end, her throat too swollen for drink, her tiny chest rattling. She had fought the fever as best she could, writhing with the pain of it. Just before dawn, she turned blue and her eyes fell fixed. Emmett's mother screamed at the moment of Sarah's passing. His daddy had to pry the child from her arms. But the next morning, she appeared dry-eyed and resolute, boxing up every toy and piece of clothing that had belonged to her little girl. Over the course of the next few days, Emmett's mother buried her only daughter, then gave away every last one of Sarah's possessions. When she was done, she had looked at her son and said, "No more tears in my house." Emmett never shed another tear, but he stole one of his sister's little shoes from the cardboard box before his mama hauled it away.

Now Emmett placed his sister's shoe in the dresser drawer under a short stack of freshly laundered t-shirts. June knew of the shoe. She had since they'd married. But Emmett had always been quick to poke fun of her superstitions, and he'd sound a hypocrite for sure if she knew of his attachment to such a thing and how he had taken to carrying it around in his pocket. Truth be told, his need for it had grown tenfold since the amputation, and that scared him some. Emmett had not cried for Sarah since her death, but lately his grief for her and Leonard seemed tangled together. He couldn't make sense of that either.

"Daddy?" Leonard cracked opened the bedroom door.

Emmett shoved the dresser drawer shut. "Get out!" He heard the unusually sharp tone of his own voice.

"Sorry." Leonard pulled the door nearly closed. "Mama wanted me to tell you supper's ready."

Emmett stared at the man in the mirror who seemed a stranger this evening. He drew a deep breath. "I'll be there in a minute." He hoped he sounded kinder. He took a last sip from the near-empty bottle of whiskey before stashing it in the dresser's bottom drawer. Then he reached for a tube of Brylcreem and squeezed a dab of it onto the palm of his hand. He fingered it through his hair and, with a plastic comb, fixed a straight part. The grown man staring back at him was ready for dinner, dull-eyed and emotionless.

# — Azalea —

 LITTLE HENRY PULLED a crayon drawing from his pocket and flattened it against the library table. Azalea studied the picture of a boy with his arms outstretched and his face turned toward a blue sky, one leg looking sticklike. Twelve little birds fluttered about his head.

"You drew Jesus," she said.

"It's Leonard, but he did work a Jesus-like miracle in me." Little Henry handed the paper to Azalea and leaned against her shoulder. "I know it ain't nothing like a real photograph," he whispered, pointing to a figure in the distance. "That's you over there, and me standing next to you."

"I don't know much about Jesus." Azalea studied the picture, tracing Leonard's shape with her finger. "But I don't think burying your birds qualifies as a true Jesus miracle."

"Does to me." Little Henry promised to swear it on a Bible if Azalea would fetch him one. She offered him a Webster's dictionary instead. "Make a joke if you like," Little Henry said, puffing up his chest. "But I ain't so different than Lazarus."

The librarian walked by their table, pushing a cart loaded with books, her left eyebrow raised in warning. "Quiet," she said, pressing her finger to her mouth, then disappeared between the stacks laden with novels and encyclopedias.

"Who's Lazarus?" Azalea asked, opening a book and pretending to read.

"A man Jesus raised from the dead."

"How you figure He did that?"

"It's a miracle. That's what I'm saying. There ain't no more explanation for it."

Azalea nodded. "Okay, but how do you figure what Leonard did for you is anything like a Jesus miracle?"

"Leonard gave me a fresh start. A rebirth. Just like Jesus did for Lazarus."

"But you weren't dead."

"My birds were dead."

"But Leonard didn't bring them birds back to life neither."

"These are just technicalities." Little Henry took a blue pencil from a vinyl pocket snapped inside his notebook and filled in a patch of bare sky on the paper's upper-right corner. "Mama used to say that some people are already dead even while they're living and breathing here on earth. She called them living ghosts." Satisfied with the drawing, Little Henry returned the pencil to the notebook. "That was me, one of them ghosts." He looked at Azalea and smiled. "Now I'm a living boy again."

When it came to burying his pain, Azalea knew Little Henry had trusted every bit of it to Leonard. Whether the change in his attitude was a credible miracle or not, the service on the hilltop had done the boy some good. She wasn't sure about a rebirth, but she had seen a transformation in Little Henry, at least a hint of it, a twinkling in his eyes. Leonard had buried the boy's sadness and guilt deep in the ground where no stray dog or Little Henry could get to it. But three weeks later, Azalea was growing tired of hearing him carry on about it, as if he really were a modern-day Lazarus. Surely Little Henry's troubles would circle back around. Ain't nobody that lucky. Her own worries weighed against her constantly, and Leonard could do nothing about any of that.

———

WEEKS PASSED, AND Azalea learned to ignore Little Henry as he told everybody about the miracle on the hilltop. Before long, word of what Leonard had done for him spread throughout school, so it was no surprise when Icky Greer stopped Azalea in the hall, bearing a slingshot shaped together with a piece of dogwood and a length of rubber tubing. He had bet his little sister, Mavis, that he could shoot a tin can out of her hand. "Just hold it steady," he'd told her. With his very first shot, Icky hit Mavis square in the eye. She hadn't been able to see properly since. His daddy had whipped him good. His mama hadn't stopped crying. But Icky was feeling worse and worse about it every day. He wanted the same as Little Henry. Absolution — to be free of the guilt that had left his heart hurting.

"Will you ask Leonard for me? Ask him to bury this?" Icky handed her the slingshot. "Bury it on the hilltop like he done for Little Henry." Icky explained that he wanted a service exactly like Little Henry's, one with some Scripture reading and hymn singing, ordering it up like a burger and fries.

"Ask him yourself," Azalea said, handing back the slingshot.

"I ain't always been that nice to Leonard." Icky pulled on the slingshot's rubber band and let it snap against his palm. "Called him Peg Leg when he first got hurt." Icky took a few steps with an exaggerated limp. "He got no reason to do me a favor. But he'll do it if you ask him. Everybody knows he's sweet on you."

"Leonard ain't like you. He don't hold grudges." Azalea tugged on her dress collar. "And he ain't sweet on me."

"Please," Icky said, his voice warbling, his eyes watering up.

Shocked to see Icky cry, Azalea considered it for a minute, then moved her books to her other arm. "No," she said. "Like I told you, ask him yourself. It's about time you start being nice to Leonard."

That afternoon at recess, Azalea and Little Henry played hopscotch while most of the boys, clustered like bees swarming a hive, huddled around Eddie Burl and Icky organizing a game of kickball. The girls batted at a tetherball or jumped rope or climbed the jungle gym. Emily and Julia sat huddled against the fence, likely sharing secrets again. Azalea wondered what more those two girls could talk about.

She tossed a beanbag into the hopscotch court. Before jumping into the first box, Azalea rearranged her skirt, another one of Rose's hand-me-downs that fit too loosely about her waist. One. Two. Three. She jumped from one square to the next, stopping on her right foot halfway up the court to pick up the beanbag before finishing her play.

Little Henry clapped for her. Azalea tossed the beanbag again and started up the course.

Out on the field, the boys began choosing teams. Eddie Burl held the ball under one arm and pointed to Hoyte Lattimer, who was clamoring to be picked first. Then Icky stepped forward. "Leonard Bush," he hollered, and some snickering snaked through the crowd. Leonard jerked up straight, looking surprised to hear his name called.

"Yeah, you, Leonard," Icky said. "You still got your good kicking leg."

Leonard pushed past the other boys, beaming as he took his place beside Icky.

Azalea laughed. *Icky must be feeling real bad about Mavis*, she thought.

———

THE FOLLOWING SATURDAY MORNING, Azalea walked up the hill to the Bush cemetery carrying Atlas on her hip. Leonard walked beside her. She kept her pace slow. He had called the night before and asked her to come. "Icky wants a hymn."

"I might need to bring Atlas," she'd warned. "Mama ain't feeling right."

Now Icky followed behind them, carrying the slingshot in one hand, the shovel in the other. Eddie Burl tagged along.

"You didn't tell me *he* was going to be here," Azalea said loud enough for Eddie Burl to hear.

"I didn't know he was coming either. I swear." Leonard held up his hand, proving he had nothing to hide.

Azalea shifted Atlas to her other hip. "I don't get it, Leonard. How come you're doing it?" she asked, lowering her voice. "Icky's a fool."

Leonard shook his head. "I don't know. Maybe it's what I'm meant to do. Got that tugging in my gut like I did when I first lost my leg. I can't explain it more than that." He tickled Atlas's chin. "Your mama sick again?"

"Sort of." Azalea dismissed Leonard's concern before he could ask any more questions. Her mama's condition was an embarrassment she didn't want to share. "I'm singing the exact same hymn I did for Little Henry. Ain't learning a new one for Icky," she said.

"It's a mighty fine song," said Leonard.

They walked farther up the hillside among winter jasmine and forsythia, studded with tiny buds and the promise of more color to come. Azalea looked toward the sun, and Atlas dropped his head on her shoulder, his little hand worming its way up Azalea's neck and tugging on her lip. She pretended to gobble his hand in one bite, forcing a wave of giggles.

At the cemetery, they gathered near the spot where Little Henry's birds were laid to rest. Fresh grass had already sprouted on the grave and beside it a large patch of daffodils brightened the nearby landscape. Azalea spread a blanket on the ground and set Atlas on top of it. A few feet away, Icky dug a hole, the earth softened by early spring showers. Underneath the giant oak, Eddie Burl jumped up and down on the very spot where Leonard's leg had been buried several months ago. "You feel that?" Eddie Burl asked, looking at Leonard.

"It don't work that way," Azalea said and handed Atlas a milk bottle she'd carried in her pocket. Eddie Burl jumped hard one more time, his eyes fixed on Leonard. When Leonard ignored him, Eddie Burl walked to the blanket and plopped down on the other side of Atlas. He made a funny face and stroked the bottom of the baby's foot with the tip of his finger. Azalea scooped Atlas onto her lap.

Leonard pulled the Bible from his pants pocket while holding the slingshot in his other hand. A sudden shout of wrens marked a first round of hymn singing, Azalea joining in at the end. When she was done, she bowed her head and fingered the fine blond hairs springing up on top of Atlas's head.

"He shall not delight in the strength of the horse nor take pleasure in the legs of a man," Leonard shouted, nearly knowing the lines by heart.

Icky cut Leonard a puzzled look.

"It's in the Bible, Icky," Leonard said, pointing to the Scripture. "Forgiveness is God's to give," he continued, "and Icky Michael Greer has come for that, for a giant helping of God's forgiveness. He wants a fresh start. A new beginning. He wants to do right by his baby sister." Leonard carried on with his sermonizing, repeating the same message and prayer he had offered Little Henry.

Eddie Burl shuffled from one foot to the other, then gathered up a rock and tossed it downhill. Azalea cut him a mean look, and he bowed his head. When Leonard proclaimed a final amen, he dropped the slingshot in the grave. "There," he said, "it's done." Then he scribbled an X in his Bible, marking the spot of the slingshot grave, and snapped it shut.

In that very instant, Icky stood taller and straighter. He smiled and shouted, "Amen!" Maybe not as dramatic as walking on water or healing a leper or raising a man from the dead, but the change Leonard had triggered in Icky was immediate. Eddie Burl sat still, his mouth gaping open.

Azalea realized that Little Henry was right. It was downright *miraculous*. She didn't know much about God, and she didn't understand what was happening on the hilltop or if God had anything to do with it. She doubted Leonard did either. But she'd seen a change in Icky with her own two eyes.

Icky ran down the hillside. Eddie Burl took off after him. Azalea shook her head, then filled the hole, packing down the raw earth while Leonard kept watch over Atlas. Neither she nor Leonard spoke about the service or the change in Icky. But even Leonard looked a little different. She couldn't define how exactly, but Little Henry's crayon picture came to mind, a boy so special that birds would light on his arms. When all was done on the hilltop, she gathered up Atlas, and she and Leonard walked out the cemetery gate.

"Wait a second," she said and handed the baby to Leonard. She sprinted back to the far side of the hilltop to grab a fistful of daffodils, her mama's favorites. Maybe something from this holy ground would bring the Parkers good luck.

# — Emmett —

 HEAVY RAINS HAD settled over the farm most of the week, keeping Emmett penned close to the barn and milking parlor. Now with a clear sky overhead, he hopped off the tractor on the north side of the pond. He had combed nearly twenty acres already, counting his herd. But he was missing one, and she was known for lazing about in the water even when the temperatures were mild.

He stomped through grasses already inches taller than his last visit, nurtured from the rain and bright sun. Redbuds promised a show in the days to come. At the pond's edge, two bullfrogs were busy mating. They ducked under water when Emmett stepped closer. He laughed. *When the world starts warming up,* he thought, *it goes full steam ahead.*

The cow was not in the pond. Still, he walked its perimeter, scanning the landscape, and soon spied her farther up the hill, resting behind a band of scrubby cedars. "Good girl," he said, and turned for the tractor, nearly stepping on a duck's nest, neatly constructed of twigs and reeds and quilted with down. Emmett stooped closer and counted nine pale green eggs. A mallard's perfect clutch. He wondered where the mama might be. Marveling at the beauty of the nest and eggs, he considered running back to the house for June and Leonard. Emmett never tired of such a wondrous sight.

His breath caught in his throat. Twenty-six years ago, he had shown his baby sister a similar nest, tucked into this very curve of the pond's bank. He had warned her not to touch it, explaining that it was up to the mama duck to tend to her eggs until they hatched. Sarah had squatted down to study the nest. She pointed at the eggs but never touched them. Such a good girl. As the memory of his little sister took hold, his chest tightened and pressed against his heart. He tried to shake it off, but Sarah would not leave him be. Instead she tugged on his hand and begged Emmett to untie her laces so she could wade into the water to catch tadpoles.

"Please, Emmy," she'd begged.

Mama had said Sarah was not to go near the water. She had been fighting a cold for days. "Don't need a sick child to tend to," she'd said before he and his sister had left the house. Emmett explained their mama's concern to Sarah. But she lifted her left foot in the air. "I won't tell." At four, she was a secret-keeper, too, and Emmett couldn't say no. He untied her laces, pulled off her boots and her socks. Sitting on her bottom, she wiggled her sweaty toes and splashed her feet in the cool water. She hiked her dress up around her waist and waded thigh-deep into the pond.

Emmett kept a close eye on her, reeling her back anytime she stepped too far from the bank. When she was done playing, he dried her feet on his shirttail, tugged on her socks, and laced her boots, then carried her piggyback to the house. The winds had shifted. The air had grown cold. He bucked and neighed like a wild horse. Sarah hugged his neck tight and begged him to run faster, her teeth clattering from a sudden chill. He could still hear her voice ringing in his ear and feel her breath on his neck. And he could still feel the weight of the panic and sadness that fell over the house that night when she spiked a high fever.

Two days later, she was dead. The doctor said it was scarlet fever, but Emmett had forever connected her loss to that afternoon at the pond.

JUNE HATED RUNNING to town for nothing but a can of motor oil, at least that's what she told Emmett when he asked her to go. Lately, she felt as though he was always trying to shoo her from the farm, sending her on errands willy-nilly—a can of motor oil, another roll of barbed wire, a tub of udder cream. *Didn't that man ever think of making a list?*

She was in her sewing room watching *The Guiding Light* and mending a pair of Leonard's school pants when Emmett hollered for her from the kitchen. "I ain't your errand girl," she shouted back, then put down her sewing and picked up her pocketbook. She didn't mind going as much as she carried on, although she wasn't willing to admit that outright. She needed a box of Miracle-Gro anyway. Her beet seeds would be going in the ground soon, and she wanted to have her supplies on hand. Besides, if she timed her shopping right, she could pick up Leonard from the picture show and save Hoyte's mother the trip. School was closed for spring break, and the boys had gone to see *Swiss Family Robinson.*

June was barely a quarter mile down the road when she spotted Little Henry skirting the shoulder, kicking a tin can a few feet, then chasing after it. She slowed the Impala. Guilt from her last encounter with the boy still gnawed at her. She owed him an apology. She pulled to the side of the road and rolled down the window.

"Where you headed?" she asked.

Little Henry looked up, a grimace of fear spreading across his face. He toed the can and nodded down the road. "Home."

"Get in and I'll drive you." June leaned across the seat and opened the car door. "Got to be careful on this stretch of road. Trucks go flying through here and might not see a little thing like you."

Little Henry hesitated. He glanced to his left, then his right, as if he were hoping someone else might come along and offer him a better ride.

"I ain't going to snap at you. I promise." June smiled to show she meant well.

Little Henry slid onto the seat and shut the door, his gaze locked on the road as if he were afraid to venture even a peek at June.

"Where you been today?" she asked.

Little Henry kept his gaze fixed straight ahead. "Nowhere really."

"That sounds like something Leonard would say. I'd like to know where this *nowhere* is. You think I could find it on a map?" June smiled. Even under the weight of a bulky sweatshirt, Little Henry looked to be a scrawny thing. He probably hadn't had a decent meal since Margaret passed. The thought caused new twangs of guilt.

Little Henry bit at his thumb. "Big Sugar mostly. That's where I was at."

June nodded. "I don't see a fishing pole. What were you doing down there?"

"Throwing rocks. Messing around." In that moment, Little Henry grew excited. "I saw a sandhill crane the other day. Daddy didn't believe me, said it was too early yet. But it ain't. It's already March, and I saw one for sure." A grin brightened his face, but the happy expression quickly fell flat.

June spied a faded bruise just below his left eye. "What happened to your face?" she asked, pointing to her own cheek.

Little Henry shrugged and turned away. "Wrestling with my brother."

"Hmm," June said, adjusting her grip on the wheel, keeping one eye steady on Little Henry. "How is your brother?" she asked.

Little Henry shrugged again. "Okay, I guess. Says he's joining the army, but Daddy says he ain't old enough or big enough. Daddy says the army don't take runts."

June nodded. "Well, you and your brother have suffered a tremendous loss. I guess it's natural he'd like a fresh start. Go somewhere new. I understand that."

Little Henry stared out the window. The sound of tires spinning against asphalt softened the quiet that fell between them. June had heard talk that the sheriff was beginning to suspect Wayne Reed of Margaret's murder. He just didn't have the proof to lock him up. What more did he need than a smoking gun? When she made a right onto the dirt road that led to Little Henry's house, she slowed the car, careful not to stir up dust and trigger Wayne's attention. "How's your daddy doing these days?"

Little Henry fell a shade paler. He scooched forward and peered over the dashboard.

"You okay?" June asked.

Little Henry picked at his thumbnail some more.

June reached for his hand and squeezed it. "Little Henry, you okay?"

He pulled his hand free and tucked it in the pit of his arm, then slumped against the seat and sighed, releasing a long, slow, aching sound that caused June to shiver. She knew the boy missed his mama. After her own mother died, June often did the same, sometimes drifting away from a conversation, desperate to recall the shape of her mama's eyes or the lilt of her smile.

Little Henry gave a small nod. "Mama and Daddy used to argue a lot," he said.

"That's hard to listen to — fussing and fighting."

"Daddy says Mama shouldn't have been riding his back every damn day."

June shifted into park.

"Mama said Daddy was a two-timing cheat."

June placed her hand on Little Henry's shoulder. "Your mama's dying wasn't her fault, and don't you forget that. She was a wonderful mother and a true friend." June's voice cracked. "And she loved you very much."

Little Henry wiped at a tear.

June reached for a tissue in her pocketbook. But Little Henry flung open the car door and nearly tumbled out.

"Thank you for the ride, Mrs. Bush." He took off running toward the house, his arms pumping hard at his sides just like that morning when June had scared him away. A few feet closer to the house, he slipped behind a thicket of rhododendrons and disappeared.

June regretted treating him rough like she had. She wasn't sure she'd ever be able to make things right with him or Margaret. Using the tissue she'd offered Little Henry, she swiped at her own tear, then slapped the wheel. "Dammit," she said and shifted the car into reverse. Back on the main road, she sped toward town. Emmett would be looking for his motor oil and the boys were likely waiting outside the picture show.

# — Azalea —

IN THE WEEKS following the first burials of birds and slingshot, Leonard went to the cemetery three more times, Azalea always by his side.

Laura Kilgore, pale-eyed from worry and fear, stole a tatted collar from the old woman who hired her to do laundry. "Mrs. Tucker nearly lost her mind looking for this," Laura admitted, handing the collar to Leonard. The sturdy lace, with its sequence of rings and chains, had been in the Tucker family for generations, stitched by Mrs. Tucker's great-great-grandmother. Laura had not known the history of the collar when she slipped it inside her apron pocket, although she had no good explanation for not returning it once she did. Mrs. Tucker died before Christmas without ever knowing the truth, and Laura worried that the stress she'd caused the old woman had contributed to her death. "I have blood on my hands," she confessed to Leonard. "I can't pay you nothing for the burial, but I could do some washing and ironing for you. Or for your mama."

"There ain't a charge for this," Leonard said, passing the collar back.

Laura nodded, her lower lip trembling, while Azalea held onto Laura's three-year-old daughter.

As Leonard read Scripture and Azalea sang, the young mother clasped her hands together, head bowed and eyes closed, looking more like a river reed being pushed around in a strong wind than a girl who'd been married at sixteen and widowed ten months later. When Laura's husband Bobby was killed in an explosion at the fireworks plant in Benton, Azalea remembered thinking that his death must have been both tragic and spectacularly beautiful at the same time. Rose had told her that there was nothing left of the body, that the casket had only been for show. Azalea wondered if that had made it harder on Laura, knowing her husband's grave was empty.

Leonard dug a tiny hole with June's garden spade while Laura fidgeted with the lace collar, fingering it feverishly as though she were attempting to iron it out one last time. "I just wanted one pretty thing for my girl," Laura said before placing the collar in the ground.

Two weeks later, Warren Gilbert, a middle-aged man who worked at the feed store unloading trucks and stocking shelves, came to the hilltop carrying a motel key from the Sweetwater Lodge. "Room number four," he said, his grin hinting at pride rather than shame. His clothes were rumpled. His breath reeked of whiskey. Azalea knew the stench of a man who had been cheating on his wife, and she wondered if Warren had walked to the hilltop cemetery directly from the motel. For a moment, she worried that he had done business with Rose in the past and might admit that in front of Leonard. "I've wronged my wife," he said, clutching the key tight. "But I swear I've done it for the last time."

"Yeah, I bet that's right," said Azalea, snatching the key from his hand.

Warren avoided her stare, kicking at the ground like he was searching for something in the grass.

"This ain't a hiding spot, Mr. Gilbert," Leonard said, taking the key from Azalea.

"Oh, I know it ain't, boy. Trust me, I'm sincere. My regret is true." Warren drew an exaggerated X over his heart.

The red-tailed hawk glided overhead, screeching wildly before swooping below the hilltop. *Liar, liar* was what the bird was saying. Azalea was sure of that.

By the time the forsythia fully bloomed and the dogwoods dotted the roadsides with splashes of white, Berta Holland Tate had called on Leonard. Her grandson Icky promised that Leonard had a special knack for making things right, and she figured there was no harm in trying.

Azalea stifled a laugh when she saw Berta standing at the cemetery gate. Bald-headed but for a wisp of white hair, she looked more like a Kewpie doll than a crone. She carried a basket of eggshells and admitted she'd been stealing from her neighbor for months. Berta seemed to feel no shame for it. Had a fox not killed her only hen, she claimed, she'd never considered taking another's eggs. Berta attended church every Sunday and most Wednesday nights when the weather was good. And though she argued that the neighbor's hen was divinely sent, Berta figured it was best to take every step to right her wrongs before she breathed her last.

"You know. Cross every t. Dot every i," she said, handing the basket to Leonard and three good eggs to Azalea. "A little thank you for your effort." When she smiled, her dentures shifted. Berta pushed them back into place with her thumb. Then, brushing her wisp of hair back against her head, she turned to Azalea. "I hear you got a pretty singing voice."

Leonard dug a fifth grave in the far corner of the cemetery and read the familiar Scripture from Psalms about the strength of horses and the legs of men, no longer needing to look at the page for reference.

"Icky warned me that some of your talk don't make a lick of sense," Berta said. "You sure you ain't making that up?"

Leonard offered her the Bible for proof, but she refused it. "God will need to explain that one in the hereafter."

When the service was over, Leonard buried the eggshells near Icky's slingshot, Laura's lace collar, Warren Gilbert's motel key, and Little Henry's box of birds. Azalea hummed a note and began to sing. Halfway through the first verse, Berta clapped her hands. "That's good enough for me," she said and pulled two more eggs from her apron pocket. "Might as well get rid of these while you're at it," she said, handing them to Leonard, then took off down the hill.

Leonard and Azalea laughed, watching the old woman go. "Not sure what I should do with these." He held up the eggs. "Scramble them or bury them?"

"Scramble them," Azalea said, taking the eggs from his hand and adding them to the others in the basket.

Leonard filled the tiny grave with dirt and stomped it down with his good foot. Azalea lay in the grass, her arms folded beneath her head, her eyes closed tight against the brilliant sun. "Do you know why people are coming to you like they are?"

Leonard lay down beside her. "I guess they just want to put their sadness somewhere so it ain't gnawing on them night and day. Except maybe for Miss Berta. I ain't sure that was her concern."

"Little Henry thinks you're a miracle worker." Azalea rolled onto her side and met Leonard's gaze. "I'm thinking maybe you are, too."

"Well, I ain't that."

"Ain't you the least bit worried by all this? People coming to you like they are?"

"It won't last." Leonard rested his head on his hands. "Whether a leg or a mistake, there's just something about burying a piece of you in the dirt. It's like dropping a lit candle in water. Snuffs it right out. But others coming? That will pass."

Azalea plucked a blade of grass and held it to her lips. She blew through her grass whistle before tossing it into the air. "Wonder if the preacher's heard about your services? Doubt he's going to like you doing his work."

"I ain't doing his work. I'm just filling in the gaps."

"What about your mama? What does she think?"

Leonard plucked another blade of grass and handed it to Azalea. "Mama don't know about it. She don't like nothing that's different, and I'm already that."

Azalea placed her head on Leonard's shoulder. "I don't know nothing but different." She opened her hand, and the blade of grass flitted through the air like a whirligig.

Leonard pulled a pencil from his pocket and placed another X in the back of his Bible. The pages were beginning to look like a map of sorts. A map of woe.

# — June —

 FOR THE FIFTH year in a row, June intended to grow the biggest and tastiest beets in Monroe County. The previous blue ribbons she'd won hung on the kitchen wall beside the refrigerator, proof of her green thumb. Her picture had run in the *Sweetwater Herald* with each first-place finish, rare moments when June enjoyed others' praise and attention. She kept those clippings in the family scrapbook.

Now the first week of April, the *Farmer's Almanac* confirmed the last threat of a hard frost had passed, early for east Tennessee. June set about planting her seeds, along with a row of bush beans. Beets always performed better with beans nearby.

Emmett said June worked the dirt as much with her heart as with her hands. That was the real reason her beets responded like they did. June nurtured them from a speck no bigger than a flea, but she credited her true success to a mixture of manure, Epsom salts, eggshells, and Miracle-Gro. The proportions mattered as much as the ingredients, and she kept her recipe a secret, even from Emmett. She liked thinking of her husband's compliment as she stepped into the tilled dirt, her blue jeans rolled up above her ankles, a trowel in one hand, the bucket of fertilizer in the other.

In early fall, June had considered abandoning her garden, figuring Leonard would demand her full attention. But Emmett had disagreed. "He's fine," he'd told her. "Besides, mothering a one-legged boy ain't going to win you another blue ribbon at the county fair." Emmett had kissed her on the cheek. "Trust me," he'd said, "tending to the garden will be good for the both of you."

June knew he was right, but she didn't dare admit it.

A goldfinch showing off a feathery yellow coat flitted past. A squirrel scratched at the trunk of the pin oak. June set the bucket of fertilizer in the dirt and knelt down beside it, the earth cool against her knees. She shaped a small hole, then another two inches from the first. Her wide-brimmed hat cast a shadow over her face and the ground she worked with the trowel. She reached for seeds in her apron pocket. "Grow big for me," she said, blowing on her balled-up fist before sprinkling a cluster of seeds in the ground. She doused them with fertilizer before gently covering them with fresh dirt.

Emmett had offered to buy her a pair of canvas gloves speckled with tiny blue flowers, knowing how she had complained of working her daddy's tobacco bare-handed. But June had refused them. This spot of earth nurtured her as much as it did the beets, and unlike raw tobacco, beets were an easier plant to tend — never leaving her dizzy-headed or requiring her to cake her bleeding hands with a soothing paste of cornmeal and baking soda.

In a few months' time, she would pickle the first of her crop, serve the tender green leaves in salads, and boil up the bigger, tougher ones with an onion and meaty ham bone. Not a bit of her efforts would be wasted. Beets were good for the blood, she'd remind Leonard and Emmett when they grumbled about their frequency on the dinner table.

She struck the ground with her trowel again, slicing an earthworm into two pieces. Each half wiggled around as if trying to find the other. June smiled, knowing this might be the very spot where her prize-winning beet would take root. She doused the seeds with an extra handful of fertilizer before burying them in their earthy womb.

As she carved out the next hole, a woman's voice called from behind her. "June! June Bush!"

June spun around, tilting the brim of her hat so she could see better. "Vivienne," she answered back, surprised to see Eddie Burl's mama standing on the far edge of the garden. The two women had never been friendly, even though the boys had played together since babies in the same church nursery. June thought Vivienne put on airs, always bragging about her husband's executive position at the paper mill thirty miles down the road in Boaz. She figured the only reason Vivienne had bothered to come to the leg funeral was out of curiosity, something to talk about at her luncheon parties. June could picture the whole scene in her mind — ladies sipping spiced tea and nibbling on chicken salad sandwiches while Vivienne chattered nonstop about June Bush holding a wake for a leg.

"You startled me," June said, dropping the trowel to the soft earth. Vivienne wore a pillbox hat, stockings, and narrow high heels. *Boastful to be wearing Sunday shoes on a Friday*, June thought.

"No one came to the door. Thought you might be hanging laundry." Vivienne pursed her lips, painted a deep ruby red. "But here you are. On your hands and knees."

Straightening up, June noticed the dirt beneath her nails and slid her hands in her pockets. "What can I do for you?"

Vivienne hesitated, then gave an airy wave with her white-gloved hand. "To tell you the truth, I came to see Leonard."

"Leonard?" June noted the paper sack in Vivienne's other hand. "Why on earth do you need to see him?"

"It's not important," Vivienne said, cocking her knee forward as if she were posing for a picture. "Just figured your boy didn't stay after school for sports these days and this might be a good time to find him at home." She offered up an exaggerated frown that quickly slid into a proud smile. "Eddie Burl's starting pitcher for Little League."

June's jaw tightened up. She crossed her arms and took a step forward. "Only because Leonard ain't on that field."

Vivienne crossed her arms, a mirror to June.

"Why are you here?" June asked. "If you have business with *my boy*, you might as well say it."

"I'll catch up with him some other time. Really, it can wait." Vivienne turned to leave.

June stepped closer to this woman who riled her, nearly standing toe to toe. "I asked what you want with Leonard. As his mother, I got a right to know your business."

Vivienne smirked. "Lord, June, you'd have to be blind not to know what Leonard's been doing up there on the hilltop right behind your house. Eddie Burl says everybody's talking about it."

June's cheeks fired hot. For months, she'd wanted a reason to knock Vivienne Ford off her high-heeled perch and force the woman to acknowledge what Eddie Burl had done to Leonard. She grabbed Vivienne's arm. "Tell me what you want with my son."

Vivienne yanked her arm free. "What is wrong with you?" She rubbed the spot where June had grabbed her. "If you want to know what your boy's up to, then ask him yourself," she said, squaring her stance. "I don't understand you, June. I've never done a thing to you."

June pushed forward, her fists clenched at her sides. "That's right. You've never done a thing. Not a single thing. When I was new in this town and had no friends, you just turned your nose up at me." June glared at Vivienne, refusing to flinch. "You never once invited me to your home, not even for a single cup of coffee."

"Oh heavens, June, we ain't in high school no more. That was years ago. I'd think you got bigger things to worry over these days." Vivienne turned and walked away, her hips swaying gently, her weight perfectly balanced on those fancy shoes. At the corner of the house, she stopped and looked back. "My boy had nothing to do with Leonard stepping on that glass, June Bush, so you best find somebody else to blame."

June picked up a clod of dirt and cocked her arm. She hated Vivienne for ignoring her. She hated her for knowing something about Leonard that she didn't. She hated her for refusing to see that Eddie Burl, at least in part, was to blame for their family's tragedy. Most of all, she hated Vivienne Ford for strutting around town in her heels and a pillbox hat, dressed like Jackie Kennedy from head to toe. June hurled the clod of dirt. It landed just short of Vivienne's pretty shoes.

———————

JUNE SPOONED A BIT of sugar into her cup of afternoon coffee, dirt still caked beneath her nails. She desperately wanted to know why Vivienne Ford had come looking for her son. She added another two teaspoons of sugar, then pushed the coffee aside, not bothering to taste it. According to the clock above the sink, Leonard should have been home an hour ago.

Not a moment later, the awkward beat of uneven footsteps sounded across the front porch. June swallowed a deep breath. She had rehearsed the conversation in her head a hundred times, her anger building with every going-over. When Leonard stepped inside the kitchen, she slapped her hand against the table. "Where on God's green earth have you been?" she asked.

Leonard froze in the doorway. "Nowhere." He dropped his satchel and opened the cabinet where June kept a tin of graham crackers.

*Nowhere ain't a place. Why do you boys keep saying that?*

Leonard reached for two crackers and poured a glass of milk.

"I asked where you been. The school bus came by an hour ago."

"Got off a stop back." Leonard broke a cracker and dipped it into the milk.

"Why?"

"Me and Little Henry were messing around."

"He lives in the other direction."

Leonard took a swig of milk.

Struggling to tamp down her anger, June drained her coffee down the kitchen sink and rinsed her cup clean. "You keeping the truth from me is the same as lying." She turned to face Leonard, her eyes narrowed.

Leonard shoved the rest of the cracker in his mouth, washing it down with a swallow of milk. He set the glass on the table and wiped his mouth with the back of his hand. "I ain't lying." But he wouldn't meet June's eyes.

"Mrs. Ford came by this afternoon. Said she needed to talk to you." June lifted his chin and held his gaze. "Look at me when I'm talking to you. What business would Vivienne Ford have with you?"

Leonard shook free. "I don't know, Mama." He reached for the milk pitcher, but June grabbed it first and set it back on the counter.

"She said you been spending time up on the hilltop. Why is that?"

Leonard looked at the floor for a long minute, then shifted to his mama. "Just helping a friend or two."

"At the cemetery? How do you help a friend up there?" She pinched his chin to keep his gaze and sniffed his breath. "You been drinking? Is that what you and Little Henry been doing?" She smelled his neck, catching a whiff of sulfur. "You been playing with firecrackers again? You ain't allowed to do that no more."

"No," he said, pulling back from June. "I was burying some things. Little things."

June frowned. "What kind of *little* things?"

"I don't know. Things that make them sad. Stuff they worry over." Leonard placed his empty glass by the pitcher of milk. "Just trinkets."

"Is that why Vivienne Ford came looking for you today here at the house? You promise to bury something for her?"

Leonard stared at his mama, his lips locked tight.

June set her hands on her hips. "Nothing's making much sense, but I got a good hunch you're meddling where you don't belong. You got no right to be burying anything in that cemetery without me or your daddy knowing of it."

"I don't go hunting for things, Mama. They just come to me. People bring them."

"Why would people bring *things* to a twelve-year-old boy?"

Leonard patted his stump. "They want what I done for my leg. A burial. A letting-go." He looked away. "I'm just trying to help," he said, his voice trailing off.

June pointed her finger a few inches from his nose. "That ain't your place, son. And that ain't helping. Burying. Forgiveness. Salvation. That's the Lord's work. Ain't that of a boy." Her eyes remained fixed on Leonard's. "And don't you keep secrets from your mama no more. You hear me? It's already cost you a leg." She turned to the sink and opened the faucet, letting the water run until it was scalding. Barehanded, she reached for Leonard's empty glass and washed it and her coffee cup clean, ignoring the steaming heat.

Leonard grabbed his satchel and shoved his way out the back door.

Wiping her hands on a dishcloth, June hurried after him. "You ain't burying nothing else, Leonard Marlowe Bush. Hear me? Not another thing. We'll talk about this with your daddy at supper."

June stepped inside and closed the door, her heart thumping hard in her chest. Her son was keeping secrets. Somebody would pay the price for that sin sooner or later.

# — Leonard —

HIS MAMA WAS WRONG, at least about the burying of things. True, he and Little Henry had been firing off Black Cats like she'd suspected. But they were playing army with Little Henry's plastic soldiers, and there was no other way to battle without lighting up some firecrackers. He didn't expect a mama to understand that. Of course, he knew that wasn't all she was mad about either. She said he had no business tending to people's sins and sorrows, that was the preacher's work, and he was headed down a dangerous path. It was his burying of things that steamed her most.

Leonard couldn't fully explain why he did it. But it was not to offer anyone eternal salvation. That was for Jesus to do. He understood that. He merely wanted to help his friends and neighbors leave their guilt in the past. Move on, like the leg surgeon and so many others had advised him to do. Maybe he was offering an earthly salvation of sorts. He wanted to explain that to his mama, the difference between the two. But he lacked the right words, and she'd likely never understand. She'd start reciting Scripture and demand the names of those who had gone to the cemetery and what they had buried there. She might order Emmett to dig up that patch of ground and report his findings to Brother Puckett. Then Leonard would have the preacher to contend with, and no one in Sweetwater, Tennessee, would ever trust him again.

Each little grave was a secret, a guarded secret he'd shared only with Azalea. It was not their story to tell. It was not their secret to expose.

At supper, June had her say. "You got a right to know what your son's doing on that hilltop, Emmett Bush."

She served up fried potatoes and green beans, knocking the plate against the table with such force Leonard feared it might break. He scooted his chair a few inches away from his mother.

"Emmett, make our boy explain why Vivienne Ford came here looking for him today." She served up two more plates. "I ain't ever believed you should take a belt to a child, but I could be wrong. Spare the rod and you know what happens." Her eyes cut to Leonard. "A boy keeping things from his mama and daddy ain't right."

Emmett smiled at Leonard. "Our boy ain't in need of any belt."

"I ain't done nothing wrong," Leonard chimed in. He picked up a fork but didn't touch his food.

June gave Leonard a punishing look. "My daddy never spared the rod."

"You want me to whip the boy for doing good?"

"You think he's doing good?" June crossed her arms. "He's misleading people is what he's doing. Thou shalt not bear false witness."

"Don't start quoting Scripture. I'm trying to eat."

"Emmett, he's burying things for people. Says it brings them peace. That's the Lord's work last time I checked." She flicked a napkin open and placed it across her lap.

"I'm sure the Lord don't mind a little help every so often."

"Brother Puckett ain't going to like it if he finds out."

Leonard tried to block out his parents' voices. Not long after Berta Holland Tate buried her eggshells on the hilltop, Mrs. Ford had stopped Leonard outside the school auditorium and confessed that her husband had lost his job three months back. They had yet to tell Eddie Burl and his older sister, Kate. Instead, Mr. Ford left the house at half past seven every morning, returning home for supper a few minutes after six. At first, he'd spent his days looking for new work, driving as far south as Chattanooga. Then he stumbled into a pool hall in Athens and began drinking and gambling what little savings they had left.

June cut her beans into tiny bites, her knife scraping against the plate.

"You trying to mash them beans, too?" Emmett asked.

"Ain't in the mood for your jokes." June pushed her plate aside. "Like I said, Brother Puckett ain't going to like this."

Leonard wondered if the preacher already knew about Mrs. Ford, who had complained about skimping and cutting coupons. In a moment of weakness, as she called it, she'd swiped a gold necklace while browsing at Cox's Department Store. "I wanted that necklace," she'd admitted to Leonard. "I deserved it." She hadn't worn it much for fear of getting found out, but she couldn't bring herself to return it either. Later that afternoon, Mrs. Ford and Leonard had walked to the hilltop together, just the two of them. "Here take it," she pulled the necklace from her purse and handed it over. "Just put it in the ground," she'd told Leonard. "Don't need any Bible reading or hymn singing."

"Leonard." June thumped the dinner table. "You listening to what I'm saying?"

Now that he'd heard his mama's story about Mrs. Ford showing up with a paper sack, Leonard figured she might have stolen more than a gold necklace. He also figured his mama might feel a tad kinder toward Mrs. Ford if she knew the truth of her hardship. He smoothed the mound of potatoes with the back of his spoon, making a tiny well for gravy. "I just bury little things in that far corner by the fence, Daddy. I don't disturb the family."

"What kind of things, son?" Emmett scooped up a bite of meatloaf and beans.

"It ain't for me to say."

Emmett nodded, swallowing the last bite of potatoes. "Leave him be, June. The boy ain't doing no harm."

June untied her apron and flung it across her chair. "Fine. But you better hope Leonard ain't flirting with the devil." She stormed out of the room with her dinner plate. A moment later, the sewing room door slammed shut.

Emmett spooned another serving of potatoes onto his plate and a second piece of meatloaf. "Better be careful up there," he said, nodding toward the hilltop. "I ain't questioning what you're doing, but don't take on more than you can chew." He forked a large bite of beans, potatoes, and meat into his mouth. Leonard snickered, knowing his mama would scold his daddy for stuffing his mouth like that.

"And don't be playing with firecrackers." Emmett squeezed Leonard's shoulder. "I know it ain't no big deal, but maybe give your mama one less thing to worry over."

---

NO ONE CAME looking for Leonard for days after that. Given his mama's mood lately, Leonard was glad of it, although he worried she might have scared people off. Then two weeks later, when the moon broke nearly full, Warren Gilbert returned with a second key from the Sweetwater Motor Lodge—a token, he readily confessed, of his ongoing infidelity. "I just can't help myself," he said, handing over the key. "It ain't my fault really. My wife, God love her, ain't interested in the marital bed, if you know what I mean."

Azalea made a face. "Maybe she just ain't interested in a man like you." She stomped off to the far side of the cemetery, refusing to sing for Warren a second time. Leonard agreed with Azalea, at least in part, and for a moment considered the value of burying a second motel key. The hilltop wasn't meant to encourage Warren's bad behavior.

Warren tucked his hands in his pockets and kicked at the ground, acting like a boy who'd been caught stealing apples. "I ain't perfect, Leonard, but name a man who is."

Leonard couldn't think of one, other than his daddy and Jesus, and he guessed that was Warren's point. "Okay then," he said, pulling the tiny Bible from his jeans pocket and opening it to the familiar verse from Psalms. He read about the strength of horses and the legs of men while Warren got down on his knees and begged for another round of forgiveness. Azalea kept her back to them. Sometimes Leonard could hear her humming, likely trying to drown out the service taking place a few feet away. Leonard talked faster and skipped the closing prayer. When it was done, he buried the key under a foot of dirt and packed it down extra hard. Using a stubby pencil, he marked the burial spot, right next to the first key, on the Bible's last page.

For days, the woeful continued their pilgrimage to the hilltop. Myrtle Haskins brought an empty bottle of George Dickel, Floyd Davis a Ouija board, Hoyte Lattimer a gold coin he'd stolen from a visiting uncle last summer. Mildred Hamilton came with a pair of silk stockings, slipped into her purse when shopping in Knoxville. Macon Sanders offered a tin of tobacco and Jessie Tribble his collection of *Playboy* magazines. Then Warren Gilbert returned with a third key and an announcement that his wife of fifteen years had moved in with her sister in Johnson City.

Leonard guarded their secrets, every one of them, even Warren Gilbert's — although he'd stolen a peek inside one of Jessie's nudie magazines before filling the grave.

# — June —

"YOU TAKING THAT fried chicken home to Emmett and Leonard?" Brother Puckett called from the church door. June was steps from the car, carrying a plate wrapped in tin foil, when the preacher struck a match to her good mood. She'd done everything she could to avoid him at Wednesday night supper, worried he might have heard about Leonard's recent shenanigans at the family cemetery. The Fords were upstanding members of the congregation, and Vivienne might have blabbed about Leonard's trips to the hilltop. June knew right from wrong and didn't want Brother Puckett's counsel. She'd tend to her son in her own way.

Brother Puckett hurried down the steps. "Would be a sight better if Emmett and Leonard came to church for their own chicken dinner. I hate you having to come by yourself." He reached for her arm and led her across the parking lot. "Can I have a word with you, Sister June?" he asked. "Privately, that is."

She eased away from the preacher's grasp. "What can I do for you, Brother Puckett?"

He shoved his hands deep inside his trouser pockets. "From what I've been hearing, it seems the second coming has arrived in Sweetwater." His woodsy cologne left June feeling nauseous. "Leonard's growing quite the reputation around town. Folks been calling him a preacher. A healer. A miracle maker. Whatever name you want to put to it, what your boy's been doing ain't right." Brother Puckett jingled his pocket change. "Surely you know that."

"Well," June said, casting off an awkward laugh, "he ain't none of that."

The preacher glanced back at the church. For a moment, June wondered if he was looking for one of the deacons or anyone else who might strengthen his case. "I've been praying for Leonard," he said. "I've been praying for your boy since the day you called me from the hospital. There's no need to remind you, Sister June, the Almighty looks to you and Emmett to guide him down a righteous path."

June fished through her purse for the car keys. In the evening's waning light, she hoped Brother Puckett couldn't see the embarrassment coloring her face. "No need for you to worry. I've already talked to Emmett and Leonard both about it."

"And?"

"Emmett's taken care of it." June forced a small smile. "Excuse me, Preacher. My husband will be looking for his supper."

"Take heed of the Scripture, Sister June. Book of Exodus, chapter twenty, verse three," he said, his voice stern. "You shall have no other gods before me." He watched June as she settled behind the steering wheel, then pretended to tip a cap that wasn't there and walked back to the church, his admonition lingering in the air.

June gunned the engine and sped from the church lot. The preacher's words replayed in her head. *No other gods before me.* Emmett might have been right. Was Brother Puckett referring to God Almighty or himself? Her own suspicions took hold, stoking her anger. Brother Puckett had read that very Scripture during the evening service. He'd pounded his fist against the pulpit with every syllable spoken, and suddenly June understood why. He had been reading it to her. When he pointed his finger at the congregation and thundered on about sin and evildoings, he had been chiding her.

*I've been praying for Leonard. I've been praying for your boy.*

Racing along the two-lane highway, June tossed those words into the night, letting them catch hold of the wind and blow across the pastures. But even with the window rolled down and the cold air slapping against her face, anger licked at her faith and good sense. She'd been afraid of what Leonard was doing on the hilltop from the start. Didn't like it one bit. But she didn't take kindly to the preacher's reprimand.

June had warned Leonard more than once that Brother Puckett would not approve of a boy taking salvation into his own tender hands. "A boy might not see a wolf in sheep's clothing," she'd argued. But Leonard promised he was doing nothing wrong, only helping others. "Let the boy be," Emmett had told her. She should feel justified in Brother Puckett's concern. Instead, she found her anger growing bolder. She pushed the accelerator and raced toward home.

When Leonard had collapsed in her arms burning up with fever that September morning, June had trusted Brother Puckett with her fears. She had trusted him with her faith. But tonight, he'd called her out like a child dragged to the front of a classroom and punished for not memorizing the weekly spelling words. She had done nothing but put her trust in the preacher and the Lord. Now the preacher was accusing her son of wrongdoing — and her of poor mothering. June was tired of feeling at fault for their circumstances. If Emmett had listened to her, Leonard would be walking on two legs, and the preacher would not be faulting her son. *When are you going to heed my concerns, Emmett Bush? When?*

Glad to be home, June dropped her purse, Bible, and plate of chicken on the kitchen counter and called out for Emmett and Leonard. Neither answered. She walked to the back of the house and called again. She could see a light in the barn. Emmett was working late for the fifth night in a row. She marched across the open space between home and dairy and pulled on the milk room door. It wouldn't budge. She tugged harder, and the door suddenly slid open with ease, almost dragging her to the ground. She righted herself and stepped inside.

Sitting at his desk, Emmett jerked upright — his eyes big, full of surprise. He tossed something into the bottom drawer and slammed it shut. He scooted closer to the desk, scattered with papers, receipts, and the electric adding machine. The television was tuned to a station June couldn't see. Emmett fiddled with a knob, adjusting the staticky sound.

June said, looking around the barn, "Where's Leonard?"

Emmett flipped off the television. "He and Little Henry caught a couple of bass this afternoon, took them over to Miss Ooten." Emmett glanced at his wristwatch. "Reckon she's made him sit with her and watch her programs. You know how she is."

June crossed her arms against her middle.

"Before you say anything, I was with them the whole time." Emmett picked up a pencil and scribbled some figures in a notebook. His hands were shaking.

"Are you okay?"

He continued writing. "Why wouldn't I be okay?"

June picked up a paper, a bank statement, and pretended to read it. Then she handed it back to Emmett and leaned her hip against the desk. "Preacher stopped me at church this evening."

"That don't surprise me." Emmett erased a figure and penciled it again, still not bothering to look at June. "Got to get these books balanced, Junebug. Can we talk later?"

"This is important, Emmett. Brother Puckett ain't concerned about Leonard's health no more," she said. "He's concerned about his soul."

Emmett tapped the eraser against the notebook, the beat growing faster and faster.

"Listen to me." June snatched the pencil from his hand and tossed it on the desk. It skittered across the top and fell onto the floor. "I told you no good was to come of Leonard going up on that hilltop, treading where he shouldn't. I told you."

"Junebug." Emmett shaped a soft smile.

"Don't Junebug me."

"This is ridiculous." Emmett dropped his head in his hands and tugged on his hair like he was trying to pull it from his scalp. "Leonard ain't hurting a living soul. Just helping some the way I see it." He looked at June. "He's a good boy. And you're a good mama. Preacher's just guarding his job."

June patted her chest, trying to calm her nerves. She could feel the anger boiling up inside her. She took a deep breath and patted her chest harder. "Mark my words, Emmett Bush, the preacher's warning is a sign of something more to come. I feel it in my bones."

"Here you go again." He reached for her hand, but she jerked it away.

"Dammit, Emmett, listen to me. I was right about Leonard fishing that day, and I'm right about this." She stormed toward the door like a human funnel cloud but stopped to make her point again.

Emmett looked at her, wide-eyed and silent, his typical response when she wanted more from him — more anger, more joy, more disappointment. More of anything that hinted at what he was feeling. But like always, Emmett gave her nothing. He was always calm. Always even. Always practical. Just like his own mama. Old Lady Bush had never raised her voice to anyone. Never confronted her pain either.

But June held back nothing, her anger washing over the milk room like an ocean wave pounding onto the shore. "Say something, Emmett. Dammit. Say anything."

But Emmett said nothing. Instead he thrust his hands inside his pants pockets.

"Why you acting so strange? Something's been off since the moment I walked in here."

Emmett laughed. "There's nothing strange going on. I'm just tallying the books like I do every day."

June eyed him closer. "What's your hand doing in that pocket? Lord, Emmett, are you pleasuring yourself right here in front of me?"

"Good god, June, no." Emmett stood up, then flashed both hands in the air.

June and Emmett locked eyes, but he couldn't hold her gaze.

"Don't lie to me. I ain't a fool."

"I know that." He stood and pulled June into his arms.

She pushed against him. "Tell me the truth. I ain't enough for you anymore, am I? You been running around with another woman." June pressed her hand to her forehead. "Oh lord, is it Vivienne Ford? Is that why she came around the house the other day? She wasn't looking for Leonard. She was looking for you, wasn't she?"

"I ain't cheating on you, Junebug. I promise. You're all I need, and that's all there is to it. Get the family Bible and I'll swear to it right here and now." Emmett reached for her hand, his grip both strong and tender. She wanted to believe her husband, but lately it seemed nobody spoke the truth.

She yanked her hand free. "I brought you a plate of fried chicken," she said, her voice faltering. "It's on the kitchen counter." Then she slipped out of the barn, thinking about Emmett's nervous laughter.

# — Leonard —

 LEONARD PUSHED THROUGH a patch of Carolina Buckthorn, its berries not long from ripe. Alone at Big Sugar for the first time since the amputation, he was eager to cast a line before the sun dropped below the horizon. The sky had been clear all week, and the water quiet. He hadn't told his daddy or mama of his plans, knowing his daddy would say yes and his mama no, and a fight between them would be sure to follow. He quickened his steps, the trusted Shakespeare spinning rod on his shoulder and the metal tackle box in his hand. Up ahead, beyond two skinny oaks, the water narrowed before sweeping toward the west. Someday Leonard hoped to follow the river beyond that bend, away from the land that bound him so close to home. Out there, not a soul would know Leonard Bush and the secrets he kept.

The river teased him into dropping a hook where most considered the water too shallow for bass and too warm for trout. The first time Leonard had fished this spot with Emmett, he'd caught a small bream with his second try. He was barely four years old, and they decided then that this was Leonard's lucky spot. Through the years, it proved to be just that. This afternoon he squatted low on the bank and turned his ear to the current. The iron-colored water was glassy except for one jagged, rippling seam slicing through the middle. He opened the tackle box and searched among the red and blue and black-hackled lures for his favorite rooster tail, the one Emmett had tied himself and given to Leonard on his twelfth birthday. Its downy costume, made up of saddle feather from their very own roosters, disguised its vicious trident hook. "It's a mean lure," Emmett said when he'd given it to Leonard. "But you're old enough to handle it."

Leonard pinned it to his shirt and picked up his rod, threaded with a heavier nylon than needed for catching smallmouth, but he wasn't in the mood to change it out. The sun, dawdling above the horizon, would be gone soon and he wanted to get some fishing in before it set.

He tied the rooster tail to the end of the fishing line and stepped to the bank's edge. Opening the reel's bail, he spied his target and in one swift motion pushed his spinning rod forward. The lure arced low across the water's surface before dropping into the far side of Big Sugar. Leonard tightened the line and edged behind some scrubby cedars, keeping his hand steady as he worked to tease a bass into thinking the rooster tail was a worthy meal. He reeled in the line and cast again. Whether he caught a fish or not made no difference. Being at Big Sugar on his own was enough for Leonard.

---

A BRANCH BEHIND him snapped. Then another. Leonard figured it was most likely a deer coming out to feed. He tugged on the line. The crackling came closer. Leonard leaned in toward the ridge. Maybe some high schoolers were headed to the river to pass around a bottle of their daddy's whiskey. For a moment, the river grew quiet. Suddenly, a high-pitched shriek pierced the woods, rolling past the trees and brush, popping out in sharp, sporadic bursts before morphing into a shrill, consistent cry.

Leonard ducked, hiding from something he couldn't see. A squirrel with an acorn clenched between his teeth stood frozen a few feet ahead. Another cry pealed, and the squirrel scampered up a nearby pine. Leonard wound the reel until the rooster tail bobbed at the end of the rod. He'd never once felt afraid at Big Sugar, despite his mama's fears and the stories she'd shared about men bootlegging by the river. But this time was different. Leonard's senses had heightened, his muscles tensed. Every breaking branch cracked louder. Each whiff of cedar and water smelled stronger. Even the warm evening light shone clearer, brighter.

Another scream, and Leonard slumped to the ground. He spied a flash of white farther up the bank and shimmied up a short rise on his belly, dragging the spinning rod along behind him. Spindly oaks and hickories blocked his view. A high-pitched voice shouted, "Leave me alone!" A second voice, much deeper, drowned out the first. A girl with red hair ran past, gasping for breath. A stocky, long-haired man chased after her.

*Azalea.* Leonard lurched forward, then thinking better of it, eased backwards. His heart beat fast, the pulse of it thundering in his ears, nearly drowning out Azalea's pitiful cries. The rush of Big Sugar fell mute. Leonard burrowed further behind a clump of river oats. He gulped down a deep breath, desperately trying to steady his heartbeat.

From his hiding spot, Leonard watched as the man reached for Azalea's shirt but grabbed only air, then stretched his stride and reached again. This time he caught her. She hit the ground with a hard thump, and the man dropped on top of her. Azalea squirmed beneath him, kicking at the ground and scratching at his face.

Leonard's thoughts swirled. His body trembled. Even his missing leg seemed to shake. Sizing himself up against this stranger, Leonard felt puny.

"Stop fighting me, girl." The man slapped Azalea's cheek. She cried out in pain. The man reached under her shirt. When Azalea's cries swelled, the man pressed his hand over her mouth and hollered at her to shut up.

Leonard rose onto his knee, careful to keep his cover behind the grassy oats. Azalea's eyes were huge white spheres set in a pale face. She struggled to sit up, but the man shoved her back. He pinned her arms to the ground. He smashed his mouth against hers. Azalea turned her head, begging him to stop.

Leonard shouted at the man. *Stop! Get off her!* But no words had formed on his tongue.

The man unbuckled his pants.

Leonard's stomach churned. Long ago, Emmett had reassured him that a man was not measured by his size or shape. Lord, he hoped his daddy was right because today his leg felt like a weighty burden. Leonard rolled onto his bottom, knowing he needed to measure up right now. The man held Azalea's face in a mean grip.

"Come on, girl, your mama loves this." Azalea screamed again.

Swallowing another deep breath, Leonard stood up and dug his toes into the wet clay. *Steady, steady*, he told himself, aiming the rod at the man's head before beginning his cast. Then he raised his arm and pushed it forward. The reel hissed as the line gave way. The rooster tail sped above the brush and grasses and through a narrow opening formed by two twiggy oaks. Just as the line passed the man's head, Leonard flicked his wrist. The trident hook caught hold of flesh and clawed its way through the man's ear.

"What the hell?" The man grabbed his ear.

Leonard yanked on the line.

The man jumped to his feet and zeroed in on Leonard. "Shit, kid, the water's the other way!"

Satisfied to see a line of blood running down the man's neck, Leonard hollered for Azalea, keeping both hands steady on the rod. The man lurched forward. Leonard wound the reel tighter. The man yelped in pain, flip-flopping like a snagged fish. The rooster tail had hooked him good. His ear was gushing blood now, a sight that gave Leonard pleasure. He kept the line taut while the man jerked along, at once both obeying the tug of the line and trying to pull away from it.

"Damn, you son of a bitch! Let me go!"

"Probably going to need a doctor to cut that out," Leonard shouted, careful to keep his distance.

"No shit I need a doctor." The man stared at his blood-stained shirt then pressed his hand to his ear. "Cut the damn line."

Afraid if he cut the man loose he might come after him, Leonard hesitated. "Azalea," he called, his voice steady, "come here." She stumbled toward him. Leonard gripped his fishing knife, jerked the line hard one more time, then sliced it in two, waving the knife in front of him, a final warning to the man.

The man scrambled up the bank, tripping as he hopscotched along the ridge, finally disappearing among the taller oaks and pines near the road.

Leonard waited a moment longer to be certain the man was gone, then he dropped his rod and went to Azalea. Her cheek was swollen, her arms claw-marked, her hair tangled with dried leaves and twigs. She gulped back tears, but her sobs grew louder, echoing across the water. Azalea cried until she retched. When she was done, she sat hunched over, covering her face with her hands.

Leonard had seen his mama cry too many times, but never like this. Azalea's sobs made him feel gut punched. His fake leg gave way, and he slumped to the ground beside her. "Are you hurt?" he asked.

She touched her finger to her lip and winced. "Don't go telling no one about this," she finally eked out.

Leonard nodded. He'd watched as that man chased after Azalea, slapped her face, tugged on her shirt. Replaying it in his head, none of it made any sense — a grown man acting wild like that. He wanted to tell his daddy and his mama, but he knew that if June found out she'd be furious — with Leonard for fishing alone and for taking on such a creep. She'd hurl her anger at Emmett for letting their son go to Big Sugar. She'd holler and pray and start a vigil, looking high and low for another stroke of bad luck. She'd talk bad about Rose Parker and likely claim Azalea was no better. Nothing good could come of his mama or his daddy finding out, but it seemed the sheriff ought to be told.

"Promise you won't tell?" Azalea asked again, her voice still trembling.

"You know that man?" Leonard asked her.

"He's a friend of mama's." Azalea kept her eyes fixed on the ridge. "Been hanging around the house most of the week. Said we'd catch some fish for supper."

"I don't think he's coming back."

Neither spoke. Soon the bullfrogs began to croak, their calm baritones filling the silence along the riverbank. Leonard wanted to comfort Azalea but refrained from putting his arm around her. He picked up a rock instead, rolled it between his thumb and forefinger, then tossed it into the woods.

Azalea wrapped her arms around her legs, curling up into a tight ball. Leonard wasn't sure what to say, but he could see clear enough that Azalea was shaken up bad. He picked up another rock, figuring she'd talk when she was ready. She pulled her long hair over her face, then slapped at a mosquito dancing too close to her ankle.

When the light began to dim under the trees, Leonard softly called her name. Azalea looked at him. Even in the gloaming, he could see her nose was red from crying, her cheek swelling with a bruise. "You going to be okay?"

"I don't know."

"You need a doctor?"

"No, I don't need a doctor. That ain't what I mean." Azalea stared at the water.

Leonard nodded. He reached for a dried leaf and crumbled it in his hand. "You need your mama?" he finally asked, scattering the leafy pieces like feed.

"No, dammit, I don't need my mama neither." Azalea kept her gaze fixed on the water, resting her chin on her knee. "That man," she started. "That man's gone and gotten Mama pregnant." She closed her eyes.

Another long silence lingered between them. Leonard wasn't sure what to say. He picked up a second leaf and crumbled it like he had the first. Finally, he spoke up. "Guess you ain't wanting another baby brother or sister?"

"Course I ain't." Azalea opened her eyes. She stared straight at him. "Mama can't take care of the one she got."

"Anything I can do?"

Azalea coughed up a laugh. "Always eager to help, ain't you?" She swatted at another mosquito buzzing about her head.

Leonard looked to the sky where an osprey circled overhead, scanning Big Sugar for fishy prey. From the corner of his eye, he spied Azalea fingering a heart-shaped pendant dangling about her neck, rubbing it feverishly as if she were trying to conjure a genie from a bottle.

"Make it go away," she whispered. "You tend to everybody else's misery. Can't you take care of mine?"

Leonard knew that Azalea took care of Atlas more than their own mama did. He figured another baby would likely be Azalea's responsibility, too. With no brothers or sisters, he didn't know much about caring for a baby, but he knew from bottle-feeding a newborn calf on a regular schedule that a new baby would be a weighty job. And he knew for certain this was a situation he couldn't bury on the hilltop and *make go away.*

Leonard reached for his spinning rod. The full moon had already risen, while the last hint of sun clung to the horizon. He wished he could bury Azalea's pain, give her family the fresh start he had promised so many others. But there was nothing he could do about a baby. Surely Azalea understood that. "We better get home," he said, searching the darkening sky. "Stars will be out soon, and our mamas'll be getting worried."

Azalea stood up and brushed the leaves from her jeans. "Guess Little Henry was wrong about you," she said. "You ain't a miracle worker after all." Then she yanked the pendant from her neck, walked to the edge of Big Sugar, and flung it into the water. "Now we can go."

# — Azalea —

AZALEA HOPED TO hide her fat lip, coming home in the dark, but Rose was sitting on the porch swing when she stepped into the clearing, lamplight blazing in the early evening. Azalea hesitated, even considered diving behind a cedar and playing possum until her mama left for bed. But Rose caught sight of her and waved her home. Azalea dreaded facing her mama, scared to admit what had happened at Big Sugar and terrified to think Mack might be inside, waiting for her return.

"Get up here, girl," Rose hollered, one word sliding into the next in a drunken jumble. "Where you been?" She slapped the porch swing. "Come sit with me."

Rose's sugary sweet tone left Azalea feeling raw. She wondered if her mama already knew what had happened at the river, how Mack had thrown her to the ground and climbed on top of her. She stepped onto the porch and settled next to her mama on the swing, checking for signs of Mack. Rose rocked the swing and patted Azalea's thigh. Cigarette butts and empty Falstaff cans littered the porch floor.

Rose wrapped her arm around Azalea's shoulder and pulled her close. "What happened to Mack?"

Azalea's body stiffened against her mother's soft flesh. "Nothing."

"Nothing?" Rose's voice rang with an eerie calm. "Then how come he showed up here bleeding like a stuck pig? Wouldn't say what happened, but he called you a little devil, packed his bag, and took off. Didn't leave me a dime and been here three days." The bare bulb burning by the screen door exposed a trail of blood on the plank floor.

Azalea's stomach churned, and she feared she might vomit again. "Don't you want to know what he done to me?"

"To you?" Rose sighed, her words gaining strength. "Honey, I was counting on that man to put food on the table." She pinched Azalea's arm. "You got money for the baby's milk?"

Azalea jerked her arm free. "He hurt me, Mama!"

Rose fumbled for a cigarette inside her robe pocket. "Get me a match." She pointed to an empty box on the floor. "I'm all out here."

Dizzy-headed, Azalea fetched a book of matches kept ready by the stovetop. On her way out the screen door, she spotted more blood on the wood floor and smiled, thinking of Mack dancing at the end of Leonard's line. She struck the match and held the flame to her mama's cigarette. Rose took a long drag, closed her eyes, and relaxed against the porch swing. "He was after me, Mama. He tried to get in my pants."

A gentle breeze rustled the treetops, and the cigarette smoke trailed into the clearing. Rose held up her hand. "Men like Mack don't want to fool with a child."

"But he did, Mama." Azalea's voice quivered as she struggled to make sense of what her mother was saying. "If Leonard hadn't come along..."

"That cripple boy saved you? Is that what you're saying?" Rose pumped her feet against the porch floor, and the swing glided higher.

"Yes, ma'am."

Azalea turned away from Rose. "He snagged Mack with a fishing hook." She scraped at a spot of Mack's blood with the toe of her shoe. She would never wash that stain from the wood, preferring to let it age and grow faint, a comforting reminder that Mack had been hurt, too.

Rose hugged her body with arms so thin the bones stood out. A long piece of ash dangled from the end of her cigarette, threatening to fall on her bare thigh. Atlas cried out from the bedroom. Azalea glanced back at the house. "Get the baby," Rose muttered and flicked the ash into the yard.

Azalea hesitated at the screen door. "Mama?"

Rose fixed her attention on the clearing.

Could her mama really be looking for Mack? Could she really want him back? The thought of Mack standing in the space of their little house caused Azalea to shudder. Atlas cried out again. As Azalea stepped inside, Rose gasped, a panicky sound like she was drowning in deep water and finally punched through the surface for air. Azalea didn't linger on the porch. Atlas was bawling, and she needed to see about him. But she heard Rose crying through the open window. For now, that was comfort enough.

---

COME MORNING, WITH the sun scrambling above the tree line, Rose ordered Azalea to open up the house. "Hot as hell in here and I ain't even had my coffee," she said, fanning her face with a magazine. Before she'd gone to bed, Azalea had checked the front and back doors and shut every window, setting their locks despite the thick, stale air inside the house. She wedged a ruler between the window sashes in her bedroom as an extra precaution and pulled Atlas's crib right up next to her bed. She was worried Mack might come back. Rose had seemed worried that he wouldn't.

On her way to the kitchen, Azalea noticed her mama's belly round and full beneath her gown. "Bring me a cold cloth, hon," Rose whined. Stretched out on the couch, her head wrapped in a damp towel, she didn't seem to notice the ripe bruise on Azalea's cheek.

Azalea took Atlas to the kitchen to give her mama some quiet. A blue bird flitted outside the window and some purple-topped joe-pye weed scratched at the screen. There was no sign of Mack or his big rig, but Azalea trembled at the thought of his body on top of hers, his foul breath in her face. Hopefully, he was miles down the road on his way to New Mexico. She fished in the sink water for another bottle while Atlas sat in his high chair banging a wooden spoon against the metal tray. A knock at the front of the house startled Azalea. She dropped the bottle in the water. Atlas squealed.

"Come on in," Rose called.

"It's locked."

Azalea started to panic as she recognized Leonard's voice.

"Shit fire," Rose said. "Azalea's got this house locked up like Fort Knox."

Azalea held her breath, listening as her mama shuffled across the room. The lock clicked and the door creaked open. "Look-a-here at this fine young gentleman come to pay us a visit."

"Yes, ma'am. It's me, Leonard Bush."

"I know who you are."

Azalea dried her hands on her jeans and rushed to the front room, desperately wishing Rose were more like a normal mother. Rose had already plopped down on the sofa, dressed in an orange bathrobe, her hair pinned loose on top of her head, yesterday's mascara smeared under her eyes.

"Come in here, Leonard Bush," Rose said. She pressed the damp cloth to her forehead. "I ain't seen you since you lost your leg."

"You feeling okay, Mrs. Parker?"

"Headache is all." Rose's robe hung open, revealing her nightgown, sheer and low-cut.

An empty bottle of Four Roses that Mack had brought to the house sat on the table by the sofa. Azalea thought about the beer cans and cigarette butts scattered across the porch. She hadn't had time to clean the mess. She looked around the room. The windows were thick with dust. The threadbare sofa sagged in the middle where Rose sat with her tits practically hanging out of her gown. Azalea would never have noticed any of these things if Leonard hadn't shown up. Why hadn't he called first? The telephone was working this month.

"Azalea," Rose said, "this here is Leonard Bush, the crippled boy."

Azalea rolled her eyes. "I know who Leonard is, Mama. And don't call him that."

"Leonard? Or crippled?" Rose laughed.

"Mama, stop it."

Rose motioned him inside. "How you doing it, Leonard Bush? Standing there on two legs like that when you only got the one. Is it a magic trick?"

Leonard took a step closer. "No, ma'am. It's fake. See?" He pulled up his pants leg, revealing the wooden limb, laminated with a creamy white finish.

Rose nodded and slumped back on the sofa. "Ain't that something. I remember seeing your picture in the newspaper when you got hurt. On the front page. Full color. It was a real good picture. You were in the hospital bed smiling like nothing had happened. Funny how I remember that." She held the damp cloth in her hand, waving it like she was signaling surrender. "You were grinning like it was your birthday or something. And look at you, strutting around my house all normal."

"Shut up, Mama."

Rose glanced at Azalea and gave her a half smile. "Don't mind her, Leonard." She patted the sofa cushion. "Come on over here. Let me see you walk some more."

Leonard took a couple more steps.

"Stop it, Leonard," Azalea said.

"It's okay." He smiled. "If you ain't ever seen a fake leg before I guess it's kind of interesting." He took another step.

"Damn right, it's interesting." Rose clapped her hands, then waved Leonard closer.

Azalea wanted to scream. She had never intended Leonard to see her mama like this. Hungover and acting like a slut. And now she wanted him to leave before Rose embarrassed her any more. She took her mother a cold glass of water, grabbed Leonard's hand, and pulled him into the kitchen.

Atlas was fussing and squirming in his chair. Azalea put a cracker on the metal tray. Atlas shoved it into his mouth. She told Leonard to sit down, then began washing last night's dirty dishes. The dried-up beans in the soup pot proved a challenge, and the smell of stale grease and cigarettes lingered despite the open window and cool morning breeze. Leonard scooted his chair closer to Atlas and started playing peekaboo with him.

"Why you here, Leonard?"

Atlas dropped his cracker on the floor. Leonard picked it up and gave it back to him. "I was worried about you," he said. "Looks like you got a pretty good shiner."

Azalea touched her cheek. "You didn't need to come here. You could've called."

"But the phone..." Leonard started.

"Phone's working," she said sharply. "And I'm fine. Just fine." She scrubbed the pot one final time and set it on the drainboard to dry. "You've seen with your own two eyes that everything's fine." Azalea added more hot water to the sink. "You don't need to stick around."

Leonard reached for an old checkered dishrag, upping the stakes for peekaboo with Atlas. The baby laughed whenever Leonard dropped the rag and fussed when Leonard hid his face.

"You mad at me?" he asked, tossing the rag over the baby's head.

"I didn't ask you to come here."

"I just thought after last night..."

"I didn't ask you to save me." Azalea wheeled around, pressing her back against the sink. "You can't be everybody's hero."

Atlas tossed the cloth to the floor. Leonard stared at Azalea, then picked up the cloth and put it on the table. He stood and patted the baby's head. "I just wanted to make sure you were okay." Leonard nodded slightly, his eyes fixed on Azalea. "Looks like you're fine." He walked into the living room and said something to Rose. She mumbled a goodbye, and the screen door creaked closed. Atlas squealed, grabbing for the cloth just barely out of his reach. Rose called for more water. Somewhere in the distance, a dog barked. Even with all the noise, the house was oddly quiet without Leonard in it.

# — Emmett —

 THE NEXT DAY Emmett dropped a quarter in the tin can on the counter at Mitchell's Hardware. He'd never noticed the Easterseals collection before today or the camp advertised on the can's label. Certainly, he'd never given such an organization much thought, and he'd never considered his own son crippled. But Leonard might benefit from the Easterseals, and he might enjoy this camp come summer. Emmett reached in his pocket for more change. At the clang of the coins, Agnes Mitchell looked up from the register and smiled. Her husband, Lytle, pushing a large broom at the back the of store, paused to wave hello. Emmett asked Agnes for a pen and paper and jotted down the number on the tin can.

Strange, Emmett thought, when one of his cows had birthed a calf with crooked front limbs, he'd put her down before she ever had a chance to suckle. It was the humane thing to do, he'd explained to Leonard, barely nine years old at the time. Now Emmett wondered if Leonard had worried, even for a second, that his father might have considered doing the same to him. Emmett brushed the thought away as he picked up a roll of chicken wire and tossed it across his shoulder. He thanked Agnes and waved goodbye to Lytle.

Cars rolled down the two-lane street, anchored by the Sweetwater Savings and Loan to the left and Peoples Drugstore to the right. Passersby chatted as they walked along the sidewalk, some stopping to gaze in store windows. Across the street, men and women bustled outside Cox's Department Store for its annual clearance sale, rifling through bins of socks and linens, shoes and housewares. Emmett wanted to dip his toe in this current, to be swept up in the town's energy and carried along far from the responsibilities waiting for him back home. Instead, he watched two ladies pass, tipped his cap, and hefted the wire into the back of his pickup.

By the time Emmett parked the truck near the feeding barn, the sun was already low in the sky. Hundreds of starlings were perched on telephone lines tying his house to every other in Sweetwater. Emmett left the chicken wire in the truck and walked toward the milk room, looking up at the sky, marveling in the beauty of the starlings. When he opened the door, the starlings took flight, a swarming black veil that bobbed and swayed above the pasture before heading farther east. Emmett stopped in the doorway to watch their flight.

Inside the milk room, he turned on the little black-and-white television. The local news flickered on. He adjusted the antennae for a better picture. A white-haired newscaster said a teenaged boy had held up a bank in Johnson City, stolen two thousand dollars before disappearing in the Smokies. Police were looking for him as far west as Maryville and as far south as Athens. Emmett would keep this news from June, knowing she'd worry, poking him throughout the night every time the house settled.

After a quick glance over both shoulders, Emmett pulled his sister's shoe from his pants pocket. He squeezed it first, as he always did, then rubbed the toe against his lips once, then a second time, before setting it aside. Like swallowing a swig of liquor, he immediately felt his body calm a tad. Still, he glanced over his shoulders one more time before grabbing a small key from his top desk drawer and wiggling it into a padlock secured to a metal cabinet where he stored medicines and vaccines. He pushed past bottles of penicillin and sulfur and reached for a paper bag tucked in the far back. He placed the bag on his desk and opened it up.

Inside were Leonard's baseball cleats — the ones he'd worn only days before the amputation. The shoes had been left on the back porch, too muddy to be brought into the house. June had overlooked them during those first few days home from the hospital, so Emmett had scooped them up and hid them in the milk room.

When she'd asked about the cleats a couple weeks later, Emmett pretended he knew nothing about them. He still wasn't sure why he'd lied. Maybe he was afraid June might give them away like she'd done Leonard's bicycle. No matter the reason, Emmett had taken the cleats and locked them away in the metal cabinet for safekeeping. That was all there was to it.

All these months later, he took the shoes out of the bag and set them side by side on the desktop. He had cleaned and polished the black leather to a high shine the day he'd first brought them to the milk room, taking extra care to remove every speck of mud from the soles, even using a toothpick to clean around the metal studs. They looked nearly new.

Emmett closed his eyes, picturing the warm afternoon last May when he'd taken Leonard shopping for new cleats at Cox's Department Store. Usually June did Leonard's clothes shopping. But athletic shoes — this was Emmett's territory. Leonard was pitching now, and his batting was strong. As he laced up the cleats for Leonard to try them on, Emmett smiled and promised that all the greats — Hank Aaron and Willie Mays and Mickey Mantle — wore the very same shoe. Leonard laughed. "Ain't no other baseball shoe than Riddell, Daddy." When they left the department store, they stopped at the Dairy Dip for a burger and chocolate shake. Leonard was hoping to start as pitcher this season. The coach had indicated he would.

Emmett rubbed his eyes, eager to brush off the memory, but his thoughts quickly circled around to that damn bottle cap lure. He'd dangled it in front of his son that morning, promised him the fish would go for it. June was right. The loss of Leonard's leg was his fault. *No one else was to blame but you.* On the television, as the news broke to a commercial, the weatherman teased about a fast-moving cold front, barreling in from the west by week's end.

Emmett scooted his chair back. He stared at his feet, then at Leonard's cleats. He rotated his left ankle and wiggled his toes. He pressed his foot flat against the floor, then kicked it out in front of him. He still blamed himself for Leonard's loss. *I made the bottle cap lure. I told him to fish Big Sugar. I told June to quit babying the boy.*

"Stop it," he shouted. But the guilty thoughts kept swirling through his head.

Emmett kicked off his work boot. He tugged off his sock. With his left foot bare, he glanced at the milk room door. The lock was secure. He took a shallow breath, then forced his foot into Leonard's cleat. His toes were jam-packed and his foot ached from the tight fit, but Emmett didn't care. For one brief moment, he wanted to touch what Leonard's left foot had touched. He wanted to feel the shoe's leather that had once hugged his boy's foot hug his own. Strange behavior, even for a grieving father. And like sneaking a cigarette or a swig of whiskey, he felt guilty for doing it. But for some reason he couldn't explain, it calmed him, just like touching Sarah's shoe.

In Knoxville, according to the television news anchor, a mother and father had been arrested for leaving their three-year-old son alone at home while they went out drinking at a local honky-tonk. Emmett wondered why a parent would do such a thing. He flipped off the television, calling up memories of Leonard at that tender age, a chubby-cheeked little boy who followed his daddy around the dairy, nipping at his heels like a puppy. *Two peas in a pod*, June would say. She dressed them in matching overalls and flannel shirts.

Emmett looked at his foot. "You ain't right," he said. "You just ain't right." He yanked off the shoe and tucked both it and its mate in the paper bag. Then he got up from the desk, hid the bag in the metal cabinet, and secured the lock.

A full moon colored the clearing between barn and house an eerie blue, and a mockingbird began a scolding rasp. Emmett crossed his arms against his chest and hurried for the kitchen door. Careful not to make a sound, he slipped inside a silent house.

June had left the stove light burning and a clean glass on the counter. Emmett ended every day with a glass of bedtime buttermilk to help him sleep. Especially tonight, he was touched by June's kind gesture. He tiptoed to the refrigerator, poured the glass full, and finished it off. Despite their frustrations with one another, he loved June and hated lying to her about his feelings and odd behavior. He was quick to rinse and dry the glass, knowing she'd chastise him come morning for leaving it dirty in the sink. Then he flipped off the stove light and walked down the hall to Leonard's room, floorboards creaking underfoot.

Leonard lay on his side, looking small curled up in sleep, a precious reminder of the three-year-old boy he had once been. Not even a teenager yet and he'd already suffered a terrible loss. He didn't deserve a warped daddy on top of everything else. Emmett pulled the door closed and leaned against it, drawing in a ragged breath. He longed for something more to offer his son than hollow words of encouragement.

He stepped across the hall and stripped bare, dropping his jeans, t-shirt, and underpants on the tile floor. He turned on the shower and held his hand under the water until it ran hot, then stepped into the tub. When he had scrubbed himself clean, he pulled on a pair of freshly pressed boxer shorts and slipped under the covers next to June. He kept to his side of the bed — afraid he'd wake her, afraid she'd smell the guilt oozing from his pores. Her chest rose and fell, keeping a steady, gentle beat. Was she lost in a sweet dream where she and Emmett were walking across a pasture together, hand in hand, like they so often did when they were young, imagining their lives together? June was suspicious now, and for good reason. Before long, she'd learn the truth. She'd pick and dig at Emmett's secrets until she finally exposed them. Then what? Emmett's heart started racing, his breathing rapid. He got up, remembering the pint bottle he'd left hidden in the dresser after tangling with the posthole digger. Tonight, he needed something much stronger than buttermilk to help him sleep.

# — Leonard —

 A FEW DAYS LATER, Emmett waved an envelope as he walked into the kitchen. The United States Postal Service had a special delivery for Mr. Leonard Bush, he said, sounding proud or curious, Leonard wasn't sure which. Emmett held the envelope up to the window. "Looks mighty official," he said, then handed it to Leonard. In the past, the only mail Leonard had received were birthday cards from the preacher and Miss Ooten and an end-of-the-year report card from school. But his birthday was months ago, and school was weeks from being over. Leonard studied the envelope. No one had ever referred to him as *mister*.

"You might ought to open that up while your mama ain't around," said Emmett, peering over Leonard's shoulder.

With his bedroom door locked shut, Leonard opened the letter. It was from a Mr. Albert Coyne who, according to the return address, lived thirty miles north in Oak Ridge. A scientist, he admitted working on the H-bomb during the war. "Very hush-hush. Couldn't even tell my wife the real reason I had dragged her from our lovely Virginia home to live in the Cumberland Mountains of East Tennessee," he wrote. "Claimed I was making a new synthetic tire for the army. But I don't think she believed me."

When the atomic bomb was dropped on Hiroshima on that August morning in 1945, Mr. Coyne admitted to celebrating. And when Japan surrendered a few days after the second bomb was unleashed on Nagasaki, he'd let out a cheer. "People were calling me a hero. For a while, I believed them." At the time, Mr. Coyne confessed not being overly concerned with the number of Japanese lives lost, only the number of American lives saved. "My only brother died at Iwo Jima."

When peace was declared the very next month on the deck of the USS *Missouri*, Mr. Coyne's thoughts immediately turned to family. And a little more than nine months later, his wife, Estelle, birthed a six-pound, blue-eyed girl. "Once Julie arrived, our lives seemed perfect," he wrote. "But holding our sweet baby, gazing into her twinkling eyes, kissing her tender cheeks got me to thinking. Thousands of babies had been killed on the other side of the world, and I had played a part in that killing." Soon, guilt consumed him, festering and strengthening every day, pressing down on his heart until he found it hard to work, to sleep, even to breathe.

He spoke with preachers, Methodists and Baptists, and the five psychiatrists stationed at Oak Ridge, but none of them offered any lasting help. Late last year, his wife divorced him, said she could no longer live with a man who was tethered to the past. "I don't really blame her. Guess I wasn't much of a husband. But I'm tired. Worn out. Lost."

It was his second cousin, related to Laura Kilgore by marriage, who suggested he contact Leonard. "I heard what you did for Laura, although snatching a lace collar from an old woman seems like child's play compared to what I did," he wrote. "I must confess that I feel rather ridiculous reaching out to a boy for this kind of help. But I'm desperate."

Leonard folded Mr. Coyne's letter and taped it to the back of his desk drawer. Then he ripped a piece of notebook paper from his binder and sharpened a number two pencil. "We learned about the war in school this year, but I've never met a real scientist," he started. "I'm not sure I can be of much help. But the hilltop is a special place, and I welcome your visit." Leonard suggested they meet Saturday at the cemetery gate. At the bottom of the paper, he drew a map, showing Mr. Coyne where to park on the far side of the dairy and how to find their meeting spot without June catching wind of his coming and going. Leonard hated sneaking around his mama, but he mailed the letter anyway, then considered phoning Azalea for a favor.

More than a week had passed since Leonard had fished that nasty man off of his friend. And more than a week had passed since he'd visited the Parkers' house to check on her. He'd tried calling Azalea a dozen times since, but no one answered. She hadn't been at school either. Leonard was growing worried. And although he knew Mr. Coyne was suffering, Leonard was glad he had a reason to call Azalea one more time. He dialed her number. Again, no one answered.

The following Saturday, Leonard arrived at the cemetery a few minutes before Mr. Coyne. Even though he knew Azalea wasn't coming, he still kept an eye out, hoping to catch a flash of her red hair.

At twelve noon, Albert Coyne arrived, right on schedule, with a yellowed copy of the *Knoxville News-Sentinel*, dated August 6, 1945, tucked under his arm. He wore a black suit and tie and a matching black hat that he tipped when he offered a quick hello. "I wasn't sure what to bring for the burying," he said, his words coming out in stuttered bursts. He held up the paper. "Guess this explains most of it."

Leonard nodded, then asked to see it. "Our teacher said nearly two hundred thousand people were killed," he said, scanning the front page. "She said that's the same as forty or fifty Sweetwaters."

Mr. Coyne reached in his coat pocket for a handkerchief and patted his eyes. "I'm afraid your teacher's right about that," he whispered.

Leonard folded the paper, then tapped Mr. Coyne on the arm. "I'm sorry," he said. He opened the iron gate and motioned for Mr. Coyne to follow.

The two walked to the far side of the cemetery where Leonard had already dug a tiny grave with a trowel he kept tucked behind the oak. Mr. Coyne's shoulders shook, and he wiped away a flood of tears. Leonard looked to the sky, desperately searching for the right words for a man with such a heavy heart. He worried that the hilltop might not have enough to offer Mr. Coyne and wished there could have been at least some music to soothe the situation. Leonard reached for his wrinkled hand. "I can't promise that putting that newspaper in the ground is going to change anything," he said. "But you've suffered long enough, and you've come a long way to be here today." He nodded toward the grave. "Why don't you let the hilltop swallow your pain?"

Without Azalea there to sing, Leonard hummed the first notes of "Amazing Grace," his mama's favorite hymn. Mr. Coyne dropped to his knees and reached for a handkerchief. The white cloth looked like a dove against his black jacket. Leonard eased to the ground beside him, balancing on one knee. "Go ahead," he said and nudged Mr. Coyne. "Let it go." Leonard hummed the refrain.

Leonard scooped up some dirt and dropped it on the newspaper, then again nudged Mr. Coyne, encouraging him to do the same. The old man pressed his palms into the freshly tilled earth.

Leonard recited the familiar verses about the legs of men and the strength of horses. He spoke about repentance and love, then offered a prayer and a whispered, "Amen." The wind kicked up, brushing over the hilltop. A shiver ran down Leonard's spine. He remembered his mama's warnings about the dead standing guard nearby, this time figuring she was right.

Mr. Coyne turned to Leonard. His features had softened, and he didn't seem so full of grief. He tossed a handful of dirt into the grave and repeated the amen.

The hillside fell quiet except for the wind rushing through the leaves. Leonard did not budge. Mr. Coyne sat back on his heels. "Could it be?" he asked, stretching his arms open wide. "Could it truly be that the awful weight pressing down on my heart for so long has been lifted? Just like that?" He stood, puffed up his chest, and took a deep breath. As he exhaled, his smile grew wider. He lifted his face toward the sun. He scratched his head. "There's no reason for this to work. No science to explain it."

"This ain't a science experiment," said Leonard.

The two of them stood together, silent and still. Then Mr. Coyne tapped Leonard on the arm, raising an eyebrow as if he'd come to a conclusion.

Leonard shook his head. "No, it ain't me either."

"It just can't be that simple?" Mr. Coyne stared at the grave, then at the sky, as if he was searching for an answer for this transformation somewhere between heaven and earth.

Leonard got to his feet, plucked a pencil from behind his ear, and began scribbling at the back page of his Bible. "You think maybe grown-ups just make things too hard sometimes?"

"Maybe," Mr. Coyne said, still gazing at the sky.

"Go on home, Mr. Coyne. Leave your troubles here and go home."

Mr. Coyne took another deep breath and doffed his hat. "Okay," he said. "I'll be on my way." He turned for the gate.

"Wait a minute," Leonard said. "After all you've been through, I hate to ask you to keep a secret on my behalf. But maybe it's best if you don't talk about this. My mama really don't like people coming around too much."

Mr. Coyne nodded. "I understand. That's the least I can do for you, but I'm not sure this is the kind of secret that should be kept," he said, smiling in return.

Leonard watched until Mr. Coyne disappeared down the hill. Then he began filling the grave, tamping down the earth with his hands. He hoped Mr. Coyne had found a lasting peace. An American hero, he surely deserved it. Too much of his life had been wasted already, choosing guilt over his wife and daughter. Leonard thought of his own parents' constant fighting, of Vivienne Ford's stealing, of Rose Parker's drunken fits, and the new baby Azalea feared was growing in her mama's belly. The adults in his life were making a fine mess of everything.

Leonard tucked the Bible in his rear pocket. When he got home, he'd try calling Azalea one more time.

# — June —

 WHEN A LIGHT frost chalked the land white, June found Little Henry Reed standing at the mailbox for a second time. Much like those Mexican jumping beans Emmett had brought home from a dime store in Chattanooga, Little Henry hopped around the foot of the drive, kicking at the wood fence post and tossing rocks. A busy bee or beaver, June wasn't sure which the boy was, but he never stopped moving.

Little Henry stared back at the house but didn't hightail it when he saw her. June didn't shoo him away either. Since she'd driven Little Henry home a few weeks back, there had been no obvious signs of bad luck hovering about the boy. No deaths, no fevers, no lost or broken limbs. Everyone she loved and knew was healthy. Talk around town about the tragedies that had trailed behind Little Henry in the weeks following his mama's passing had subsided. These days gossip swirled about his daddy, Wayne.

Supposedly the sheriff hauled him into town for questioning last week, even confiscated his shotgun. Still, Wayne was a free man, and June worried about Little Henry being anywhere near him. But tempting fate was always dangerous. Letting Little Henry in the car was one thing, but allowing him in the house was altogether different. She'd only have herself to blame if she invited him inside and another tragedy beset her family. She sipped her coffee, careful not to take her eyes off him.

Emmett was at the dairy, well into the first milking of the day. He'd likely never know if she went inside and shut the door, drew the curtains, pretended she'd never seen the boy. But the thought of Margaret circled back around. Not a day passed that June didn't think of her friend. Some days she swore she heard Margaret calling to her. When the two of them finally met up in heaven again, how would June ever explain her bad behavior toward Little Henry?

June looked up to the sky, heaved a heavy sigh, then stepped into the yard and motioned to him to come around. Little Henry came running, his arms pumping at full tilt like always. June wondered if given a few more yards he might not take flight.

"What are you doing out so early?" she asked. Didn't Wayne know a growing boy needed sleep? She glanced at her wristwatch, not yet seven o'clock. No wonder Little Henry was such a runt. "Your daddy know where you're out at this hour?"

Winded, Little Henry hung his head. "He says come home by dark. He don't ever say nothing about leaving." He stood grinning, his hair shaved short, too thin in patches, too long in others. June wondered if Wayne or Little Henry had done the cutting.

"It ain't barely light yet," June said, leading Little Henry into the living room. "Leonard will be up soon enough. You can watch cartoons if you want." She pointed to the television and went to the kitchen. Little Henry followed close behind. "You want some eggs? Maybe a biscuit or two? You ain't got a lick of fat on you." June spun around and squeezed his arm. Little Henry winced.

"Goodness, did I hurt you?"

"Just a sore spot." Little Henry rubbed his arm, covered in a long sleeve.

"You been wrestling with your brother again?" June reached for Little Henry's hand, but he slipped it into his pants pocket. "Or something else?"

"Daddy says I'm just an accident waiting to happen." Little Henry scooted close to June. "Can I have some scrambled eggs?" He beamed up at her with a crooked grin.

Last time June hesitated to press the conversation further, but she worried about the boy. More every time she saw him. June looked him square in the eye. "Would you tell me if somebody was hurting you?"

Little Henry's smile faded.

"Your daddy's a tough man," June said, her voice soft. "Your mama knew that."

Little Henry looked away. "He just don't like me crying over mama no more. Says it's time to move on."

"*Moving on* is hard work." June stroked Little Henry's chin with the tip of her finger. "It's natural to miss your mama, hon. I miss mine, and she's been gone twenty-odd years."

Little Henry's eyes widened. "That's a long time to go without a mama."

June nodded. "Yes, it is."

Little Henry looked toward the window. "Mama wouldn't want me crying neither. She said, 'Blessed are the peacemakers.'"

June smiled. *And blessed are those who mourn, for they shall be comforted,* she thought, imagining Margaret beside Little Henry, kissing his head. "That sounds like your mama all right." June reached for her apron and tied it around her waist. "You sure you don't want to watch cartoons? Tom and Jerry are a lot more entertaining than me scrambling up some eggs."

Little Henry flopped down at the table. "I used to watch my mama cook. Sometimes she let me help."

June poured Little Henry a glass of orange juice and cracked a half dozen eggs. While she worked, he pulled a paper from his back pocket and flattened it on the tabletop. "I drew this one for you, Mrs. Bush. I was fixing to leave it in your mailbox if you hadn't come out and found me." He held it up. "See? It's you and my mama sitting at our kitchen table like y'all used to, eating pie and drinking coffee and talking."

June dried her hands on the apron and picked up the drawing. There on the crumbled piece of paper were two women — one in a red dress, the other in pink, one with brown hair, the other yellow — both sitting at a table, cups and saucers and a whole pie in front of them. Overhead, birds flitted through a cobalt blue sky dotted with a couple of white puffy clouds, and a giant rainbow stretched from one edge of the paper to the other.

Little Henry pointed. "That's you there."

June swallowed hard and nodded.

"And that's my mama," Little Henry pointed. "And that's one of them pies you used to make and bring over."

"I bet it's apple," June said. "Your mama's favorite."

"Mine, too." Little Henry licked his lips. "You ain't got any of that pie around, do you?"

June laughed. "No, not today, hon. Ain't apple season. It'll be time for strawberries before long."

"I like strawberry."

June wiped at a tear with the hem of her apron. "I got some strawberry jam," she said, returning the picture to Little Henry. "You want some of that on a biscuit?" She opened the far cupboard.

Little Henry nodded.

June showed him the jar, and Little Henry grinned. "The picture's for you to keep," he said. "Mama used to tape hers to the refrigerator."

"Thank you. I'll put this one right here so Emmett and Leonard can admire it, too." June rummaged through a kitchen drawer for a spool of Scotch tape. She fixed Little Henry's drawing to the refrigerator door, then stepped back to the stove and commenced her cooking. Little Henry was a sweet boy, but she'd burn some cedar and sage after he left, just to play it safe.

# — Leonard —

WHEN LEONARD AGREED to bury a piece of cat's tail for Roy Martin, he didn't mention Azalea's pretty singing voice or offer any hymn singing for that matter. He hadn't talked with Azalea since the day he went to see her. Probably for the best now. Roy's meanness, tying a bottle rocket to the tabby's tail, would have only upset her. Leonard knew her tender heart. Despite her stern talk at times, she'd rather catch a fly and set it free than smack it dead with a swatter.

"What the heck were you thinking?" Leonard asked Roy outside the cemetery gate.

Roy pulled on his ear. "I just wanted to see what would happen," he said. He handed Leonard a rolled-up newspaper with something thick inside. "Didn't think it'd take its tail off like that." Roy cracked a sneering grin. "You should have seen that cat run. Took off fast as lightning. Swear it."

Leonard skipped the Bible reading and went straight to praying, reminding Roy that even an old cat should be treated kindly. "Do unto others, even the four-legged ones, as you would have them do unto you," he said. Roy twitched at the words, but Leonard went on. "Please, God, forgive Roy Martin. Set him on a better course. Teach him that it's wrong to hurt any living creature. Teach him that meanness ain't ever right." Flashes of the tattooed man tackling Azalea ran through Leonard's head. His cheeks flushed, his temper blistered. He found himself hating Roy Martin for what he'd done almost as much as he hated that tattooed man.

The next afternoon, Marie Pearson stood waiting for Leonard at the bus stop. Plump and gray-haired, Marie was near Miss Ooten's age, maybe a few years older. She handed Leonard a paperback book with the picture of a leggy nurse on the cover, a handsome doctor standing behind her, his nose nuzzling her bare neck. "It's a Harlequin," she said. Reading it had left her feeling uneasy. *Tingly*. She was certain she had sinned somewhere between pages 235 and 242. She had marked those pages with a paper clip.

"I wanted hymn singing," she said. "You sure this burying will work just as well without any hymn singing?" she asked.

Leonard offered to call Miss Ooten.

"No, that ain't necessary. Don't need everybody in town knowing my business," Mrs. Pearson said, plucking the book back from Leonard, staring at its cover. "That book is dangerous. It emboldened me. I flirted with Lytle Mitchell at the hardware store, and Agnes not five feet away, before I even finished reading it." She waved her hand. "No, let's just get it done before I change my mind."

Two days later, Larry Ross came bearing a ticket from the Tennessee Theater in Knoxville. He'd paid for it fair and square. That wasn't the issue. *Elmer Gantry* was playing again for the weekend only, and Larry greatly admired Burt Lancaster. After the picture show, he'd stopped for a spaghetti dinner at the S & W Cafeteria. He paid for that in full and left twenty-five cents on the counter for the waitress. But he hadn't checked his gas tank. With only a dime remaining in his pocket, Larry couldn't afford a full gallon. He filled his tank and sped away without paying, the movie ticket and single dime the only evidence of his thievery.

"Sometimes, Lord, we just don't plan ahead as well as we should," Leonard said, winking at Larry with the final amen.

"It was a mighty fine service," Larry said, just what he needed. Leonard marked the burial in the back of his Bible, but he missed Azalea standing beside him.

The sun soon faded, and a full moon rose in the evening sky. Leonard reasoned that was the cause for the recent spate of burials. June always said a full moon made people lose track of their better senses. Three fresh, tiny graves seemed proof enough for Leonard.

He wanted to tell his mama about Azalea but remembered how she'd shooed Little Henry away after his mama died. Then a few days ago, she'd fed him breakfast, and later he and Little Henry had played outside the feeding barn. June brought them a snack of apple juice and cinnamon toast. Leonard wasn't sure what to think, but he knew his mama had loved Margaret Reed. On the other hand, June thought Rose Parker was a Jezebel. She'd be furious if she found out Leonard had visited their home. But seeing Azalea's beat-up house and her strung-out mama — bloodshot eyes, tangled hair, her big boobies spilling out of her nightgown — made Leonard wonder if he should tell June how desperate things were for his friend. His mama was right. His earlier secret-keeping had cost him a leg.

When Azalea finally returned to school, the bruise on her cheek had faded from purple to yellow. She told the teacher she had run into a door fetching Atlas a bottle in the dead of night. Miss Roberts must have believed Azalea, because she made the class stay in their seats a little longer at the end of the day while she lectured about home safety and emergency preparedness. Finally the last bell rang, and Leonard caught up with Azalea behind the gym where the older kids gathered to smoke and make out. "I been real worried about you," he said.

Azalea took his hand and pulled him closer. Leonard hoped she intended to kiss him like the high schoolers were doing. "I need you to do something for me," she said.

A little disappointed, Leonard asked her what.

"Bury this." Azalea pulled a piece of notebook paper from her pocket, folded in a tight, tiny triangle. She placed it in Leonard's palm. "Bury it on the hilltop."

"What is it?"

"Does it matter? Just get it in the ground."

Leonard turned it over in his hand, trying to decipher its meaning.

"It's a note to God." Azalea chewed the loose end of a tendril.

"You wrote God a note?"

"Just because I ain't a regular at church don't mean I think God's a phony."

"But a note?"

"It's more like a letter, Leonard. One the post office can't deliver. But you can."

"You ain't making any sense." Leonard worried Azalea was not fully recovered from her ordeal with Mack.

A couple of teenagers walked past, muttering something about little kids trespassing on high school property. Azalea grabbed Leonard's arm and yanked him toward the playground. "I told you that day at Big Sugar I needed your help. This is what you can do for me. I don't want another baby in the house. This explains it. It's simple — plain and simple."

Leonard shook his head. "Okay. But I still don't understand the note."

"Seriously, Leonard. Are you that thickheaded?" She set her hands on her hips just as Leonard had seen June do when she was riled. "Your mama makes you brownies and sandwiches and gift wraps them in wax paper. My mama can't do anything for herself, much less me and Atlas. I ain't taking care of another baby. And I sure as hell ain't taking care of Mack's. It'll probably come out with horns and a spiked tail." She pointed to Leonard's hand. "That note spells it out for the Lord, so there's no misunderstanding what I need from Him."

Leonard's eyes lit up. He'd never heard Azalea cuss.

Azalea touched her bruised cheek, then pulled her hair across it. "Truth is I don't know that much about God. But I been watching you on the hilltop, and I figure He's my only hope since Santa Claus ain't real." Azalea twirled some stands of hair around her finger. "You got a special connection. Everybody knows that. So I figure if I write down what I been asking for and you bury it up there on the hilltop, then God will have to pay me some attention. He can't ignore what's been prayed over."

Leonard studied the note in the palm of his hand, unsure of what to say.

"We got to keep that baby from growing." Azalea closed his hand around the note.

"Maybe I ought to show this to my mama instead."

"Are you crazy? You blab to your mama and no telling who'll show up at my house — the preacher, the law."

Leonard scratched his head. "Just seems like a grown woman might be better at handling woman things like this."

Azalea took his hand and squeezed it. "Bury this one thing for me, Leonard, like you do for everybody else."

Leonard felt sorry for her. More than that, he loved her. "Okay," he said, stuffing the paper in his pocket. "It just feels like this might be going too far."

"How you figure that? I'm asking you to put my prayer in the ground so God will know what I need. It's up to Him what to do about it. Not you."

Leonard's missing leg started to ache. Maybe Azalea was right. Maybe he did have a special connection to the Almighty. He'd never thought of it like that, but people sure were lining up to see him, traveling all the way from Oak Ridge and Niota, thinking he had something to offer that nobody else could, not even Brother Puckett. When they buried his leg, friends and neighbors had prophesied that he was special, touched by God. Is this what that meant?

"You say you're my friend," Azalea piped up, "but if you won't help me, I'll bury it on my own."

"You can't do that. That ain't your place."

"You ain't God. And you sure ain't telling me what I can and cannot do." Azalea snatched the note from him.

Leonard snatched it back. "Fine. I'll take care of it."

"Fine."

"You going to sing?"

"Why not? I need to do whatever I can to get His attention." She pressed up against Leonard and kissed him on the cheek. "Thank you," she said and stomped off, her long hair sawing back and forth.

Leonard's stomach and groin twitched. Is that what Marie Pearson had meant by feeling *tingly?* Maybe, Leonard thought, if he buried Azalea's note, she'd kiss him proper, on the lips, with their tongues touching like the high school kids did.

Later that afternoon, standing on the hilltop beneath the old oak, Leonard dug a small hole while Azalea sang the first verse of the familiar, "On the Wings of a Snow White Dove." When she finished, Leonard took her hand, and they bowed their heads. "Lord, Azalea has been trying to get Your attention for some time," he said, opening his eyes to sneak a peek at her. "She's trusting that by placing this note in the ground, You'll finally take notice of her troubles."

Leonard held the paper triangle above his head and waved it around a few times, hoping God might see it from heaven. Together, they said, "Amen." Azalea covered her prayer with dirt, and Leonard made another X on the last page of his Bible. Then they walked out of the gate and headed home. For the first time, Leonard wanted to tell his mama what he had done.

# — Emmett —

 EMMETT KICKED BACK in his recliner, the evening newspaper spread across his lap, the day's last glass of iced tea on the small table beside him. June sat opposite on the sofa, reading glasses perched on the tip of her nose. A long piece of blue thread dangled from her teeth. She had been quiet through dinner, speaking mostly to Leonard and only asking him about school. When he told her that he had made an A on a recent math test, "Good," was all she'd said.

Now Leonard was in the kitchen doing his homework while in the living room Walter Cronkite eased the awkward silence between husband and wife. The Kennedys were hosting a state dinner at the White House in honor of the Western Hemisphere's Nobel Prize winners. The day's greatest scientists and artists were already arriving in Washington. Emmett glanced at June, knowing how she admired the First Lady. He thought of complimenting her sewing but thought better of it. He doubted Jackie Kennedy did needlework of any kind.

Lately, June seemed to be working her anger like dough — kneading it, then letting it rise until ready to shape into a string of harsh, hateful words. Emmett turned the page of his newspaper and began reading the birth announcements out loud. "Looks like the Wilmots finally had that baby girl they been hoping for," he said, peeking over the top of the paper. "Luther said Janine's been wanting a girl so bad she even dressed the last boy in pink for the first month or two."

June pulled a stitch through the heavy denim.

Emmett continued with the obituaries. "Oh my. Poor old Mr. Harvey passed. Figured that day was drawing near. Ever since his daughter took him over to Nashville I hadn't heard a word of him. Guess we should send a card."

June held her sewing closer to the lamplight.

Emmett read a while longer, then folded the paper and stared at the television. "Looks like a right smart crowd's gathering in Washington, DC, tonight."

June snapped the thread and tied a knot. She looked up at Emmett. "Quit making small talk. I know what you're up to."

Confounded by his wife's accusation, Emmett tossed the paper on the floor. "What am I up to?"

"Don't play dumb with me. You're trying to butter me up."

"I ain't playing dumb. I got no idea what you're talking about."

June pushed her sewing aside, pricking the sofa arm with the needle. "You got no recollection of telling Agnes Mitchell that you plan on sending Leonard away to some camp for the disfigured?"

"What?" Emmett recalled the tin can on the counter in the hardware store. "I took down a number. Nothing more."

"A number to that camp."

"I thought Leonard might enjoy it. It ain't like I signed him up."

June jumped to her feet. She walked from one end of the room to the other, pacing off her anger in equally measured steps. "You should've talked to me before you talked to Agnes Mitchell. You ought to know by now I don't want to learn about my son from another woman."

Emmett wanted to reach for June's hand but knew better. "Listen to me, Junebug. I asked her for a piece of paper and a pen. That was it. I promise. I ain't made a call." He reached for June again. She crossed her arms.

The shrill tone of the telephone startled them both.

"I got it," Emmett said, jumping from the recliner and stepping into the kitchen. "Hello," he said into the receiver, his eyes fixed on June who stood firm in the next room. She frowned. *Brother Puckett*, he mouthed in return. June stepped closer.

"Sorry to bother you on a Sunday night, Emmett, but I thought I'd call before leaving the church. Kept thinking I'd see you here or in town. I would prefer talking to you in person, but what I got to say can't wait any longer." The preacher coughed and then apologized for needing to take a sip of water. Emmett pressed the receiver to his chest, shaking his head as he looked over at June. "Here comes nothing," he whispered to her. He was not in the mood to talk to Brother Puckett, especially not on the heels of an argument with June. When the preacher returned, his voice was scratchy and lower-pitched. "As I was saying, I kept looking for you in town."

Emmett switched the receiver to his other ear. "Yeah, I got that, Preacher. You got something to say?"

"I'm calling about Leonard."

Emmett stiffened. "What about him?"

The preacher laughed, but Emmett knew he wasn't joking. "I'm talking about what he's been doing up there in your family's cemetery. Berta Tate told me about her stealing eggs and trying to atone for it. You know how she talks. But she says there's been others to go to the hilltop. Two she knows of, and I got a hunch they're dealing with something much more serious than nabbing a few eggs." The preacher paused for another sip of water. "I tolerated it in the beginning, figuring Leonard was just learning how to be one-legged, part of the adjustment to his loss. I tried to talk to June about it at Wednesday night supper. But this has gone on too long."

June pushed up close to Emmett, trying to press her ear against the receiver. "What's he want?" she asked.

Emmett turned his back on her.

"Your boy's doing a preacher's work, Emmett. I'd say he's stepping out of line."

Emmett's neck flushed hot. First June and her accusations, now this. Contrary to June's way of thinking, no preacher — Baptist, Methodist, or Church of Christ — had the right to tell a man how to raise his own son. "Seems to me you're the one stepping out of line here, Brother Puckett."

June yanked on Emmett's arm. He shook her off.

"When anyone, even a child, is misleading people on the path to the Lord, then it is very much my business."

"Who said he's *misleading* anybody?" Emmett paced as far as the phone cord would allow, refusing to look at June. "My boy ain't done nothing but help a few people move on with their lives. You best accept it. And that's all I got to say about it, Brother Puckett. Goodbye." He slammed the receiver down and faced June. "What?" he asked, feeling the heat of her angry stare.

"What's the preacher want?"

"You know what he wants, and you can guess how I feel about it." June clenched both fists. "I don't know who you are anymore, Emmett Bush. I've told you from the start it ain't right what Leonard's doing up there on your family's land."

Emmett took a deep breath, hoping to ease the anger building up inside him. He patted his shirt pocket, looking for a cigarette, but it was empty.

"You never want to face anything head-on." June pointed her finger at Emmett's face. "Such a big man you are, standing up to a preacher on the other end of a telephone line. You can't talk about Leonard losing his leg. You can't talk about your baby sister for that matter neither, and she's been dead nearly thirty years." June pushed on, her voice rising to a shrill pitch. "Hell, Emmett, you can't talk about anything but the damn cost of milk."

Emmett's jaw tightened. "Stop it, June," he said.

"You won't listen to me. Fine. But you better listen to the preacher, Emmett. You better choose right over wrong. I'm tired of being our boy's only parent." June stormed out of the kitchen. Down the hall, the bedroom door slammed shut while Walter Cronkite reported on a nuclear test somewhere in Nevada.

Later that night, Emmett lay awake, and in the pitch dark, his baby sister came to him. She held up a bucket and begged him to take her to the pond to catch tadpoles. She tapped his shoulder, took his hand, then led him to the far pasture. Emmett jerked upright in bed. Cold sweat beaded down his back. A few days before Sarah died she'd done that very thing.

Beside him, June slept soundly. He lay back down and tried to slow his breathing. When daybreak came, he was already in the barn tending to the day's chores, trying not to think about his baby sister or the argument with June or Sarah's little shoe that was already tucked in his pants pocket or the pair of baseball cleats locked in the metal cabinet behind his desk.

# — June —

COX'S DEPARTMENT STORE advertised a spring sale in the Saturday morning paper, along with a coupon for an additional five-dollar discount. It had been months since June had treated herself to something pretty—a new dress or a bottle of Jean Naté. She clipped the coupon and tucked it inside her wallet, energized by the thought of shopping on her own, although she might look for a new pair of church pants for Leonard, too. She'd been lenient with his attendance since the amputation. But after the preacher's call, he'd be sitting next to her on the front row come Sunday. She checked her hair in the hall mirror, then walked out back and hollered goodbye.

Emmett was lying halfway under the tractor. Leonard stood beside it, holding a can of motor oil. She tapped the Impala's horn. "I'll be back late afternoon," she called. Emmett slid free of the tractor and Leonard waved goodbye, their fulsome grins identical, their arms cocked at the elbow exactly the same. *Birds of a feather*, she thought, and slipped the key into the ignition. No doubt the two of them would gather their fishing gear and head out for Big Sugar before she got clear of the mailbox.

June tied a brown-and-white-dotted scarf about her head and reached for her sunglasses. Still rankled from her fight with Emmett the night before, she pumped the accelerator. The engine roared, something she knew annoyed him. Then she backed out of the driveway. The clematis planted on her first wedding anniversary, already brimming with pink-toned blossoms, scraped against the side of the car as she pulled away from the house.

On the main road, she switched on the radio to her favorite Top 40 station. The pavement was spotted with puddles. Heavy rains had come through during the night, leaving behind a fresh spattering of daffodils and quince. Spring seemed to have arrived just this morning in a blast of floral fury. She rolled down the window, breathing in the honeyed scents. On the radio, Del Shannon sang "Runaway," and June joined in the chorus. Rare moments like this, she felt like a teenaged girl burdened with nothing more than a desire to hang out with girlfriends at the Dairy Dip and flirt with the older boys who wore greased-back dos and bore the hint of beer on their breath. She slowed the car, wanting to stretch the drive a little longer. But soon, she saw the Sinclair station with its lumbering dinosaur and turned right onto Main Street.

June parked the Impala in front of Cox's. She checked herself in the rearview mirror, applied a dash of lipstick, and smoothed her bangs before stepping out onto the sidewalk. Down the street, Vivienne Ford was walking into the bank. June rolled her eyes at the thought of a meetup with her nemesis. Vivienne acted so high and mighty, but she couldn't even raise her son right. June doubted she'd ever get an apology for Eddie Burl's role in Leonard's misfortune. She grabbed her pocketbook and hurried into Cox's before Vivienne caught sight of her.

In the women's department, June spotted a sleeveless drip-dry cotton print with a spaghetti bow looped around the waist. The sales lady, a young woman June didn't recognize, thought it fit perfectly and held up a recent copy of *Look* magazine. A brunette model on the cover wore a similar style. "Put it in a box please, with the hanger," June said and handed the clerk a twenty-dollar bill along with the newspaper coupon from her wallet. On her way out of the store, June stopped to look at a pair of pearl studs. The earrings would be an extravagance, but June could already imagine them with her pretty new dress. And Emmett wouldn't dare question her spending when trying to make amends.

She held one to her ear, admiring her reflection in the tabletop mirror, when Vivienne Ford sashayed past, seemingly unaware of June. Vivienne laid a hatbox and garment bag on the counter. "I need to return these," she said to the sales lady.

The clerk pulled the dress from the garment bag. "What's wrong this time, Mrs. Ford?" she asked, holding up the dress and looking it over.

"Excuse me?" Vivienne raised an eyebrow. She leaned forward and lowered her voice to a harsh whisper. "Do we need to call your manager?"

The sales lady fell silent and rang up the refund.

June thought the exchange odd. Vivienne was often rude and bigheaded, but her reaction to the saleswoman's question seemed excessive. She ducked a little farther behind the mirror where she could listen without being seen.

Vivienne tucked several bills in her pocketbook and snapped it closed. She hurried out of the store, not even bothering to thank the sales lady who seemed to keep a close eye on Vivienne until she was out the door. June returned the earrings to the display, the strange interaction between Vivienne and the clerk scratching at her memory. She had seen that dress on Vivienne just last Sunday at church.

Down the block at Peoples Drugstore, the lunch counter was bustling, the smell of burgers and onions frying on the griddle a welcome scent. June found a free stool at the end of the counter and decided on a grilled cheese and a Coca-Cola. Every couple of minutes, the waitress shouted out a new order or the register announced another sale. The man beside her rapped his knuckles against the wooden counter, then pointed to his empty coffee cup. A pimple-faced boy crowded up beside her and ordered a burger to go. "Burn one more," the waitress called to the cook behind her. The buzz swept June back to her youth working at the diner in Sylva. She considered a hot fudge sundae, just so she could linger a while longer, but thought better of it. Tomorrow she'd go to church, and she wanted to wear her new dress without a girdle. She fished for a few dollars inside her wallet, slid them under her lunch plate, and left for the IGA grocery, idly wondering what Vivienne Ford would wear to Sunday service.

# — Leonard —

SATURDAY MORNING CARTOONS were over, Leonard's chores at the dairy done. He was finishing a second bowl of Frosted Flakes, poured more out of boredom than hunger, when he heard a loud knock at the front door.

"Come over to my house," Eddie Burl said, standing outside the door, looking as bored as Leonard felt. "You ain't got nothing better to do."

Even with June gone to town, Leonard glanced over one shoulder, half expecting her to appear out of thin air and chase Eddie Burl away.

"Can't fish Big Sugar with the water running high like it is," Eddie Burl said, grinning big, revealing a newly chipped tooth. "But I got a full box of BBs for shooting, and we can dig for worms for fishing later. Mama's got a patch of garden that's swarming with them. Big, fat ones."

Leonard hadn't spent a Saturday with Eddie Burl since the amputation, mainly because he knew June would pitch a fit. And if he were being honest, he'd have to confess to still harboring a little anger at Eddie Burl for tossing his shoe in the river. And for taking his place on the pitcher's mound. But Leonard being Leonard found holding a grudge too tiresome. Besides, Eddie Burl was his best fishing buddy. His aim with a BB gun was pretty sharp, too.

"Hey," Eddie Burl said, thumping a finger against Leonard's head. "You in there? I asked you a question. You coming to my house or not?"

Leonard shrugged. "Sure. Like you said, ain't got nothing better to do." He hurried to the kitchen and hollered out the back door to Emmett who was busy feeding chickens at the far side of the clearing.

"Be home by three," Emmett said, scattering another handful of grain.

Leonard waved goodbye, then caught a strong whiff of the Jergens lotion June kept at the sink. He drew in a deep breath. Leonard froze, his eyes closed, listening for his mama's footsteps or the sound of her Singer whirring at the back of the house. He glanced out the window toward the drive. She had gone to town. Her Impala was not parked in its usual spot. *Just imagining things.* He shook off his worry and chased after Eddie Burl.

"Can't believe your mama's letting you go," Eddie Burl said, holding the bike steady while Leonard climbed on the rear fender.

"She ain't home." Leonard found his balance on the metal, sticking his fake leg out straight. "Can't believe your mama's letting me come over."

"She ain't home neither."

The boys howled with laughter. Then Eddie Burl let out a *whoop, whoop, whoop!* and Leonard echoed it. Eddie Burl straddled the bike and pushed off with his foot, standing tall on the pedals, straightening one leg, then the other, powering the bike faster and faster with every step. Leonard stretched out his arms, grabbing hold of Eddie Burl only when he felt his balance give way. Once past the Bushes' farm, Eddie Burl settled on the seat and coasted downhill. The tires hummed against the pavement. Pastures of spring switchgrass sweetened the air. Up ahead, a grazing cow nodded as the boys flew past. Just before Christmas, June had declared bike riding too dangerous for a one-legged boy and promptly gave Leonard's bike to a poor family the church helped with food and clothing. But with his mama not around, he broadened his wingspan, his arms gliding across the crests and troughs of a warm breeze like the red-tailed hawk soaring over the hillside. "Faster," he hollered, "faster."

Eddie Burl leaned forward, rocking the bike from side to side with every pump of the pedal, sweeping Leonard back to a memory of racing his own bike against Eddie Burl's. His thighs had burned, but he had pedaled harder, each boy trying to nose out the other.

Leonard laughed thinking of it now. Everything with Eddie Burl was a contest. Just then Eddie Burl pointed to a dead possum, swollen twice its size, bringing Leonard's attention back to the present. They cruised another hundred yards before the bike began to slow. Then without warning, Eddie Burl braked hard and jerked the handlebar to the left. The tires skidded. The bike and the boys leaned too far into the turn. Eddie Burl rolled into the grass. The bike landed flat on the Fords' gravel driveway. Leonard lay underneath it.

"Oh shit," Eddie Burl said, his eyes wide.

Leonard's elbow was scraped raw, his fake leg twisted at a gruesome angle. Eddie Burl scrambled across the loose rocks, stopping just short of Leonard. He poked at the prosthetic. "You feel that?"

"Of course I don't feel that. It ain't real." Leonard sat up and examined his elbow.

"Does the real part hurt?"

"Not as much as my elbow." Leonard straightened out his elbow, then his prosthetic. He rolled up his jeans until the fleshy tip of his stump poked through.

Eddie Burl bit his lower lip. "You going to need your mama?"

"Hell no." Leonard brushed his skin clean of any dust or bits of gravel. "But I can't set the leg right without my sock."

"You need a sock?" Eddie Burl looked back at the house. "I can get you a sock."

"Not that kind of sock. It's special, made for the stump." Leonard turned the prosthetic upside down and gave it a hard shake. A bit of grit dusted his lap. He eyeballed the inside of the leg, then wiped it clean with his hand. "I put the sock on my stump, my stump in the leg, then I pull the sock through this hole here at the top of the leg. Creates suction. That's what keeps it on good. Keeps it from rubbing against my thigh."

Eddie Burl inched closer. "Can I touch it? The stump?"

"Sure."

Eddie Burl hesitated, then pushed his finger into the fleshy part of the nub. "Feels normal."

"It *is* normal," Leonard shoved his stump into the prosthetic, hoping the fit would prove snug enough. He may have known Eddie Burl since birth, but he wanted to walk on his own. Eddie Burl held out his hand. Leonard ignored it. Balancing on his hands and knee, he kicked out his right leg and pushed himself up. He dusted his pants, then dabbed at the blood trickling down his arm.

"Sorry about that," Eddie Burl said, picking up the bike.

"It's okay."

"No, it ain't." Eddie Burl looked down at a bent spoke, avoiding Leonard's eyes. "I'm sorry about everything, I guess. I shouldn't have thrown your shoe in Big Sugar."

Leonard inspected his scrape again.

Eddie Burl fiddled with the bike, still not looking at Leonard head-on.

But for the first time since that day at Big Sugar, Leonard believed Eddie Burl was truly sorry. In that moment, his heart lightened. "Forget it," Leonard said, taking a small step, already noticing the fit was a touch loose. "I should've shown the cut to my mama."

The boys started down the drive, Eddie Burl walking the bicycle, keeping his pace in rhythm with Leonard's slow steps. By the time they reached the house, Leonard's stump was already aching, the skin rubbing against the prosthetic, likely red and blistering. Leonard rested on a rear porch step while Eddie Burl ran inside to fetch his BB gun and two bottles of Yoo-hoo. After chugging the chocolate drink, Eddie Burl set up a half dozen tin cans on fence posts, then loaded the gun's chamber with the tiny metal balls. "You're company, so you go first," he said, handing the gun to Leonard. "Shoot from right there if you want."

Leonard grabbed hold of the porch rail and pulled himself up. He cocked the gun's lever, steadied the stock against his shoulder, and pulled the trigger. He missed his first and second shot but knocked the third can from the post.

"Not bad," Eddie Burl said, but Leonard knew he was humoring him, probably still regretting the spill on the bike. Eddie took the gun, fired, pumped the lever, and fired again. When he was done, not a single can was left standing. "Hey, put one of them cans on your head."

"Hell no."

Eddie Burl laughed, then fired at a nearby oak. A flock of starlings took off from the leafy canopy. "Thought I might've snagged one. Could've given it to Little Henry for his collection."

"How'd you know about that?" Leonard asked, pretending to hold a gun and firing off a perfect shot.

"Everybody knows about Little Henry and his birds. Killing runs in that family, at least that's what my daddy says."

Leonard nodded. "My mama says the same thing, but Little Henry ain't a killer."

"Yeah, right, he's a painter." Eddie Burl chuckled, but his smile quickly faded away.

When Leonard looked up, he saw Mrs. Ford steering her Lincoln into the drive, a cloud of dust trailing behind. Eddie Burl rushed to meet the car. A tall woman, Mrs. Ford towered over Eddie Burl in her high heels.

"Need any help with the groceries, Mama?" Eddie peered into the back seat. "You get me some potato chips?"

"No," she said, her tone crisp. "Didn't have time for grocery shopping." She patted his head, then quickly shooed him away. Eddie Burl pressed his face against the car window, clearly checking to see if his mama had been teasing.

Leonard scooted to the far edge of the step, averting his eyes. He had not seen Mrs. Ford since he'd buried a necklace for her and later a silver charm bracelet. Suddenly he felt uneasy keeping her secrets. But despite her failings and June's distaste for her, Leonard had always liked Mrs. Ford. She'd come to the leg funeral and brought Eddie Burl, never once staring at Leonard with weepy eyes or speaking to him in saccharin tones as so many mothers had that day. Besides, no other mama in Sweetwater kept her refrigerator stocked with Yoo-hoos.

"Well, hello, Leonard." Mrs. Ford said, her voice almost a whisper. She stepped closer, pushing her pocketbook farther up her arm, then grabbing hold of the porch rail. Leonard shrank back, trying to put a few more inches between himself and Mrs. Ford, wondering if she felt uneasy, too. He knew better than to mention her recent visits to the hilltop, particularly in front of Eddie Burl. "Saw your mama in town," she said. "She know you're here?" Mrs. Ford smiled, then walked up the porch steps, not waiting for an answer. Leonard let out a breath he hadn't realized he'd been holding. At the door, Mrs. Ford paused. "Don't shoot your eyes out, boys."

Eddie Burl took aim at a squirrel scampering past. His BB hit the dirt, and the squirrel raced up a tree. "I missed him on purpose," he said.

"Sure you did." Leonard knew he was probably right. "Let me have a turn," Leonard said, reaching for the gun. He raised the stock to his shoulder. "That scarecrow in your mama's garden ain't got a chance."

"No way. It's farther than the cans."

"Bet you a Yoo-hoo." Leonard fixed the scarecrow's head in the gun's front sight and fired. The scarecrow shook. Leonard smiled.

"Nailed it. But we ain't got anymore Yoo-hoos." Eddie Burl grinned in a sheepish way.

Leonard laughed and cocked the gun's lever. He was scanning the landscape for another target when the sheriff's black-and-white barreled down the road out front and wheeled into the drive. Official, even though the lights weren't flashing. Eddie Burl froze. The front door opened, and Mrs. Ford stormed out of the house. She stopped at the edge of the porch, her hands fisted on her hips, not seeming to remember that Eddie Burl and Leonard were standing nearby. The sheriff stepped out of the car, adjusting his hat squarely on his head.

"No siree! You take him straight to jail, Sheriff. If that man is drunk again, I don't want him here."

"Come on, Vivienne, you don't want me taking Charlie to jail. You two been married a long time. You're just going through a rough patch." The sheriff pulled Mr. Ford from the back seat. His shirttail hung out of his pants. A days-old beard darkened his face. This man stumbling about looked nothing like the Mr. Ford Leonard knew.

"I mean it," Mrs. Ford shouted. "I don't want him in my house reeking of whiskey. Put him back in that car." Her last words came out in a sob.

"Come on, baby." Mr. Ford smiled, his speech slurred. "I ain't been drinking." He tottered to one side, then fell to the ground laughing. The sheriff jerked him up to his feet.

Leonard felt bad for being there, an eyewitness to both Mr. Ford's condition and Mrs. Ford's anger. He glanced at Eddie Burl huddled next to a cluster of jasmine near the rear of the house.

"I said get him out of here, Sheriff." Mrs. Ford went inside and slammed the door.

The sheriff dragged Eddie Burl's daddy up the porch steps and pushed him through the door. "He's all yours, Vivienne," he said, swinging the door shut. He nodded to Leonard as he climbed back into his car.

Leonard limped over to Eddie Burl and the two boys watched the squad car pull out of the driveway. Mrs. Ford's anger boiled into the yard where the boys stood, still in shock. "You're a no-good drunken fool, Charles Ford. Can't keep a job. Too good to stay home and help with the chores. I wish I'd never met you."

Eddie Burl elbowed Leonard's ribs. "You ain't ever going to say a word about this."

Leonard shook his head. He saw the hurt in Eddie Burl's eyes. "I won't tell."

"You hear me?" Eddie Burl grabbed Leonard's shoulders. "Swear it! Swear you're never going to say nothing about this!"

"I said I wouldn't." Leonard shoved Eddie Burl away.

Eddie Burl grabbed Leonard's arm. "Ain't none of your business."

"What the hell is wrong with you?"

"Say it." Eddie Burl tightened his grip.

"Shit, Eddie Burl, I said I won't tell nobody."

Something crashed inside the house. "You're a lying son-of-a-bitch!" Mrs. Ford's voice rang from the living room.

Leonard glanced at a side window. His parents argued, but they'd never fought like this. The Fords were going at it like something he'd seen in the movies or on a TV show but not in real life. Eddie Burl's face turned crimson. He slugged Leonard.

Leonard doubled over, gasping for air. "Damnit, Eddie Burl. What'd you do that for?"

Eddie Burl dropped his head. He turned toward the garden, but not before Leonard saw him swipe at his cheeks with the back of his hand.

"Go home," Eddie Burl whispered.

Leonard held his bruised stomach. "Every family's got their troubles, Eddie Burl. You don't have to hit me for it." He hobbled to the road and began the long walk home, wishing June hadn't given away his bike.

# — June —

 THE WIND RATTLED the metal glider on the back patio as June opened the trunk of the Impala. Murky gray clouds veiled the dairy. The air had turned musty. Both were sure signs that another rainstorm was brewing nearby. June wrestled two sacks of groceries from the back of the car and carried them into the kitchen, her Cox's shopping bag and pocketbook dangling from the crook of her arm. She called for Emmett and Leonard. Neither answered. She set everything on the counter, then removed her sunglasses, slid her headscarf to her neck and knotted it at her throat.

"Emmett," she hollered again as she stepped back outside, surveying the space between house and barn. She wanted help unloading the rest of the groceries and was eager to tell Emmett about seeing Vivienne Ford in town. Surely he and Leonard weren't at Big Sugar at this hour, knowing she'd be home and ready to get supper on the table. Besides, the cows were quiet, almost too quiet for this time of day. They must have been milked and fed and turned out for the evening, a good hour earlier than normal.

In the distance, a whippoorwill called, reminding June she was not completely alone. Still, she grew anxious, fear stoking her imagination. Emmett's and Leonard's fishing poles rested against the metal shed at the far end of the carport. The pickup and tractor were parked inside the barn. She called their names again, but only the whippoorwill answered back. Heart thumping faster, hands trembling, she walked toward the milking parlor. She never used to be like this, her nerves turning jittery at the slightest thing. Leonard's amputation had changed that.

When she opened the door to the milk room, Emmett was sitting at his desk, leaning back in his chair. Arms crossed against his chest. The overhead light was off, and in the dimness of the room, she couldn't tell if he was dozing or lost in faraway thoughts. She opened the door a little wider. "Emmett," she said in a whispered tone, not wanting to startle him.

He spun around. "What are you doing back so soon?"

"What do you mean?" She glanced at her wristwatch. "I'm running late if you want supper at five-thirty."

Emmett ran his hand through his hair, then looked toward the window.

June walked up to the desk. "Where's Leonard?"

"Over at Miss Ooten's." Emmett leaned forward, curled up as if he were in pain.

June's eyes flicked to an empty bottle of whiskey and a single cigarette within Emmett's reach. He wasn't acting right, and she didn't like it. "I need help putting groceries away," she said, her anger rising.

"I'll get to it in a minute."

"You been drinking?"

"A little."

"And smoking?" June tugged on his shirt collar, leaned down, and sniffed his neck. "What's going on?"

"Nothing," he said. He held up his empty hands as proof.

June glanced about the room, then sized up Emmett from top to bottom. The sky was growing dark. She reached for a switch on the wall behind her. The bare bulb hanging from the ceiling snapped on. In the harsh white light, June found a paper bag and a work boot on the floor. Emmett's left foot was bare, two-thirds of it shoved into a baseball cleat, his heel hanging out the back. "What are you doing?"

Emmett's face went from beet red to turnip white. He stammered, "Nothing. I ain't doing nothing wrong." Emmett kicked off the cleat and scrambled to cover his foot with a worn sock, his hands shaking so hard that he fumbled and dropped it on the ground. "I can explain." He bolted out of the chair.

June tugged at the scarf around her neck as if it were choking the life right out of her. "You some kind of pervert, Emmett?"

"Hell no." He reached for June. "That ain't it. I swear it."

"Then what the hell is·it?" June fixed her eyes on Emmett's bare foot.

"It's hard to talk about."

"Hard to talk about? Is that it? Just like it's hard to talk about Sarah? Instead touching her baby shoe all the time like it's a damn rabbit's foot."

Emmett stammered. "It ain't what you think."

"What I think is that you been bottled up since the day we met. I accepted it in the beginning, but I knew someday you'd explode." June shook her finger at Emmett's face. "And now you've gone and done it. Kaboom!"

"You don't think you do weird things?" Emmett slapped his hand against the desk. "You hang a cloth over a mirror for no good reason and Clorox the kitchen floor three times a day till the smell of it damn near burns my nose." He kicked at the desk. "I can't explain it, June." His voice turned softer. "But since Leonard lost his leg, I go through the day like someone's holding a pillow to my face. Can't catch my breath. But when I put on my boy's shoe..." Emmett paused again. His eyes shifted to the floor. "I don't know. I can breathe."

June's cheeks burned fiery hot. "Shut up, Emmett. Just shut up. You ain't making sense, and I ain't in the mood to hear you out right now. I got a supper to fix. A child to look after. Damn you, making a fool of me like this." June grabbed the cleat off the floor and flung it across the room, the sole grazing Emmett's forehead, a metal cleat slicing the tender skin above his right eye.

"Shit." Emmett fell back into the chair.

June didn't flinch, not even when a streak of blood bubbled up over Emmett's eye.

She walked back to the house, leaving Emmett to tend to his cut. For a minute, she wondered if she'd imagined her husband's foot smashed up in Leonard's shoe or if, in her worry over her son and her marriage, she'd conjured a strange vision. Perhaps a warning of a future evil. Standing at the kitchen sink, she wasn't sure of anything except trying to calm her spinning thoughts. She leaned against the counter. Splashed cold water on her face while on the other side of the drive the milk room fell dark. *Who are you Emmett Bush? Who did I marry?* She threw up the window sash, desperate for a cool gulp of air.

# — Azalea —

 AZALEA TICKED OFF another box on the Esso calendar that hung over her bed. She should have heard from God by now. It had been too many days since she and Leonard had buried her note on the hilltop cemetery. A full moon had come and gone, Atlas had turned one, and still she had no answer from Him. Last night, when lightning strikes fired up the sky and thunder rocked the house, Azalea believed He was dialing her up. She lay awake, waiting for a clear connection. But morning came bearing neither angels nor divine messengers, only the sweet smell of Carolina jessamine and the sound of Rose bumbling about in the kitchen.

In another minute, Rose called Azalea to breakfast. She held out a plate of scrambled eggs and buttered toast. Was it a peace offering or an answer to prayer? Azalea wasn't sure, but she was glad for something to eat. She gobbled it down while Rose sat at the table, spooning small bites of egg into Atlas's mouth. When the baby finished eating, Rose carried him into the front room and sat on the sofa, sipping a cup of coffee and smoking a cigarette while Atlas played on the floor at her feet. For a few minutes, Azalea believed God's hand was indeed upon them, guiding them to a better place. Rose flicked a bit of ash into the lid of a mason jar.

Glad of a lovely spring Saturday, Azalea buttoned up her favorite green blouse and tied a green-and-pink-striped ribbon around her head for no special reason other than she liked it. She smiled at her reflection in a small mirror tacked to her bedroom wall. She slipped on a clean pair of blue jeans and laced up her nearly-too-tight sneakers when the sheriff's car cruised into the clearing. No lights or sirens, only the crack of gravel against tires announced his arrival.

"Girl!" Rose hollered from the front room.

Azalea didn't need any more direction than that. She ran toward her mama and grabbed Atlas from the floor. Rose dropped her cigarette in her coffee cup and knotted her robe closed. Azalea fled out the back door, tripping on an old mop left to dry in the yard. "Dang it." She kicked the mop aside and took off running.

The sheriff came to the house from time to time, either threatening to toss Azalea and Atlas in foster care or Rose in jail. Sometimes both. More often than not, he hauled Rose away, then brought her home an hour or two later — hair mussed, mascara smudged underneath her eyes. Azalea knew better than to ask where they went or what they did, but when the sheriff came for a visit, both mother and daughter knew the drill.

Azalea darted through rhododendron, oak, and pine, keeping one eye on the woodsy trail that wound toward the main road and the other eye on the house. Even from a distance, she could see the sheriff adjust his belt and don his hat before walking up the porch steps. He was a big man like Mack, but more fat than muscle, and he loomed over Rose, who stood at the door, fiddling with her robe's collar. The sheriff removed his cap and stepped inside. Rose scanned the clearing then closed the door.

Atlas wiggled in Azalea's arms, wanting to be set down. Since he'd started toddling, he was a constant effort, always running and grabbing at anything within reach. "You ain't going nowhere little brother." She tightened her grip and skirted the clearing, then ducked under the forsythia. Her heart pounded hard, the sound of it nearly drowning out the robins and chickadees chatting at a new day. Inside her twiggy cave, Azalea rolled onto her back and pulled Atlas on top of her. He squirmed, grabbing at her ribbon. "Stop it." She shoved his hands away. He reached for the ribbon again, this time pulling it free. "Dang it, Atlas, let me be." She popped his hand. He held his breath. His face turned red and his body stiffened. Soon, his face faded from a bright red to a pale shade of blue. Panicking, Azalea shook him until he coughed up a wailing cry. "I'm sorry, baby." She rocked him as fat tears trailed down his thin face. "Shh. Got to be quiet. Shh." Atlas sucked on his fingers until his sobs weakened into sporadic breathy gasps. Azalea blew on his neck and stroked his back until his crying finally ceased.

In a few minutes, the patrol car came barreling down the dirt path, sirens blaring and lights flashing. Atlas startled as if he'd awoken from a deep sleep and began crying again. Azalea caught a glimpse of the sheriff as he sped away, his lips spread into a sickening grin. Rose sat in the back seat, still wearing the orange bathrobe. She glanced out the rear window, then dropped her head against the seat.

Azalea scrambled out from her hiding place, pulling Atlas along with one hand, her green blouse smeared with dirt and grass, the green-and-pink ribbon left unnoticed under the bushes. The patrol car grew smaller and smaller until it was a tiny speck on the horizon. In Azalea's mind, the sheriff and Mack were no different. One wore a badge, the other tattoos. One threatened Rose with the law, the other with his knuckles. Azalea hated them both, but at least Mack paid money for her mama's time.

Atlas squirmed on Azalea's hip. She switched him to her other side and headed back toward the house. She'd been certain that burying her note to God with great ritual would garner His attention at last. Everyone else who'd hauled their sins up that hill had found relief. Berta Tate, Laura Kilgore, Little Henry. Even Icky Greer. They had walked to the cemetery hunched and teary-eyed, then trotted back down a few minutes later happy and seemingly free of their worry and pain.

Azalea knew enough about God to know He was capable of changing anything from wrong to right, even Rose Parker. At her most desperate, Azalea had trusted Him, the only man other than Leonard she'd ever dared rely on. But the sheriff's afternoon call seemed proof of His continued indifference. Had it all been a lie?

Had she been a fool to believe in Leonard's ritual on the hilltop? He was only a boy. She could forgive him. But God? If He was truly that great, how could He let this happen? How could He let Rose birth another baby? Could He not hear Atlas in his crib at night, crying for a milk bottle when all Azalea had to give him was tap water? Could He not hear Mack grunting at the back of the house, having his way with Rose? Could He not hear Azalea sobbing into her pillow, desperate for a mama who wore pretty dresses and smelled of Ivory soap?

Azalea was worn out — exhausted in equal measure from worry and caregiving. She decided it really might take losing a limb like Leonard Bush or getting shot in the chest like Margaret Reed to garner God's attention. She set Atlas in his crib and wandered into the kitchen, the baby's complaints pulsing in her ears. She searched the kitchen drawers for a knife sharp enough to do some good, ran her index finger down the dull side of a blade, pricked her skin on its tip. A drop of blood bubbled up, crowning her finger with crimson. When the church ladies had come to the house, they talked about being washed clean in the blood of the lamb. *Washed clean. Washed clean.* How much of her own blood would it take to make things right?

# — Leonard —

IF A MAN was meant to be king of his castle, then Leonard didn't understand why his daddy had moved out of their house and into the milk room. A worn leather suitcase, the hot plate June stored in a high cabinet, Emmett's faded blue reclining chair, one box of Zane Grey novels and another packed with high school football trophies seemed to be the sum total of his father's possessions, other than his clothes and shaving kit. Leonard had watched his daddy carry one load after another, never offering an explanation for his leaving. Nor did June.

In those first days following the Great Departure, as Leonard came to call it, his mama took to cleaning with a vengeance. Even on the Lord's Day, she filled the kitchen sink with water, Clorox, and a dash of lemon, then wiped down the cabinets, counters, and stovetop. The next day, she dusted the wood hutch and two end tables in the front room before vacuuming the drapes and sofa cushions. And when that was done, she turned her attention to the floors, mopping the hardwoods and scrubbing the linoleum.

June loved a clean house, but Leonard had never seen her work so hard to rid it of something no one could see. By the time she was done, the house reeked of bleach. Leonard felt woozy-headed. His throat burned. When he complained, June opened the windows and told him to hush.

"Mama, your hands are going to crack and bleed if you keep this up," he said, standing in the kitchen doorway, watching her empty the mop bucket.

"Take your concern up with *him* not me," she answered, nodding toward the dairy. *Him. Your father. That man.* June refused to speak Emmett's name, as if the mention of it soured her stomach. When

Leonard pressed her for an explanation, she screamed at him to leave her alone. He confided in Little Henry, confessing that Emmett had moved into the milk room. Little Henry suggested that perhaps Emmett was only protecting his herd. "Maybe he spotted a bear. Plenty enough around these parts." Little Henry acted concerned, even drew a picture of Emmett standing in the middle of a pasture, holding a rifle in both hands. "Your daddy needs to keep a lookout. Stay close to his cows. My daddy says a good milker is worth her weight in gold."

Leonard knew that wasn't the case. And nothing could explain his mama's behavior. Once June finished her zealous bout of cleaning, she took to her bedroom and drew the floral curtains shut, not opening them even when the sun was shining bright. She didn't venture from the house much, and when she did, she left through the front door. She wasn't hiding from a bear. She was hiding from her husband.

Like his mama, Leonard kept to his room most days, too. Sprawled on his bed, he pulled back the curtains and kept a lookout for his father. He worried about his daddy. He was quiet-natured. A man of few words, June would say. But Leonard knew Emmett didn't take to being alone, particularly at night. After supper, he loved sitting with the family either on the porch reading the clouds until the stars popped out or in the front room watching *What's My Line?* on the television. Sometimes Emmett just sat in the recliner and watched June sew or crochet, her every stitch seeming to please him. But tonight, the thought of Emmett alone in the milk room caused an ache in Leonard's belly.

Yesterday, he spotted his father walking the edge of the pond. He hollered and waved, but Emmett hustled onto the tractor and drove away. His daddy had said once that every man needed a hiding place. "Someday you'll likely have one of your own." He had laughed then, calling it a universal secret among men. But Emmett had never holed up like this before.

By evening, the milk room window lit up. Leonard caught sight of his Daddy pacing the small space like the caged lion Leonard had seen on a school field trip to the Chattanooga Zoo. Emmett stopped in front of the window, and Leonard wondered if he was looking back at the house, hoping to catch a glimpse of his family.

In the absence of any explanation, Leonard decided his parents' separation was his fault. They had argued fiercely since the day he woke up in the hospital, groggy from anesthesia. And every day since, their arguments had swelled — never turning as violent as the Fords', but constant and loud. Now they weren't speaking. His daddy was living in the barn, not appearing to blame anyone or grieve for what could not be undone, while his mama groused around the house, seemingly determined to blame someone — anyone — for her loss. First Eddie Burl, then God, then Eddie Burl's mama, then her own husband. Leonard figured they both needed some of what the other lacked.

Thinking on it tonight, he wondered if burying his leg on the hilltop had been as much for his parents as it had been for him. Had he hoped, perhaps unknowingly, that the offering might have brought peace to them all? Since the leg funeral, he'd buried other folks' miseries and regrets while June's and Emmett's had simmered, then boiled to overflowing. Months from that September day when he'd come home with a cut and bloody foot, it was clear Big Sugar had cost him much more than a leg.

Leonard switched off the bedroom light, and looked out into the distance, desperate for one more sign of his daddy. He wished he could send Emmett a signal — flash a light on and off, tap out Morse code — somehow let him know that his son loved him.

June knocked on the door and, without waiting for an answer, stuck her head inside the room. "What are you doing in the dark?" She flicked on the overhead light.

Leonard flipped over, squinting at the sudden light. "A growing boy needs his sleep. Ain't that what you're always telling me?"

She kissed Leonard's cheek and held her palm to his forehead. "But this is mighty early for you to be in bed."

He pulled back. "I'm fine, Mama. Just tired."

She frowned, stroking her forearm as if to comfort herself. "You do look a little flushed."

He craned his head toward the window. "Why won't you let Daddy come home for good?"

"Why do you think it's me keeping him at bay?"

Leonard shrugged.

"You're daddy's a grown man. Believe me, he's fine."

"But it must be lonely out there, especially at night."

June drew the curtains closed. The panels were decorated with cowboys riding bucking horses, lassos wound in their hands. She'd made them as a present for Leonard's sixth birthday, half his lifetime ago. "Spending time alone can be a good thing," she said. "It takes peace and quiet to ponder right and wrong." She opened a dresser drawer and pulled out a fresh set of pajamas. "You're right to turn in early. If you're at the start of another fever, best to ward it off." She kissed him good night and left, gently closing the door behind her.

Leonard listened to his mother move around the house as he dressed for bed. When she finally settled in her sewing room, the sound of her Singer whirring down the hall, he slid the window open, lowered his crutches to the ground, and climbed outside. His mama was wrong about his daddy. Spending time alone was not good for him. Leonard grabbed his crutches. The evening was ripe with the raw smell of cattle and fresh-cut hay and the chant of Big Sugar thundering beyond pasture and pines. In the darkness, bullfrogs readied for a night of courting. Leonard scooted across the clearing, then, resting on one crutch, rolled the milk room's wooden door open.

Emmett hopped up from the recliner.

"Hey Daddy."

Two shirts and a pair of blue jeans hung from a hook on the front wall. On a metal shelf with a small mirror perched above it, a bowl stored a toothbrush, toothpaste, razor, and can of shaving cream. A carton of Salems, two cans of Spam, some peanut butter crackers, and a half-empty bottle of Coca-Cola cluttered a second shelf below it. A blanket and pillow made up a camping cot pushed into the far corner, the books and trophies carried from the house still packed in a cardboard box beside it.

"Your mama know you're here?" Emmett turned off the television.

Leonard shook his head. "No, sir. She wouldn't like it."

"You better get on back to the house then."

Leonard balanced on his crutches, letting his body dangle in the air, a trick he'd gotten good at, although it always made June mad. "I just want to visit for a minute."

Emmett tapped the recliner. "Sit," he said and pulled up another chair for himself. He reached for a near-empty packet of Salems on the desk, then downed the last sip from a pint bottle of Evan Williams before tossing the empty bottle into a trash can. It clanked loudly against the metal, and Leonard jumped at the sound. He'd never seen his daddy smoke or drink, at least when he wasn't trying to hide it.

"I come to tell you I'm sorry," he said.

"About what?"

"This." Leonard felt his throat close up. "And you out here."

Emmett sucked on the cigarette, the tip of it burning red, an airy cloud of smoke rising above him. He leaned back in the wooden chair until the front legs lifted off the ground and he was gazing up at the rafters. "This ain't your fault," he said. He shifted his weight forward, and the chair rested square on the concrete again.

"But you and Mama started fighting the day the doctor took my leg." Leonard pushed his weight against the back of the recliner like his daddy had done and stared at the ceiling, too. "They took my leg, Daddy, not my ears."

Emmett crushed the cigarette beneath the toe of his boot. "Lord, son, we started arguing the day we said 'I do.'" Emmett shook his head and smiled. "Trust me. This ain't your fault. Your mama and I got problems of our own making." He stood up. "Come here." He pulled Leonard into his arms. "You haven't caused any of this. You hear me?"

Leonard collapsed against his father's chest. Emmett hugged him tighter, nuzzling his chin into the top of Leonard's head. "You are not to blame for one bit of this, but you better get on back to the house before your mama finds you're out here." Leonard locked his arms around his daddy's waist, not ready to let go. "Trust me, son," Emmett whispered, "Your mama and I are both so proud of you." He kissed Leonard's head, then walked him to the door, keeping his son close, and slid it open.

The moon shone over the dairy brighter than Leonard had ever seen it, as if God was shining a flashlight on it. He'd never seen such a beautiful night and longed to share it with the ones he loved most in this world — his mother and father. Maybe Azalea. When he was six, life was all cowboys and bucking broncos, like those on his bedroom curtains. Now life grew more complicated with each passing day. "When are you coming home?" he asked, glancing back at his daddy.

"Someday."

"You can't live out here forever."

Emmett nodded. "I know."

Leonard stepped into the open air and fixed on the moonlight shining across the pasture. It caught on the evening dew, lighting the grass like a million stars. "Someday sounds like a far-off time, Daddy," he mumbled. "Too far off."

# — June —

THE NEXT SUNDAY morning, June dressed for church early, her cotton shirtwaist ironed and laid out on the ladderback chair in her sewing room. An hour from daybreak, both the milk room and milking parlor were dark. Emmett had moved out of the house a week ago, the two of them unable to talk about what pained them most. June had grown accustomed to the silence, she guessed, but the thought of Emmett's foot jammed into that baseball cleat left her queasy. She had tossed fitfully most of the night, waking dry-eyed and tired. Relief came from knowing that this was the Lord's day. She needed to be in God's house, with other true believers, and Leonard was going with her.

June opened the top dresser drawer where Emmett had kept his comb and underwear before moving out. As much as she hated to admit it, she missed his presence in the house. A heartsick feeling for him bothered her every waking moment. Fingering the neck of an old t-shirt he'd left behind, she pictured him dressing in the morning, his body lean and muscled. She held the shirt to her nose catching only the scent of her own lemony fabric softener. In all her righteous cleaning, she'd scrubbed Emmett's smell right out of the house.

As she returned the shirt to the drawer, something in the far back corner caught her eye. She pulled the drawer out farther and dug past a few more undershirts. There, in the corner, lay the small brown ankle boot with matching brown laces that Emmett kept with him most every minute of every day. June knew Emmett's mama had removed toys, photographs, clothing, anything that had belonged to her baby girl. June had always pitied Emmett for that. Her own daddy was a rough man, but at least he'd let her cry for her dead mama, never once telling her to hush her grieving. In some ways, Emmett was no different from Little Henry, their pain stomped down inside them.

From the start of their marriage, June had known better than to talk about the little shoe. After all, she wore her mama's thin gold wedding band on her finger. She figured the shoe was not much different, a kind of sacred keepsake. But wearing Leonard's cleat was taking his grief to a strange, unsettling place.

June covered the little shoe with Emmett's t-shirts just as she had found it and shut the drawer. Later at church, she'd commit her fears and concerns to the good Lord, let Him sort this one out.

Beyond her bedroom window, the sky was turning light at its eastern edge. She'd need to wake Leonard soon, but for now June shook off her questions about Emmett and colored her lips a soft shade of pink. Then she settled at the kitchen table with a strong cup of coffee and the family Bible, the wall clock ticking away the seconds. For a few minutes, she tried to focus on the Scripture, but the baby shoe nagged at her thoughts. She'd have to solve the mystery of it later. Church would be starting soon, and she didn't want Brother Puckett peeking into her heart, knowing anything about her husband and those baseball cleats and the baby shoe in his dresser drawer.

June's mama had taught her that everything a believer needed to get through this life and into the next was written in the Good Book. She'd start at the beginning if need be and read every word until she found the solution to Emmett's peculiar behavior. Or the absolute proof that should her marriage fail, she would not be held at fault. A cow mooed in the distance. Their proud rooster screeched a wake-up call. Chapter one. Verse one. With her index finger guiding her along, she read the Scripture out loud.

God created the world, day and night, land and sea. A dramatic beginning. A perfect start. Everything black and white. No space for imperfection — like one-legged boys who liked to bury things or a dairyman's odd behavior. Clearly, from man's first breath, woman had been bound to him, by bone and spirit. June wondered if Eve had ever wanted to part ways with Adam. Maybe leave the Garden of Eden and strike out on her own. The serpent had duped her into offering that apple to Adam, but he'd eaten it of his own free will.

Fifteen years ago, June had promised to love Emmett in sickness and in health, but this was not the kind of sickness anyone had in mind when they made that vow. Not some malady she could remedy with an herbal tea or drugstore medicine. The uneasiness she'd felt spying Emmett's bare foot in Leonard's shoe was similar to what she'd felt when she first saw Leonard's stump. Abnormal and wrong.

At half past eight, she closed the Bible, marking her place in the book of Genesis. She fixed Leonard a jelly biscuit and left it on the table, then stepped down the hall to his room. "Get up," she called, rapping on his bedroom door.

Leonard moaned.

She poked her head inside his room. "Time to get up, I said."

Last night, Leonard had argued about going to church. But June had put her foot down, fearing he was becoming too much like his daddy. She would not tolerate two backsliders.

Leonard's bedroom door swung open. June stiffened. He walked past her to the bathroom, his gait awkward and offbeat. "I put your leg by your clothes. Even polished your Florsheims extra good. Both of them," she said, before walking back to the kitchen.

"I don't feel like wearing my leg."

June added a splash of hot coffee to her cup, then a tad more sugar and stirred. "Leonard Bush," she said, her voice firm, "go put your leg on."

Leonard sat down at the table, resting his crutches against it, and bit into the biscuit; grape jelly dripped onto the plate. June pressed her hand against the Bible. Leonard swallowed some orange juice.

"I ain't going to argue with you, son. Not on a Sunday. We're going to church this morning, and we're going to look our best for the Lord."

"This ain't my best?"

"Don't smart-mouth me." June fiddled with the bow tied at her waist. "I'm wearing my new dress, and you're wearing your leg. And did you not hear me say that I polished both of your shoes?"

"Who you trying to impress, Mama? Brother Puckett? Mrs. Ford?" June slapped the table. "God dammit."

Leonard flinched, his jaw dropped.

June cupped her hand to her mouth. "Look what you've made me do—take the Lord's name in vain. And on the Sabbath. As if I ain't got enough to worry about."

Leonard wiped his mouth with the paper napkin June had left by his plate. "Don't it wear you out, Mama, carrying all that anger around in your heart day after day?"

June stared at Leonard like he was speaking in tongues. She shoved her chair back, rattling the table as she stood. She snatched up her pocketbook. "You put that leg on, young man. I'll be waiting out front."

At half past nine, June started the car. Miss Ooten would be taking her place at the piano soon, adjusting her hymnal and making sure the right pages were marked with paper clips. Once that was done, she'd play a few chords while nodding at the congregation, as if cuing them up for the Lord. June hated walking in late, to have the whole room turn around and take note. She fidgeted with her purse and checked her lipstick, then tapped the horn and pressed on the gas. "Leonard," she hollered out the window and blew the horn again.

A minute later, she shifted into reverse and spun the car around. God, Emmett, Leonard—she was beginning to doubt a single one of these men understood her pain.

# — Azalea —

THE NEXT TUESDAY, Azalea jerked up straight, wondering if she was fully awake or lingering in a bad dream. She checked her door and window and saw both were closed tight. Atlas slept soundly in the crib beside her. With the covers pulled to her neck, she sat stock-still and listened, certain a scream or some cry of desperation had awakened her. A playful shadow danced across the opposite wall. *It was a dream. That's all it was,* she told herself, then lay down, closed her eyes, and hummed herself a lullaby. *Hush little baby, hush little baby.* A low groan fractured the quiet. She bounded out of bed, tripping over the crib and waking Atlas. She ignored him and dashed toward her mother's room. Had Mack come back around? Had he turned rough with Rose? In the dark, Azalea conjured an image that scared her into thinking she might need the sheriff.

"Mama," she whispered. She cracked open the door to Rose's room, suddenly afraid to step any farther.

Rose moaned.

Azalea squinted for a better look, then flipped on the overhead light to find Rose alone, balled up in the bed, a tiny mound underneath layers of covers. Down the hall, Atlas's fussing grew stronger.

"Mama," Azalea said. She inched closer.

Rose's mouth twisted in pain, her upper lip damp with sweat. Azalea tapped her mama's shoulder. Rose's eyes fluttered open.

"Leave me be," she mumbled. Her breathing was shallow and fast.

"You sick, Mama? You need a saltine cracker?"

Rose curled up a little tighter, clutching her belly. The cries of mother and baby mingled together.

Azalea shrank back against the wall. She had seen her mama sick with fever. She had seen her drunk. But she had never seen her like this. Leonard had buried her note on the hilltop weeks earlier. She'd given up hope that God might make things right. But could this be His answer to her plea? Was the baby in Rose's belly clawing his way out early? Why else would her mama be balled up and her skin drained of color? Azalea had begged God to get rid of the baby, but she hadn't imagined the answer would come like this.

She ran for the telephone in the front room, hoping the operator might know what to do. A steady *beep beep beep* answered back. "Dang it," Azalea said, slamming down the receiver, then heading back to her room. She yanked on jeans and a sweatshirt left dirty on the floor. Atlas stood in the crib, bawling at top pitch. Azalea slipped on her shoes, not bothering to tie them, then grabbed Atlas.

"I'll be back, Mama," she yelled. She sprinted down the porch steps. In the distance, a lone rooster primed his wake-up call. Overhead, Venus glimmered on the tree line. The early morning was chilly, and Azalea pulled Atlas tight to her chest, regretting that she'd left his blanket behind. His diaper felt wet against her shirt. She raced headlong down the dirt drive, her breath fogging up white, dotting her path to the main road.

When she reached the mailbox, she slowed her pace, relieved to see the sky two shades lighter in the open. Robins and thrushes were already harmonizing with the rooster's crow. Weeks ago, when Azalea begged Leonard to bury her note to Jesus on the hilltop, he had asked her outright if she would prefer a woman's help instead of a man's, even if that man was divine. *Just seems like a grown woman,* he'd said, *might be better at handling woman things like this.* Azalea wished she had listened to him. At this early hour she had no doubt her mama needed a grown woman who knew about womanly things. The kind of woman who had nursed a wounded boy back to health. The kind who cleaned a house with an arsenal of Lysol and Clorox. The kind who cooked a perfect roast beef and won blue ribbons for growing a vegetable nobody but grown-ups liked.

Most importantly, her mama needed the kind of woman who went to church on Sundays. Rose Parker needed June Bush, and Azalea was going to fetch her.

Azalea ran across the field in front of her house to the county road that led to the Bushes' dairy. Heading east, she followed the broken white line down the middle of the asphalt that stretched a good mile from her house to June's. Atlas quickly grew heavy in her arms. His cries swelled louder. By the time she reached the Bushes' drive, her chest, sides, and arms ached. Her legs wobbled. Atlas thrashed about, his diaper wet through to his sleeper. But Azalea was too winded to tell him to hush and too tired to set him down and then pick him back up. She kept her gaze fixed on the pretty yellow house that sat proudly on a stretch of open land.

She stopped to catch her breath, now anxious that coming to June for help might have been a mistake. What would a fine woman like Mrs. Bush think of her showing up before daybreak with a wet, hungry, hollering baby in tow? True, Leonard had suggested his mama could help. But had he checked with her first? Azalea glanced back at the road. Calling the doctor from town or the school nurse were her only other options. The doctor would want money they didn't have. The school nurse never did anything much more than hand out aspirin and Band-Aids.

A flock of robins chirped a burst of high-pitched notes as if in agreement. Then a light flickered on in the Bushes' front window. It was too late for turning back. Azalea had buried the note. God's plan was in motion. She shifted Atlas in her arms and beelined it straight to the pretty yellow house.

----

JUNE ANSWERED THE DOOR in a long white bathrobe and matching terry cloth slippers. Her bosoms were fully covered. Her hair neatly pinned to the back of her head. Not a single trace of day-old makeup dirtied her face. Azalea had not considered that any mama could look this upstanding in her bed clothes.

"What are you doing here, child?" June asked. She tapped the face of her wristwatch. "It ain't even six o'clock." Azalea stepped back. Atlas clung to his sister monkey-like, arms about her neck, whimpering.

"Little Henry tell you it was okay to come to my house at this hour?"

"No, ma'am," Azalea said, her throat tightening up. "Leonard did." She pinched her nose, desperate to stifle her tears.

"Leonard?" June cocked her head. She stepped onto the porch. "Why are you running around at this hour? And with a baby in nothing but his pajamas?"

All the worry Azalea had been carrying these past few weeks, along with the fear for her mama's life, gushed to the surface with surprising force. She pinched her nose harder, but the tears came anyway. Atlas started fussing again.

June shut the door. "Hush up, the both of you. You're going to wake my boy." She took Atlas from Azalea and jostled him in her arms. "Lord, he's soaking wet. Is something wrong with your brother? Is he sick?" June held Atlas up in front of her, looking him over from top to bottom, then pressed her cheek to his forehead. "He needs a dry diaper, I can tell you that. And a pair of plastic pants, and I imagine a bottle. But he ain't got a fever." June flung Atlas over her arm, careful to keep his wet sleeper from touching her robe. She patted his back, then with her free hand, pulled a tissue from her robe pocket and handed it to Azalea. "Dry those tears and tell me what's going on."

Azalea blew her nose. "Atlas ain't the problem. It's a woman thing."

"You've got a woman problem?"

"Not me. My mama's got the problem." Azalea blew her nose again.

At the end of the drive, a blue pickup slowed to a near stop. The driver hurled a rolled-up newspaper out the window. "You best come inside," June said.

A lovely home inside and out, it even smelled of honeysuckle.

Azalea followed June to the kitchen. "Go on, sit down." June disappeared with Atlas, only to reappear a moment later with a bath towel under her arm and a jar of petroleum jelly just like they had at home. "Let's get your brother out of this wet diaper first." June spread the towel on the table, then lay Atlas on top of it. "Watch him for a minute," she said. "Don't let him fall off."

Azalea scooted closer and placed her hand on his tummy. "I ain't ever dropped him."

June looked back over one shoulder. "Well, that's good news," she said, tossing two dry dishcloths on the table and running a third under hot water. "So tell me what kind of *woman* problem your mama's got."

Azalea stared out the window, afraid to look at June straight on. She'd run the whole way here, but sitting in this cheerful kitchen with its ruffled curtains over the window and blue-speckled floor, she was afraid to tell the truth about her mama's condition — how she hadn't bled in weeks and how the baby was likely coming too soon.

Tongue-tied, Azalea watched as June glided from the sink to the table, unsnapping Atlas's sleeper and stripping the wet diaper from his body in one swift motion. "Goodness, his bottom is raw," she said, gently wiping his skin clean before smearing it with a thick coating of petroleum jelly. Atlas fussed and squirmed. But June took hold of his ankles, slid the clean dishcloths underneath his bottom, and quickly pinned them around his waist, not even pricking her finger in the process. Diapering was another thing June Bush seemed to be good at.

"Go on. Tell me about your mama," June said. She dropped the dirty sleeper and diaper in the sink, then wrapped Atlas in the bath towel and sat at the table beside Azalea with the baby on her lap.

Azalea started at the beginning without faltering and told June everything. "It's a devil baby," she said when her telling was done. "I know that much for sure."

June sat quiet for a moment, her hands firm around Atlas's chest. "You call the doctor?" she asked at last.

Azalea shook her head.

"I ain't a nurse, hon. I'm not sure what I can do for your mama."

"Leonard said you know about woman things." Azalea's voice faltered. "Please, Mrs. Bush. Can't you just come take a look at her? I don't know what else to do."

June glanced at her watch, then the wall clock. "I don't think your mama's dying. You hear me? No doubt the devil tries to tempt us at every turn, but I really don't think he's taken up house in your mama's belly neither." She handed Atlas back to Azalea. "I got a lot to do today, but I can drive you home and check on your mama. It won't take me but a minute to dress." But first June wrung out Atlas's dirty sleeper and diaper and sponged the kitchen table with bleach. "That'll do it," she said and disappeared down the hall a second time, her white robe flowing behind her.

# — Leonard —

LEONARD FOUND A note from June on the kitchen table. *Gone to the Parkers. Cereal in the cabinet. Milk in the fridge. Do your chores. Do not even think about going to Big Sugar!*

He rubbed his eyes and reread the first four words. *Gone to the Parkers.*

On his crutches, he hopped to the picture window in the front room, then returned to the back door. The Impala was gone, and the kitchen smelled of bleach, not freshly cooked bacon and scrambled eggs. The oven was cold, and the coffee pot empty. Nothing about this morning made sense. Rose Parker wasn't his mother's friend. They never visited one another or spoke on the telephone. Whenever Leonard mentioned Azalea's name, June got a funny look on her face.

Leonard headed across the clearing to the milk room. Maybe his daddy would have some answers. But the milk room was empty, and the tractor was missing from the barn. Leonard scanned the pasture, then hollered for Emmett. A cow bellowed back. Not sure where to go, Leonard stood frozen in the clearing halfway between the house and barn. The field grasses were tipped with a shiny frost. The newest calf was dozing in her pen, the chickens scrapping for the last specks of their morning feed. Over the foothills, the sun rose on cue, the sky growing a bright cerulean blue. Nature seemed perfectly normal, but from where he stood, Leonard feared his world was suddenly spinning out of kilter.

A bird in the house. A broken mirror. Those silly superstitions didn't concern Leonard like they did his mama. He never once thought that one or the other could cause nature to change its course. He had reassured Little Henry of that very thing when he came teary-eyed, bearing his box of dead birds. But burying Azalea's note had worried him from the start. She was asking God to alter the future, and Leonard had played a part in it. His misgivings nagged at him like a splinter.

# — June —

 JUNE WORRIED FOR Azalea but feared her showing up unannounced was another sign of bad luck. That child might as well have been a black cat streaking under a ladder. *Trouble*, in no uncertain terms. And like Little Henry, Azalea was not her responsibility, not her child to tend.

The poor girl, rail-thin with dark smudges blooming under her eyes, had tossed out words like *bled* and *late*, *God* and *prayer*. June agreed Rose Parker was likely pregnant. Although she doubted she could offer any help, here she was headed to the Parkers' house to take a look at Rose for herself. Even now a part of June wanted to send Azalea on her way so she could carry on with the routines of her day. She had mending and baking to do, a garden to weed, a family of her own to care for. But that little baby, whose legs were nearly as skinny as a stray cat's, needed an oatmeal bath and a warm bottle. If nothing else, June would see to that. She'd been sure to pack a gallon of milk and a brand-new carton of oatmeal.

As they sped down the highway, Azalea sat beside her as tense as a taut rubber band. June felt a peculiar shiver down her spine. Since leaving Sylva, she had tried to forget the girl she'd once been, the one who wore dirty clothes that never fit, whose hair was tangled with beggar's-lice, whose hands were rough from field work and keeping house. Now a grown woman, June had found a similar girl, almost a mirror image.

When she turned left onto the Parkers' dirt drive, Azalea finally spoke up. "How come you know where I live?"

*Everyone knows where Rose Parker lives, child.* June slowed the car, navigating around overgrown laurel and cedar. "Your mama got any idea I might be coming?"

Azalea shook her head.

June sighed and cut the engine. The house stood quiet. A cracked windowpane, missing roof shingles, mounds of kudzu smothering the clapboard siding. June's heart broke.

Azalea bolted from the front seat, leaving Atlas in the car for June to carry. He pulled up on the steering wheel, then wobbled his way onto June's lap. It had been such a long time since she'd held a baby. She stroked his sweet head, fingered his wispy hairs. "Everything's going to be okay, little one," she said and rattled the car keys in front of him.

Azalea reappeared on the porch. "Mama's in bed. Says she has a bad headache." Azalea knotted her arms about her. "Mama says I was wrong to bother you. Says you should go home unless you got some aspirin or cigarettes." Azalea looked down at the floor. "She don't mean any of it."

With Atlas straddling her hip, June reached into the back seat for a canvas bag, sensing another fight ahead of her. "Where's your mama at?"

Azalea nodded toward the house. "Down the hall. On the left. But mama said..."

"Take your brother." June handed Azalea the baby and the canvas bag. Atlas buried his face in Azalea's neck, only clutching his sister tighter when June tickled his thigh. "I packed some meat loaf and mashed potatoes in there with a gallon of fresh milk. Why don't you fix him a bottle, and I'll check on your mama."

"She ain't going to like you being here."

"You knew that when you came looking for me." June marched up the porch steps and followed Azalea into the house.

Inside, empty beer bottles crowded the tabletop by the door. At the foot of the sofa, a wet diaper was left on the floor, an old jelly jar half-filled with milk not far from it. The room reeked of stale tobacco, the lingering stench of it already burning June's nose.

Whether Rose had a headache or not, June was primed to have it out with her for neglecting her children and her house. Spying a mop on the front porch, she went to fetch it, already regretting she hadn't brought her own. This one stunk of mildew. She left it on the porch and went to check on Rose. Cleaning this house would have to wait.

June eased the bedroom door open. Inching her way forward in the darkened room, she knocked against the foot of the bed.

"Quit that, girl. I told you I got a headache."

"It's June Bush." She reached for the lamp and switched it on.

"Dammit." Rose appeared from behind the pillow, a hand shielding her eyes. "Turn that thing off and go away. You got no right to be here."

"Your daughter invited me."

"Lord, you're just as bothersome as she is." Rose sat up, her hair a stringy mess. "I told Azalea, unless you got some aspirin, I don't need your help."

June pulled the shade up. "Azalea's worried about you. Seems to think you're miscarrying."

"What's it to you?" Rose asked, tugging on her low-cut gown, worn almost bare in places.

"Not much, I reckon, other than you're a child of God from what I can see," June said, picking up an empty bottle of Orange Crush and a half-eaten cracker, "you need some help. And your children need a mama who knows where they are at the crack of dawn."

Rose slumped back under the covers. "God's little foot soldier, come to wage battle on the town whore. Ain't that grand?"

June stood by the side of the bed, wishing she had Scripture at the ready to fling back at Rose, but her mind called up the "Battle Hymn of the Republic" instead. "If you are pregnant, Rose, then this baby is taking a terrible toll on you. You ain't got an ounce of fat on your bones. That ain't good for you or the baby." June clasped her hands together. "So go right ahead, think of me as God's foot soldier, come to the rescue. Glory, glory hallelujah!"

Rose shook her head, pinching her lips in sarcasm. "I don't need God. I don't need you. And I ain't pregnant."

"Are you sure about that? Azalea's pretty convinced you do." June pressed closer. She studied Rose's eyes for the truth.

"Hell, she don't know what's what." Rose looked away, her voice turning thin. "Let's just say a man that called himself a doctor down in Athens took care of all that business the last time I got knocked up."

"Oh god, Rose."

"Don't *oh god* me. Atlas about did me in. And I ain't got a good man like Emmett Bush providing for me like you do." Rose yanked the covers about her waist. "You got a mighty fine life from where I'm sitting, June Bush." She closed her eyes.

June stood quiet and let that comment sink in. She looked around the bedroom, just as filthy with dirty clothes and half-spent cigarettes as the front room, but here the smell of nicotine and stale beer mixed with a wisp of gardenia. On the dresser top, a bottle of perfume and three tubes of lipstick stood in a neat row, behind them a pearl-handled brush and a Revlon compact. June couldn't make sense of any of it, because down the hall, a young girl was scrounging for something to eat and doing her best to mother her baby brother.

In the past, June had seen Rose as nothing but a whore. But what if she'd been wrong? What if Rose was doing the best she could? In that moment, June's judgment softened. She'd never faced mothering alone. She'd gone straight from her daddy's house to Emmett's, never once worrying about a roof over her head or food on her table. Maybe Rose was right to point a finger. If Emmett had not come along, June's life might look very different. It might look more like Rose Parker's. Who's to say that a chance meeting in a diner wasn't the only thing separating one from the other. Life wasn't fair. She'd learned that when her mama died. And most times, we don't get what we deserve. Leonard losing his leg was proof enough of that.

Despite their recent fighting, June had always trusted Emmett's fidelity to her and his family. Steady. Dependable. Rock-solid. That was Emmett Bush. Finding him with Leonard's shoe on his foot had rattled her understanding of him, left her wondering what other secrets might be wedged between them. But standing beside Rose Parker, she felt an unexpected pang of tenderness for her husband.

June caught her reflection in the mirror set above the dresser. The woman staring back at her looked worn out. She fingered her bangs, then leaned closer and traced a line worming its way across her brow. Maybe she'd stop at Peoples on the way home for a jar of Ponds. Silly to be thinking of herself with Rose huddled up in bed and no one but a child to care for her. She shook off the notion and turned her attention back to the need at hand.

Rose shivered, her body shaking and her teeth clattering from a sudden chill. She stretched for a blanket just out of reach. June placed it over her body. Then she picked up a towel from the floor and flicked off the bedside lamp. "I'll be back in a few minutes," she said and stepped into the hall, calling to Azalea for cleaning rags and bleach.

June spent the next hour scrubbing the tub, toilet, and bathroom floor with a bottle of vinegar Azalea found underneath the kitchen sink. A band of scum around the tub proved particularly stubborn, but June doused the rag with extra vinegar and rubbed at it until her arm ached, even stepping into the tub at one point to better her reach. Sometimes she caught Azalea peeking at her from behind a doorframe. When she was done, she ran a tub of hot water. The bathroom smelled like pickling brine, but the faded tiles gleamed from June's cleaning.

"Your bath's ready." June walked into Rose's bedroom. She pulled back the covers. "Come on before it gets cold."

Rose shooed her away. "What do you think you're doing?"

"Cleaning you up. You're a sight." June held out her hand. "And you stink. So come on."

Rose shrunk back. "I ain't your mission work or some sinner looking to be saved." Rose narrowed her eyes. "Surely you done enough already today to feel good about yourself."

"I ain't here to save you." June pitched a hand on one hip. "But your own girl came to me for help this morning, and she was right to do it. Have you even been out of this bed today? Yesterday? Your children don't need to see their mama looking like this." She pulled Rose upright, then lifted her gown over her head, exposing her gaunt frame and pale, yellowish skin. June hid her shock and hurried to wrap Rose in a towel. She didn't argue as June led her into the bathroom.

Rose sank into the water, releasing a slow, satisfied sigh. She closed her eyes and rested her head against the back of the tub. June washed Rose's face and arms with a soft cloth, then handed her the soapy rag, telling her to wash her privates, and left her to soak.

In the next room, June stripped the sheets and blanket from the bed and tossed them in a metal tub out back. "You got another set?" she called to Azalea who was rocking Atlas on the porch. "Found a bottom sheet for your mama's bed but not a top."

"No, ma'am," Azalea hollered back.

June set the spare sheet on the mattress and covered it with a quilt, thinking she might have an extra at home. She dusted the window sills, dresser, and bedside table, straightening Rose's magazines into a neat stack and carrying a half dozen empty glasses to the kitchen. When she was done, she ran back to the bathroom to check on Rose.

"Water's starting to cool," Rose said, her teeth clattering.

June turned on the faucet, adding hot water to the tub. "Let's get your hair washed real quick so we can get you warmed up." Using a measuring cup, she poured fresh water over Rose's head, then squeezed shampoo into her own hand and began scrubbing Rose's scalp.

Rose moaned. "Ain't never had someone do that for me. Not since I was a little girl and mama washed me for bed proper."

"Everybody needs a little mothering on occasion, even grown mamas," June said. She poured one last cup of water over Rose's hair before helping her out of the tub.

Back in the bedroom, Rose pulled a clean gown over her head. June towel-dried and combed her hair.

"Sheets are getting a good soak, too," June said, careful to work out the tangles without tugging too hard. "I'll hang them on the line shortly. Won't take long to dry. Then I'll remake the bed right." She set Rose's hair in a braid, tying the end with a rubber band.

"This is good," Rose said. She settled back against the pillows, her body still shaking from a chill.

"I got a washing machine at home. I'll take the rest of the laundry with me and bring it back tomorrow." June reached for Rose's hand and rubbed it warm. "For now, get some rest while I make you something to eat."

Rose nodded. "Ain't a lot in there. But I ain't hungry for much neither." She palmed the top of the bed. "You see my cigarettes?"

"You need to eat something." June had slipped the pack of cigarettes in her apron pocket when she made the bed. "I brought food from my house. You like meat loaf and mashed potatoes, don't you?" She didn't wait for an answer but flipped off the overhead light, then went to the kitchen and fixed a plate. She heaped on more meat and potatoes than she knew Rose would eat, but that woman and her two children needed to gain some weight. June gave the plate to Azalea to carry to her mother. "If she argues with you, tell her I'll spoon-feed her like Atlas if I have to."

"Yes, ma'am." Azalea smiled and bobbed down the hall.

June glanced at her wristwatch, then attacked the kitchen counter and stove with dish soap and vinegar, all the while wishing for a full bottle of bleach. Azalea had done her best, but tending to this house, her mother, and a baby brother was just too much for a girl her age. June couldn't imagine Leonard handling half of the things Azalea did. When she finished the kitchen, June bathed Atlas in the sink filled with soapy water and ground-up oatmeal. She fed him a few spoonfuls of mashed potatoes and another full bottle, then rocked

him to sleep while Azalea took her turn in the tub. By late afternoon,
June pulled the sheets from the line and went to check on Rose.

"I'll come back tomorrow morning," she said. "But I'm thinking it
might be best if we get you into town to see Dr. Mathews."

"I told you I ain't pregnant."

"I know. Let's just be certain of it." She handed Rose a cup of tea,
brewed from chamomile and valerian root she'd raised in her own
garden and thought to bring at the last minute. "In the meantime,
this should help you sleep and ease those shakes some."

Rose took the mug and rested it on her lap. "You didn't need to
do all of this."

"I think I did."

# — Emmett —

EMMETT'S CONCERN FOR June had doubled, then tripled since morning. She was never late. When she'd come to the milk room early that morning to tell him where she was going, she'd promised to be home within an hour or two. Azalea Parker had been in the car. What the hell was June doing with that child? By midafternoon, his worry had taken a deeper turn, knowing the kind of men that crossed Rose Parker's door. His imagination whirled out of control, leaving him to fear that June might be wrecked in a ditch. Or worse.

Not long after sunup, Leonard had tracked him down outside the milking parlor. He waved a note from his mama, wondering what it meant. Emmett had lied, said Rose was running a fever and had sent Azalea to fetch June for help. Leonard said that made no sense, that his mama and Rose weren't friends. Emmett told him to go do his chores. But at four o'clock with Emmett's worry for June building, he rounded up Leonard and they got in the truck.

Just as Emmett started up the engine, June pulled the Impala behind the house. "Where the hell have you been?"

"Parkers'."

"All this time? Why didn't you call?"

"Their phone ain't working."

"I was worried sick."

June rested her head against the steering wheel.

"June?"

Emmett touched her shoulder. "What's this about?" In all their years of marriage, he had witnessed June pitch an angry fit or blubber like a spoiled child too many times to count, but he had never seen her look so deflated. He opened the door and offered his hand. When June leaned against him, Emmett let out a breath he'd been holding for weeks.

"What's wrong with Mama?" Leonard looked troubled, but Emmett would deal with him later.

"Son, why don't you go turn on my TV in the milk room? Got some cold Coca-Colas in the little fridge." He watched his boy go inside. "Come on, Junebug," he said. "Let me fix you some coffee."

June nodded. "I could use a little company right now."

Emmett placed his hand at the small of her back and guided her toward the house, only now noticing that her cleaning apron was still knotted about her waist. Emmett had never known June Bush to leave the house wearing an apron.

He started a pot of coffee and set a small pan of milk on the stove to heat. While he waited for the milk to warm, he pulled a half-pint of whiskey from his pocket. It had been a source of comfort since moving out of the house. He added a generous splash of the amber liquid to the two mugs and sat down at the table opposite June. "What's got you so upset?"

"I don't know."

"Well, it must be something big 'cause you're still wearing your cleaning apron."

June glanced down at herself. "Oh my goodness, I stopped at Dr. Mathew's office on my way home to make an appointment for Rose. No wonder his nurse looked at me like I had two heads." She quickly untied the apron and dropped it on the chair bedside her.

Emmett smiled. "You look beautiful in that apron."

"Stop it," she said, but a small smile crept across her face, too. She wrapped her hands around the mug as if warming them up. Her eyes glazed with sorrow.

"Talk to me, Junebug."

June swallowed hard. "There ain't nothing right about what's going on over there at the Parkers'." She paused to catch her breath, her finger tracing the rim of the cup. "It's been so easy to judge from a distance. I don't know. Maybe it is Rose's fault, but there ain't no husband or sister or relative of any kind to help her. I don't know that I could do any better if I were in her shoes."

Emmett sipped from his mug.

"But no matter the reason, those children shouldn't have to suffer. It ain't their fault." June stared out the window as if searching for her next words somewhere in the pin oak. "That poor Azalea is trying to manage everything on her own. All of it. Barely keeping the house in order, washing clothes in a metal tub out in the yard. I ain't had to do that since marrying you." She reached for a paper napkin and wiped her nose. "She reminds me of myself, taking on so much, so young. Once Mama died, I cooked three squares for Daddy and cleaned up his mess." June's voice faltered. "But this is worse, Emmett. She's raising a baby not her own, and she's no more than twelve years old."

Emmett nudged June's mug closer. "Take a sip. It'll calm you some."

"There ain't nothing in here but whiskey."

"Go on, take a sip. It ain't a sin."

June hesitated, smelled the whiskey, then took a small sip. She coughed and made a face.

Emmett grinned.

June reached for Emmett's hand. "I know this is a lot to ask given the state of our marriage, but would you consider going to the Parkers' with me tomorrow? Something just don't feel right, and I'd really like you there with me."

Emmett's heart swelled at June's request. "Soon as I tend to the cows," he said, fighting the urge to pull June into his arms and to reassure her that everything would get better. He squeezed her hand, then let go. "First, how about you let me fix you something to eat?"

She made another face. "You fix supper? Not in my kitchen." June stood up from the table and tied a fresh apron about her waist. "You ought to stay, though," she said. She pulled three plates from the cabinet, glancing over one shoulder.

Emmett set the table, taking extra care to place the napkins and silverware the way June liked them. While she cooked, he sat at the table and watched, letting his imagination take him someplace nice, a special place where they were a family again.

# — Leonard —

POTS AND PANS clanked in the kitchen. Cows in the field lowed to be milked. From Leonard's room, the morning sounded exactly like it should.

June had been upset after returning from the Parkers', leaning mightily on Emmett for comfort. They ate supper as a family for the first time in weeks. Once or twice, Leonard caught his parents exchanging a wink or a twist of the lips as if they were trying to communicate in secret code. Later, Emmett watched some television, sat next to June on the sofa with his arm around her shoulder. Leonard figured his daddy had spent the night and woke contented, knowing that at least one part of his life was returning to normal. But when Leonard went to the kitchen for breakfast, June stood at the stove alone.

"Good morning," she said and added three slices of crisp bacon to a plate of eggs and toast and handed it to Leonard. "Sleep well?"

"Where's Daddy?" he asked, noticing the newspaper rolled up on the counter.

"Packing the truck."

Leonard took a bite of bacon. "Did he sleep here last night?"

"No, hon." June paused and fingered Leonard's bangs. "For now, your daddy's where he wants to be." She kissed his head, then pulled a casserole wrapped in tin foil from the freezer.

Leonard shoved the plate aside. "No he ain't. You're the one made him go. You're the one wants him out there."

"Watch your tongue," June said, adding the casserole to a wicker basket on the back porch. "Your daddy's got his own mind." She called for Emmett to come for the diapers and other supplies stacked by the door, then reached for a pitcher of orange juice from the refrigerator and set it on the table. "Look-a-here, Leonard, we're going to the Parkers', and we might be gone a good part of the day." June grabbed her pocketbook on the counter. "So when you're done with your breakfast, wash your dishes, clean your room, and feed the calf and whatever else your daddy asked of you before you even think of turning on that television set. You hear me?"

"Where you going?"

"I told you. To see about the Parkers." June pulled a scarf from her purse and snapped it closed.

Leonard scooted back his chair, anxious for Azalea. "Can I go?"

"No." She knotted the scarf under her chin. "This don't concern you." She blew Leonard a kiss. "Be good," she said and hurried out the door.

The truck's engine roared, slowly fading as his daddy steered down the drive, then turned onto the highway. Leonard didn't know what to make of his parents' marriage. And even though he was worried sick about Azalea, he was grateful her mama's condition had brought some harmony to his house. Maybe that was the silver lining Emmett was always talking about. He rushed to dress, not finishing his breakfast or washing his plate as June had asked. His mama didn't like him working the dairy, but he'd never washed a dish in his life. He wasn't sure what to make of that either. All he thought about was his mama and daddy and Azalea—and why his parents were headed her way.

Leonard secured his stump inside the fake leg and headed to the pens outside the milking parlor. Feeding a newborn calf on schedule was one chore he could not ignore. The calf gulped the milk as if she knew Leonard would rather be someplace else. When she was done, he dropped the empty bottle in the parlor sink, forgetting to wash it as Emmett had taught him to do. That strange feeling in his gut was churning up again, calling him back to the hilltop.

In bed last night, he'd listened to his parents talking about Rose, but he could only decipher bits and pieces. June had gossiped about

Rose Parker in the past, but this discussion was different. He was pleased his parents were talking to each other again but worried their conversation was sparked by something bad.

Halfway up the hill to the cemetery, he stumbled on a loose rock and fell. When he hit the ground, his front tooth sliced into the soft flesh of his tongue. He winced and rolled onto his back. A cloud scuttered across the sky. Tasting blood, he pressed the tip of his tongue, already feeling thick, against the roof of his mouth. Maybe he deserved a split tongue for talking harsh to his mama this morning, but he missed his daddy and wanted him home. He wasn't sorry about that. Leonard raised up on his elbow and spit. He wiped his mouth on his shirtsleeve, then steadied himself on his feet. By the time he reached the cemetery's iron gate, his limp was strong, his tongue pulsed, and a persistent breeze had pushed the lone cloud farther east. He leaned against the rail and rested.

In the far corner of the cemetery, a smattering of daisies hid a small patch of ground still raw from a recent burial. Leonard walked to the tiny grave where Azalea had buried her note and dug at the earth with his hands. This was the very same spot where she had picked daffodils for her mother back in the early spring. He dug deeper until the tip of a paper triangle appeared.

Azalea had come to him afraid that Rose was pregnant, and he'd barely offered any consolation in return. The note, she said, was for God. He was the only one who could undo what was done. Leonard resisted burying it at first, not because he doubted the power of the hilltop, but because he believed in it. Azalea was asking God for too much, but he had played a part in that request.

He held the folded paper like an artifact unearthed from a mummy's tomb, opened it fully, and blew dirt from the creases. The paper was damp, the writing smudged.

*He shall not delight in the strength of the horse nor take pleasure in the legs of a man.* The Bible verse came to him, playing again and again in his head like a scratched record, the Lord Almighty's words mingled with the pleas of a good friend needing his help. He wished Azalea were with him, singing about that snow-white dove. He wished he were knee-deep in Big Sugar, casting his concerns into its winding waters. He wished he weren't the boy who buried people's secrets.

At the very least, he owed Azalea his trust. He loved her, but his love had not been enough. The hilltop had not been enough. Now his parents were on their way to the Parkers' house to make things right, and he hoped God was paying attention. He glanced up at the sky, then returned the note to its grave.

"Leonard," a man's voice called out. Leonard scrambled to fill the hole with fresh dirt, then spun around to find Warren Gilbert standing just inside the cemetery gate. Warren waved and called his name again.

"What are you doing here?" Leonard asked.

Warren dangled another motel key from his hand, grinning like a mule. His wrinkled shirt was untucked, and a scruffy beard darkened his face. "Thank the good Lord you're here. I was hoping you might be able to help me with this."

"I helped you with that already. More than once."

Warren kicked at the ground. "I did a little backsliding last night. Thought it best to jump right on it before God or Elizabeth catches wind of it."

Leonard's cheeks fired hot. When he had buried his leg, he could not justify the reason for it. There was simply a need, something chafing at his soul. Maybe he needed to bury the boy he'd been so he could move on, like the doctor had prescribed. Then, before he could make sense of it, all these others starting showing up — Little Henry, Laura Kilgore, Berta Tate, Warren, even Azalea — thinking he could help them feel better, too. He never dreamed burying his leg would come to this.

Leonard snatched the key from Warren's hand. "Who are you trying to hide that key from?" Leonard asked, "God or Mrs. Gilbert?"

Warren took a menacing step forward, stopping to swat at a wasp. "What's that supposed to mean?"

"It means I ain't burying another dang motel key for you."

Warren reached for the key, then ducked from the wasp that kept circling about. "You can't turn a man away just because he drank too much and made one little mistake. That ain't godly."

"I ain't God."

"Maybe not, but you're the next best thing."

Leonard handed back the key. "Leave me be," he said and shoved past Warren, who was weaving and bobbing to avoid getting stung.

"You mind if I bury it myself?" Warren hollered after him. "Hey, you hear me?"

Leonard didn't answer. He walked down the hill and set about his chores.

# — Azalea —

 JUNE RETURNED TO the Parker house, just as she had promised Azalea she would. Warblers and sparrows chattered wildly, seeming to announce her arrival. Azalea watched from behind a blanket tacked to the front window while June unpacked the truck. Mr. Bush stood beside her, holding a basket of laundry, clean and neatly folded. He carried it to the porch and returned for another load.

Casseroles, a dozen eggs, a bundle of cloth diapers, and two bottles of bleach, plus a tub of fresh butter, cans of beans and meats, peanut butter and jars of jelly, two loaves of bread, and boxes of instant pudding and cornbread mix — the Bushes stacked a wealth of homemade and store goods by the screen door — all foods easy for Azalea to prepare. When they were done, Emmett leaned against the hood of the truck and watched his wife. June removed her sunglasses, then knocked on the Parkers' door.

Azalea had longed for help, prayed hard for a ministering angel. Now she saw the answer to that prayer dressed in a gathered skirt and pale pink blouse. Rose always said that nobody does a good deed without wanting something in return. So what did Mrs. Bush want from them?

When Azalea ran to June's home for help, she was desperate, terrified her mama was dying. Yesterday, June reassured her that wasn't so, yet she had fretted over Rose, kept checking her for fever, even mentioned calling the doctor. And today she'd hauled more food to their house. All of this frightened Azalea. She stood behind the screen door, refusing to unhook the latch. "Mama said she isn't up to a visit. She ate that food you brought and spent the night on the pot." Behind her, Atlas crawled to the sofa, pulled himself up, and squealed with delight at the sight of June.

June tapped the toe of her shoe against the porch floor. "It ain't my food making your mama sick. Me and Emmett ate the same thing last night. As I recall, you did, too, and the three of us are standing here no worse for wear." She looked back at Mr. Bush, then leaned closer as if she intended to share a secret. "Azalea," she said. "We need to get your mama to the doctor so we'll know for sure what's making her sick." June rapped the doorframe with one knuckle. "Come on, honey, open the door. You want your mama to feel better, don't you?"

Azalea kept her hand steady on the latch. Atlas dropped to his bottom and crawled toward her. June was right. Azalea had eaten the meat loaf, and she felt fine. She nodded toward the laundry and the haul of food and supplies. "Why are you doing this? And why did Mr. Bush come with you?" The baby slapped his hand against the screen and Azalea pulled him back.

"I just thought we might need a little help getting your mama to and from the car."

Azalea looked at June hard. "Mama can walk just fine. He don't need to be here."

June glanced back at Emmett. "You ever seen him here before today, honey?"

Azalea shook her head.

June smiled. "Good. Like I said, just thought we might need a strong arm."

Azalea couldn't make sense of these people standing on her porch coming to help in such a big way. They left her feeling jumpy, but she was well aware that the refrigerator was empty and nothing but a few saltines left in the cupboard. "Little Henry said you chased him off with a shotgun after his mama died."

June opened her purse and reached for a clean tissue, reminding Azalea of her schoolteacher, Miss Roberts, always ready with a Kleenex tucked under her sweater sleeve. "That was wrong of me," she said. "I was scared. Leonard had just lost his leg, and I wasn't thinking straight. But I didn't have a shotgun, for what that's worth." June blotted her nose with the tissue.

Atlas clung to Azalea's leg and cooed.

"You know, I ain't so unlike you." June brushed the back of her hand against her cheek. "I pretty much raised myself, despite having a daddy."

"You got a mama?"

June nodded. "She died when I was ten."

"How'd she die?"

"Doctor said it was a stroke. At least that was the best he could figure. But bad luck had been circling our part of the mountain for weeks. Granny passed a month before Mama. Aunt Lorraine broke her foot falling down a mountain trail." June balled up the tissue in her hand, working it into shreds. "Mama was getting over a fever but seemed to be feeling better. She got up from bed, thirsting for coffee and wanting to see the sun come up over Waterrock Knob." June paused; her gaze seemed fixed on a faraway memory. "One, two, three," she whispered, "And she was gone."

Leonard often complained about his mama as if she were a chigger that got under his skin. But Azalea felt sad for June, and she was mad at Leonard for falling short. He had never once mentioned her kindness or generosity or the suffering she had known as a child. "You miss her?"

June nodded, pressing a hand to the screen. "Let me in, sweetie. Can't you see I'm just a grown-up version of you?"

Azalea hesitated, then lifted the latch.

# — June —

ROSE CRAWLED INTO the back of June's Impala, her teeth clattering harder than ever.

"Another reason to get you to the doctor." June sat in the front seat beside Emmett. Looking back at the house, she spied Azalea peering out the front window. June had promised they wouldn't be long, that tomorrow she'd be back to care for Atlas so Azalea could go to school. The year would be ending soon, and the girl likely had catch-up work to do. "Come summer, I'll teach you to cross-stitch if you want," June had said.

Settled in the back seat, Rose closed her eyes, her head against the warm vinyl. With every rattle and bump, she moaned in pain. Emmett glanced in the rearview mirror, then slowed the car, and June promised they were almost to town. A half mile farther up, Emmett turned just past Peoples Drugstore and found a parking spot near the doctor's office.

"We're here," June said and reached for her pocketbook.

Emmett helped Rose from the car while June ran ahead to open the door to Dr. Mathew's office. Inside, Estellene Pearson and her twin, Lorraine Allen, sat on a far bench. When Emmett and Rose stepped into the waiting room, Estellene straightened up and poked her sister in the ribs. The sisters smiled at June, their mannerisms as identical as their appearance. June brushed past them, muttering a weak hello, and wrote Rose's name on the patient log.

Estellene cleared her throat. "How is Leonard? We've been hearing some talk about him lately. Had no idea he was such a curious boy." Lorraine nodded along, punctuating her sister's talk, as twins will sometimes do.

"He's fine. Thank you very much," June snapped. She didn't want to discuss Leonard and his hilltop work. She took her place between Emmett and Rose.

The sisters began whispering, and June imagined they were either wondering further about Leonard or commenting on Rose. Either way, she didn't like it. She kept a firm look fixed on the sisters until one picked up a magazine and the other fiddled with the straps of her purse.

A moment later, a nurse appeared at the door that led to the examination room. "Mrs. Parker, come this way, please."

Emmett wrapped his arm around Rose's waist and helped her to her feet. "I'll wait here," he said.

June took Rose's hand, and the nurse led them down a brightly lit hallway to the last room on the left. The same room, June noticed, where Leonard had been examined, his foot red and swollen and his body burning hot. June paused outside the door, her legs weak, her hands trembling, the fear she had felt all those months ago washing over her again.

"Mrs. Bush, you doing okay?" the nurse asked.

June smiled. "Of course." But thoughts of Leonard, limp in Emmett's arms, swirled in her head. She patted her chest a couple of times to calm her nerves, then followed Rose and the nurse into the room.

The nurse pointed to the scale, "Step up here, Mrs. Parker." She jotted down her weight and slipped a thermometer under Rose's tongue. "How long you been running a fever?" the nurse asked a minute later when she checked the thermometer.

"Not sure exactly," Rose said. "Off and on for a while, I guess."

Next, the nurse fitted Rose's arm with a blood-pressure cuff, then pumped the rubber bulb. When she was done, she removed the cuff and handed Rose a gown. "Everything off, please. Put this on and have a seat on the examination table. Dr. Mathews will be in shortly."

June unzipped Rose's dress and eased it off her shoulders. She unhooked Rose's bra, then tugged off her panties. Rose stood in the middle of the room, shivering as June guided her arms into the cotton gown and tied it at the neck. The room was cold and smelled strongly of rubbing alcohol. June draped her sweater across Rose's shoulders and promised the doctor would be coming soon as she helped Rose onto the examination table. June pictured Leonard stretched out in that same spot. She saw his pale face and glassy eyes. The memory of that afternoon made her shake in rhythm with Rose.

Since the amputation, June had grown convinced her life was cursed, that death and loss were her constant companions. Faith in God or her granny's superstitions hadn't saved either her mama or Leonard's leg. In the aftermath of both, June had grown angry, always expecting someone else to better her life. But women like Estellene and Lorraine reminded her that most people were more interested in themselves than helping anyone else. June figured she'd done no better at times and would need to make amends for that. She looked at Rose, scared and quivering like a dog left in the snow. Rose's condition only convinced June that there was no escape from pain or judgment. But Leonard was doing well. June was married to a loving man. The good Lord had been kind. She just hadn't seen it until today.

When the door opened, June took a deep breath and squeezed Rose's hand.

A bald-headed, thin-framed man with wire-rimmed glasses perched on the tip of his nose, Dr. Mathews smiled and held out his hand. "Rose Parker and June Bush in the same room." A manilla folder was tucked under his arm. He handed it to the nurse and adjusted the glasses on his nose. "Rose, haven't seen you in quite some time. What's brought you in today?"

Rose bowed her head. June answered for her. "Mrs. Parker ain't got any appetite. Eats about as much as a chipmunk and don't seem able to keep down what she does eat for very long." June paused and looked at Rose's bones poking at her from inside out, the skin an unnatural shade of gray. Maybe the florescent ceiling light was to blame for some of her sickly appearance, but Rose looked worse today than she had the day before. "She's been running a fever off and on." June instinctively placed her hand on Rose's forehead. "But don't know for how long."

The doctor nodded and began his examination — checking Rose's pulse, eyes, ears, and throat, then listening to her heart with the stethoscope dangling about his neck. He pulled a paper sheet from a cabinet and placed it over her lap. "Lie down," he said and tugged on a pair of latex gloves. "Spread your legs for me, Rose." As the doctor continued his examination, he kneaded her belly, pressing deeper a second time around. Rose winced and squeezed June's hand tighter.

"Is she pregnant?" June asked.

Rose looked up at June. "I told you that ain't possible."

The doctor tossed the gloves in a trash can, took the chart from the nurse, and scribbled down some notes. "No," he said. He looked up at June with kind eyes, "Mrs. Parker is not pregnant."

"I told you I got an angry uterus." Rose smiled, seemingly pleased she had been right.

"We need to run a few tests though," Dr. Mathews said and tucked his pen in a coat pocket. "We can do a couple here, but you'll need to go to Knoxville for the rest."

"Why?" Rose asked.

"We don't have that kind of fancy equipment in Sweetwater." He patted her hand. "Besides, one thing I learned long ago is that in both medicine and home repair, it's always good to get a second opinion." The doctor grinned. He pushed his glasses farther up his nose.

"Why do I need tests?" Rose asked, her voice rising in panic. "What's wrong with me?" She pulled herself up on one elbow, looking to June to help her the rest of the way.

"I don't want to make guesses until we know more, but I felt something in your belly, and we need to rule out anything serious. Could be any number of things."

"I got something serious, don't I?" Rose grabbed hold of June's hand. "That's what he's trying to say, but he's too chicken to come out with it."

Dr. Mathews placed his hand on Rose's shoulder. "I'm not saying it's anything serious. I'm just saying we can't make a diagnosis until we know more." He handed the chart back to his nurse and asked her to get blood and urine samples. "It's a good thing June brought you in to see me, Mrs. Parker. You're lucky to have such a friend."

June's heart raced, her hands started to shake. The doctor had used the same kind, even tone with her when he surely knew Leonard's leg would have to be amputated. She tucked her hands under her arms to hide her nerves from Rose while the nurse tied a rubber tube just above the bend of Rose's elbow and swabbed it with alcohol.

Dr. Mathews nodded toward the door. "Will you join me in my office, Mrs. Bush?"

"Don't leave me in here alone," Rose whispered. A tear spilled down one cheek.

June patted her hand. "I'll be right back. I promise."

The doctor paused in the hallway. "I've been practicing medicine for a long time," he said. He glanced at the door, then leaned in close and lowered his voice. "You need to prepare yourself," he said, "and Rose. I don't think the outcome is going to be very good."

"You just told her not to worry, that it could be any number of things."

"She's not ready to handle more than that today." Dr. Mathews touched June's shoulder just as he had Rose's. "But you are."

June thought of the ramshackle house the Parkers called home, pictured Azalea's worried eyes, and Atlas's pinched face. "Rose ain't got no one to help her. Not enough money to put food on the table. What's she going to do? She's got two kids counting on her. One's just a baby."

The doctor slipped his glasses into his coat pocket. "Seems to me, she's got you."

———

BACK AT THE PARKERS' HOUSE, June put Rose to bed while Emmett fed Atlas a bowl of warm applesauce. June wanted to speak with Rose alone, but Azalea followed her mama through the house tighter than a shadow, then climbed onto the bed beside her and snuggled close. "You want me to brush your hair? Or get you some soda crackers and ginger ale?" Azalea asked.

"She needs something more to eat than that, honey," June said. She placed a second pillow underneath Rose's head. "I brought some..."

"She ain't hungry for your food," Azalea interrupted. She readjusted the pillow. "What'd the doctor say, Mama?"

"Well, there ain't *no* baby," Rose said. "Just like I been telling you both." She flashed a small smile at June.

"Did he give you some medicine?"

"He gave me some aspirin for the fever." Rose pressed her index finger to her temple as if she were trying to pinpoint an ache. "But he wants another doctor to take a look at me."

Azalea snapped up straight.

June sat down on the edge of the bed. "So I'm going to take your mama to Knoxville Monday morning." June smoothed the old quilts covering Rose. "Then we'll know more."

Azalea tugged on the quilts. "I don't want you going to Knoxville."

"It's just for some tests," Rose said, her voice sounding tired.

June tapped Azalea on the leg. "Would you do me a favor, hon?" she asked. "Would you mind checking on Emmett and Atlas? If I know Emmett Bush, he'll have a fishing pole in that boy's hand before he can talk good if we don't keep a close eye on him."

Azalea didn't budge.

"Sweetie, you hear Mrs. Bush?" Rose asked.

"Atlas is fine," Azalea said.

"I'm sure he is," June said, "but it's been a long time since Emmett cared for a baby. Thought he might need a little extra help from an expert like you."

"You ain't my mama. I ain't got to do what you say."

"Girl." Rose smacked Azalea's hand.

Azalea flinched.

"You do as Mrs. Bush asked," Rose said, her voice wobbly but stern. "What's got into you?"

Azalea rubbed the back of her hand.

"Don't make me get rough with you again. I ain't got the energy for it. Go on, do as Mrs. Bush asked," Rose said, her voice a shade softer. She closed her eyes, settling deeper into the pillows, then opened her arms. "Come here."

Azalea fell into her mama's hug. "She was supposed to make you better," she cried. "I wouldn't have brought her here if I'd known she was going to take you to Knoxville."

"It's okay, baby. It's all going to be okay." Rose kissed Azalea's head. "It's just going to take a little time," she whispered, kissing her again. "But right this minute, I need you to go check on our boy for Mrs. Bush. Okay? Be a good girl and run on." Azalea lay against her mama a minute longer, then she dried her eyes on Rose's terry cloth robe and slipped past June.

In that moment, June's heart broke for Rose and Azalea both. Atlas was the lucky one. A tiny boy would likely never remember his mama taking ill, but Azalea was at such a tender age. Outside the bedroom windows, the afternoon light fell across the sky and trees in lovely shades of blue and green as if everything in the world was perfectly fine. Once she heard the screen door in the front room shut, June took Rose's hand in hers.

Rose's bottom lip quivered, then her whole body.

This time, June pulled Rose into her own arms.

"I'm dying. Ain't I?"

"We don't know that." June held Rose tighter, her tears damp against June's neck.

"I know it. I've known for a long time things weren't right. Kept thinking it would pass. Or just didn't want to admit it, I guess." Her words choked with a palpable fear. "It's my fault it's come to this."

"This ain't nobody's fault," June said. "Trust me, sometimes there just ain't no rhyme or reason to this life here on earth." She brushed Rose's hair from her face. "We really don't know anything yet." But June knew she was lying. She'd seen death before — its ashen skin, dull eyes, hollowed cheeks — and that old trickster was lying right there in the bed beside her. "Let's just take it day by day. Right now, I'm going to put on a kettle and brew you some special tea. Brought some dried greens from my beets and a little ginger."

Rose held onto June's hand. They exchanged a look, and June had a hunch they were asking the same awful question. *What would come of Atlas and Azalea?*

# — Leonard —

LATER THAT AFTERNOON, Leonard spied Elsa Foster and Henrietta Ooten waltzing up the drive. Miss Ooten had warned him earlier in the week that Elsa was in desperate need of his services, but he had brushed the request aside amidst his mama's and daddy's talk of Rose Parker's condition. Leonard ducked behind the living room curtains, in no kind of mood to go back to the hilltop, not even for Miss Ooten. Besides, neither Azalea nor Warren Gilbert had fared any better after trusting their woe to him. If anything, they seemed worse off.

The women chattered like two squirrels as they walked to the porch. Leonard couldn't make sense of a word said. He slipped another peek from behind the curtains.

Wearing a large-brimmed hat and a bright yellow dress, Elsa stood at the front door looking as showy as a summer wildflower. Henrietta stood beside her, plain in comparison with her long gray hair knotted in a tight bun at the back of her head. Both women were short and plump, alike in so many ways, although Elsa was a widow, a fancy dresser, and her right ankle was stained with a large reddish-brown birthmark in the shape of Florida. Henrietta carried her Autoharp.

A heavy knock came at the door. Leonard held his breath, frozen in place like a scared rabbit. Another knock came louder than the first, then a steady pounding. Miss Ooten had likely kept a close eye on the house and knew he was home alone. She'd go to the back door next, maybe even bust in the house if she feared Leonard was hurt or in trouble. Blood kin or not, she loved him like a grandson.

Realizing he was cornered, Leonard pushed aside the curtains and opened the door.

"Hello there, young man," Elsa said. Her broad smile revealed a shiny gold tooth. "Henrietta wasn't sure you'd be around today, it being a Saturday. But I told her let's give it a try, and here you are." She talked at high speed, barely pausing to take a breath. "Got this silly little thing I need you to tend to for me this morning. Can't seem to let go of it on my own. Just picks at me." She started rummaging through her pocketbook. "Henrietta said you'd take care of it lickety-split. Bury it out of sight for me so I can rid myself of some guilt that's been eating at me for a while now."

"I didn't put it quite like that," Miss Ooten said, cutting her eyes toward Elsa. "The boy ain't God, for heaven's sake."

"Well, I know that. Just look at him. If he were God, he would've fixed that bum leg a long time ago."

"Elsa." Henrietta nudged her friend.

Leonard's left thigh started to ache. "This really ain't a good time. I got chores to do before Mama and Daddy come home."

"When is a good time?" Elsa asked. She held a tube of lipstick in the palm of her hand. "I'd think your hilltop work would come before chores."

Leonard looked at the lipstick, then back at the curtains, wishing he'd never left his cover. He had a good hunch Elsa Foster wouldn't leave either until he saw to her need. "We better hurry along then," he said, shutting the door behind him.

Barely on their way up the hillside, the two women stopped to catch their breath. Miss Ooten set down her Autoharp and tugged on her dress.

"Don't you want to know why I want that lipstick buried?" Elsa asked between winded gasps.

"Not really." These days Leonard preferred not knowing, leaving the truth only for God to judge. He had always tried to be impartial, but that was proving harder the more he discovered about his neighbors.

"My husband, Frank, died two years back," Elsa said. She started up the hill again. "He was a good man and a good provider."

"Yes, ma'am." Leonard kept a steady pace despite their foot-dragging. He glanced over his shoulder. Miss Ooten was fanning her face with her hand, and Elsa was adjusting her hat.

"I always had what I needed, but considering my weekly budget, Frank didn't give me a lot of wiggle room for extras," she hollered. She motioned for Miss Ooten to hurry along. "I could make a pound of ground beef into three suppers. You hear me, boy?"

Leonard nodded. "Yes, ma'am. Three suppers."

"I don't expect you to understand what that means, but your mama can tell you that's an impressive accomplishment. That's why I like your mama. She's as resourceful as I am."

Leonard's fake leg rubbed at his stump. The path to the cemetery grew steeper, the afternoon warm for May. Miss Ooten and Elsa still lagged behind, stopping every few feet to rest, Elsa drying the sweat beading above her lip with a hankie.

"Anyway, when Frank died, come to find out he had thousands of dollars stashed in the bank. *Thousands,* I'm telling you." Elsa shook her head, and her hat flopped forward. She adjusted the brim again. "That man let me wear the same pair of nylons for months, runs stopped with nail polish. I had to beg before he'd ever give me money for a new pair."

Leonard nodded.

"Until you're grown, you might not understand any of this."

"It ain't up to me to understand."

When they reached the gate, Elsa grabbed Leonard's elbow. "After my husband died, I thought about that money for a long time. Then one morning I went to the bank and withdrew most of it. Went on a three-day shopping spree in Knoxville. I bought every-thing I wanted, whether I needed it or not." She blushed. "The very next Sunday the preacher took to the pulpit and delivered a sermon about vanity and lust. It was like he knew what I'd done, how I'd sinned against God and my husband." She opened the tube of lipstick and smeared some on her mouth, then puckered up her lips. "It was like the preacher was in cahoots with my husband."

Leonard rubbed his thigh some more, "Yes, ma'am," he said.

Miss Ooten opened the case and tuned her Autoharp. Discordant notes wafted down the hill.

Elsa handed the lipstick to Leonard. "Parisian Nights has always been my favorite."

Leonard knew Mr. Foster had been a good man, a hardworking banker folks in town respected. He handed out sticks of chewing gum to kids for no reason. Maybe he had been tightfisted. Maybe Mrs. Foster was a spendthrift. Leonard didn't know, but it seemed the longer a husband and wife lived together the muddier the truth became. His parents were a prime example.

The three of them walked to the corner of the cemetery where Miss Ooten plucked out a hymn. Leonard recited his script by rote, and Elsa smiled through it all. After the service, Miss Ooten invited Leonard to her house for oatmeal cookies and vanilla ice cream.

He thanked her for the invitation but claimed his mama needed him home. When the women disappeared down the hillside, he walked to the headstones and began pulling weeds. Like his daddy had done back before the leg funeral, he got down on his knee and cleared each grave of the finger grasses and chickweed, leaving dandelions and shepherd's purse because he thought they were pretty. He was in no hurry to go home. He missed Azalea. She'd hardly been to school since she buried her note on the far side of the hilltop. Here, he felt like she was near. He didn't think her mother was a bad person, whether a baby was coming or not. And he didn't think less of Azalea for not wanting another brother or baby sister. He wished she would come up the hill so he could tell her these things. He wished his mama and daddy would quit whispering about the Parkers and tell him the truth of what was happening. In the distance, the sun glinted off Big Sugar. Leonard closed the gate and headed for the dairy. Surely his parents would be home soon, and his chores were still not done.

THE FEEDING BARN reeked of manure, but Leonard didn't mind the smell, the sign of a true dairyman, according to Emmett. Leonard thought of his daddy's compliment as he scraped the floor with a pitchfork. He was nearly half-done, when Icky Greer walked up behind him. "I come for a redo," he blurted.

Startled, Leonard jumped back, his fake leg giving way. He stabbed the floor with the pitchfork, grateful for the rubber muck boots that gave his feet traction, and regained his balance.

"What are you talking about?"

"I said I come for a redo. So you need to wave a wand or do some more of that hocus-pocus — whatever it is you do up there on the hilltop. I ain't any better off than when you buried that damn slingshot. It's been months, and Mavis ain't hardly talking to me. She can't see any better neither, and Mama ain't stopped her crying over her blind eye."

Leonard tightened his grip on the pitchfork. He had to finish mucking the barn floor and wash a half dozen glass bottles. He was in no mood to deal with Icky Greer. "Sorry about that," he said.

"Sorry? That's all you got to say? Hell, you said you'd make this bad feeling go away. And it ain't."

Leonard widened his stance. "Look, I never said I could make anything go away. It's up to you to make peace with Mavis."

Icky bumped his chest against Leonard's. "Get your Bible out and do what you got to do to make this right. You promised I'd feel better, and I don't."

Leonard pushed back. "I never said that, Icky. I never promised you anything."

Icky grabbed Leonard's collar and yanked him close. "You may be able to fool Little Henry, but not me."

Leonard didn't flinch, although he knew Icky, like Eddie Burl, could deliver a mean punch. "You going to beat me up, Icky? You want to add to the list of things you feel guilty about? Go on. Do it."

Icky jerked him closer, then let go, but he held a mean look in his eyes. "I told you from the start your guilt ain't up to me to get rid of," Leonard said. "I did what you wanted. I buried the slingshot."

"You told me there was magic up there."

"Dammit, Icky, I never said such a thing. You're the one came begging for help. You're the one believing that there's magic in that hilltop."

Icky puffed up again. "What a waste. Turns out, the cripple ain't good for nothing after all." Icky gave Leonard one more shove, then tore out of the barn.

Leonard balanced his hands on his thighs. He had stood his ground, but he was shaking from the effort. He had felt bad for Icky when he first came to the cemetery bearing the slingshot, full of regret for what he'd done to his sister. Now Leonard was scared of Icky. Not of being bullied. He was afraid Icky spoke the truth. That Leonard Bush wasn't so special after all.

In the beginning, Leonard had buried the woes of other people for the right reason. He believed that in his heart. But maybe he'd continued for the wrong one. He'd come to the hilltop with Little Henry to help a friend. But later? People just kept coming to him, asking for such a simple favor, something a damaged boy could do. *Take my pain and hide it in the ground.* They left happy, claiming Leonard had done them some good. Mulling it over now, maybe he'd been wrong to let folks think he could affect such a change. Had he tarnished his family's sacred ground for a selfish need to feel better about his own misfortune? His missing leg throbbed, and he wondered if the phantom pain was a direct message from God, telling him to pay attention. His mama would say that it was. His daddy would say otherwise.

# — Emmett —

THE DASHBOARD CLOCK read half past four. Emmett sped down the road, drumming out a fast, steady beat on the steering wheel, a nervous tick that bubbled up whenever he was away from the dairy too long. June set her hand on his thigh. "Slow down. Cows ain't going nowhere." Emmett nodded, flipped on the radio, and spun the dial from one end of the AM band to the other. Notes blurred with static, then a man's rich, steady voice spit out bits of news and local crop reports — recent rainfall was holding up corn planting in the county, but wheat was coming in strong.

"Don't need a weatherman to tell me that." Emmett turned off the radio and glanced at June. She hadn't said a word since they'd left the Parkers'. She was worried. He was, too. His drumming started up again.

"You planning on taking Rose to Knoxville on Monday?"

"Don't know how else she'd get there."

"Need me to go?"

"I don't know how long it'll take. You best stay here." She patted his forearm. "You got the dairy and Leonard to keep an eye on," she said, gazing out the window. "I need to find somebody to look after Azalea and Atlas."

"Miss Ooten?"

"Atlas is a handful."

Emmett stopped at the railroad tracks and rolled the window down halfway. "I don't understand you no more. Ain't you afraid Rose will bring more bad luck our way?"

June sighed. "I'm worried sick. But bad luck is coming one way

or another. All I can do is keep a close watch." She turned back to
Emmett. "Good luck comes around, too, you know. Maybe not in
threes. But it comes." She breathed in the smell of fresh-cut grass.
"You know Leonard's sweet on Azalea?"

"Yeah, I know." Emmett grinned. "Didn't know you knew." He
laughed, cutting a quick look at June. "About time he started noticing pretty girls."

"Not my baby boy," June said.

They passed the Greers' farm, a dairy fifty head larger than Emmett's. A little farther down the road, Laura Tate stood in front of
her trailer, her baby girl toddling nearby, dragging a rag doll behind
her. They both looked like children. Laura had buried something on
the hilltop. Emmett had seen her come and go. He tapped the horn
and waved. "Reminds me of when Leonard was little bitty."

"Those days are gone for good." June looked down at her hands,
fingering her wedding band. "I feel so old."

Emmett glanced over at her. "You're more beautiful than ever,
Junebug," he said, shifting his eyes back to the road. He suddenly
wanted to drive out of Monroe County and the state of Tennessee.
Head north, straight to Ohio where his mother's people were from.
Sometimes when he was alone in the milk room, he wondered if
there might be another living Bush like him somewhere above the
Mason-Dixon Line — one who kept weird secrets from his wife. Emmett was desperate to start fresh with June. He wanted her to look
at him doe-eyed again, the way she had in the early years of their
marriage.

He rolled up the window, and the car fell quiet except for the hum
of the motor and the tires spinning against the road. The white line
grew blurry. He cleared his throat and drummed hard at the wheel.
"I need to tell you something," he said. "About Sarah. About that
baseball shoe of Leonard's ..."

June raised her hand. "Not now, Emmett. Please. Not now." She
leaned against the window. "I got enough to deal with today without thinking about that."

"Okay," he said, gripping the wheel, careful not to look at her. He was ready to move back into the house. He missed kissing Leonard good night and waking with June beside him, but he needed to know she could love a flawed man. He turned on the radio again, this time louder, and raced toward home.

# — June —

JUNE OPENED THE kitchen window a little wider despite the warm day. The pot roast slow-cooking in the oven was nearly done, the pan-fried potatoes browned and crispy. She always served dinner an hour early on Sundays and figured its aroma was all the invitation Emmett needed. Ten minutes after four, he had yet to knock on the back door. She glanced out the window, then dialed down the oven's temperature another few degrees.

Although June had tried not to dwell on it, Rose's illness was likely the first bout of more bad luck to follow. Her calculations weren't going to change her plan to drive Rose to Knoxville tomorrow morning. Still, she had to keep a close eye on her family. Leonard was in his room, wrapping up a science report. She went looking for Emmett, calling for him as she neared the barn, then the milk room, careful not to step inside without warning. She knew Emmett had wanted to talk about his secrets. But the Parker family needed her, and she couldn't focus on her own issues until theirs were settled.

June walked farther up the dirt path that wound its way toward the pond. Up ahead, she spied Emmett tracing a stretch of fence line.

"Dinner's ready," she hollered.

Emmett pulled off the thick leather gloves he wore whenever working with barbed wire. "I sure got an appetite tonight," he shouted back. "Could eat one of them cows."

They laughed as they walked toward one another, June suddenly remembering an afternoon when they were first married. Emmett had carried a picnic basket near this very spot. They'd spread a blanket, eaten ham sandwiches, and watched the sun set. Chiggers had feasted on her bare ankles, but she never complained, not wanting anything to end their romantic date.

Emmett lifted his head and sniffed in an exaggerated way. "Pot roast?"

June smiled. "Your nose ain't that good."

"You got a nose for tobacco. I got one for pot roast."

"Can that nose of yours tell you what kind of pie I got?" Grinning, June tucked some loose hairs behind her ear and started walking toward home. Emmett followed. They stopped when a black sedan pulled up outside the kitchen door. Brother Puckett stepped out of the shiny black car and walked into the house.

"Dammit to hell," Emmett said, "I ain't in the mood for this tonight. Acts like he owns the damn place." Emmett slapped his work gloves against one thigh.

"Nah, he's just got a nose like a hound dog. Smelled my pot roast from the church."

They walked a little faster.

As they neared the house, June grabbed Emmett's shirtsleeve. "No matter what the preacher wants, Emmett Bush, don't you go cussing in front of him."

"Now why in the hell would I do that?" Emmett winked at June. She couldn't help but smile in return.

The kitchen was empty when they stepped inside the house, but Brother Puckett's voice rang loud in the front room, his words sparking hot. June couldn't tell if he was leading someone to the cross of salvation or to the fiery gates of hell. Either way, she didn't like the sound of it, and she could tell Emmett didn't either.

"Brother Puckett," he called out, stepping into the front room.

Wide-eyed, Leonard sat on the floor, his fake leg stretched out straight, a cartoon on the television playing behind him. The preacher knelt in front of him, spewing words of evildoing and idolatry. June couldn't make sense of it, but she clearly understood that the preacher was branding her son a sinner.

"Brother Puckett," Emmett called out again. The preacher abruptly stopped praying and jerked around. Seeing Emmett, he stood and stuck out his hand. "What are you doing here?" Emmett asked, ignoring the offered hand. The preacher straightened his belt. "I come to pray for your son."

Leonard scooted backward, well away from the preacher's reach. "He just showed up," he said.

"You okay?" Emmett asked. Leonard reached for his crutches. June bent to help him up.

Brother Puckett squared his shoulders and lifted his jaw. "Icky Greer's mother came to see me this morning before service," he said. "Seems Icky ain't doing so well. Blames himself for Mavis's blind eye."

"He shot his sister with a slingshot," Emmett said. "Everybody knows that."

The preacher held up his hand as if ordering Emmett to hush. "Mrs. Greer says your son convinced Icky he could wipe his slate clean if he buried that slingshot in your family's graveyard — as if that's some kind of special place. Now Icky thinks God is punishing him because he didn't trust our Lord and Savior with his salvation. Turned to a boy instead." Brother Puckett pointed at Leonard. "Whatever you did up there on that hilltop has him believing he don't deserve God's glory no more. His mama's never seen him so despairing, says she's afraid to leave him alone for fear of what he might do." He clenched his hands as if he were praying. "Even a sinner like Icky is deserving of salvation."

Red-faced, Leonard looked up at Emmett. "I never promised Icky nothing. He came by yesterday begging for a *redo*, and I told him *no way*."

Emmett put a steady hand on Leonard's shoulder. "I think you best go, Preacher."

The preacher wiped his brow with a folded handkerchief, then stuffed it in his pants pocket. "You know I'm speaking God's truth,

Sister June. Leonard needs to stop pretending to be something he ain't before it's too late."

June had warned Emmett not to cuss, but anger flickered in his eyes, and she wondered if he'd be able to hold his tongue. A part of her hoped he wouldn't.

Brother Puckett opened his worn Bible, a page marked with a thin gold ribbon stitched to the spine. He placed his other hand on Leonard's head and began to pray for the boy's salvation.

June slapped the preacher's hand away. "Don't touch my son."

Emmett wedged himself between June and the Preacher. "I told you once—you need to leave!"

Brother Puckett cocked his finger again and took aim. "You and your family, Sister June, ain't welcome at the church until you make this right. I can't allow it no more. I got an entire flock to look after, and if I got to sacrifice one for the many, then so be it." He pushed past Emmett and walked back through the kitchen. Emmett followed him to his car, and June hurried behind as far as the porch. "I'll be praying for you," Brother Puckett said. He shoved his belly behind the steering wheel. "I'll being praying for you all."

June and Emmett watched the car disappear around the house. Brother Puckett's words lingered in the air, so bitter June could taste them. Shaking, she stepped toward Emmett, and he slipped his arm around her waist and drew her close.

# — Emmett —

JUNE TOOK EMMETT'S hand and led him back to the kitchen door. "Come inside, supper's ready."

He shook his head. For years, he'd expected the preacher to call him out, to point his finger at Scripture and expose him as the sinner who needed God's most immediate attention. Emmett had always worried the preacher saw straight into his soul, eager to crack it wide open and expose the meat of his wrongdoing.

Emmett had never doubted God. A thick fog, a gentle rain, a suckling calf were all the proof any man should need of the Lord's existence. But as strong as his belief in God, Emmett reasoned that a confession of his own iniquity would never be enough to please either the preacher or the Almighty. He saw himself as the most twisted kind of sinner, well beyond salvation. No Scripture addressed a man who kept a baby shoe instead of Scripture in his pocket for comfort or jammed his sweaty, swollen foot into his son's shoe for comfort.

"You and Leonard go on and eat without me." Emmett put his arm around June's shoulders. He'd never meant to hurt her. He'd loved her since that day in Sylva when he spotted her at the diner. He smiled thinking of that now. But if she'd only known his secret-keeping then, his inability to talk about what pained him most, she never would have married him, no matter how desperate her desire to leave her daddy's tobacco farm behind. And now that she'd discovered Leonard's shoe on his foot, he felt both relieved and terrified. Would she ever be able to love and respect him as she had before?

"You got to stay for supper," June said. "Me and Leonard can't eat that pot roast on our own."

"I ain't hungry," he said.

"Don't let the preacher ruin your appetite," she said, nodding toward the house. "Leonard needs his daddy tonight. Here, at home."

Emmett felt a tightness in his chest. "He's got his mama."

"He needs his daddy, too," she said. "Especially tonight." She wiped her hands on her apron, then pressed the cotton smooth.

Emmett smiled at her small gesture, something he had watched her do a thousand times. Tonight, with the stars glimmering in the sky, she looked beautiful. Emmett wanted to accept her supper invitation. He wanted to be a family again, but the preacher's visit had shaken him into doubt. "Just got a lot on my mind," he said. "Things I need to sort out. I'll check on Leonard in the morning." Emmett waved, then walked to the dairy.

Newborn calves nestled in beds of straw outside the milking parlor scrabbled to all fours when they saw him coming. They lunged for Emmett's attention, and a dozen cows ambled toward the milking barn, their udders full. Emmett patted a calf's head. "I know you're hungry, but you're going to have to wait a minute longer." The calf licked his hand.

Emmett locked his office door and reached for the key in his desk drawer. He jiggled it into the padlock latched to the metal cabinet, then took a deep breath and exhaled. He kicked off his left boot and sock and shoved his foot into the cleat. It pinched his toes, but his heartbeat slowed. Peace washed over him.

Losing his baby sister had hurt Emmett to the bone. Leonard losing his leg had left Emmett damn near paralyzed. But the thought of losing June was unbearable. He pulled a pack of cigarettes from the desk drawer, struck a match, and sucked in the smoke. Further relief came from the first long drag. Moonlight tinted the walls a cool blue. On the far side of June's garden where her beets grew, a light in the kitchen window glowed warm. Emmett finished the cigarette and crushed it with the tip of the cleat.

The shoe hurt like hell tonight. Emmett slipped it off and pulled his sock back on, wiggling his toes against the damp cotton before tugging on his work boot. He noticed a tiny scuff on the heel and reached for a clean cloth and a tin of polish in the desk's bottom drawer. Carefully, he dabbed the cloth with the black-colored cream. Holding the cleat in one hand, he polished the leather, making sure the mark was cleaned away completely. He reached farther into the drawer for a soft brush and buffed the athletic shoe to a high shine. "Almost as good as new," he said, then wrapped the shoe with its mate in a paper bag and set them back in the metal cabinet for safe-keeping. A calf bleated for dinner. "I know. I know." Emmett slipped the padlock through the cabinet's handles and clicked it in place.

# — Azalea —

 WHEN THE MOON rose high above the clearing, Azalea took to her bed, watching the familiar shadows skip across the bare wall opposite the window. Tonight, they jumped and flexed, their gyrations growing wild. Cedars and pines fought against a gusting wind.

Atlas slept soundly in the crib beside her, but worry kept Azalea awake. The shadows' dance only agitated her more. She dozed some, dreaming of a ghoulish monster that rose up from Big Sugar and grabbed at her feet. Morning came with the shrill crow of a neighbor's rooster. Azalea covered her head with a pillow and tried to go back to sleep. Atlas stirred and babbled her name, but the crunch of tires rolling over gravel in the front yard jangled her fully awake.

She shimmied into a pair of jeans and an old t-shirt and lifted Atlas from his crib and onto her hip. "Mama," she said, poking her head inside Rose's room, "Mrs. Bush is here."

Rose sat on the side of the bed, buttoning her blouse. She stopped halfway, exhausted from the effort, Azalea thought.

"You need some help?"

"No, taking care of Atlas is help enough." Rose twisted another two buttons in place. "How do I look?"

Azalea set Atlas on the bed and smiled. Her mama had always been a pretty woman, her auburn hair falling in soft waves past her shoulders, her copper-brown eyes large and kind. Even now, despite her withered frame and sallow color, she was still a beauty. "You look real good, Mama. Real good."

Rose reached for a sweater.

Azalea had believed Dr. Mathews would fix her mama the minute she went to see him. Give her a bottle of pills. Tell her to rest for a week or two. Then she'd feel better. Instead, she seemed worse, and now June Bush waited outside to take her to Knoxville to see another doctor. A specialist. Azalea's stomach churned at the thought of her mama going so far. She never should have buried that note on the hilltop. She never should have turned to God for help.

She handed Rose her favorite lipstick, but Rose frowned. "No thanks. Ain't much interested in impressing folk." Azalea couldn't remember a time when her mama had left the house without color on her lips.

A quick knock came at the door.

"I'm learning real fast that June Bush is never late," Rose said. Azalea reached for Atlas, then helped her mama to her feet. "My legs are a little shaky this morning." Rose stroked Atlas's cheek. He grinned, wrapped his legs around Azalea's waist, then buried his face against her neck. "That boy loves you like a mama," Rose said. She kissed Azalea's cheek, then the top of Atlas's head. "Run on and tell Mrs. Bush I'm coming."

June stood on the porch, holding a plate of cookies. That woman never showed up empty-handed either, Azalea thought, but was glad she'd come with chocolate chip, her favorite. Miss Ooten stood beside her, tapping one clunky black shoe against the plank floor. Azalea ignored her. She was in no mood to listen to that Autoharp and feared the instrument was packed inside the trunk of the Impala.

"Good morning," June said through the screen door. "Miss Ooten here wanted to come with me. Thought she might be of some help to you, Azalea."

"I don't need no help."

June opened the screen door and stepped inside, followed by Miss Ooten. "You do a fine job taking care of Atlas, but it's tiring work, even for a young girl like yourself. And me and your mama may be gone a good part of the day."

Azalea hugged Atlas tighter. "He won't go to her."

Miss Ooten smiled as Rose came into the room. "Then how about I take care of you, Azalea. How's that sound?"

Rose pressed close to her daughter. "Be a good girl," she whispered.

June passed the plate of cookies to Miss Ooten and turned her attention to Rose. "I got a blanket in the car and some hot chocolate in a thermos." She reached for Rose's hand.

"It ain't winter," Azalea said.

Rose glanced at her with fierce eyes, and Azalea felt her face turn hot.

"Sooner we get going the better. Emmett figured it'd take us a little more than an hour to get there." June guided Rose outside and down the porch steps. Miss Ooten clucked her tongue and tickled Atlas's chin. Azalea jerked him away.

She ran after June and Rose. "Can't I go?"

"If you go anywhere, sweetheart, I think you need to be going to school," June said. She guided Rose into the front seat and tucked a blanket across her lap.

Rose lifted her head. "I need you to stay here and help Miss Ooten with the baby. Can't you do that for me, honey?"

Azalea nodded.

"Don't you worry," June said as she slid behind the steering wheel. "Everything's going to be fine."

Azalea stood in the clearing holding Atlas. Her mama looked so fragile in the front seat next to June. For months, she'd believed another baby was sucking Rose dry. Now she could see that her mama was very sick. She yanked open the car door. "Please, Mama, let me go with you. Atlas won't be no trouble." She knelt in the dirt and dropped her head on Rose's lap. "Please say I can."

Rose stroked Azalea's back. "We talked about this."

"Please."

"Shh," Rose said, "stop this." She lifted Azalea's chin and brushed the hair from her face. "I love you, baby girl, but you need to let me go."

Atlas fussed. Miss Ooten wrapped her arm around Azalea and gently pulled her from the car, and Rose shut the door. "Go on," she mouthed and turned her eyes away. Atlas started crying. His grip around Azalea's neck tightened.

Azalea fought against Miss Ooten, but the old woman's hold was strong. "You're going to be okay," she said over and over, nearly singing the promise. At last, Azalea collapsed against her soft, round belly, Atlas squeezed in tight between them. The Impala disappeared through the thicket of cedars and pines. A cool spring wind skimmed across the treetops.

"Come on, honey," Miss Ooten said. She led Azalea back to the porch swing where they sat together, the baby on Azalea's lap, the swing screaming under their combined weight. Atlas squealed and flapped his arms like a little bird whenever Miss Ooten pushed her foot against the plank floor, rocking the swing higher. "You like that, don't you?" she asked, again tickling Atlas under the chin. Her knotted fingers made Azalea think of a witch's hand.

Azalea didn't like Miss Ooten being there. She didn't like her old lady shoes or her wattled neck, the way it shook every time she spoke or laughed. She didn't like her sunny disposition or the blue tint to her hair. Azalea fixed her gaze straight ahead, wishing Miss Ooten would go home.

When Atlas lunged for Miss Ooten's beaded necklace, she scooped him up and let him gnaw on it like a dog with a bone. "I think your brother's getting hungry," she said. "How about you?" She patted Azalea's thigh.

Azalea ignored her.

"Well, I'm going to fix your brother some oatmeal. Let me know if you change your mind," she said and took Atlas into the kitchen to feed him breakfast.

For most of the day, Azalea kept to the porch, waiting for any sign of her mama's return. June Bush had promised everything would be okay, but Azalea feared it had been a lie. By late afternoon, she lay down on her mother's bed and pulled the quilt over her head. Rose's scent comforted her, and she drifted off to sleep. When she woke, a thin sliver of moon had climbed above the tree line, and June Bush was sitting on the sofa, her legs crossed, her face blank. Miss Ooten sat beside her, Atlas sleeping in her arms.

"Where's Mama?" Azalea asked, rubbing her eyes.

"Come here, honey," said June. "Let's talk."

# — Leonard —

 A KNOCK AT his bedroom window woke Leonard just after daybreak. *Tap. Tap. Tap.* Leonard knew it was Little Henry. Who else came calling in the dark hours of the morning? He opened the window. Little Henry crawled through and tumbled onto the floor.

Leonard yawned and scratched his belly. "Why don't you come to the front door like a normal person?"

Little Henry scrambled to his feet. "And have your mama chase me away with a shotgun again? I don't think so."

"Mama never chased you with a shotgun. She don't even like guns." Leonard grinned, thinking of his mama chasing after Little Henry that day back in the fall and wondering what she would've done had she caught him.

Little Henry pulled a piece of paper from his back pocket. He'd drawn a picture of two angels. A big orange sun punctuated the blue sky behind them. A cloud below their feet. "I heard Azalea's mama is real sick," he said. He handed his artwork to Leonard.

Leonard nodded. "She's at a hospital in Knoxville. Mama says she'll be home day after tomorrow."

"Daddy said she's going to die."

"Mama says only God knows who's coming and going."

Little Henry sat down next to Leonard. "That's what I come to talk to you about. Going."

Leonard held his hand to Little Henry's forehead like June when checking for fever. "You okay?" he asked. "Because here you go again. Not making a lick of sense."

Little Henry shoved Leonard's hand away. "I ain't sick."

"Then what is it?"

"Daddy says we're moving to Texas."

Leonard's eyes widened. "Why?"

"Daddy says we got family down there in Brownsville, but I ain't ever heard talk of any Texas kin before yesterday." He picked at a fresh scab on his knee. "You know, Brownsville ain't far from Mexico."

Leonard shook his head and leaned back against his pillow. "Didn't know that."

"I looked it up on a map at the library." He lowered his voice. "Daddy thinks I don't know about Mama. But I do."

Leonard stared at Little Henry. He'd heard June and Emmett whispering about Margaret and how she died. June had never believed Wayne Reed's version of the story. Leonard didn't know what to think. As much as Little Henry liked to talk, he had never mentioned it.

"Someday," said Little Henry, his voice sounding like it might crack. "I'll make it right."

"What are you talking about?"

"Talking about my birds is all." Little Henry brandished a toothy grin. "Since I'm leaving town, I just want to be sure you'll look after the gravesite. You know, keep it nice, visit it from time to time. Maybe sprinkle a little birdseed in the winter for the daddy whippoorwill."

"That daddy don't go and visit the grave."

Little Henry picked up the drawing and folded it back into a square. "If Mrs. Parker don't make it, will you give this to Azalea?" He handed the paper back to Leonard. "It's a picture of our mamas in heaven together. I know Mrs. Parker and Mama weren't friends, but when the time comes, just let Azalea know I'm sorry."

Leonard nodded. "That's real nice."

The boys talked about Texas and cowboys. But when June's footsteps drew close, Little Henry slipped out the window and took off for home. Two days later, the sheriff came by the house asking questions about the Reeds' whereabouts. By then, Leonard figured, Little Henry was halfway to Texas.

JUNE SAT IN her sewing room, guiding blue cotton beneath the presser foot of her Singer. The needle rose and fell with the motor's steady hum. The tiny room, not much bigger than a closet, was hot from the afternoon sun and hours of the Singer running fast. Still, June shook off a chill, mouthing the harsh words she'd flung at Brother Puckett over a week ago as if rehearsing for a play. He'd come to help, she was sure of that, but he'd left pointing his finger, swearing Leonard was bearing false witness and blaming his parents for his sin. Maybe there was a time when June would've seen it that way, a clear right and wrong to every action, but everything seemed different now. Rose was dying. Emmett was living in the milk room. No, the preacher owed her an apology, not the other way around.

Emmett said reliving that afternoon's encounter was a waste of her time. "You got bigger challenges ahead," he'd said. June agreed, and she'd tried hard to forget the preacher's accusations. But then she received a two-page letter from him, reminding her that she was responsible for Leonard's salvation. If the preacher couldn't let it go, then she wasn't about to either.

June lifted the presser foot and snipped the thread binding cotton to metal. The new romper for Atlas was adorable, if she said so herself. She had promised Rose a summer outfit for the baby and a pleated skirt and matching blouse for Azalea, but since their return from Knoxville, she hadn't had much time for sewing. Rose's care demanded most of her energy and attention. The specialist in Knoxville said the cancer was spreading fast. He had wanted to keep Rose in the hospital longer, but she refused, fearing she'd never get home to see her children again. "Then make her comfortable," he'd said. "That's the best we can do at this point." Miss Ooten was at the Parkers' today, and June was grateful for the respite.

Outside, thousands of starlings flew over the house, shouting in rounds, their noise climbing to a fevered pitch. June dropped the romper on the chair and walked to the back door. Any other day, the murmuration of starlings would have annoyed her. Today as she watched their undulations, she was glad of their company.

When Leonard first lost his leg, he'd rambled on about the hilltop calling to him. June hadn't understood her son's ranting then and was quick to blame it on the infection. She had blamed all of it on anyone in her line of sight — Emmett; Little Henry; Eddie Burl and his mama, Vivienne; even God — unable to accept that Leonard's loss was an accident. Nothing more. And while there was no one to blame for Rose's cancer, now June felt her own peculiar calling. She stepped out onto the stoop. The starlings that had settled in the shade trees suddenly took flight, massing into one dense, black body that swooped and whirled, crisscrossing the hillside before disappearing from sight.

She set her sewing scissors on the porch railing and followed the direction the birds had taken, drawn to the hilltop, scarcely noticing the steep climb. She had not been to the cemetery since the leg funeral, telling herself the memories of that day were too painful to relive. When she reached the iron fence, the gate stood open, almost like an invitation. The sky glowed a peculiar pink. Overhead a hawk circled. June walked to the old oak, pausing beside the grave that held Leonard's leg. A wooden cross Emmett had shaped from one of the tree's branches marked the leg's final resting spot. She bowed her head, fingering a tissue in her apron pocket, but the consuming sadness she feared never surfaced. She glanced at the Bush headstones, smiling at the one with the little lamb on top as she walked to the corner where the purple-crowned thistle was in full bloom.

Tiny swatches of raw dirt and sparse new grasses showed evidence of Leonard's recent work, a patchwork of guilt and redemption. How many people had come here, trusting their shame to her boy? June knelt down and placed her palms on the ground. Holy earth. Hallowed ground. She could feel its power radiating through her body, warming her hands, her arms, her chest. From this vantage point, she could see the entirety of her life. At every turn, she had fought everybody and everything since her own mama died. Was it time to put down the heavy cross she'd been carrying and bury it in this very spot?

# — Emmett —

 THE CALF CAME sometime in the dark hours after the last milking. Emmett had brought the first-time mama in from the field the day before yesterday in preparation for the birth and put her in a stall padded thick with straw. Before leaving the barn shortly after sundown, he'd checked her heart rate and breathing. Nothing indicated labor had commenced, no wringing of her tail or kicking at her belly. Last night he'd laughed, remembering the young man he'd once been, alone in a hospital waiting room, pacing the floor, desperate for a cigarette and news of his own baby's arrival.

The next morning he woke late to the sounds of the cows clamoring to be fed. Outside the milk room's lone window, a chalky sky seemed to swallow the earth whole. Emmett yanked on his boots and headed to the feeding barn. Mornings like this, as he shoveled silage into troughs, he wished he'd studied to be a doctor or a lawyer, anybody who wore a suit to work instead of boots and overalls.

An hour passed before he found the cow and calf in the stall, the newborn curled up tight beside her mother's belly. Emmett took a short step closer and squinted for a better look. Licked clean, the calf should have been standing, suckling her first milk. What Emmett saw turned his stomach. His heart sank. The calf's head was swollen twice its normal size, and she looked to have two noses instead of one. The cow nodded, lowing softly as if to confirm that she'd birthed a monster. Then she licked at her newborn's head some more, urging the calf to stand and prove her wrong.

In all his years of farming, Emmett had only lost one other calf. That one had come into the world with crooked legs and a shriveled-up body. Weak and odd looking, certainly, but not a freak of nature. He squatted beside the newborn. "Damn," he said.

Leonard came up beside him with a pitchfork in one hand, ready to clean the stall. "What's wrong with her?" he asked.

"Don't know exactly." Emmett studied the calf, flinching when it gasped for air.

Leonard knelt down next to his father. "She going to die?"

"Afraid so."

Leonard reached out to pat the calf's head, then withdrew his hand. He bit his lip and inched closer but kept his hands at his sides. "What's wrong with it?"

Emmett scratched his temple, longing for a glass of water and some Goody's headache powder. "Sometimes things just don't go right," he said. "Mama might've eaten some hemlock early on." He picked up a piece of straw and broke it in half. "We'll never know for sure."

Leonard reached for the calf again, caressing her head as if his touch might break her. The calf opened her eyes but didn't stir.

"I'm surprised she's lasted this long." Emmett tapped Leonard on the back. "Come on. Let's let nature take its course."

Leonard rubbed the calf's ear some more. "I ain't leaving her."

Emmett shook his head. "You can't change this, son. Watching it die won't make it any better."

"No," he said sharply, then closed his eyes and mumbled something more. Emmett wondered if his son was praying for a miracle. "I can't get nothing right," Leonard finally said.

Emmett gently took the pitchfork from Leonard and placed his hand on his son's shoulder. Leonard leaned against him. Emmett pulled him close. "You think you caused this?"

"No. Not really. Maybe."

"What do you mean?"

"I don't know. People keep asking me to bury things, telling me I got some special purpose. Maybe I let that kind of talk get to me. Lead me to do things I got no right to do, just like the preacher said."

Leonard wiped his eyes with his shirtsleeve. "Azalea's mama is sick, and this calf is dying. Everything's wrong, and I can't make it better."

"This ain't your fault, son. We're farmers, not healers. And farmers can't blame themselves for things they can't control. Calves die. People get sick. And sometimes boys lose a leg."

"But everybody kept saying something good would come from the loss," Leonard said, his voice wobbling. "So I do what they ask me to, but bad things keep happening."

Emmett stood and stabbed at the floor with the metal end of the pitchfork. "Bad things are always going to happen. Trust me, this ain't your fault." He mussed Leonard's hair. "And we ain't burying this calf on the hilltop so don't you start getting any ideas."

Leonard cracked a smile.

"We just have to get on with things," Emmett said.

"Get on with things? Like everything's normal? You ain't even in the house with me and Mama. That ain't normal. Losing a leg ain't normal." Leonard turned back to the calf and stroked her ear. "We ain't normal, Daddy."

Emmett hesitated, his throat closing up. "You can stay with her as long as you need to," he said. Then he stomped into the feeding barn and tossed the pitchfork like a javelin, barely missing a cow lingering at the trough. Leonard was right. Emmett had never once asked him how he felt about losing his leg or Emmett moving out of the house. He had just carried on, acting like nothing had ever happened, just like his own mama had when Sarah died. This morning Emmett didn't know what angered him most — the calf dying or Leonard's emotion or his inability to fix either one of them.

# — June —

 JUNE SAT ALONE in the Parkers' living room, flipping through magazines she'd bought for Rose when she went to the grocery store last. She skimmed articles about makeovers and diets, her thoughts wandering away on every page. Rose had fought sleep this evening. Atlas had fussed with a gassy tummy. Leonard was home alone, Emmett still sleeping in the milk room. A few minutes past midnight, the wind picked up and the overhead light flickered. June didn't rattle easily, but her nerves were frayed. When Rose called for her, June rushed to her side.

"Talk to me," Rose said. She held out her arm.

Rose was too weak to leave the bed. Once the sun faded and the world grew dark and the children slept, she grew anxious, never wanting to be alone. The doctor said this was normal at the end. June spent every night with Rose Parker now, sitting upright in a chair, singing hymns or reading from the Bible until Rose dozed off to sleep. June adjusted the bed pillows, then added another blanket to the already thick layer of covers.

Again, Rose reached for June. "Please," she said, "just talk to me."

June scooted the ladder-back chair closer to the bed and held Rose's hand, afraid she might snap a bone if she squeezed too hard. Rose had been more alert today than yesterday. She'd even held Atlas for a short while and fed him a bottle. But tonight, her breathing was labored, and every movement seemed to exhaust her. June began humming a familiar hymn. Rose's face pruned up.

"Are you hurting?" June asked.

Rose nodded.

June slipped a pill on Rose's tongue.

"You're a good friend," Rose said at last.

June smiled. "I'm glad I've been some help."

"Help," Rose said. "So you're not my friend?"

"I didn't say that."

Rose closed her eyes, her chest rattling with every breath. "You think in another time we might've been friends?"

"Maybe."

"If I were a better person?"

"Or if I was," June said.

In the faraway distance, a siren wailed.

"I ain't ready to die," Rose said.

"Nobody's ever ready."

"I ain't right with God. I ain't even right with my kids." She coughed on the last of the words. June held a glass of water to her lips. Rose took a sip. "You're a good person, June Bush," she said. "Like it or not."

"God loves you, Rose Parker. Don't doubt that." June dabbed Rose's lips with a dry washcloth. "And so do your children."

Rose stared up at the ceiling as if she were searching for something, then looked at June. "I didn't want either one of them. At least not at the start."

June's eyes widened.

"Oh, come on. Don't look so surprised. I ain't meant to be a mother. Azalea's a much better mama than I ever was."

"She loves you very much."

"I made life so hard for her."

Across the hall, Atlas whimpered but quickly settled down.

"How'd it come to this?" June reached for Rose's hand again. "I know this ain't what you wanted."

"No, it ain't," Rose smiled.

"I saw the picture of Azalea and you and a man taped to her closet door. Is that her daddy?" June leaned forward, resting her elbows on the mattress, still holding Rose's hand.

Rose fell quiet.

"It's okay. You can tell me. I don't shock as easy as you might think."

Rose nodded, drawing a shallow breath. "Azalea's daddy wasn't a good man," she started. "And that picture ain't of her daddy. Just an old friend. Made up a story about her real daddy. Made him a hero." Rose paused, already seeming to need a rest. "She don't need to know the truth about her real father."

"Her *real* father?"

"I was sixteen. Met a man at the Dairy Dip. Bought me a strawberry shake. Told me I was pretty and offered me a ride home." Rose's voice quivered. Her breathing turned irregular.

June worried the truth-telling was too much for her. "You don't need to go on."

Rose pointed to the glass of water, and June offered her another sip. "But I do," Rose said and sighed. "He stopped the car a mile from the house. Yanked up my skirt. I begged him not to. He said if I'd quit fighting, I'd like it." She turned her face to the wall. "But I didn't."

"I'm so sorry." June kissed Rose's hand.

"A few months later, Mama and Daddy kicked me out of the house. Said I was a tramp." Rose's body shook. She closed her eyes. "Atlas's daddy wasn't much better. Made up a story about him, too."

June pulled the covers to Rose's shoulders, offering a silent prayer for the right words to give her friend, even a small measure of peace. "You didn't deserve to be treated so poorly."

For a while, neither woman spoke. Then Rose grimaced. June offered her another pill. Rose waved it away. "Probably best I die, get out of the way before something worse happens. The men that come around here can't be trusted."

"Don't say that. Your children need their mama."

Rose shook her head. "Promise me you'll take my kids. Raise them right," she said, her voice suddenly gaining strength. "I don't want them going to an orphanage. Or split apart. They shouldn't have to suffer any more on account of me."

June's eyes welled up. Her heart hurt for Rose, but she couldn't make any promises without talking to Emmett. And she couldn't lie to her either. She didn't know what to say. In the dark, a whippoorwill began tuning his night song. June smoothed the covers over her friend, who looked like a child scared by a bad dream. She gently kissed Rose's forehead as she had Leonard so many times when he was a small boy fighting sleep. "Don't worry about anything right now. Just try to get some rest."

---

ROSE PARKER DIED in her sleep just before sunrise. June held her hand as she breathed her last, offering steadfast prayers for comfort and promises of an easier life ahead. In the end, it was a peaceful passing. A few shallow breaths. A final gasp. June knew Emmett wouldn't believe her, but she was certain Jesus stood in the room with them, waiting to escort the town's whore through the pearly gates of heaven.

*Three minutes after four o'clock.* June jotted down the time of death on the back of an envelope in case the sheriff asked for it later. Then she set about preparing Rose for her children's viewing. She washed Rose's face, arms, and legs, careful to keep her covered with a blanket. Rose hated the cold.

The house creaked and popped, bending into the howling wind. June wasn't skittish as she dressed Rose in a clean white gown, pressed and starched days ago with a hot iron. If nothing else, Rose Parker would look presentable when her children saw her for the last time. She combed Rose's hair, damp with bathwater, and dabbed a little foundation under her eyes. Rose had looked haggard for a long time. Now she looked peaceful, but pale. June rubbed a hint of rouge into her cheeks and a bit of Revlon pink on her lips.

She reached for a bottle of sweet-scented perfume that she'd ordered from the Avon lady as a gift to Rose when she was first diagnosed. June didn't want Atlas and Azalea smelling the cancer on their mama, only iris, freesia, and her favorite gardenia. She paused and admired her handiwork. Rose Parker was a pretty woman, even in death.

Across the hall, Atlas and Azalea still slept. June knew from her own experience how their young lives had changed. "They don't yet know the half of it," she said to Rose who looked like Sleeping Beauty. June covered her mouth with one hand. "Listen to me, talking to a dead woman." Lord, but she was tired. She straightened Rose's bedcovers one last time, opened the window shades, then closed the door behind her.

Tears came as she checked on Azalea and Atlas, their bodies clinging to each other. "Sleep a little longer," she whispered and pulled a tissue from her apron. She pressed the tissue to her nose while easing their door shut. *Got to be strong, June. Got to be strong.* But when she sat on the sofa, she doubled over, her grief for Rose wed to the grief she felt for her own mother and the worry she carried for Atlas and Azalea. She cried hard. And when she was done, she wiped her eyes and nose dry and went into the kitchen to telephone Emmett.

# — Azalea —

 AZALEA TUGGED ON the frilly collar that scratched her neck. The new dress June had sewn for Rose's funeral already rubbed on her nerves. Made of white organza and pink linen June said she'd been saving for a special occasion, this was the fanciest dress Azalea had ever owned, and it was proving to be a bother. She sat sandwiched between Miss Ooten and Leonard on the Bush's living room sofa opposite the big picture window that overlooked the front yard.

Miss Ooten jostled Atlas on her lap as if he were riding a bucking horse. He laughed and waved his arms, quick to whine whenever she slowed her pace. "You're going to wear me out, boy," Miss Ooten said and started up again.

Poor brother, Azalea thought, he don't know he's an orphan, his daddy unknown and his mama buried in the Bush cemetery. After the burial, Azalea had fought leaving the hilltop, although Emmett and June promised that her mama would have a peaceful resting place alongside generations of Bushes. Emmett had insisted on that. Still, Azalea worried Rose would be scared up there among folks she didn't know.

"Your mama ain't there, child," Miss Ooten had told her. "She's gone to be with the Lord, likely sitting at the right hand of His heavenly throne as we speak." But Azalea fretted for her mama. Rose had never been comfortable around strangers despite what others might think. Azalea tugged at the collar again, swallowing a fresh wave of sorrow.

Outside, Emmett stood in the yard speaking with the funeral director. He'd delivered the casket early that morning and stayed on the hilltop until his men had covered the grave. Emmett patted him on the back, shook his hand, then turned for the house.

Leonard had offered to play tic-tac-toe with Azalea or a round of Go Fish. "Ain't in the mood for games," she'd said, then apologized for her rough tone. Now he read a comic book while Miss Ooten entertained the baby and June worked in the kitchen. When Atlas started fussing again, Miss Ooten handed him a teething biscuit. Azalea couldn't remember a time she hadn't been the one to care for him.

"Sorry for the wait," June said. She carried a tray topped with a pink frosted cake and a small stack of china plates. "Coffee's brewing. It'll be ready in another minute if you want some, Henrietta." June set the tray on a table and began slicing the cake. Leonard dropped the comic book on the floor and licked his lips.

"My, my, June, you needn't go to this much trouble for us. Bringing out the good china. We're all family here, ain't that right?" Miss Ooten kissed Atlas's head.

June hesitated, then tendered a slight smile. "Why, yes, we are," she said and handed Azalea the first piece of cake.

"How come we're eating in here?" Leonard asked. "You always say we can't bring food in the living room."

"It's a special occasion." June cut two more pieces of cake. "Goodness, I never thought serving cake on my good china and eating it in the living room would cause such a fuss." She handed a plate to Leonard, took the baby from Miss Ooten, and offered her a plate.

Miss Ooten took a bite and cooed. "I didn't think it was possible to taste anything better than your strawberry cake, but eating it formal like this certainly makes it a touch sweeter."

June pinched off a piece and tucked it inside Atlas's mouth. His eyes widened as he chewed, then he opened his mouth like a baby bird begging for more. "I didn't make this cake."

"Don't tell me it's a Betty Crocker." Miss Ooten winked at June.

"Lord no. Never again. Actually Vivienne Ford brought it by this morning," June said, feeding Atlas another bite. He gobbled it down and patted June's cheek with his hand. "It was awfully kind of her, don't you think, Azalea?"

Azalea nodded, almost smiling as she watched Atlas and June. Emmett walked into the room, stuffing his handkerchief into his rear pocket. "Heating up out there." He eyed the cake and grinned. "Dessert in the living room?"

June swatted his backside.

Emmett cut a thick piece and sat on a kitchen chair placed at the end of the sofa. "Sure is tasty. When did you find time to make it?"

"Vivienne Ford made it."

Emmett raised his eyebrows. "Vivienne Ford?"

"She's a darn good cook, I'd say," June said and gave Atlas another bite.

"It was a lovely service," Miss Ooten said. She balanced the plate on her belly and took another bite. "And Leonard, that prayer of yours was mighty fine. Didn't you think it was mighty fine, Azalea?"

Azalea nodded, licking a dollop of the creamy pink frosting off her fork. "Thank you for playing your Autoharp, Miss Ooten. You did a real nice job."

Miss Ooten looked sideways at Azalea and beamed.

Emmett set his plate on the table, then loosened his tie. "I'm going to get out of these clothes and check on the herd," he said. "Son, come give me a hand." Leonard stuffed the last bite of cake into his mouth and followed Emmett out of the house.

Straddling Atlas on her hip, June walked to the picture window, pointing to a red bird splashing in a bucket filled with rainwater.

Azalea tugged on the scratchy collar again, but something much worse was bothering her. She felt responsible for Rose's death, at least in part. And none of the day's pretty service or fancy lunch had changed that. As a last-ditch effort, she had begged God to turn her mama into an upstanding woman, one like June Bush. When that didn't happen, Azalea had accused Him of not caring about her or Atlas. With Rose buried in the Bushes' cemetery in one of June's best Sunday dresses, He'd gone and gotten even. Azalea didn't know many Bible stories, only the few that Little Henry had told her, but she knew enough of Adam and Eve and Issac and Esau to understand that God could be as mean as He could be nice.

Sitting in the Bushes' living room on a pretty blue sofa with matching pillows, eating cake with pink frosting, she could see no other good reason for her mama's passing. If Little Henry was right, and his mama was always watching over him, she worried hers was doing the same. In heaven, Rose likely knew the full truth of what she'd done and might want to settle the score with her daughter, too.

Miss Ooten set her empty plate on the table and squeezed Azalea's hand. "Your thoughts have carried you someplace far from here, haven't they?"

Azalea thumbed away a tear, not wanting Miss Ooten to know her secret.

"There's no explaining these things, honey. Why the Lord calls some home early and others like me later on," she said, "but your mother is in a good place, and you'll be happy again one day. You'll see."

Azalea bristled at Miss Ooten's words. She knew the old woman meant well, but she was tired of her talking about the Lord picking her mama for heaven like she'd been chosen homecoming queen. "You really think my mama's happy without me and Atlas there with her?"

"In heaven, you ain't got no choice but to be happy." She brushed a strand of hair from Azalea's face then turned to June. "Give the baby to me. Sounds like he needs a nap, and I imagine you need some rest, too."

Azalea scooted to the far end of the sofa.

"Probably needs a diaper change," June said. "Clean diapers and a tube of Desitin are on my bed."

Miss Ooten gathered Atlas into her arms and disappeared down the hall.

June began collecting plates and cups and stacking them on the tray. "You didn't eat nothing but the frosting," she said to Azalea. "You didn't like the cake?"

"Ain't really that hungry."

"Your appetite will come around soon enough," June said.

Azalea followed her into the kitchen. The afternoon light streamed across the kitchen floor, and the linoleum sparkled like Big Sugar on a summer day. Azalea sat at the table, sunshine warm on her legs. June tied an apron over her dress and scraped the plates clean before dropping each one in the dishwater to soak. Anytime she was near June, Azalea felt closer to her mama, even if Rose had never served cake on pretty china or cleaned a kitchen until it gleamed. She hoped her mama knew how much she loved her.

The sound of a car engine drew her attention outside.

"Oh lord," June said, glancing out the window. "Of all times." She untied the apron and straightened her skirt just as Brother Puckett hollered a hello from the back stoop. His wife, Edna, carrying a Pyrex dish wrapped in tin foil, followed behind. June opened the door and welcomed them inside. Edna wore a syrupy grin, her lips smeared with a bright pink. Brother Puckett put an arm around his wife's waist and offered his other hand to June.

"Didn't expect to see you today," June said. "Or you, Edna."

"Of course, we'd come pay our respects." Brother Puckett offered a saccharin smile, then nodded at his wife.

"That's right. We wanted to pay our respects," Edna said. She held up the casserole. "Chicken noodle. Figured the children would like that." Azalea slid behind June.

"You're a shy one," Brother Puckett said. He took the Pyrex from his wife and handed it to June. "Everyone at Piney Grove Baptist Church wants these newly orphaned children to know that we're thinking about them at this difficult time." He pulled two small Bibles from his suit pocket. They looked just like the one Leonard carried to the hilltop. "June, in your hands, these children finally have a chance for a true relationship with their Lord and Savior." The preacher looked at Azalea. "Here, child, take these. One for you. One for your brother. Read from it every day. These words will guide you to the Lord." Azalea took the Bibles. She didn't have many books of her own, and certainly not one like this, bound in leather and embossed with gold lettering. She had always admired Leonard's, and whether it led her to the Lord or not, she was glad to have it.

June set the casserole on the table. "Thank you for the meal and kind thoughts and the Bibles. All are appreciated," June said. She took Azalea by the hand. "Henrietta was just saying, Brother Puckett, that you'd offered to come and pray for Rose before she died." June tightened her grip on Azalea. "Funny, I never saw you come around, even at the end. But maybe you came while Henrietta was sitting with her, and I just missed you."

Brother Puckett toyed with his pocket change. "Prayer can be said from a distance, June. God don't care where you are when you call on His mercy."

"We've both been down on our knees," Edna said. She stroked Azalea's cheek.

Azalea buried her face in June's side. She had met this woman one other time, when Atlas was a newborn. Mrs. Puckett had come to her house along with a bevy of fine, upstanding church women. They had prayed over Rose, for her salvation, but it hadn't done any good. Azalea didn't know how to reach God. Her few attempts had failed. But Brother Puckett and his wife were experts. Had they truly bothered to bow their heads and get down on their knees for Rose Parker surely it would have made a difference. Azalea doubted they had prayed for her mama like they claimed, and judging by the tone of June's voice, she doubted it, too.

"Praise God, June Bush," Brother Puckett said, "you sure have earned yourself another jewel in that heavenly crown of yours, providing such tender care to a woman some might say wasn't so deserving."

Azalea's body tensed at those words, anger boiling up inside her. She'd had it with finger-pointing and name-calling. The preacher had no right to judge. Whether he had prayed for her mama or not, she didn't care. Her mama deserved to rest in peace, and the preacher was disturbing her peace.

June patted Azalea's back. "Rose Parker loved her children," she said. "Let's remember that."

"Of course she did," Mrs. Puckett said. She glanced toward the living room. "Where's the baby? I sure would like to hold him."

"Napping," June said with a snap in her voice.

The preacher wiped his brow with a neatly ironed handkerchief, then took his wife's arm. "We best be going, Sister June. You're a busy woman these days, lots of decisions to be made." He leaned down to speak to Azalea, but she turned her head.

"Well, then, call if you need anything." Brother Puckett led his wife out the door. Just beyond the stoop, Edna Puckett spun around. "Probably best if you warm that casserole in a three-hundred-degree oven for thirty minutes or so."

June waved from the kitchen door. "Thank you," she said. She smiled until the Pucketts drove away, then she shut the door and stroked Azalea's cheek just as the preacher's wife had done. "So what do you think we should do with Mrs. Puckett's chicken casserole?"

Azalea looked at the dish. "She came to our house when Atlas was born."

"The preacher's wife?"

"Yes, ma'am." Azalea tugged on the collar, scratching at her neck again.

"Oh, did she?"

"She wanted to take Atlas home with her. Said Mama didn't need another mouth to feed."

June nodded. "Well, isn't she thoughtful," she said, reaching for her apron and knotting it at her waist. "Not really in the mood for chicken tonight, are you?" Without waiting for an answer, June picked up the casserole and tossed it in the garbage.

Azalea gasped, then laughed at June's rebellion.

"Don't go telling Miss Ooten." June pressed her finger to her lips. "It'll be our little secret." Azalea smoothed her dress the way she'd

seen June do. "Thank you, Mrs. Bush. For everything." The tears
starting in her chest expanded to her throat and up her nose.

June stroked Azalea's cheek. "Think maybe it's time you started
calling me June?"

Azalea looked toward the hilltop. "June," she whispered.

# — Leonard —

 A DAPPER-LOOKING MAN in a dark suit showed up at the Bushes' home bearing hairbrushes, toothbrushes, toilet brushes, moth blocks, laundry soap, brooms, and mops. When Leonard came to the door, the gentleman doffed his hat while holding a red-handled broom in his other hand. A brown leather case rested on the porch floor by his feet. Out in the drive, a shiny black car baked in the hot sun.

"Good afternoon, I'm the Fuller Brush man. May I speak with the lady of the house?" he asked, his voice lilting.

"The who?" Leonard answered through the screen door.

The gentleman smiled. "Is your mother home?"

"No, sir. She's in town." June had taken Azalea and Atlas to Cox's for new summer shoes. Not even the promise of a chocolate shake from the Dairy Dip had been enough to tempt Leonard to spend the afternoon shopping. What a shame, he thought now, that his mama was not home to meet this man dressed in a starched shirt and bearing just the kind of cleaning tools she loved.

"What about your daddy?" the man asked. "Is he home?"

"He's at the barn," Leonard said.

The Fuller Brush man cleared his throat. He glanced back over one shoulder, then leaned in closer. "Truth is, I came to see you. You're Leonard, right? Leonard Bush?"

Leonard narrowed his eyes, wondering how this stranger knew his name. "Yes, sir," he said, carefully doling out his response.

"Excuse me for not introducing myself. My name is William T. Jones," he said. "But my friends call me Bill." The man reached inside his suit pocket and pressed a card with his name and address printed on it against the screen. "I'm from Gadsden, Alabama. You ever been to Gadsden?"

Leonard stared at the print on the card.

"Well, I guess no real reason to go to Gadsden unless you got family there or passing through," the man said. "I don't normally travel north of Chattanooga myself. This isn't my territory. But I heard of you. Down in Alabama."

Leonard's eyes grew wide. "Me?"

"If you're the same Leonard Bush who lost a leg and buried it on a hilltop and walked away transformed, then yes, you." The man seemed to be looking Leonard over from head to toe, trying to determine which of his legs was fake.

"That ain't all true." Leonard scratched at a fresh mosquito bite on his forearm. "But how come you know of me? I don't understand."

"You got a reputation, son," the Fuller Brush man said and adjusted his tie. "And as it turns out, I'm in desperate need of your saving graces." He dropped his head, hiding his eyes from Leonard's view. "I need you to bury something for me. A small little thing really. But I'm getting married next month and need to turn over a new leaf before I take a wife." The man patted his lapel, then fished inside his suit pocket and cupped a pair of dice in the palm of his hand. "Been carrying these with me for some time, trying to figure out how to make things right. Just a couple of days ago, one of my best customers down in Anniston told me about you." The man slipped the dice back in his pocket. "Once I heard of you, I knew I had to come to Sweetwater straightaway."

Leonard unlatched the screen door and stepped onto the porch. No one had come looking for him since Rose Parker's funeral nearly a month ago. Although quiet periods had come and gone in the past, this time Leonard figured people had quit coming for good. Burying the town prostitute in the Bush family cemetery likely had turned them away. Leonard reckoned a lot of folks had changed their opinion of the Bush family. He didn't know this for certain, but he knew how people had once gossiped about Azalea and her mama. He figured Rose's death hadn't changed that.

It was for the best really, that people quit coming around. June smiled more these days, happy with two more children in the house. And even though Emmett was still sleeping in the milk room, he came to the house every day—ate breakfast, lunch, and supper with them and tarried some nights, watching TV or playing dominoes. Atlas even called him Daddy, or some baby talk that sounded a lot like it. Leonard's leaving the hilltop work behind must have been the reason for the change. He couldn't think of another explanation for it.

"I ain't really burying things for folks anymore, Mister." Leonard hated to disappoint anyone, especially someone who'd traveled so far, but he didn't want to go to the hilltop either.

"Excuse me?" Bill's smile quickly faded.

"I sort of gave it up."

The man's face turned pale. "What do you mean *gave it up*? You can't *give up* what you're called to do. I've come from Gadsden, Alabama, just to see you."

Leonard kicked at the porch floor. "I just ain't sure what I been doing up there is my calling really. At least not anymore it ain't."

The man shook his head, now holding the red-handled broom like a giant exclamation point. "Look. This is my calling, being a Fuller Brush man. It's who I am. You, on the other hand, from what I've heard, ease people's suffering. That's what you do. You can't just up and quit it."

Leonard grinned. "Thank you for the compliment, but I'm really not sure that's what I've done. Ease suffering, I mean."

"It's not a compliment, son. It's a calling. Don't you hear what I'm saying?"

*Calling.* Leonard had heard the word buzzing around since that September day when he'd buried his leg among friends and neighbors. They'd prayed for him then, swearing the Lord had a purpose for his loss. Leonard had fought the idea at first, then secretly longed for it. His *calling*. For a while, as one person after another walked to the hilltop alongside him, he had come to believe they were right. God had orchestrated his amputation for a greater purpose. He had been handpicked to do God's work on earth. How silly, he realized, that he had thought so grandly of himself.

In the quiet following Rose's funeral, he'd watched June assume the role of Azalea's and Atlas's mother — drying their tears, making them new clothes, preparing their meals. Leonard came to understand that God hadn't chosen June to do His work. It was the other way around. June had volunteered, choosing love in the middle of a tragedy. That was truly divine. Watching his mama do the Lord's work, Leonard regretted ever misguiding anyone for his own selfish purposes, to feel better about his misfortune.

The man leaned the broom against the side of the house and opened his satchel filled with every type of brush imaginable. "Just hear me out," he said. "I've come a long way, and my heart is heavy." He pulled out a small brush and handed it to Leonard. "If you'll listen to my story, the whole of it, I'll leave this very fine vegetable brush with you, a complimentary gift for your mother."

Leonard scratched his arm again. "Mister, you really don't need to tell me the right and wrong of what you've done."

The Fuller Brush man hung his head. "If I don't, I'll explode."

"Don't want that," Leonard whispered, then invited him inside and offered him a glass of cold water. He would help Bill Jones from Gadsden, Alabama. But he knew his calling was truly over after today.

His mama's would continue, though. And she would be thrilled with her new brush.

# — Emmett —

EMMETT FLICKED THE last of a cigarette into the yard. He'd promised June he wouldn't buy another pack. This time he meant to keep his word. He glanced at the long shadows creeping across the pasture and then at his watch. He'd told Leonard to meet him at the milk room, and the boy was running late. Emmett patted his shirt pocket, reminding him of the pack of Salems tucked inside it.

"Coming, Daddy," Leonard hollered. The sight of his son loping across the clearing filled Emmett with pride. He waved and stepped into the milk room. "Hey there," he said when Leonard came inside. He offered the boy a cold Coca-Cola from the ancient refrigerator. Leonard settled in the recliner and took a swig from the bottle.

"What'd you need, Daddy?"

Emmett combed his fingers through his hair, then adjusted a top button, watching Leonard take another sip from the bottle. He'd grown so much in the past year, not just taller but fuller in his heart. Emmett cleared this throat.

Leonard drained the last of the Coca-Cola in two long gulps, then let out a big belch and laughed at the sound.

"Lord, son, don't let your mama hear you doing that." Emmett leaned back in his chair, his foot tapping fast against the floor. "I'll get right to the point. I need you to bury something for me. Up on the hilltop with all them other things folks brought you." Emmett reached inside his overall pocket and held out a single, beat-up little boot, the impression of a child's toes still cast in the leather. "I need you to bury this."

Leonard set the bottle on the ground and reached for the shoe, but Emmett jerked it close to his chest, unable to hand it over just yet. "It was my sister's."

Leonard nodded. "How come you want to bury it? Now, after all this time?"

Emmett looked away, his cheeks turning red. "Is that important?"

"Guess not." The hollow sound of his voice echoed through the room. "Can I touch it?"

Emmett hesitated, then handed the shoe to his son. He placed his open palm on his thigh to steady his nerves. "It's the only thing I got left of Sarah. Just this one shoe," he said. "I can't rightly explain it, but I think it's the root of some other troubles. Bigger troubles." He reached for another cigarette, his leg shaking again. "I don't expect it to make a lick of sense to you, and I can't really explain it more than that. I just think we need to bury it."

Leonard admired the shoe, turning it around, inspecting every inch of it, even fingering the laces woven through a series of metal eyelets. He handed it back to Emmett. "I don't know, Daddy. Seems to me that a memory like this ought to be kept close. Maybe even bronzed. Like you and mama done to my baby shoes."

"Bronzed?" Emmett admired his son's insight, wondered at his own lack of it.

Leonard nodded, his eyes brightening. "You could keep it on your desk. Like a paperweight."

Emmett held the shoe to his nose. "There was a time when I could smell my baby sister in these shoes."

Leonard tapped his fake leg. "There was a time when I felt my real leg. But that don't happen much lately."

"Do you miss it?"

"Sometimes. But I think some good can come from losing something."

"How so?" Emmett set the little shoe on the desktop, then picked it up again.

"Losing something forces you to look at things another way. You still miss it, Daddy. Ain't no sin in that. But you miss it more with your head. Not your heart." Leonard reached for the empty Coca-Cola bottle. "If you really want to go to the hilltop, we got a little bit of daylight left."

Emmett saw strength in his son's spirit. He imagined the man Leonard would become one day and felt the pride a father feels for his son. "Let me think on it."

"Sure, but I told Mama I'd help with Atlas. He's cutting a new tooth. Been fussing since he woke this morning. Mama and Azalea are worn out."

"How you doing with all that?" Emmett asked. "Them coming to stay with us. It's a busy house lately."

Leonard held the bottle to his lips and blew across the opening. The eerie piping swelled through the barn. "As long as I don't have to share a room with Atlas, it's good."

Emmett nodded, his lips curling into a small smile. "You better go on then."

Leonard stood up and took a short step. "Nothing's going to be right till you come home." He set the bottle on his daddy's desk. "Mama said you need time to sort things through. It's been more than a month. Seems like you've had plenty of time for that."

Emmett watched his boy walk back to the house, his fake leg looking as though it needed to catch up with every step. It was hard to remember him two-legged. The image of his son before the amputation had turned fuzzy. He remembered their friends and neighbors at the leg funeral, swearing that God had a plan for Leonard. He knew Leonard had cringed at those words then. Emmett let out a deep sigh. He was beginning to understand.

---

THAT EVENING, EMMETT and June sat in the living room, watching *The Jackie Gleason Show*. Atlas dozed in June's arms. Azalea and Leonard slept at the other end of the house — Leonard in his room, Azalea in June's sewing room on a pallet of blankets. "It's time we make a proper room for Azalea. Buy a mattress. Maybe paint the walls pink or a pretty yellow. I can make curtains. What do you think?" June asked.

"Is this what you want, Junebug?"

"I can't imagine handing them over to strangers to raise." She leaned down and kissed Atlas on the forehead. "They're beginning to feel like my own."

"You ain't got any worries about Leonard and Azalea growing up under the same roof? You said yourself he's sweet on her."

She looked up from the baby. "Maybe it's a good thing she'll be his relation. Law ain't going to let a brother and sister marry." She cast a sharp eye toward Emmett. "But let's go ahead and add on that room at the back of the house that we been talking about for years. Azalea's going to need a space of her own."

Emmett laughed. "He's going to marry someday, June. Steel yourself." He watched her cradle Atlas, adjusting the blanket around his body, admiring his sweet face. The baby was growing like a dandelion in a spring pasture with June's constant nurturing. He reached out and touched the baby's foot.

"For now, Atlas can sleep in our room," she said. "Till he's a little bigger."

"Leonard will be relieved to hear that. He's afraid they might have to bunk together, and he ain't keen on that notion." Emmett knew June was already imagining the baby's new room, the color of the walls, the fabric she'd buy and sew into curtains, the rug she'd order from the Sears & Roebuck catalog. He wanted her to have every bit of the life she wanted. He went to the television and flipped it off.

"The show wasn't over."

Emmett knelt in front of her and took her hand in his. "You got any worries about us, June? We shouldn't bring more children into this family if you do. It wouldn't be fair to them or Leonard neither."

June squeezed his hand in return. "I know you love me. And I know you ain't ever been unfaithful."

"But the shoes . . ." Emmett faltered.

June pulled Emmett's hand to her chest. "I don't fully know what to make of it. We all bear our losses in our own way. If those shoes help you, I won't be scared of them anymore."

Emmett leaned across the baby and kissed her, remembering the excitement of a little one in the house. He'd known from the start June intended to keep the Parker children, to raise them as her own. He marveled that life could hold such surprises. "Then we better go to town tomorrow and buy whatever you need."

Atlas stirred in June's arms.

"You woke the baby," she whispered.

Atlas kicked his legs and clenched his fists, building up to a strong cry. Before he got too wound up, June pitched him over her shoulder and rubbed his back. "He's been waking so fitful like this the last couple of days." He reared backwards, and June reeled him in, tickling his lower lip with the last of a bottle.

"Leonard said he was teething," Emmett said.

June pushed her finger in his mouth and rubbed it across his gums. "That's what I was thinking. Can't really tell." She bounced him up and down. "You reckon a baby this young knows his mama's dead? Reckon he misses her?"

"Hand him to me," Emmett said. "He's probably working on a tooth. You just can't feel it good yet. Probably needs some paregoric. We got any?" Emmett held out his arms and June passed him the baby.

While June went to fetch the medicine, Emmett took Atlas outside. Under the glow of moonlight, pines in the near distance gave way to a westerly wind. Big Sugar's song blended with the baby's fussing, washing over the pastureland in one plaintive note. Emmett paced the porch, jostling Atlas with every step and humming in his ear. The baby grew calmer, his sobs laced with breathy cries. Emmett couldn't help recalling the sleepless nights when he'd gentled a fitful Leonard on this porch.

June appeared, holding a small glass bottle. "Here," she said, and rubbed some of the amber-colored liquid on the baby's gums. "That should help." She wiped his lips with a clean diaper before tiptoeing back inside the house. Emmett paced another two laps. Atlas finally dropped his head against Emmett's shoulder, his breathing slow and steady. The notes from Big Sugar drifted on the wind. Had Atlas heard it, too? Had the river, not Emmett's efforts, lulled him to sleep?

Emmett lowered Atlas into the crook of his arm. He'd forgotten how sweet a toddler smelled, how soft the skin. Maybe June was right about Atlas. Maybe he knew his mama was gone, the pain from that loss already poking at his heart. He rocked Atlas in a steady rhythm as he walked another lap.

June hadn't said much about Leonard's cleat. Emmett wondered if she ever would. Lately, they ate meals together, watched television together, even knelt together in her garden, weeding between rows of beans and beets, glancing at one another like flirty teenagers. In many ways, their life had returned to normal, but Atlas was a reminder that in every other way, it had flipped upside down. Emmett turned his ear to the river. Yesterday's heavy rains had filled Big Sugar to the brim, and she roared tonight as she coursed her way to deeper waters. The baby whimpered. "Hush," Emmett whispered. "Hush now." Atlas burrowed deeper into Emmett's arms.

Emmett had replayed the conversation with Leonard in his head a hundred times in the hours since his visit to the milk room. If there was any hope for his marriage and his family, Emmett needed to make things right. He crept inside and settled Atlas in his crib, then waved good night to June and headed for the milk room. A lone cow mooed in the distance. The newest calf, a healthy one, rustled in her pen. Emmett unlocked the metal cabinet and grabbed Leonard's cleats.

Stalks of corn towered above his head as he passed through the field with the shoes, wrapped in their paper bag, tucked under his arm. He crossed a paved road and dipped into the woods where the cedars and white oaks mingled with pine and hickory. The moon slid behind thick clouds. The air cast a chill.

Emmett felt his way to Big Sugar. The river called louder, guiding his steps. Soon, the moon reappeared, and just as the land pitched downward, Emmett caught sight of the river, sparkling in the moonlight as if diamonds had been scattered across its surface. He skidded down the slope to a hard stop at the river's edge. The water lapped at his boots. Downstream, bits of white cap crested over rock as the river shifted westward.

He stepped into the water and pulled the shoes from the bag. At first, he'd thought ridding himself of Sarah's boot would somehow ease the need for these cleats, too. But in the end, he'd been too ashamed to bury any of his secrets among his long-dead family, even though so many others had seemed to gain peace from visiting the hilltop. Whether it was watching Leonard gain strength on one leg or watching June rock a crying baby to sleep, Emmett had come to understand that his attachment to Sarah's and Leonard's shoes was more punishment than comfort. He'd been wrong for hiding his pain. His mama had been wrong, too. Refusing to accept a loss never made the sadness go away. It only made it fester.

Emmett cocked his arm and flung Leonard's shoes into the rapids. The cold water pushed against his thighs. The river's roar suddenly turned softer. Nearby, a crappie or bass broke the surface, likely scouting for an evening meal. Emmett sucked in the cool air, his lungs pushing against his ribs. He exhaled as the moon slid behind another bank of clouds.

He and June were making a fresh start. They needed to trust one another with the good and the bad—every bit of it—not invest their fears in silly superstitions and shoe-styled talismans. He reached inside his pocket and pulled out Sarah's little boot. He smelled the toe one last time and rubbed its leather across his lips.

*Enough now,* he said, *enough.* Then he cocked his arm a second time and flung the shoe into the water. He shouted his sister's name and the echo of it danced across the water.

"Sarah!" He yelled a second time. "Sarah Elizabeth Bush!"

Emmett stepped deeper into Big Sugar. The water gently lapped against his thighs. The baritone call of a hooting owl encouraged him further. He bobbed beneath the surface. The cool water washed over his head. He rooted his feet in the river's muddy bottom. His lungs burned, but he resisted the urge to surface. Then he sprang out of the water. He spit and gasped for air. But the hushed grief Emmett had carried in his chest since his sister's drowning was gone. He drew in a deep breath. He slapped the water. H shouted his sister's name again. This time, a joyful cry, one he'd not heard in years. He lay back on the water and gazed up at the moon, the peace of Big Sugar having set him free.

When he reached the house, June stood on the porch, gazing at the night sky.

"Why are you soaking wet?"

He wanted to tell her what he'd done but couldn't find the words. "Just making things right."

"You've done enough of that, Emmett Bush," June said. "Leave your wet clothes on the porch and come to bed. It's time you come home for good."

She walked into the house, leaving the door open behind her.

# — Azalea —

 LEONARD SAT ON the back stoop, cleaning out his tackle box while Azalea and June pinned bedsheets to the line. Atlas tottered around the yard, chasing squirrels and collecting sticks, always coming back to June to hug her leg, laughing when she played peekaboo with a hanging sheet. June had a working clothes dryer, but she claimed sunshine on fresh-laundered sheets guaranteed a good night's sleep. Azalea believed it to be true. She'd slept better in her new house, in her tiny room, than she had in a long time.

Today she wore a halter top, one she'd made herself with June standing over her as she worked the sewing machine, carefully guiding the presser foot to set a straight seam. The top was a bright blue cotton dotted with white-and-yellow daisies. Azalea loved it. June promised they'd make a matching skirt before the week's end. Azalea's bare shoulders were turning red as she held the clothespins, doling them out to June on cue without her asking.

On a hot day like this, cows in the pasture huddled under the oaks. Nearby a sprinkler spat cool water on pink- and orange-topped zinnias June had nurtured from seed. Emmett had stopped by for a cold glass of lemonade before heading back to the barn to work on the tractor. Leonard swatted at a horsefly on his neck, then grouped his soft-plastic baits according to color and size. Looking across the yard, Azalea wished she had a snapshot of this very moment.

More than a month had passed since her mama's death. At first, Azalea had cried as much as Atlas cutting a new tooth, her eyes always red and swollen. And she clung to June nearly as much as Atlas did. The preacher and his wife had never circled back around as they'd promised June the day Rose was buried. Azalea was glad. The preacher's wife left her queasy, and she still hadn't squared her mama's death with the Almighty. But June made them bow their heads at every meal and thank the Lord for the nourishing food and the strength to face another day. She always ended the prayer with a resounding "Amen."

A few days ago, Emmett and June had gone back to the Parkers' little house to clean things out. June had asked if Azalea wanted to come along. "You know, say goodbye."

"No," Azalea said, her response resolute. Before bed, she'd scooted close to June and whispered in her ear. "Would you bring me two things?"

A day later, Azalea woke to find the black-and-white photograph of her parents and her mother's pink satin bathrobe at the foot of her bed. Azalea taped the picture to the back of a closet door just as she had done at her old house. Then she took June's sewing scissors to her mama's robe and cut a tiny scrap of it before throwing the rest of it away. Even now, pinning clothes to the line, that bit of robe was in her front pocket.

"Why don't you two go play?" June called to Azalea and Leonard, clipping the last pillowcase to the line. "Go on. Summer will be over before you know it." June reached for Atlas and settled him on her hip, nuzzling his furred head. "I'm going to start supper once I put the baby down for a nap. Emmett's begging for pork chops again, and I need to get them started." She picked up the laundry basket, resting it on her other hip.

"Closer to time, would you come in and set the table?" June asked Azalea.

"Yes, ma'am." Azalea loved working in the kitchen with June. She particularly liked setting the table, handling June's pretty dishes, every piece matching the other, and folding the paper napkins with the edge of her palm, just like June had shown her, to ensure a sharp crease.

"You two be good," June said, and the screen door shut behind her.

Azalea plopped down in the grass near Leonard and started picking yellow dandelions, twirling the stem of one between her forefinger and thumb before knotting it below the head of another. Leonard foraged for dandelions with extra-long stems and handed them to Azalea. She worked fast, stringing them together without breaking a single one. "There, what do you think?" she said, holding up a long chain dotted with yellow blooms.

"Pretty."

"Just wait." She twisted the two ends together with a final knot then slipped it over her head so that it fell around her neck.

"Even prettier," Leonard said.

"You want me to make you one?"

Leonard laughed. "Nah," he said, shading the afternoon sun from his face.

Azalea adjusted her halter top. "What do you want to do?"

Leonard shrugged. "Walk to the hilltop with me?"

"Thought you gave that up."

"I have. But I promised Little Henry I'd set out birdseed, and I haven't done it in a while. Saw that hawk circling around up there earlier and made me think of it."

"June said to have fun. That don't sound like fun."

"I still got to do it."

"No, I said."

"Fine." Leonard leaned forward and reached for a stick Atlas had dropped nearby. He flung it across the yard. "How come you don't ever go up to your mama's grave?"

"Why do you care?"

"Just curious."

Azalea fingered her dandelion necklace. "What's the point? Miss Ooten says Mama ain't there anyway. Says she's up in heaven."

Leonard nodded, rolling his knuckles against his fake thigh while Azalea picked another dandelion and started a second chain. For a while, neither spoke. The sound of pots and pans clanking together inside the kitchen interrupted their silence. One particularly loud cicada sounded like it was clamoring to be heard above the storm of others.

Leonard cleared his throat. "Do you blame me for your mama dying?"

"How you figure that?"

"Because I buried the note."

"You done what I asked you to do. I don't blame you. I blame myself. I'm the one who wrote God. I'm the one wanted the note buried."

Leonard plucked a dandelion that had gone to seed. "Just like I told Little Henry, ain't nothing we can do here on this earth, even up on that hilltop, to cause nature to change its course. You didn't cause your mama's cancer no more than he could turn a whippoorwill into a morning songbird."

Azalea pulled the scrap of shiny satin from the front pocket of her denim shorts and held it in the palm of her hand. "You know why I keep this bit of mama's robe with me?"

Leonard blew the dandelion fluff and watched it float in the air. "Guess you feel like you got some of your mama with you."

"No." She held the satin to her cheek. "It's so I don't forget. Any of it. All the hell we lived through in that house. When I start blaming myself, I pull this out. Then I remember." Azalea closed her hand around the fabric. "I love my mama. Always will. But everything's easier now." She tucked the scrap back inside her pocket. "I ain't hungry no more. I ain't scared. I ain't tired. For the first time in a long while, I'm happy. Most of the time." Azalea stood, her body casting a shadow across Leonard. "So whether I caused her cancer or not, there's a little part of me that's glad of it. I know that sounds terrible, but it's the truth." She looked toward the hilltop. "So I ain't going up there. Not today."

Leonard reached for his tackle box. "Fine."

Azalea yanked the flower chain from her neck and threw it on the ground. "Quit judging me, Leonard Bush. Not everybody needs to bury their grief."

"Dang it, Azalea, I ain't judging you. I was trying to help."

"I don't want your help. Don't you get it?" she shouted.

June came to the screen door. "Everything okay out there?"

"Just leave me be, Leonard." Azalea pushed past June and slumped into a chair at the kitchen table.

June watched her for a moment, then stirred a pot of beans on the stovetop and turned down the heat. "What's going on out there?"

"Nothing."

"Didn't sound like nothing," June said, setting the spoon on the counter.

"Leonard is what's wrong."

"Ah." June wiped her hands dry on a dish towel draped across her left shoulder. She poured Azalea a glass of cold water from the pitcher kept in the refrigerator and joined her at the table. "You know, I thought of my own mama today when you and me were hanging laundry."

Azalea held the cold glass to her cheek. She was mad at Leonard and wanted to tell June why but knew better than to interrupt.

"When I was a little girl, older than Atlas but younger than you, my mama took me to the five-and-dime and let me pick out anything I wanted." June tapped her fingers against the tabletop as she called up the memory from someplace far away. "You know what I picked?"

Azalea shook her head.

"A baby doll. I named her Sally." June laughed. "Sally had yellow curly hair and blue eyes that opened and closed. Mama made a doll bed out of a shoebox and sewed a little blanket for her. It was years later, long after Mama died, that I realized how hard she must have saved for that baby doll. What she must have given up so I could have her. My family had nothing to speak of, and that baby doll was no little thing." June reached for Azalea's hand. "You got a memory like that, honey?"

# — Leonard —

LEONARD LEFT FOR the cemetery without telling anyone where he was going. He carried a pocketful of birdseed, a small spade, and his tiny Bible.

That peculiar tugging in his gut had returned, stronger this time. More like an electrical current coursing through his body, popping and snapping as it flowed through limbs, fingers, and toes. He had felt a tingle of it after the Fuller Brush man's visit, but the sensation had grown more intense since he and Azalea had exchanged their harsh words earlier that day. He'd been wrong to push her toward the hilltop when she wasn't ready. Maybe it was his own lingering guilt over her mama's death that had caused him to encourage her so.

Leonard had shared their argument with his daddy. "Give her time," Emmett had said. "Just give her time."

Halfway to the cemetery, Leonard stopped to catch his breath. Below, near the feeding barn, Emmett was filling the troughs with fresh water. In the garden, his mama was picking the ripest tomatoes, putting them in a split-oak basket that Azalea carried for her. A billowy white cloud assuming the shape of a giant hawk floated overhead, reminding Leonard of Little Henry. He wondered if his friend had seen a real cowboy yet or discovered some strange Texas bird not known in Tennessee. Little Henry had promised to send a postcard, but none had arrived.

Leonard thought of Little Henry's drawing of his mama with Rose Parker, floating against a golden sky. If Little Henry was right about his own mama looking down from heaven, maybe Rose was doing the same, two winged angels admiring Atlas and Azalea from above.

Maybe she was tucked up inside that cloud hovering overhead. He waved, then felt silly for doing it.

He started up the hill again, recounting the verse Brother Puckett had read at the leg funeral. It had taken him the better part of a year to figure out what that King James talk of legs and horses truly meant — a man wasn't defined by his bodily shape or physical power but by the strength of love in his heart. Emmett had said pretty much the same thing right after the amputation, but he'd said it in simple English. Funny, Leonard thought, that it had taken him this long to connect the Bible verse with his daddy's words.

When he reached the hilltop, he flung the cemetery gate open and headed to the far corner where so many people had come to bury their woe. A light breeze cooled his neck. The hawk reappeared, carving a loopy path over the old oak. With every step, Leonard scattered birdseed, just as he'd promised Little Henry he'd do. When his pocket was empty, he gathered up sticks and sat down in a thick patch of grass.

He opened his Bible and flipped to the last page. Studying the penciled markings, dozens of them now, he placed a small stick on each grave to mark it. Like a diviner searching for water, he found the sweet spot among them and began digging a fresh hole. Satisfied with his work, he set the spade aside and picked up the Bible again. Right or wrong, he hoped he had helped the folks who had come to the hilltop, even if he lightened their load only a little.

Leonard tore the map from the Bible's spine and set that page in the new grave. A song floated up behind him, the tune and voice both familiar. He spun around. Azalea strolled up the hill, singing about a snow-white dove.

"Thought you said you weren't coming up here no more," Leonard said when she finished the verse.

"I never said never. I wasn't in the mood when you asked me last."

"You're in the mood now?"

"I'm here, ain't I?" Azalea opened her hand. The scrap of satin cloth lay on her palm. "You're burying the wrong thing," she said, swapping the Bible page for the piece of her mama's robe. "Put this page back where it belongs."

"I think I'm finished with this business. People got to work out their wrongdoing on their own. Mama calls it a journey. The long walk with God."

"Maybe." Azalea pulled the stubby pencil from inside the Bible and marked another X on the very last page. Then she tucked the paper inside the tiny book and handed it back to Leonard. "But there ain't nothing wrong with giving people a little head start."

Azalea filled the grave, then sat beside Leonard and dropped her head on his shoulder. He listened for the sound of Big Sugar and looked up at the white cloud hanging steady over the hilltop.

# Acknowledgments

With heartfelt gratitude to the following:

Lynn York and Robin Miura and everyone at Blair and Pine State Literary.

Anne Edelstein, the patient, encouraging, and steadfast agent and friend.

Ruth Pettey Jones, gifted writing partner and confidant in all things.

Darnell Arnoult whose wise instruction inspired me to start over, one more time.

Michael Kindness whose support has never wavered.

Melissa Hennessy, niece and business partner, always generous with her time and understanding.

Singer-songwriter Belinda Smith who inspires me with every note.

And to my big, wonderful family—I love you all. Special thanks to my husband, Dan; my amazing daughters, Claudia, Josephine, and Alice; sister, Hall, and brother-in-law, Tom; and my three grandsons, Quentin, Harlan, and Duncan, who bring laughter and joy to every day.